MUSLIM
WRITERS

Also by Jamilah Kolocotronis

Echoes Series:
Echoes (Book 1)
Rebounding (Book 2)

Innocent People
Islamic Jihad

Turbulence

Book Three of the *Echoes* Series

by

Jamilah Kolocotronis

Muslim Writers Publishing

Tempe, Arizona

This work is a work of fiction. Names, characters, places, and incidents are
the product of the author's imagination or are used fictitiously and are not to
be construed as real. Any resemblance to actual events, organizations, locales,
or persons, living or dead, is entirely coincidental.

Published by Muslim Writers Publishing
P.O. Box 27362
Tempe, Arizona. 85285
USA
www.MuslimWritersPublishing.com

Library of Congress Catalog Control Number: 2007922581

ISBN 0-9793577-0-5
ISBN 978-0-9793577-0-1

Book cover designed by Zoltan Rac-Sabo
Book layout design by Leila Joiner
Editing by Pamela K. Taylor

Printed in the United States of America

Turbulence

Dedication

This book is dedicated to all who search and struggle.
May you be guided to peace.

I also dedicate this book to my little granddaughter, Aisha Jamilah.
May your path always be smooth.

Author's Note

This story begins on Friday, December 15, 2017—five days after Brad Adams' forty-seventh birthday. Although the events are set in the future, my concentration was on spirituality and human interactions, which are timeless. I have included some subtle references to life in the future. Please don't let my few small attempts at fortune-telling distract you from the story.

Acknowledgements

Alhamdulillah, the saga of Brad Adams has been completed through the help of many.

First I must recognize the mercy of Allah, Who sustains me.

My family supports me and sometimes makes sacrifices so I can continue to write.

I received technical assistance from Empish Thomas, a fellow writer who has dedicated her life to helping those with disabilities. She patiently explained how the special circumstances faced by the disabled affect the entire family.

I always appreciate the continuing support of Pamela K. Taylor, who patiently edited this book, and Linda D. Delgado, who approaches her role as publisher with true professionalism.

Finally, I need to mention Judy Kaber, who read early drafts of Turbulence and provided me with invaluable advice.

Table of Contents

Prologue

Kyle and I fought again this morning. This time it started when he walked into the kitchen and said he needed fifty bucks.

"I just gave you fifty bucks last week," I said, sipping my coffee. "And what about the money you earn on the weekends?"

"I'm taking Amy to the Winter Dance, and Christmas is coming. You know how much everything costs."

"I'm not giving you any more money until you start helping out around here."

"What do you want me to do? I have football practice after school, plus my homework, and my job at the grocery store. I barely have time to see Amy."

"Do you think your life is tough? Wait until you start supporting yourself. Then you'll find out what hard work is."

"You think I don't work hard? My team is headed to the state finals. I gave you another straight A report card. Not that you noticed. I think I deserve a little appreciation."

"Appreciation? Why should I reward you for what you should be doing anyway? Do I get appreciation for the things I do for you? No. It's my duty as a father."

"What do you ever do for me?"

"Do I need to make you a list?" I shouted.

Beth walked in. "Can't we have just one peaceful morning in this house?"

"Talk to your son. He needs to get over his sense of entitlement."

"All I want is a lousy fifty bucks. I know you can spare that."

"I don't have any cash on me."

"Yes, you do," said Beth. "I saw you counting your money last night."

"Will you stay out of it? This is between Kyle and me."

"Not when your fighting disrupts the entire household. Give me your wallet."

Five minutes later we went our separate ways. I had a tension headache. Kyle had fifty dollars. We need to stop spoiling that kid.

Lightning and Turbulence

And ever has it been known that love knows not its own depth
until the hour of separation

—Khalil Gibran

My head pounds as I sit in traffic on the expressway. I rub the back of my neck and pop in a CD. Sounds of the ocean fill my car. Gradually the tension disappears. I've never been to the ocean. I need to go someday.

By the time I walk into my office, I'm ready to work. Tamara smiles. "Good morning, Mr. Adams. How are you?"

"What do I have scheduled for today?"

"You're meeting Mr. Nelson for lunch."

Good. I told him I'd see him at that place around the corner. Angelos. I love Italian.

I open my files and get to work. Ideas fly on to the paper. I'm soaring.

At noon, I head to the restaurant where I wine and dine Nelson over rigatoni. Good company and great food.

On my way back to the office, I dream about the weekend. I'll change into something more comfortable and convince Beth to join me in a bottle of wine. One of my best vintage. I plan to sleep late tomorrow. And I plan to talk Beth into skipping her monthly seminar and sleeping late with me.

I slip behind my desk and take a few minutes to dream about the weekend. My cell phone jolts me from my reverie.

"Hello. What can I do you for?"

"Hello, Brad. It's Karen."

I haven't heard from any of my stepsisters in over a month. "Beth and I were just talking about you. We'd like you to come to the house sometime next week. And don't forget to bring Doug, of course. What day would be good?"

"I don't know how to say this."

"What? I have bad breath? Or is it my dandruff?"

"No, Brad. Listen. Their plane is missing."

"Whose plane?"

"Dad and Evie's. Air traffic controllers lost contact with their flight somewhere over the Pacific."

I close my eyes and rub the back of my neck. "Um, it's probably just a satellite glitch. It happens all the time."

"Maybe. But they should have landed in Honolulu by now. Their flight never arrived."

"There must be a rational explanation."

"I hope so. Anyway, I thought you should know."

"Thanks for calling. I'll get back to you about that dinner. After we find Mom and Walt."

Their plane is missing. No, it's just a glitch. They'll turn up somewhere. Nothing can happen to Mom and Walt.

My hands start shaking. I stare at my crystal paperweight and concentrate on regaining control. Mom is missing. But she'll come back. She'll never leave me.

I go to my sink and wash my face. Everything's okay. I browse my messages. Eighteen unread emails and five calls which absolutely must be returned, but suddenly I don't know what I have to say that is so important. Except that my mother's plane is missing.

First I call Beth. I get her voice mail. "Call me right away."

I need to tell my brothers. Chris doesn't answer. "Call me."

Joshua answers, but all I can say is, "Mom's plane." The words stick in my throat. I hang up.

I feel nauseated. I shouldn't have eaten Italian for lunch.

I scan my to-do list. A short report to turn in Monday. Two projects due next Thursday. A presentation in Indianapolis next Friday. I put the planner in my briefcase, along with the necessary papers and CDs, and tell Tamara I'm going home.

"What should I say if someone asks for you?"

I give her a half-hearted wave and head for the elevator.

I try Beth again when I'm on the expressway, but my eyes blur and I can barely see where I'm going. I pull off onto the nearest exit and sit in a parking lot until I have my emotions under control. When I go back to the expressway, I concentrate on the dotted white line leading me home.

I pull my Lexus into the garage and walk into the house. Everything looks the same, but nothing is. I walk into the living room, fall into our green couch, and close my eyes—trying to picture Mom.

Five minutes later Beth calls. "I heard about the crash. Was that their plane?" she says softly.

Crash?

"Come home, Beth."

"I'll try. I absolutely must get this report out today, but I'll come as soon as I can. I love you."

"Come home," I plead. My eyes blur again. I hang up.

Three minutes later, the school bus pulls up outside the house. Matt walks in and glances into the living room.

"Dad? Why are you home?"

I wipe my eyes and shake my head. I don't know what to say to him. He's only nine.

"Dad? What's the matter?"

I walk away and go through the kitchen into my home office, closing the door and turning on the computer. "Breaking News: Plane Crash."

I'm still staring at the screen when the doorbell rings. Matt gets it. "Where's your dad?" It's Chris. His dress shoes click across the beige kitchen tiles. I have just enough time to pop a breath mint before he walks in.

"They say they've found the wreckage," he says quietly. "They're sending out teams to search for survivors."

"Do you think?"

"I don't know."

We turn back to the computer.

We're still searching forty-five minutes later when Joshua walks in. I don't hear his footsteps because he always removes his shoes at the front door.

"How you doing, man?" He hugs us both. We all turn away when our eyes become moist. "I heard the search has started. I don't know what they found."

An hour and ten minutes later, the front door bangs opens. Kyle drops his things and yells at Matt. After two minutes the fighting stops, Matt goes back to his video game, and Kyle dashes up the stairs. Three minutes later, I hear water running through the pipes.

Fifty-five minutes later someone honks. "See you later," Kyle calls.

"Be home by midnight," I shout back. The door slams.

Two hours and seventeen minutes later, Beth walks in. She'll tell me the report took longer than she expected and she had to answer her emails. I don't care. She should have been here.

"Where is your father?"

"In his office." Matt pauses his game. "He came home early. Do you know why?"

"He hasn't told you?"

"Told me what?"

"Nothing. I mean, it's something. Let me talk to your father."

Nothing? Is that what this is to her?

Her heels tap lightly across the kitchen tile. She walks in and puts her hand on my shoulder. "How are you, Brad honey?"

Does she care?

I make her wait while I read a new post, then quickly turn. "It's about time you got home," I shout. "Where the hell have you been?"

"I told you, I had work to finish."

"Mom's plane went down. Who gives a damn about your work?"

"I'm sorry. I'm here now. You haven't told the boys yet?"

"No."

How could I?

"I'll talk to Matt. What about dinner? Have you eaten?"

What is she talking about?

"For God's sake, Beth, Mom's plane went down. Nothing else matters. Can't you get that through your head?"

"Let me know if you need anything." She sighs and walks away.

"Listen, man, I need to get home," says Joshua. "Aisha is waiting for me."

"And I need to get back to Melinda and the kids," says Chris. "Call if you hear anything."

"You don't have to leave."

"No, really, Aisha wants me to come home."

"Melinda will be calling any minute. I'll talk to you later."

My brothers leave. I pause for thirty seconds before returning to my search.

At twelve minutes after eleven, Beth walks in. "Do you want something to eat? You must be hungry."

"No, I'm fine."

"I'm sorry, Brad." She holds me.

"Yeah. Sure."

Eight minutes later, she decides to head upstairs. "Are you coming?"

"Not yet."

"Don't stay up too late." She kisses me. I'm alone again.

Kyle walks in the front door two hours and twenty-six minutes later. An hour and forty-six minutes past curfew. I listen as he sneaks up the stairs. Tomorrow I'll tell him he's grounded.

I keep searching. I know the amount of force involved in a crash of that magnitude and the odds of surviving that kind of impact, but there must be survivors. Mom and Walt are among them. I can't look for them in the waters of the Pacific. I keep searching the net.

Seven minutes past three and I can barely keep my eyes open. I lay my head on the desk. Just for a minute.

Beth kisses me. "Wake up, Brad honey," she says sweetly.

I reach for her, but I'm not in bed. Two seconds later, I remember. I glance at the screen. Nothing new.

"How are you?"

"I don't know."

"I'm sorry I didn't come home sooner. I should have been here for you."

"You're here now." I hold on.

Four minutes later, she pulls away. "I'll fix you some eggs before I leave."

"Where are you going?"

"My monthly seminar. It's today, remember? I'm giving a presentation on health care for the elderly."

"My mother's plane went down. Doesn't that mean anything to you?"

"Of course it does. I'm worried about Evie and Walt, too, but they're depending on me. I'll come home as soon as I can."

She walks away. "I'm depending on you, too," I whisper, turning back to the computer.

I check several sites. Nothing new. Beth brings coffee and scrambled eggs, and kisses me on the cheek. "I'll be back soon, honey."

I eat a couple bites of eggs and down the coffee. My stomach started growling sometime last night. That should keep it quiet.

At 11:47 AM, the bulletin flashes in bright red letters. Two words. "No survivors."

Kyle walks in five minutes later. I'm still staring.

"I need a ride to the game, Dad."

I can't answer.

"Dad? Come on, I can't be late."

I turn around. "Do you think your damn game is so important? Look at that."

He reads. "So? What's the big deal? People die all the time."

I choke back the tears. "That was Gramma's plane."

He reads it two more times and starts sobbing. "No. They're okay. That wasn't them. They have to be okay. That wasn't their plane. You're lying." He sits on the floor and cries.

I probably should reach for him, but I don't want him to see my tears. I turn away.

When Beth walks in, we're still crying. It's not much later, but it's too late. "I just heard the news. I can't believe it."

Matt comes in. "What's going on?" Beth takes him aside and gently tells him. She holds him while he bawls.

"No survivors." The words scream at me through cyberspace. I turn away and walk slowly up the stairs. I haven't changed my clothes since 6:45 Friday morning. It doesn't matter. I crawl into bed and pull the covers over my head.

Beth stays with the boys. They need her.

In the evening, my brothers come with their families. I lie in bed and listen to them talk about Mom. Melinda and Aisha are crying, but not Beth.

After a while, Chris and Joshua walk into the bedroom. "Hey, man, come on out of there." Joshua tries to pull away the covers. I hold on.

"I know you can hear us." Chris shakes my shoulder. "We need to be together now."

I don't want to talk about Mom and I can't let them see me cry. I hide under the covers until they go away.

I fall asleep with their voices in the background. No dreams. I almost never dream.

I wake up at 6:18. Twenty-eight minutes later than usual. Beth is sleeping next to me. I reach for her. Then I remember. It all comes crashing down on me.

My stomach growls. I haven't eaten since yesterday morning. I guess I'd better take care of it. I go to the kitchen and look around, settling for coffee and a bagel. Just enough.

I clean up my dishes and change my clothes. The shirt I was wearing when I heard about the crash, the pants I had on when I knew Mom was dead. I throw them into the laundry chute. Good riddance.

I peer out the living room window. It snowed again. The newspaper lies on the lawn, half buried. Beth can get it later if she wants.

Usually, on Sundays, I tackle my work right after breakfast. I look at my briefcase and think about opening it. Not this Sunday.

Maybe I should go to church. People are supposed to turn to God at times like this. I haven't gone in fourteen weeks. It might help, but I doubt it.

I think about crawling back into bed with Beth and holding her close, but it doesn't seem right. How can I ever enjoy life again?

I walk to the couch and sit. It's too soon. It's too sudden. When Mom told me she had breast cancer, I knew she might die. It was too soon, but I would have had time to say goodbye.

Beth walks in an hour later. She doesn't have anywhere to go. She sits with me.

We move through the day slowly. The phone calls start in the afternoon. Mom's name was in the paper. And Walt's. No more hope.

Our pastor calls first, offering empty platitudes about heaven. Then some woman who says she's Kyle's girlfriend's mother goes on and on about how sad I must feel. Then Charlene, Mom's old business partner, who can't say much of anything. Then Celia, my half-sister, who says, "I'm sorry" and sounds like she really means it.

I take the first four calls before asking Beth to deal with it.

Chris and Joshua each call. Beth tries to hand me the phone, but I push it away. There's nothing to say.

Jean calls too. Walt's oldest daughter. Beth forces the phone on me. I say I'm busy and hang up.

Beth sits with me for four hours and fifteen minutes. Then she cleans the house, does the laundry, and goes out to buy groceries. Life goes on, I guess.

In the evening, she tells the boys to get ready for school.

"Don't you think they should stay home tomorrow?"

"No. It's better if they return to their normal routines as soon as possible."

I'm too tired to argue. I go to bed.

I hear the boys heading out for school in the morning. Kyle grumbles and argues with Beth, but she's adamant, as always. I don't hear Matt. He's been quiet lately.

When they're gone, I crawl out of bed, pour some coffee, and sit at the breakfast bar. Beth walks through the kitchen, carrying her briefcase.

"Where do you think you're going?"

"I have to get to work."

"Stay with me."

"You're not going to work?"

"My mother died. What part of that don't you understand?"

"I'm sad too, Brad, but I can't wallow in it. Life goes on, whether we like it or not. As it is, I can barely keep up. I can't afford to take a day off. In fact," she says, glancing at her watch, "I need to get out of here. I have a meeting in thirty-five minutes. If traffic is bad, I'll never make it." She kisses me on the cheek. "I'll see you tonight. Maybe I can get away early."

I grab her hand. "Not today. They can get by without you today."

"No, they really can't. You couldn't imagine how hectic it's been at the hospital lately." She pulls her hand away.

I study my White Sox World Series mug as she walks out the door. "I'll see you later," she calls in a voice sounding much too cheerful.

I carry my mug to the green couch and I sit. I make one phone call. I answer the phone once. I'm tired.

I'm sitting when Matt gets off the school bus. When Kyle comes home from football practice, I give up and go to bed. I listen for her. She comes ten hours later. I'm glad she could get home early.

She calls my name. I don't answer. Finally she walks into the bedroom, carrying take-out.

She leans over and kisses me on the cheek. "How are you, honey? Did you have a nice day? I got cashew chicken, your favorite."

I open my eyes and stare at her.

What is wrong with this woman?

"I didn't stub my toe or have a bad day at work. I lost my mother."

"I just want to make you feel better."

And she thinks cashew chicken will do it?

"I wish I could have stopped her from getting on that plane."

"Is there anything I can do?"

"You can stay with me."

"You know I can't do that. I have too many responsibilities at work. You're going back to work tomorrow too, aren't you?"

"I called Ted. He gave me a one-month leave, with pay. I haven't taken vacation time or sick leave in nineteen months, so I have it coming. Oh, and Tiffany called."

"I'm glad. You need a break. But I simply can't take time off. What did Tiffany want?"

"She thinks we should plan a memorial service for my mother and her father. We're supposed to meet tomorrow evening at her house."

"Good. I'm sure that will give you closure."

"Don't you understand? There is no closure." I pull the covers over my head.

"What are you doing?"

"Going back to sleep."

"What about the cashew chicken?"

"Stuff it."

We go to Tiffany's house, but I don't know why. A few nice words, a song or two, and they're still gone.

While my two younger brothers and her two older sisters discuss the details of the service, I nurse a wine cooler Tiffany offered. I rarely drink in front of my brothers, but they don't seem to notice.

I ask Tiffany for seconds, and after a few minutes I'm feeling more comfortable. They're debating loudly. I decide to listen.

"We need to have it in our church," says Jean.

Tiffany shakes her head. "Dad hasn't set foot in that church in years."

"Mom still goes there. He used to go, too, when we were little. Everyone in that church knows Dad. Besides, it's only proper to hold a mass for our father."

"I don't want to cause problems," says Chris, "but what about our mother? She never went there, and no one in our family is Catholic. The memorial service should be meaningful for everyone."

Jean frowns. "I told Dad to marry Evie in the church. You wouldn't believe what he said to me. He—"

"Excuse me, Jean, everyone." I'm relaxed enough now to contribute. "Walt and Mom weren't church people. We need to respect that."

"What do you suggest?" says Karen.

"If we have to do this, we should choose a neutral place. Let's rent a hall."

"That sounds good to me," says Joshua. "What does everyone else think?"

After a few minutes of heated discussion, they accept my suggestion. Then they put me in charge of finding a place. No problem.

I lean back and listen as they move on to arguing about the service.

"Even though we're not having it in a church," says Jean, "I think everyone agrees it must be a Christian service. Would anyone object if I ask our priest to officiate?"

"I agree," says Chris. "But we need to make the service interdenominational. I have a few songs I would like to include. My daughter, Ruth, would be willing to sing."

"I'd like to add to that," says Joshua. "Mom and Walt went to Malaysia to explore all religions. As a Muslim, I would like to include some Islamic content."

"And I want to emphasize the word spiritual rather than religious," says Tiffany. "Dad was a very spiritual person but he didn't see any sense in religion."

"No," says Karen. "He said you don't have to follow a religion in order to be spiritual."

"Whatever," Tiffany replies. "I don't think he would appreciate turning this into a high religious ritual."

"And Mom," I add, "would laugh at the idea of a priest officiating." I snicker at the thought. Jean crosses her arms and shoots me a dirty look.

Chris stands, taking his preacher pose. "So we must put together a service which will honor Mom and Walt, and still reflect our own beliefs. Tiffany, could you bring a pen and some paper? Karen, why don't you take notes?"

He takes over the process as they continue to debate. Speeches, prayers, musical program. It goes on and on. I wander into the kitchen. I'm thirsty.

An hour and twenty-five minutes later, they've ironed everything out. I wander back into the meeting.

"You'll get back to me tomorrow about the hall?" Jean asks.

"What?"

The hall?

"Yeah, I'll get back to you."

We put on our coats and head for our cars. I walk toward the driver's side. Beth clears her throat. I hand her the keys.

∼

When I answer the phone on Wednesday afternoon, a vaguely familiar voice says, "Brad, I just found out. I don't know what to say."

"Who is this?"

"Your Uncle Rob. I can't believe she's gone."

Oh yeah. Good old Uncle Rob.

"Yes, we're all stunned."

"She emailed me only a week ago. She was very happy. If only I had persuaded her to stay a few more days and take a different flight. I can't believe my sister is gone." He cries, unashamed.

"Listen, I can't talk right now. I'm in the middle of something."

"I'll let you go then. Do you have plans for a memorial service?"

I tell him what we discussed last night. Then I remind him I'm very busy and hang up.

When Beth comes home, she asks if I found a hall.

"No, I forgot."

"But they want to have the service this weekend, before the holidays." She looks into my eyes and sighs. "Never mind. I'll do it."

Jean calls fifty-five minutes later. Beth handles it. "Brad doesn't feel well. I'll take care of it tomorrow." I can always depend on Beth.

On Thursday evening, she says she reserved the hospital auditorium. "I was lucky to get anything at this late notice." She calls Jean and promises to notify Mom's friends. Then she goes to the computer to make the contacts. "You should be the one doing this."

"Can you email Uncle Rob while you're at it?"

She sighs and gets to work.

On Sunday afternoon, we climb into my Lexus and drive to the hall. Beth made the boys wear suits. Kyle tugs on his tie and gripes, "Why do I have to wear this?"

"You need to look nice. Now stop complaining," says Beth.

Michael, my favorite nephew, flew in from Boston. We nod at one another, but the words aren't there.

Mom's brother is here. My dear old Uncle Rob. He always shows up when someone dies. Only then.

They sing nice songs and say nice words about Mom and Walt. I stand in back and tune them out.

After the service, Umar walks up to me. I turn away.

He pats my back. "I know how hard this is for you. Let me know if I can help."

We've been good friends since Joshua married his sister, but I don't have anything to say to him today. I walk away.

Chris and Melinda invite the family back to their house. I'd rather go home. Beth drives. I sulk.

Casseroles cover a folding table in their family room. Kyle rushes to the food. I take my place on their couch.

We sit and talk about Mom. No, they talk. I pretend to listen as they reminisce. I wish they would all just shut up.

Uncle Rob is the worst. He goes on and on about how he misses his sister and how much she meant to him. He puts on a good show. They all shake their heads in sympathy for the old man.

I tolerate it for two hours and seven minutes. Then I tell Beth we have to leave.

"Don't you want to stay and spend more time with your uncle?"

"Why should I spend time with him?" I want to say. But everyone is looking at me. I'll be polite. "No, I'm tired." I want to crawl into bed with my wife and find safety in her arms.

We leave, but the minute we walk into the house Beth grabs her car keys.

"Where are you going?"

"I need to buy groceries, take items back to the library, and pick up some things from the cleaners. And I haven't quite finished my Christmas shopping."

"Can't that wait?"

"Tomorrow is Christmas Day. You go ahead and rest, but somebody needs to keep this family going."

"What's that supposed to mean?"

"It means you're having a hard time with this, and I understand, but the world hasn't stopped because of that plane crash. Go ahead and rest. Take all the time you need. I can't afford to slack off."

I crawl into bed alone.

I wake up at my usual time and drink my coffee on the couch. Beth and the boys are up an hour later, diving into the presents under the tree. They hand me my gifts. I set them aside.

"Open this, Dad," says Kyle. "You'll like it."

I stand up and walk away.

"Where do you think you're going?" says Beth.

"I'm tired."

"It's Christmas. This is family time. And you'll need to get dressed for church soon."

"You go ahead. I'll stay home."

"Brad, I am sick and tired of begging you to go to church with me. You need to ask God to help you through this."

Yeah, sure.

"You go on ahead. Have fun."

When Kyle asks if he can stay home too, Beth yells. "You're coming with me. Now get ready or we'll be late."

They leave in search of inspiration. I go back to bed. There is no Christmas without Mom.

Two hours later, Beth walks into the bedroom and kisses me. "Are you ready to go to Chris's house?"

It's the same thing every year. First presents and church, then dinner with Chris and Melinda. Melinda bakes turkey and ham. Mom brings the pies.

Mom won't be there. "Go without me."

"But Brad, it's Christmas. You can't just sleep the day away."

"Watch me." I pull up the covers. She walks out, slamming the bedroom door.

I remember Christmas with Mom. We had some rough years, both before and after my father left, but no matter how bad things were, Mom always made Christmas memorable. When I was eight, and our father had just walked out, it seemed like she cried or slept nearly all the time, but on Christmas morning I found a brand new bike next to the tree. All that day she cooked and baked and laughed and played with us. The next day she stayed in bed, but she always gave us Christmas.

I hear Beth and the boys walk into the house. She's laughing. Sixteen minutes later, she comes in and kisses me on the cheek.

"How are you, honey?"

I groan. She walks away.

Forty minutes later, Kyle slams the front door, shouting something about friends. I don't hear Matt. He must be playing his new video games.

Two hours and twenty minutes later, Beth lies down next to me and hugs my back. I don't respond. She moves to her side of the bed.

~

Darkness engulfs me. More than darkness. I'm falling into a void. I cry out, but no one hears. I cry again.

"Honey?"

I bolt upright, shaky and sweating, and reach around me. I'm on solid ground again.

"Go to sleep. It was just a dream," she mutters, drifting away.

It's 2:11 AM. The house is quiet and calm, but I'm still shaking.

What was it? Emptiness. Loneliness. Falling into an abyss. That's all I remember.

For two minutes, I lie on my back and stare at the ceiling. Then I get up and pace. Twenty-two minutes later, I lie down on the green couch. I switch on the TV and watch an old horror movie until I fall asleep.

I open my eyes and look around, trying to remember how I got here. I glance at the clock. Twelve minutes after nine. I never sleep this late.

I remember fear. Terror, really. What was I afraid of?

It doesn't matter. I need to snap out of this. My mother is gone, but I'm old enough to take care of myself. I've had enough of sleeping and hurting. It's time to get on with my life.

I head for the kitchen. Beth is sitting at the breakfast bar with her coffee.

"Good morning, Beth honey. Did you sleep well?" I kiss her on the cheek.

"What about you? How did you end up on the couch?"

"I don't know. Sleepwalking, I guess." I pour my coffee and heat my bagel. She's staring at me. "What's wrong?"

"Nothing. It's just so nice to see you smile again."

"Was I smiling?" I put the bagel on a plate and get the cream cheese from the fridge. "What are your plans for the day?"

"I thought I'd stay home and relax. It's nice to finally have some days off."

"Stay home? That sounds boring. Let's pack up the car and go for a ride in the country. We can take the Toyota. I haven't driven that car in months."

She gives me a long kiss. "It's good to have you back."

What? I didn't go anywhere.

~

We spend the week playing. The boys are off for winter break and Beth took vacation days. On Wednesday, we go to Lake Michigan and take in the Lincoln Park Zoo and the Field Museum. On Thursday, we sleep late. In the afternoon, I watch kung fu movies with Matt while Beth reads a novel and Kyle goes off with his friends.

On New Year's Eve, Kyle goes to a party. I drive Matt to Chris's house—they don't celebrate, but he likes playing with Jacob and Benjamin. Then I take Beth out on the town. The Palmer House Hilton has a big bash every year. I made the reservations nearly two months ago.

The party has started and the band is playing some "oldies" from our day. I take Beth out on the dance floor. We used to dance for hours, but after thirty minutes we're both a little winded.

We catch our breath and head for the buffet. Steak and seafood. Five different kinds of rice and potatoes. Papaya and kiwis. Sweet and creamy desserts. And all the wine and champagne we can drink.

This is great. The music plays all night. Sometimes we dance. Sometimes we eat. I drink. Beth abstains. At midnight I give her a long kiss. One hour and twenty-five minutes later, we take the elevator to our room on the sixth floor and have our own celebration.

We sleep late. I wake up with a headache. Beth drives us home.

The rest of the day is pretty much wasted. Kyle and I sleep. Beth picks Matt up from Chris's house and takes him to see a movie. When she comes home, I'm walking around in my pajamas, my fifth cup of coffee in hand. I watch a kung fu movie with the boys before going to bed.

I wake up suddenly at 2:09 AM. Terror. I wander through the house for thirty-one minutes, finally sleeping again on the green couch.

On Tuesday, the second day of the new year, Beth returns to work and the boys go back to school. By the time Beth is ready to go, I'm wearing my sweats.

"What do you have planned for today?" she asks.

"I thought I'd work on my car. The Toyota. She's running pretty well, but she needs a check-up."

Beth puts down her briefcase and kisses me. "Enjoy your tinkering."

She always calls it tinkering. I consider it serious work—more serious than anything I've done at the office for the last ten years. My engineering career has become an endless string of meetings and presentations, with a strong dose of politics. But when I'm working on my car, grease on my hands, man and machine—that's why I got into engineering in the first place.

I'm still working when Matt gets off the school bus, and when Kyle comes home from practice. I'm nearly done when Beth pulls into the garage.

"Have you been out here all day?"

"Just about. Your car sounds like it needs attention. When was the last time I changed the oil?"

"I don't know."

"I'll take care of it this weekend."

I spend most of my week "tinkering." My Celeste, the Toyota, needs some serious engine work. I've neglected her too long.

On Saturday, the temperature gets up into the 70s, which is great for Chicago in January. Global warming has caused major flooding in some areas of the world, but I welcome a warm winter day. I open up the garage and breathe in the fresh air while changing the oil on all three vehicles.

I'm working on my Toyota when a delivery truck pulls up and a guy jumps out with a package. I sign and glance at the address. It's for Mom. Something from Malaysia. Three days ago, I arranged to have everything delivered to my house. I wonder what it is. I can check it out later. Right now I need to finish the oil change. I throw the package into the back seat of my Toyota so it won't get dirty.

I'm nearly finished when Joshua pulls in. He has his three youngest boys with him.

"How you doing?" he calls, climbing out of his car. "We were going to garage sales and I came across this. You remember it?" He holds up a kung fu classic—*Snake and Crane Arts of Shaolin* with Jackie Chan.

"Where'd you get that? Gems like this are impossible to find."

"Like I said, at a garage sale. Does your old DVD player still work?"

"Sure. You know I've got a whole library of these classics. Give me five minutes and I'll be ready for some serious fighting."

We go inside to eat pizza and watch furniture being broken. They don't make movies like this anymore.

Nearly a week without nightmares. Our cars are all in good running order and I'm feeling great.

∼

On Sunday afternoon, I iron my ties.

"What are you doing?" says Beth.

"You know I always iron my ties on Sundays. I have to get ready for work."

"But you have another week left on your leave."

"I need to get back. The holidays are over and it's time to get serious again."

"Okay." She keeps staring at me. She's been doing that a lot lately. I must be getting better looking in my old age.

At 2:13 AM, I wake up suddenly with stomach cramps. After thirty-two minutes in the bathroom, I pace until I'm able to sleep on the couch.

Beth and I have coffee together after the boys are gone. "I'm so glad you're able to deal with this. I was worried."

"I'm fine, but I'd better go or I'll be late."

When I walk into the office, Tamara says, "Mr. Adams. I didn't expect you back yet. I'm so sorry about your mother."

"Call Ted and tell him I'm here."

I ease into my chair and turn on my computer. While I'm catching up on emails, a story pops up. "Air crash cause determined." I follow the link. The plane crashed, they say, because of lightning and turbulence. Not human error, mechanical failure, or terrorism. Lightning and turbulence. Is this some sort of cosmic joke?

I return to my emails. I need to get back to work.

The days fly. One week in New York for a conference on mass transit solutions. A few days in Toledo. Next week, I'm traveling to Kansas City. In three weeks it will be Des Moines.

The nightmares come every two or three nights. And sometimes in the middle of the day, for no reason, I feel nauseated. I'll ask Tamara to call my doctor.

I live for Saturdays when I can work on my Toyota Celica GT Coupe. I call her Celeste. Beth calls her a nuisance. Celeste is almost thirty years old, but I have her running like she was brand new. Three years ago, I overhauled her engine for the second time. I've replaced all her major systems. She has a bright yellow paint job and a fresh interior. And I've put in a new fuel system which I designed and built myself. She runs on a mixture of solar energy, battery power, and vegetable oil. A car like that can last forever.

I just came back from Des Moines, tired but tense. I pace through the house until I'm ready to drop.

When Beth wakes me, I'm on the couch again. It happens nearly every night now.

I have a big presentation this morning. They're talking about doing away with the L in favor of the underground system. Someone else can worry about the costs. I address structure, mechanics, and efficiency. The underground runs well, and it has its advantages, but I hope they keep the L. Chicago wouldn't be the same without it.

When the meeting is over, I shake hands with everyone and head back to my office. Sixteen minutes later, Ted calls.

"Could you come to see me, Brad? We need to talk."

"I was just about to head out for lunch."

"Come in before you leave."

Ted is my boss. We've also been friends for the last fifteen years. He came to the company fourteen years and three months before I did and he's close to retirement. Everyone knows I'm in line to take his place. I walk in smiling.

Ted is frowning. "Sit down. I received a call from a member of the Des Moines city council this morning. They liked the content of your presentation."

"Great. So we're ready to move forward with the deal."

"Not quite. He said the morning session went smoothly, but you came back from lunch nearly an hour late, and it was obvious you had been drinking."

"I had a glass of wine with my chicken parmigiana."

"From what this man said, it was more than one glass. According to him, you dropped your papers, and for nearly two minutes you forgot how to operate your handheld."

It wasn't two minutes. Not even one.

"You know how those Iowa bumpkins are. Would you believe they started the meeting with a Bible reading?"

"Brad, I know you drink too much on occasion. Keep it under control."

"Sure. No problem."

What is he talking about? It must have something to do with that Christmas party the year before last.

"Is there anything else?"

"No. This morning's presentation was quite impressive. You're a good engineer. Don't ruin it."

I eat Italian again for lunch, with just one glass of wine. What's the big deal over one glass?

In the morning, Curt Hendricks drops by my office. "I'm going to Little Rock next week. Do you have any pointers for my presentation?"

"You're going to Little Rock? That was my assignment."

"Ted handed it to me yesterday afternoon. Talk to him."

I know mass transit inside and out. For years, I've traveled to these small cities and helped them build their systems. I know a hundred times more than Hendricks. I call Ted on it after lunch.

"Curt is barely out of grad school. I've worked on mass transit for twenty years."

"I want to give Curt the chance to show what he can do. Don't worry about it."

I rub my neck. I have to worry. Hendricks has been after my job since he signed on. He's in a wheelchair—some kind of diving accident when he was a teenager—but he can run rings around any other guy in the department.

I decide to work late. They have to know they still need me. At twenty past eight, I save my work and walk to the elevator. I push the button and wait. Nothing happens. I try again. The damn thing breaks down once a week. I take the stairs.

I'm walking down the first flight when I trip, tumbling down the last three steps and landing on my side. I try to get up, but I'm dizzy. My heart is beating wildly. My chest hurts. I'm sweating. My God, I'm having a heart attack. I fumble for my cell phone, but it flew out of my pocket when I fell and it's out of reach. I can't move. I can't catch my breath. I'm helpless. I'm going to die here in this stairwell. I close my eyes and wait.

Ten minutes later, I'm feeling better. My head clears. My breathing slows. I don't need an ambulance. I sit up and reach for my phone. I'll call Beth. She can drive me to the hospital.

She answers on the third ring. "Brad? Where are you?"

Hearing her voice calms me. I'm almost back to normal. "I had to work late. I'm on my way home now."

"Okay, honey. I'll see you soon."

I end the call and make my way carefully down the five remaining flights.

Driving down the expressway, I relive the experience. I thought I was going to die. And once I got past the initial shock, I could live with that.

I have nightmares nearly every night now. I never remember the details, just the terror. When I wake up I am sweating, my heart racing or my stomach cramping. I pace, finally sleeping on the green couch. Classical music helps me relax.

I can't concentrate. I keep up with my work and my face remains calm, but inside I'm a nervous wreck.

I feel Ted watching me. I watch the clock and beat it to the door precisely at 5:00 PM. I can't stand the scrutiny. And I don't want to be caught in the stairwell.

Beth is watching me too. I don't know why.

A couple days ago, Hendricks returned from giving a presentation at a conference in Los Angeles. That was my assignment. I'd done all the work and I knew the figures by heart. I've been quietly fuming about it all week.

It's three minutes to five on a Thursday afternoon and I'm ready to go home. Staring at the clock and counting the seconds.

Hendricks comes in. "Adams, take a look at these figures for the Des Moines project. The cost analysis doesn't sound accurate."

"I worry about the construction. Let the accountants worry about the cost." I glance at the clock. Two minutes. I pack up my briefcase.

"Cutting out at five again?"

"Leave the file on my desk. I'll get to it in the morning."

"I always heard you were a good worker. Conscientious, dedicated, all that crap."

"I'm a damn good engineer. I don't have to stay late and suck up to the boss."

"Where did that come from? Getting a little insecure?"

"I know the field inside out. I was developing systems when you were in grade school. I'm not worried. Quality always wins."

"Except when quality has had too much to drink. Isn't that right, Adams?"

"Leave my office."

"You won't help me? I thought you were a team player."

"I know what you're doing. It won't work."

He knocks the wood on my imported desk. "Nice. I think I could get used to it."

I stand, briefcase in hand. "Leave the figures with me and I'll get to them tomorrow."

And keep your hands off my desk.

"Des Moines is ready to close the deal, but we'd better act fast. We almost lost them after your stunt." He turns his chair toward the door. "L.A. was nice. Too bad you missed it."

I kick the wastebasket across the room and pick up my crystal paperweight. "You get the hell out of here." I won't hit him, no matter how much I want to.

"I'm scared." He laughs and wheels away.

I'm breathing hard. It takes me ninety seconds to calm myself. When I look up, Ted is standing in my doorway.

"Come to my office first thing in the morning, Brad."

I grab my briefcase, look down, and rush past him to the elevators.

He's going to fire me. I have been with that company for twenty-three years and seven months, but one idiotic outburst has put an end to it.

How will I tell Beth? We can't afford our lifestyle on her salary. We'll have to sell the house and the Lexus, and learn how to do without. We've always been able to buy what we want. That's over now. I'm finished.

After Ted fires me, I won't be able to find work anywhere in Chicago. Word travels fast. Where can we go? I can't start over. They're looking for guys like Hendricks, young and fresh out of grad school. Nobody wants a middle-aged man who's been tossed out on his ass. I'll never work in engineering again.

And these damn nightmares hound me nearly every night. I can't sleep. I can barely eat. I can't live like this.

I can't live...maybe I don't have to.

I have a nice life insurance policy. Once Beth collects on that, she can keep the house. She and the boys won't have to do without.

How should I do it? Sleeping pills? Hanging? Or should I buy a gun?

Where should I do it? Not at home. Imagine if Matt found me.

Maybe I should take them with me. Guys do it all the time these days. One day they're model citizens. The next day their pictures are on the news. Another murder-suicide. Beautiful, saintly wife. Two adorable kids. Who could have guessed?

I'll buy a gun. I'll wait until they're asleep and...no, I can't.

I need to go. Just me. The question is, who will find the body?

I could kill myself in my office. Get blood all over the desk. Hendricks would love that.

But that would draw media attention. They would hound Beth. I can't do that to her.

What if no one finds me? I could jump off a bridge into the Chicago River. My body will float downstream, decaying along the way.

But every few months they find a bloated body washed up along the banks. A guy like me who couldn't take it anymore. His family has to identify him. Reporters go after the grieving widow. I won't put her through that.

I need to disappear. I will kill myself, but not in Chicago. Where?

I walk into the house and stare at Matt playing video games. He looks so innocent.

Beth walks in thirty-two minutes later. I give her a long kiss.

"Where did that come from? Someone must have had a good day."

"The best part of my day is seeing you." I hold her close, brushing her soft brown hair with my hand. I want to remember this moment.

Kyle and his girlfriend walk in forty minutes later. I talk with them while they eat the take-out Beth brought home.

"How's school going, Kyle?"

"It's okay."

"What about you, um, what's your name again?"

"Amy."

"What's your favorite subject, Amy?"

"English, I guess. Definitely not math. Kyle is the math genius."

He puts his arm around her shoulders. "I keep telling you, it's not that hard if you just concentrate."

She giggles. "How can I concentrate with you around?"

They kiss. I leave to give them some privacy. Kyle won't miss me.

At night, I hold Beth close to me one last time. I don't want to leave her but it's the only way.

I wake up at 2:15 AM, as regular as clockwork, shaking and sweating. I never did see the doctor. It doesn't matter now, does it?

I walk into the living room, turn on the radio, and listen to the music which will relax me.

I know this piece. *The Grand Canyon Suite*. Gary, one of my grad school roommates, listened to this all the time.

The Grand Canyon Suite. I haven't heard it in years. I wonder what Gary is doing these days.

I've never been to the Grand Canyon. I always meant to go one day. They say it's beautiful. And so deep it takes hours to hike all the way down.

The Grand Canyon. That's it.

I stretch out on the couch and fall asleep.

When I wake up, the boys are leaving. I watch them walk out. *Goodbye.*

Beth comes over and kisses me on the cheek. "Wake up, honey. You overslept."

I groan. "I'm sick."

She puts her hand against my forehead. "You don't feel warm, but maybe you should rest. Do you want me to call the office for you?"

"Tell Tamara I'll see her on Monday." I don't want her to talk to Ted.

Before leaving she comes to the couch, her briefcase in hand. "Do you need something? Should I make breakfast for you before I go?"

"No. My stomach's queasy. I'll get something later."

"Okay, honey. I'll see you tonight." She leans over to kiss me goodbye.

I pull her closer. "I love you, Beth."

"I love you, too." She pulls away and stares for a second. "Well, I'd better get going or I'll be stuck in traffic. Have a good day."

I look out the living room window and watch as she drives away.

I'd better get moving. It will take me a few days to get to Arizona.

After breakfast, I dig my old gym bag out of the basement and pack enough clothes to last for five days. I don't think it will take that long but it's good to be prepared. Nothing fancy. Jeans, sweatpants, sweatshirts, and old t-shirts. I add socks, underwear, and a picture of our family.

I throw the gym bag into my Toyota and walk back into the house one last time. I could leave a note, but they can't know it was suicide. Beth will need the insurance money.

I close the door and slip the house key into my pocket. I drive away, heading for the Grand Canyon.

Getting Away

When one realizes his life is worthless
he either commits suicide or travels.

—Edward Dahlberg

Part One

Driving away from Chicago, I remember my brothers. I didn't say goodbye. And what about that package in my back seat, the one for Mom? It's been back there for eight weeks, but I never got around to opening it. Should I go back and leave it?

No, I can't lose any time. If I drive straight through, I can be at the Grand Canyon in twenty-nine hours and three minutes. Dead by Saturday afternoon. No more nightmares.

I don't know if I can drive non-stop, but the important thing, really, is I'm gone. No one knows where I am. I might as well be dead.

I watch the dotted white line as it pulls me farther away from home.

While crossing the bridge into St. Louis, I think about Beth. She'll be home soon. What will she think when she finds me gone?

The sun shines a bright red, low on the horizon and below my visor. I squint. It will be dark soon. I haven't slept more than four hours a night for the last week. For the last five hours and twenty-five minutes, I've gripped the steering wheel, focused on the pavement as it rolled beneath my tires. I need to sleep. I guess I'll live to see Sunday.

No motel or hotel. I didn't bring enough cash. No credit cards either. I have to disappear.

I wouldn't mind stopping in St. Louis for the night, but I need to put more miles behind me. I'll keep heading west on I-70, looking for a rest stop. No one will bother me out on the highway.

As I cross the Mississippi River into Missouri, I glance at the Arch and head west.

I pass a rest stop soon after sunset. I can't stop yet. I need to get further away.

My stomach growls. I should eat, but I can't stand those chain-restaurant burgers they call food. I'll be dead soon. I want to enjoy the time I have left. Fifty miles past St. Louis, I pull into a truck stop in a place called Kingdom City. They say truckers know where to eat.

I sit in a blue vinyl booth and pick up a menu. Truckers sit in the booth behind me, talking and laughing. One of them is heavy-set. One is young and skinny. One might be a woman.

I give the waitress my order. Seventeen minutes later, she returns with an open-faced roast beef sandwich with mashed potatoes and green beans on the side. A good-sized plate for the money. This roast beef is delicious and it was nearly as fast as a burger. Truckers do know good food.

I'm full and getting sleepy. I drive to the next rest stop near a place called Boonville—four hundred and sixty-five miles from home. She's getting ready for bed. Does she miss me?

I park, use their facilities, get a candy bar, and crawl into the backseat. As I stretch out, I think about everything that brought me to this point. Mom's death. A Bible-thumping city council member in Des Moines. Hendricks. And the damn nightmares. I hope they leave me alone tonight.

I forgot to bring a pillow or blanket. It doesn't matter. I zip up my coat, get into a comfortable position, close my eyes, and drift off. My lullaby is the whizzing of traffic on I-70.

~

I wake up with the sun on my face. I made it through the night.

Before I am fully conscious, I listen for the sounds of my family. Then I remember. I disappeared.

A family pulls their van in next to me. They have two boys, too, but theirs are smaller. They still hold their father's hand.

I grab my toiletries from my gym bag. I nearly forgot my deodor-ant and toothbrush—Beth always packed my bags. I'll be dead soon, but I don't want to go out smelling like a bum.

I open my car door. The mother startles and takes a hard look at me while climbing back into their van and locking the doors. The father holds his sons close as I walk behind them into the restroom. Two days ago, I was a senior engineer and suburban dad. Today, I guess, I am dangerous.

The father watches me closely as his boys do their business. I don't blame him. If I were on a trip with Kyle and Matt, when they were little, and I saw someone who looked like me, I would be careful, too. But I never took Kyle and Matt on a trip. I was busy.

I take a good look at myself in the mirror. Rumpled gray sweatshirt with worn-out jeans. Hair flying in every direction. A day's growth of beard. Yeah, I look dangerous enough.

I wait until they leave to start my rituals. Brushing my teeth, putting on deodorant, taking out my razor. I rub the stubble on my chin. I thought about growing a beard once, several years ago, when I had two weeks off from work. Beth said she would never kiss a man with a beard. She isn't here now. And I'll be dead soon. I throw the razor in the trash.

Walt grew a beard. I saw the pictures. It looked good on him.

I finish up and get back on the road. Heading west.

～

I plan to drive through Kansas and Colorado, then south into Arizona. But light snow starts falling fifteen miles east of Kansas City. A March surprise. I'm tired of snow. I take I-35 south to Wichita.

And this is my life. No more presentations. No more Hendricks. No more nightmares. I eat at truck stops. I sleep at rest stops. I talk to no one.

～

I've been on the road for three days when I pass through Albuquerque. Or was it four? Does it matter?

I'm less than a day away from the Grand Canyon. I can be dead by sunset.

I spot an exit for Santa Fe. For some reason, I have always wanted to go there. I have time. I'll find authentic Mexican food. My last supper.

I pull into town, looking for the real deal. Not one of those places where all the workers have pimples. I'm driving down a busy strip, cruising along, when I hear a thump. Then another. Celeste tilts to the right. Damn. She has a flat.

I ease her into the parking lot of one of those old strip malls with boarded-up storefronts, and get out to inspect the damage.

I find the nail in her tire. Then I look around me. No service stations or auto parts stores nearby. I'll have to put on the spare and drive somewhere for a new tire. I go to my trunk and take out the jack.

The spare is on. I'm hot and hungry. The strip mall has one eating place still open. I walk in and look around.

Gray metal tables with red booths. A stainless steel counter with red vinyl stools. A juke box in the corner. This place is antique. No customers except for a guy sitting at a table in the corner. I perch myself on a stool.

An old man turns around. I mean old. Ninety, at least. "Hi there, son. What can I do for you?"

Son?

"Cheeseburger, with the works, and a coffee."

The old man bustles around the grill, and in fourteen minutes he brings me my burger and coffee. He sure moves fast for someone his age. I take a bite. This is one good burger.

I finish up and open my wallet to pay. It's nearly empty. I haven't used cash much in the last twenty years—I didn't realize how quickly it disappears. And I expected to be dead by now.

I hand my money to the old woman at the cash register and walk out, trying to decide what to do next. I don't have enough cash for a new tire. I can't drive all the way to the Grand Canyon on my spare.

I glance back at the diner. Is that a "Help Wanted" sign? I could sure use the money. Working in a diner. Wouldn't that be something? One last experience.

Before walking back in, I realize I'd better have a story. I can keep my name. Brad Adams is anonymous enough, and I won't have to worry if I'm asked for ID. But who am I? Why am I in Santa Fe, New Mexico, looking for a job? I can't say I'm suicidal. I'm glad I stopped shaving. The whiskers will give credibility to my story.

I shuffle back in toward the woman at the register and point to the sign. "Hi there. I'd like to apply for this job here," I say with a light drawl.

"Ed," she calls. "Someone wants to see you."

The old man looks up. "What's your name?"

"Brad Adams."

"Come over here and tell me about yourself."

I sit on a red stool. "There ain't too much to tell. I come from Illinois. Pulled into town this morning. Need a job."

"Where have you worked?"

"Here and there. Been working since I was fourteen. Never did finish high school. Just picked up jobs wherever I could."

"How do I know you'll stick around?"

"I like what I see so far. Sure is warmer here, I can tell you that."

Ed laughs. "You like it warm? You're going to love it in August then. What can you cook?"

"Burgers, mostly. But I can handle whatever you throw at me."

"Is that so? What do you think, Molly?"

"Where do you live?"

"In my car, for now. It'll take me a while to save up for a place."

"So you really need a job, don't you, Brad?"

"Sure do. Just about out of cash. Never did get one of them credit cards."

"I guess you'll do," says Ed. "Go put on an apron. You have a lot to learn before the dinner crowd walks in."

I did it. I just need to lose my college-level English and I'll be okay. "Sure thing, Ed. Bring 'em on."

I'm still learning when the place starts filling up. The orders come fast and furious. Ed and I work together, side by side. Someone puts money into the jukebox. Country music fills the diner.

It's not a bad place to work. Ed and Molly have owned the place for over fifty years. That's what it's called, too. The Place. They don't have much imagination, but they know people and they know food.

Ed knows just about everyone in the dinner crowd, mostly from "way back." I pick up the lingo and keep the burgers coming. When things slow down a little, I lean on the counter and trade jokes with the customers.

We're about to close when I introduce myself to the waitress. Her red hair is piled high up on her head and her makeup is an inch thick. "Hi there. I'm new to these parts."

"You did a good job for a greenhorn, darling." Ruby laughs and pats me on the back.

The Place doesn't close until eight. I forgot to ask for details. It doesn't matter. Ed and Molly are nice, I eat for free, and it's good to be someone else for a change. Not Brad Adams, the suicidal engineer. Just Brad, a guy who doesn't know much but can fry up a mean burger.

As they're closing, Molly nudges Ed and he turns to me. "You don't have to sleep in that car tonight. We've got a place up over the restaurant. It's not much, but it sure beats the backseat of a Toyota. Our last cook lived there."

"What happened to him?"

"He passed on."

I wonder what he died from. It must not be contagious. I would like to stretch out. "Sure. Sounds good."

While Molly counts the money, Ed takes me upstairs to my new home. There's a small kitchen, a slightly larger living room with a well-worn couch, and a bedroom about the size of our walk-in closet back home. Home. Is home where my heart is, with Beth and the boys, or is it where I hang my hat? I forgot my White Sox cap but I can hang my sweatshirt on the hook in the bathroom. This will do.

"We open up at seven. You need to be downstairs at around six-thirty to get the grill fired up. Molly and I come in at a quarter till. You don't work on Sunday. Molly won't let me open up on the Lord's Day. She says it's bad karma."

Talk about mixed metaphors. Now that I think of it, Ed and Molly seem like the type who did drugs in the 60s. I wonder how old they are.

Ed leaves. I stretch out on the bed. The mattress is lumpy, but after a few hours behind the counter I could sleep anywhere.

I think about my first shift at The Place. I haven't laughed that much since the plane went down. There's something in the air down here. I relax into the pillow, and I'm out.

I get downstairs at twenty-eight minutes after six. The Place is quiet. I make the coffee, pour myself a cup, and take ten minutes to look out through the plate glass window and watch the sun rise over the desert.

Ed and Molly walk in as I take my last sip. Molly takes her place at the cash register and Ed comes back behind the counter.

Ruby walks in five minutes later with a grin. "Good morning, everyone."

At 7:00 AM sharp, the bell over the door rings, the first customer walks in, and I get his eggs frying on the grill. I could get used to this.

Over the next few days, I fall into the rhythm of The Place. I learn Ruby moved here from Houston sixteen years ago, escaping an abusive husband. Her only daughter will graduate from college next May. Ben, who is always our first customer, likes his eggs over easy and his coffee black. Vanessa, who came here from Indiana because of her allergies, always orders the meatloaf platter for lunch. Miguel doesn't care what he eats, but he always has a story to tell. Maria sits at a booth in the back and talks to herself while eating her cheeseburger, hold the lettuce, and checking her email. And Lou sits at the counter, on the red stool in the middle, and talks to me while he eats his hamburgers, extra pickles, and onion rings. Whenever I have a free moment, I talk to Lou.

He's eight months and two days younger than me and has lived around here all his life. His mother and sister sell pottery to the tourists. His ex-wife moved to Memphis where his son studies pre-med. He learned how to operate a forklift when he was eighteen and has never done anything else. He orders two burgers, onion rings, and a cola every day for lunch. His hair is darker and straighter than mine, and his skin is brown—we'll never be mistaken for brothers—but after a few days, I feel he's someone I can trust.

On Sunday, I sleep until nearly eleven. It's good to be in a bed again, even one with a lumpy mattress. And the nightmares have stopped.

At twenty minutes after twelve, I hear Lou's voice. "Hey, Brad, you there?"

I'm still in my boxers. I open the window and call down, "Yeah, hold on."

Eight minutes later, I climb into his car. Ed paid me yesterday so the first thing I do is buy a new tire for my Celeste. Then Lou shows me around. We drive by an open market called The Plaza. Beth would like the turquoise. I see the state capital building and a lot of old churches. Missions, Lou calls them. Finally he takes me out into the desert to his old stomping ground. The view is incredible.

Lou laughs at my expressions of awe. "Man, you act like you never saw a desert before."

"I never have, unless you count looking out the window of a plane at 30,000 feet."

"That's just sad, man."

It's dark when he pulls up to the restaurant. Before I get out he says, "Be straight with me, man. You're no drifter. What's the story? Did you kill someone?"

I plan to cover my lies, but he's sitting there grinning and I know he won't buy it. "Not yet," I say.

"You work for the mob or something?"

"Nothing that exciting. I'm an average guy—wife and two kids. I need to disappear."

"You robbed a bank."

"If I robbed a bank, do you think I'd be working my ass off at this place?"

"Was it a woman?"

"No. I love my wife. I miss her. But I can't go back."

"What is it? You'd better level with me or I might slip and blow your cover."

"I don't know what else to tell you, but you can come up for a drink. I've got root beer in the fridge."

"No beer?"

"Molly won't allow it. And I've got one brother who's a born-again Christian and another who's a Muslim, so the whole family has gone dry." *Do they miss me?*

"Okay. Root beer will do, for now."

We sit on the tattered orange couch and I tell him about the plane crash, the nightmares, and the day I went away.

"But why did you leave?"

He seems like the kind of guy who would understand. "I've worked at the same place for twenty-three years, but I was about to get canned. If I disappear, my wife can collect on the insurance."

"She's in on it?"

"No. She's too honest. I just picked up and left. After I'm declared dead, she'll collect."

"That takes years. How long do you plan on hiding out?"

"I'm not going to hide out. I'm going to kill myself."

"Are you for real? You've got a good woman, a nice house, a Lexus, and you're leaving all that behind? I didn't figure you for that kind of fool."

"The house and the Lexus will be reclaimed by the bank once they know I can't pay for them. I hope they cut Beth some slack until she gets the paperwork completed."

"Man, you are a piece of work, coming up with a half-assed plan like that. How you gonna do it, anyway?"

I tell him my solution. "It's the best I can come up with."

He smirks. "If you're in such a hurry to get there, why are you hanging around here?"

"The flat tire slowed me down, but I think I'll stay on for another week or so. I like the work."

"You're too smart to aim so low. Isn't there anything else you want to do before you die?"

"I never swam in the ocean, but I don't see any oceans around here." Now I smirk. "And I never saw the Grand Canyon."

"You should get a real good view on your way down."

"I guess so."

He takes out a cigarette. "Want one?"

"I gave them up almost ten years ago. I'll catch it from Molly, too, if she smells smoke up here."

"What is she, your mother? Anyway, it's not that kind of cigarette."

I take a closer look. "You rolled it yourself?"

"It's a skill. What do you think? You gonna try it? Or are you too hung up about your life in the suburbs?"

"They have these in Illinois. We're not that backward."

He takes something else from his pocket. It's hard and round. "I bet you don't have this."

"What's that?"

"Peyote. You heard of it?"

"Don't tell me you're some kind of holy man."

"My uncle is. He talks about connecting with the spirit, but he never seems to notice when I sneak a little for recreation. How about it?"

Something else to do before I die. But I'm too old to experiment with drugs again. "I'll think about it and let you know."

"Man, you have been in the suburbs too long. Where are your suits? I bet you brought them with you."

"Everything is back home. It's just me, trying to get away."

"You stick with me. The peyote will take you on the trip of a life-time."

Peyote. I have heard of the stuff. What do I have to lose?

I make the deal with Lou on Monday. He brings the stuff at night.

"You don't smoke it?"

"Just chew a little. You'll see."

Maybe it's because I'm older, but this stuff is definitely stronger than the grass I used to smoke. I see visions and dream dreams. I'm free. Not a care in the world. This is great.

But in the morning, I have to go downstairs and cook Ben's eggs. I had a hold of something last night. It's gone now. And I'm tired. I overcook the eggs.

Ben complains to Ruby. "I've been coming to this diner for twenty years. You all know how I like my eggs."

"Hey, darling," Ruby yells into the kitchen. "Try again. And you'd better get it right this time. Ben is our best customer. Aren't you, sweetheart?" She pinches his cheek.

Ed frowns. "Are you all right, son?"

"I'm great," I say, frying more eggs.

Lou comes in for his burger five minutes before noon. When Ed is out of earshot, he whispers, "How you feeling, man?"

"Not too good. It was wild, but I need my sleep. I'm not a kid anymore."

"Forget about work. Vanessa can get by without her meatloaf for a day or two."

It's tempting, but I'd better pass. "I like working here. And I don't think Vanessa could get by. She claims to be allergic to everything else."

"What about Sunday?"

"Bring the stuff Saturday night. Let's see what I can find."

I spend "The Lord's Day" stoned out of my mind. The universe opens up to me and I have all the answers. I don't know where I am, but I'd like to stay.

I was a good worker for too long, though. I clear my mind by Monday morning. While I'm flipping burgers, I have visions of where

I went.

After the breakfast rush, Ruby pokes me. "What are you so happy about, darling?"

"Had a good weekend, that's all."

"You must've picked up a girl. Next time you get lonely, honey, just call Ruby."

"Yeah, I'll remember that."

I wait until Saturday night for another "experience"—I owe it to Ed and Molly to finish the week. All day Sunday, I'm floating.

This is what I've been missing. The peace. Everything is right and beautiful. No problems. No nightmares.

I take more and struggle to get downstairs. I stare at Ben's eggs frying on the grill, awed by their transformation. I'm lost in my visions and burn Maria's burger. Ed shakes his head. When Lou comes in at his usual time, Ed hovers nearby. Lou plays it cool, but I'm soaring.

And I don't want to come down. This is what I've been looking for. Lou comes by after hours and gives me more.

But something is wrong. I can't sit still. I pace the tiny apartment, the walls closing in on me. My mind races. I see fire. Our house burning to the ground with Beth and the boys inside. They scream. I can't save them. I see Kyle speeding around a curve, the car slamming into a tree. I see Mom and Walt, struggling, drowning. I bang my head against the wall, but the nightmares won't stop. Pain. Suffering. Death. I scream. I curse.

When it's over, I fall into the couch, exhausted.

"Brad, wake up."

Walt?

He gently shakes my shoulder. He's back.

I open my eyes and try to open my arms to hug him. But it's not Walt. It's Ed.

"It's almost seven. What are you doing up here?"

I groan.

Ed sighs. "I'll take care of breakfast. Make sure you get down there for the lunch crowd."

I can't answer. My head pounds.

"I'll tell Lou not to come back around here. I thought you were smarter than that."

I am a lot smarter than that, Ed. I have a graduate degree in engineering. I could run circles around you if I wanted.

"Sorry," I say.

"It's time for you to move on. You drifters are too unsteady. You're just like the last guy we hired."

Did he throw himself through the window after a bad trip?

"How did he die?"

"He didn't die. He passed on to the next town. He said he was headed for California."

I manage to get downstairs as the lunch crowd is coming in. When the rush is over, I sit down and close my eyes. My head still hurts. And I miss Lou. He was always good for a laugh.

After Ed and Molly leave, he calls up. "Hey, Brad, let me in."

I'm tempted. That was just one bad trip.

But it was bad enough. I thought the peyote would bring me peace. It betrayed me. I turn off the light and go to sleep.

Ed and Molly let me finish the week. On Saturday night, I say goodbye.

"I appreciate your kindness. I'm sorry to have disappointed you."

"You've gotten a lot smarter these last few weeks," Ed smirks. "Maybe that peyote did something for you, but I can't tolerate it."

"Didn't you do drugs, Ed?"

"No, but our boy did. Our only son. We haven't seen him in over thirty years. We keep hoping that one of the drifters we take in can tell us where he is. I search the face of every man who comes through that door, looking for him."

"I hope he comes back." I think of Kyle. We have our problems, but nothing that bad.

"Hope so. Have a good trip, wherever you're going. And stay away from that stuff."

I climb into my car and drive away. Heading west to my death.

~

I wasted more than a month in Santa Fe. I'm living on borrowed time.

I stop at a rest stop outside of Albuquerque. I'm less than seven hours from the canyon, but I'm beat.

I sleep late and stop for breakfast on my way out of New Mexico. I can still be dead by sunset.

I pull into Flagstaff in the late afternoon. An hour and forty-nine minutes from the canyon. But what's the rush? When I go over that edge, I want to be fully alive. I'll only get to do this once. I need to do it right.

I find a side street and park. One more night.

~

I eat a good breakfast before heading out. Three fried eggs, two orders of hash browns, four slices of toast, four strips of bacon, two cups of coffee. In a few hours it will be over. Who cares if my arteries are clogged?

I take the highway north to the canyon, marveling at the scenery along the way. Nothing dramatic—mostly forests—but it's peaceful. The evergreens usher me to my final destination.

I reach the Grand Canyon National Park, pay my admission, and drive another two miles without seeing anything. Where did they put it? Don't tell me I drove all this way for nothing. Man, I must still be tripping.

There it is, finally, opening up ahead of me. I drive west along the south rim, looking for a secluded place to park. I step out of my car and gaze at the canyon.

It's magnificent. I never imagined. The pictures don't do it justice.

I walk slowly up to the edge and look down. The cliffs are craggy here. I might get caught on the way down. I might survive.

I remember the package in my backseat. I'll take it with me. Mom and me, going down together. Just like in the old days.

I'm walking near the edge, looking for a place without ledges, when another car pulls in. A man, a woman, and two teenagers get out. The girl looks right at me. Does she know? Can she tell?

I'll have to wait until they leave. I watch as they take pictures of one another, standing as close to the edge as they dare. The mother frets as her son clowns. "No, Mitch. Be careful."

They're taking too long. I could go look for another spot. No, I'll wait them out.

While I wait, I actually look at the canyon, studying it. It's awesome, in the truest sense of the word. The colors. I could say it's mostly red, but that wouldn't be saying much. I never imagined so many shades of red. I concentrate on the colors. Never the same, from top to bottom or left to right. I never realized rocks could be so exciting.

Next I study the formations. A rock sculpture built from the ground up. A succession of ridges, one blending into the next. Small solitary sculptures reach for the sky. I'm amazed at the precision. What architect, what engineer, could have achieved this?

They say it was carved out by the Colorado River over millions of years, but I find it hard to believe a simple river could have produced this beauty.

I sit and gaze out over the canyon, studying the colors and formations. I analyze the structural development. I scrutinize the varying hues. I'm still staring when I feel a tap on my shoulder. I look up.

"It's time to leave. The park is closing for the night."

I glance to the west. The sun is a red orb, veiled by clouds. Shades of red and orange illuminate the horizon.

"Let's go," says the ranger. "You don't want to be here after dark."

But I haven't completed my mission.

"Sir." He issues a final warning, watching as I glance once more at the canyon before heading to my car with the package still in my arms. I climb in. He follows me to the exit.

As I drive back to Flagstaff, through the densely forested areas which begin to look eerie in the coming dark, I see it. The colors. The precision. I didn't take anything this time, but I am still flying high through the canyon.

I buy some real Mexican tacos and find a place to park for the night. Later, as I drift away, I'm still flying.

～

I wake up refreshed. Another night without nightmares. It's been over a month now—except for that one bad trip, which was worse than any nightmare.

Yesterday, I wasted my time staring, completely unprepared for the beauty of the canyon. Now I know. I'm ready.

When I pay my admission, the ranger says, "Welcome back."

She recognizes me. Will she be suspicious to learn my body was found at the bottom?

The ranger who told me to leave will recognize me, too. If they know why I came, my plan will be useless. I need to make it look like an accident. I'll leave the package in my car. They'll find the wallet on my body. I was standing too close to the edge and I slipped. Beth can collect on the insurance. No one will know. Lou won't tell. He has enough secrets of his own.

I drive to a different spot and wait a few minutes. No company. This is it.

Forty-seven years have come to this. Most of my life has been rough. Falling into a rocky canyon seems like a suitable ending.

I take another moment to look. It is spectacular. If I wanted to describe it to Kyle and Matt, I don't know if I could find the words.

I walk casually toward the edge, getting closer with each step. I look down. A clear drop to the bottom. Will it hurt, or will I die instantly?

I take another step into some gravel. My feet fly out from under me and I slide rapidly toward the edge. I grasp at the ground, trying to hold on. I grab a clump of weeds with my right hand and a large rock with my left. I've stopped, with only inches to spare. I lie on my back, trying to catch my breath. That was close.

What am I doing? It was supposed to be close. Man, I can't believe I screwed that up. Can I do it again? I don't need to fall. All I need to do is let go. The pebbles will take me down.

I'm almost there. I just need to let go.

I look up at the clear sky. An eagle flies overhead. I watch, forgetting for a few seconds why I'm here.

I have to let go. But I can't. I don't want to die.

I'm so close. I've come all this way, but I want to live.

I slowly pull myself away from the edge and carefully move into a seated position. I peer down, and shiver.

I cautiously stand and inch further away from the rim. I sit on a rock and stare at the canyon until a ranger comes and tells me I need to go.

If not for the ranger, I would stay here all night. I couldn't see the beauty, but maybe I could feel the spirit of something. There is something more important here than rocks and erosion. I wish I knew what it was.

The ranger reminds me to move along. I walk slowly to my car. As I look out over the canyon one last time, my heart bursts with a new sensation. Awe? Wonder? Faith? Faith in what? Whoever or whatever created this, I guess. Not the Colorado River. Something or someone more powerful.

Slowly, I climb into my car and drive to the exit with the ranger following.

I eat tacos for dinner again and try to sleep, but I can't relax. I set it all up so carefully—except for that distraction in Santa Fe—but I couldn't follow through. Now what am I supposed to do?

I toss and turn all night. Not quite awake, but never fully asleep. I wake up exhausted.

During breakfast I grab a napkin and jot down my options:

1. Return to Chicago. Tell Beth everything. Put the house up for sale and look for another job.
2. Go swim in the ocean.
3. Try again.

I quickly cross number three off the list. It's a good idea, and it would solve a lot of problems, but I don't have it in me to destroy myself.

What will it be? East to Chicago or west to the ocean?

I need to go back to them. We'll have to do without. So what? I've done without for the last five weeks and it's not as bad as I expected. We'll manage.

I should go home. But I'm nearly fifty years old and I have never swum in the ocean. I've come this far. Just five hundred miles more.

I'll go to the ocean first. Then I'll turn around and go home. I finish my breakfast and head west on I-40.

I can barely keep my eyes open. I'm still worn out from all that tripping in Santa Fe. I am too old for that.

I haven't seen a rest stop for many miles, and I don't think I'll find any soon. I take the next exit and pull into a discount store parking lot. Warning signs are posted every twenty feet—No Overnight Parking. I'll wake up early and head out before anyone notices.

I wake to a steady rapping noise. A police officer stares at me through the window.

I rub my eyes, reach forward, and open the door. "Hello, Officer. Can I help you?"

"What are you doing here? Didn't you see the signs?"

"I'm sorry, Officer. I'm heading to California to see my elderly mother. She broke her hip a few days ago and she's all alone in that hospital. I couldn't afford to fly and I'm trying to get there as fast as I can. She was expecting me sometime last night, but I got tired and I thought I'd better pull over in case I fell asleep and caused an accident. I hope there's no problem."

"No, no problem. It was smart of you to pull over. Be on your way then. Don't keep your mother waiting."

I climb into the front seat. He smiles and waves as I drive away.

This is great. I can be anyone I want to be, inventing friends and relatives to get me through any situation.

It's late, and I'm hungry, but I'd better eat in a different town. I don't want that policeman to think I don't care about my elderly mother.

Mom would laugh if anyone called her elderly. She didn't live long enough to be really old. Those last couple of years she looked younger than ever. That's something I have a hard time reconciling. Being with Walt made her more alive. But being with Walt, in that plane, killed her.

I drive into California in the afternoon, stop to eat at a small diner, and pull into a rest stop a few miles short of Barstow. Tomorrow, I'll go to L.A.

I wake up early and do my morning routine. I used to spend one hour and twenty minutes getting ready for work. I showered, shaved, and decided which tie to wear. If I was in a very good mood, I wore one of the corny ties my boys gave me every Father's Day. Everyone had a good laugh at my expense, but it made my boys happy.

No more ties or designer dress shirts. I can wear a sweatshirt—gray, navy, or black—or if it's warm I can just wear a t-shirt.

I haven't shaved in six weeks. I need to buy a cheap pair of scissors and trim my beard. It's getting scruffy. I haven't seen any frightened parents since Missouri, but I look scarier now. I have the drifter look down pat.

I'll drive into downtown L.A. and see what I can find. I've thought about looking up dear old Uncle Rob. He gave me his card at the memorial service. He lives in Santa Monica.

He came to say goodbye to the sister he ignored all those years. Good for him. He's old now and if I visit him he might put me in his will, but I don't need his money. I needed him when I was small and my father was beating me.

❧

I pull into L.A. in the late afternoon and cruise along a main strip. I'm stopped at a red light when I see him. He crosses in front of me and keeps on walking. I almost honk my horn. He looks like a younger version of Joshua. But he's just another Muslim.

I watch as he walks into a mosque in the middle of the block. I find a parking spot, walk back to the mosque, and enter a large hallway—looking around until I spot him in the prayer area.

He's walking out. "Assalaamu alaikum," he says.

"Hi. My name's Brad. I'm not a Muslim, but my brother is. You look like him. It must be the beard."

"I'm Abdullah. Does your brother live around here? Maybe I know him."

"No. He's in Chicago. That's where I'm from."

"Are you here on business?"

He's not Joshua, but I feel comfortable with him. "Do you have a minute?"

"Sure. Let's go back in and sit down."

I remove my shoes before walking into the mosque.

"You do know something about Islam, don't you?"

"My brother has been a Muslim for fifteen or sixteen years. And he asks us to remove our shoes in his house."

"Excuse me a moment." He turns away and calls someone on his cell.

While he's on the phone, a man with a full black beard says, "Assalaamu alaikum."

"I'm not a Muslim."

His eyes narrow. "You can't come into the masjid. You're not clean." He turns to Abdullah. "You should know better than to bring him in here."

Abdullah quickly ends his call. "Let's go." We put on our shoes and he leads me to a quiet hallway.

"What was that about?"

"Some people think non-Muslims shouldn't enter the mosque. I don't agree, but it's better not to argue." He puts down his backpack, shuts off his phone, and turns to me. "So, Brad, what brings you to Los Angeles?"

I end up narrating my entire story. The plane crash. The nightmares. Hendricks. The family I left behind and the awe I felt at the Grand Canyon. I even confess trying peyote and failing suicide. He looks like Joshua and I think I can trust him.

"Brad, my father says nothing happens by accident. I've always tried to prove him wrong, yet I met you today because I resemble your brother. I don't think our meeting is coincidental."

"Are you talking about fate?"

"Yes. I think my father is right. We were meant to meet today."

I laugh. "Why? So you can convert me?"

"I imagine your brother has already tried. But you sound like you're searching for something. Have you thought about looking for your answers in Islam?"

Searching? I just came to swim in the ocean.

"No, never. It's fine for Joshua, and his conversion helped him leave his wild life behind, but I've been a husband, father, engineer, pillar of the community. People like me don't find our answers in Islam."

"I don't think people like you travel across the country in an old yellow Toyota."

"How do you know what car I drive?"

"I noticed you when I crossed the street."

"And your father would call that fate, right?"

"Have you eaten? Where will you sleep tonight?"

"Where would it would be safe to park?"

"Come to my apartment. My mother visited last weekend, and she cooked for me before she left. Do you mind leftovers?"

"Of course not. But you're in school, aren't you?" I point to the backpack. "I'm sure you need to study."

"After we eat, I'll still have time for my studies. All I have to offer is an old couch, but it's probably more comfortable than the backseat of your car."

"I'm sure it is, but I'm a stranger. How do you know I'm not really an axe murderer?"

"I'll take my chances."

"How do I know you're not an axe murderer?"

He laughs. "You don't. But you have just driven across the country in an old car. You left your family and came within inches of plunging to your death. Someone who is willing to take those kinds of risks probably isn't afraid of much."

I have many fears. Losing my job. Dying. Facing the consequences when I return to Chicago. But I can still fake it. "We'll both have to take our chances then."

We walk to his car, and he drives me back to my car. He found a much better parking spot.

As I get out, he picks up a piece of paper and quickly makes some notes. "This is how to get to my apartment, and here's my phone number. I want you to follow me, but you'll need this in case you get lost."

We pull out into the city streets. He waits for me as the next light turns yellow. Traffic is heavy, and cars often come between us, but I manage to keep sight of his red compact. He greets me in the parking lot of his building.

"You're good. Have you ever thought about becoming a private investigator?"

I wonder if any agency would be interested in a washed-up engineer. "I know L.A. is infamous for its traffic, but it's not much heavier than what I faced going to work in Chicago. I sure don't miss that."

When we walk into the apartment he excuses himself, spreads out a rug, and stands in a corner, praying. I've seen Joshua pray. And Jeremy. And Michael. The first time I saw each of my nephews pray, I felt like grabbing them by the shoulders and shaking some sense into them. Joshua has always been different, but I couldn't understand why any red-blooded American boy would choose such a restrictive life. I think of them now as I watch Abdullah who, except for his name, is like any other red-blooded American boy.

He finishes and notices me watching him.

"I'm sorry. I shouldn't stare. You remind me of my nephews."

"They're Muslims too?"

"Two of them are. Joshua's sons. The oldest just recently converted."

"I'm sure that made your brother happy."

"Yes. I don't understand it though."

"What don't you understand?"

"It's not important. You were going to pray at the mosque, weren't you, if I hadn't come along?"

"I try to say most of my prayers at the mosque, but we needed to leave. I didn't want you to follow me in the dark. Are you hungry?"

He opens the refrigerator door, bringing out chicken and something he calls couscous. It smells great as he heats it up.

We eat at the small white table in his kitchen. The food is delicious. "Your mother is a good cook."

He laughs. "When I was younger, I felt embarrassed by my mother's cooking. My friends were eating burgers and pizza, and I was eating couscous. But, yes, she is a very good cook. She enjoys it, and I enjoy the way she spoils me."

I learn more about him while we eat. Abdullah's parents are Moroccan, but he was born and raised in California. He's in his first year of college, studying film-making. I almost laugh because it sounds so cliché.

After dinner, he shows me around his small apartment. "There's your couch. It folds out into a bed. Feel free to watch TV or browse the net. Maybe you'd like to email your family. I'll see you in the morning." He grabs his backpack and heads for his bedroom.

It's a nice place, and not that small, really, for just one guy. My student apartment wasn't much larger than this and there were three of us. One of my roommates, Chuck, never stopped talking. I don't know how I managed to study.

I stare at the computer. I could email Beth and let her know where I am. I'm safe. I love her. But what if she answers? What will I say?

I'm not afraid. That's what Abdullah said. Why should I fear my wife? I log in and start typing.

I write and rewrite the email eight times. Should I tell her everything, starting with my argument with Hendricks? If not, what should I leave out?

I finally decide to keep it simple. "My dearest Beth," I write, "I'm sorry I left you like that. I had my reasons. I want to let you know I'm alive, and I love you very much. I'll be home soon. Please understand." I sign it, "With all my love, Brad."

Before hitting the send button, I add, "Don't reply. Don't worry. I'll come home soon." I deliver the message into cyberspace and quickly log off. I know she'll write back, but I don't want to hear from her. She'll ask me questions. It will be complicated. I'll explain everything, face-to-face, after I swim in the ocean.

I miss my family. I shouldn't have left. But the longer I'm gone, the harder it is for me to think about going back.

I don't know what else to do with myself. Abdullah has a small collection of books. Most are about Islam. I pick one up, thumb through it, and quickly put it down. Most of the Muslims I've met are nice, except for some like that guy in the mosque. Arrogant. Anyway, it's not for me.

I'm bored, but I'm comfortable. I flip through the TV channels. Finally, I'm tired enough. I pull out the sofa bed and enjoy the best sleep I've had since the night before the plane crash. No nightmares. No tossing. Just peace.

I wake up to the smell of coffee. Abdullah is standing in front of the stove, making scrambled eggs. He smiles when I walk into the kitchen.

"Did you sleep well?"

"Very well. Your couch is much more comfortable than my back-seat."

"Good. We can eat breakfast together before I leave. I work a few hours in the morning, and I have afternoon classes."

"I'd better be on my way then."

"No, you can stay. In fact, I insist. I'll give you my key so you can explore while I'm gone. Try to be back by six, though, because I only have one key. Is there any place special you'd like to see while you're here?"

"I want to check out a beach. But you don't have to do that. You barely know me."

"I don't think you're an axe murderer. I'm sure you're not a thief either. Here, I'll draw you a map to the best beach in the area."

"You've done enough already."

"My parents taught me to be hospitable. It's the Moroccan way." He gives me the directions, takes a last sip of coffee, and heads out the door. "Enjoy the beach. I'll see you at six."

I clean up the kitchen and study his map. After a nice hot shower—that place in Santa Fe never did have enough hot water in the tank—I get dressed and head for the beach.

I've attended business meetings up and down the east coast, and I've spoken at conferences in San Francisco and Seattle, but I have never gone to the beach. I've seen the ocean, from a distance, but I have never experienced it.

His directions take me right to it. A large expanse of sand preceding a tremendous expanse of ocean as far as I can see. I take off my shoes and socks, and walk barefoot through the sand. Then I roll up my jeans and wade into the ocean. Cool waves beat against my legs. This is what I've waited for.

I go back to the beach, sit on a large rock, and stare into the endless blue horizon. My mind becomes free as I listen to the sound of the waves. I remember my ocean CD. This is different.

I sit on the rock for a moment or two. When I arrived, the tide was several yards away. It crept closer until it was nearly to my knees. I closed my eyes and enjoyed the sensation of the cold water against my shins. Now the water is receding again. I notice the sun has moved into the west. I've been here all day, but it felt like only a moment or two.

The clock in my car confirms it. Ten minutes after four. I'd better head back. I don't want to leave Abdullah standing outside his apartment, wondering why he trusted a complete stranger.

I take another look at the ocean before driving away. I never imagined it would be like this. I should have come here years ago. And I should have brought my family with me.

I get back to the apartment, pick up the phone, and order supper.

The pizzas arrive a few minutes before Abdullah does. He looks at the boxes on the kitchen table and smiles. "How did you know I like pizza?"

"I have kids."

He opens one of the boxes and frowns.

"What's wrong?"

"I appreciate the thought, but I can't eat pepperoni."

I knew that.

"I'm sorry. I forgot. That's what my oldest son likes."

"Don't worry about it. But you'll have to eat it." He opens the other box. "I will take some slices of this cheese pizza, if you don't mind."

"Take the whole thing."

"Did you get to the ocean?"

I nod. I want to tell him what I felt there, but I can't put it into words.

He takes another shot at conversation. "Will you go home now?"

"I don't know. I should."

"You told me what happened. But why exactly did you leave?"

I don't like all the questions. "It's complicated."

"Was it the plane crash, or was there something else?"

He won't give up.

"What would your father say about the plane crash?" I ask.

"He would say everyone has a life span. When our lives are over, we die."

"Just like that?"

"We can't live forever."

"Are you saying my mother and stepfather were meant to die on that plane?"

"I know it sounds harsh."

"Three hundred and forty-six people were killed in that crash, some of them children. You're talking about mass murder."

"I wouldn't call it that, but I believe Allah has a plan."

"A plan? Killing three hundred and forty-six people is a plan?"

"I believe there's a purpose in everything. Even in the plane crash."

"I can't accept that."

"It does sound unreasonable to someone without faith."

"That's me, then."

We finish the pizza in silence. I choke down the rest of my slice. I'm not very hungry.

Abdullah pats my shoulder. "I didn't mean to upset you. I understand how much grief you still have over your loss."

I shrug. "I'm sorry for bringing pepperoni into your home."

"Let's call it a draw." He picks up his backpack and goes into his room.

I flip through the channels, trying to forget, but I can't find any sitcom or drama to distract me. I arrange the books in his shelf alphabetically. Then I pace around the room until I'm tired enough.

He emerges from his room just as I'm pulling out the sofa bed. "I think I'd better move on tomorrow," I say. "Thanks for your Moroccan hospitality."

"I thought you might want to get going. I'd like to give you something before you leave."

It's a copy of the Qur'an. "You are trying to convert me."

"Whether you read it or not is up to you. I have only one condition. Never place it on the floor."

"I can respect that. I won't promise to read it though." I wish I had something to give him. I jot down his address and phone number. I'll send him something after I have myself sorted out.

I get up early to make breakfast. We eat and talk a little before he has to go. We shake hands in the parking lot.

"Good luck," I say. "I'm glad we met."

"Call me sometime, or email me. Let me know where you are in your search."

My search. Is that what this is?

"I'll do that."

I get into my car, wave one last time, and follow his directions out of Los Angeles.

I've experienced the ocean now. I need to go back to Chicago, but I head north toward the coastal highway instead. I won't go far. I just want to see the ocean again. I may never come back to California.

I spot an exit for Santa Monica and I plan to drive past it. I'll ignore him just as he ignored me. But I signal and stop at a gas station to ask for directions.

Nice house. One of those expansive California ranch homes overlooking the ocean.

I ring the bell. A minute later, an old man comes to the door. It's only been a few months, but he looks so much older.

"Hello, Uncle Rob. I'm Brad, Evie's oldest son."

"Yes, Brad, it's good to see you. Please come in."

He leads me through the house to the patio in back. Expensive furniture. Asian artwork. He did very well for himself.

We sit on the patio. I stare out over the ocean.

"What brings you to California?"

He's family, but he's a stranger to me.

"I'm here on business."

"I'm glad you were able to stop by. How have you been?"

I'm supposed to say, "I'm fine, thank you. What about yourself?" Mom taught me to be polite. She also taught me to control my emotions. But she's gone now and I can say what I feel. "I have been struggling to come to terms with my mother's death."

"I'm sure it's been difficult. I miss Evie very much."

"How could you miss her? You hardly ever saw her."

"She was my sister. I cared for her."

"You sure had a funny way of showing it. Don't you know how much she needed you? Why did you ignore her?"

"Your mother has always been special to me, but we both had lives of our own. She never said anything. I would have helped if I thought she needed me."

"Mom wouldn't ask for help. You know that."

"You're right. I remember one time, when she was eleven, she climbed up a tree and got stuck. When it got dark, our mother sent me to look for her. I called her name, but she never made a sound. She stayed in that tree until she could figure out how to get down on her own. She didn't want my help."

"Did you know Sam left her with three young children? Did you know he beat her? Did you know he beat me for more than three years before he left?"

"I knew he left, of course, but I didn't know about the abuse. I never felt comfortable around Sam, but your mother seemed happy."

"My mother was an actress."

"Yes. Always. Even when she was hurt she never cried. She took it."

"She took a lot in her life. Why didn't you know?"

He shrugs. "We were close as children, but there was nothing for me in Chicago. I moved out here and built a career and a life for myself. Time got away from me."

Tired excuses. That's all I'll get from him.

"You should have loved her," I scream. I walk out and get back on the freeway, heading north, gripping the steering wheel until my knuckles turn white.

He didn't have time for us, and I sure as hell don't have any time for him.

Fifteen miles out, I stop at a public beach and wade in the ocean, kicking the surf, walking back and forth until I'm too tired to go on. Then I crawl into the backseat of my car.

I wake up with a headache. I wash my face in the ocean and stare at the horizon until my mind becomes clearer.

I can still see the expression on his face when I walked out. I did what I wanted to do. I hurt him. I get back on the freeway.

He opens the door and reaches for me. "You came back."

I hug him lightly and pull away. "Look, Uncle Rob, I shouldn't have talked to you that way—I know Mom wouldn't like it—but it hurts. Would you like to get some lunch?"

"It will be my treat."

He leads me to a Chinese restaurant with a large buffet. We talk over rice and noodles.

"I miss my sister. We were very close. But life got in the way." He shakes his head. "I don't know what happened to the years, but we were in touch. Did you know we talked regularly for the last four years? A week didn't pass without a phone call or a series of emails. She told me all about you boys. I knew about her catering business and her marriage to Walt. She called me from LAX on their way to Malaysia, and even called once from Thailand."

"I didn't know that. The last time I saw you, before the memorial service, was two weeks after her surgery. You flew in for a few days. Then you left. You never stayed."

"I had my own life out here."

"Nearly every time you came, it was because of some tragedy— my grandparents' funerals, my mother's illness—but I was always happy to see you. Mom talked about you all the time. We watched your movies, and she told everyone about her little brother, the Hollywood screenwriter. You should have seen her the night you won that Oscar. She was actually jumping up and down."

I can still picture it.

"I always admired you, Uncle Rob. I used to imagine you would come to Chicago and rescue me."

"I didn't know about the abuse. If I had known things were that bad, I would have done something to stop it."

"Would you?"

"I like to think so, but time gets away from us. You know how it is. By the way, I know we're more casual out here, but I would like to know what kind of business you have been conducting in torn jeans and a t-shirt."

How much should I tell this stranger uncle of mine?

"I don't know. Things were getting rough and, well, here I am."

"Getting away from it all. California is the place for that. Is it your marriage?"

"No, my marriage is good. I don't know what it is." I study the stir-fried rice on my plate.

He reaches over and pats my arm. "I remember when my mother died. I had four years to prepare, but I always thought she would beat the cancer. When Evie called to tell me Mom was in a coma, I cried like a baby. I always thought I would have another chance. I would wrap up my projects, fly to Chicago, and we would have a good old time. I had four years to think about it, but she died too soon." He puts down his chopsticks. I see a tear.

He's old. He can afford to cry. I quickly regain control.

"It wasn't just that. I had problems at work and trouble sleeping. Things were closing in on me." I've told him much more than I meant to reveal. I swallow hard, forcing down another mouthful of rice.

"Closing in. So you stepped out for a little fresh air. What does your wife think of your vacation?"

"I left without telling her. I need to go back soon."

"But you don't want to go back yet, do you?"

I start to protest, but he stops me. "I hear it in your voice. You like this taste of freedom and you're not ready to give it up."

"But I need to go back to my family."

"I wrote a movie like this once. A man wakes up one day and decides he's had enough. He takes off to find himself."

"How does it end?"

"He discovers there's no place like home. Shades of Wizard of Oz, you know. When he returns, his wife welcomes him with open arms and his boss gives him a raise."

"A real Hollywood ending."

"I'm not finished. He tries it for a few days. Then he says to hell with it. As the credits roll, he's walking off into the sunset."

I remember that movie. I didn't know it was one of Uncle Rob's. "Did you ever feel that way?"

"When I was your age, I felt it nearly every day."

"What did you do about it?"

"I wrote screenplays. My heroes were strong men who followed their hearts. And after a good day of writing, I went home and suffered marital hell. You never met your Aunt Barb. She refused to fly to Chicago with me. Said it was too cold. She should know about cold." He snickers. "Barbed wire, I called her. That woman was torture. But that wife of yours is a real lady."

I nod. She is.

"When are you going back to her?"

"I don't know. I want to go home and take care of my family, but I need time to take care of myself."

"What will happen if you don't go home yet?"

"Beth will be unhappy. Money will be tight."

"What if you do go home?"

I speak more to myself. "I'll be tormented by nightmares. Money will still be tight. And I'll be so busy taking care of them there won't be anything left for me."

"I'm an old man, Brad. I have my health and my house on the ocean. I have my Oscar. I write a little, and I can watch my old movies and compliment myself on how well I turned a phrase. My daughter visits often enough. I finally divorced Barb and now she and I can stay in the same room without killing each other. I'd say my life is good just the way it is, but you're still fairly young, at least from where I'm standing. You have a powerful itch and you've come this far. Why don't you keep going and see where the road takes you?"

"What about Beth? Shouldn't I go back to her?"

"Of course you should. You'd be a fool not to. But take a little time for yourself first. Tell Beth you need this. She'll understand. Like you said, you're already out of a job. Think of the possibilities. You're free to explore and find yourself."

"Free to walk off into the sunset, right? What would you do if you were in my shoes?"

"I would catch the first bus, plane, or train out of here. I just cleared sixty-five last month, and now I realize life is too short to waste it on dreaming."

We finish our rice and noodles, and say goodbye in the parking lot. "I hope you find what you're looking for," he says. "And thank you for giving an old man a second chance."

We hug before going our separate ways. I head north, thinking about chasing my dreams. Driving off into the sunset.

I don't go far, just a little past Santa Barbara. I buy a sleeping bag and stretch out on the beach between the mountains and the ocean. The sound of the surf rocks me gently to peaceful dreams. The nightmares are gone.

～

I wake to the cries of seagulls. The waves pound the sand. The sun shines. I'm free.

I buy a postcard. "My dearest Beth," I start. "I miss you and the boys very much. I'll be home soon. But I need some time on my own. Please understand. With all my love, Brad."

～

I slowly work my way up the coast. When I left home, I felt rushed, pushing toward death. That changed at the Grand Canyon, when I knew how much I want to live.

Up until these last few days, I have always been rushed. First I had to learn to walk, talk, toilet train. A new skill around every corner. Then there was reading, writing, adding, subtracting. Always achieving. If childhood wasn't difficult enough, I had my father to keep me on my toes. Always waiting. Would he beat me today, or would he wait until tomorrow? Would it be something I said, something I did, or merely my existence? Always on edge.

After my father left, life should have been easier. But it wasn't. Not much. Mom shut herself off emotionally. I had to fend for myself, feed and dress Chris, and do my best to take care of the baby. When Mom did talk, she always pushed me, wanting more. If I fed the baby, I didn't do it well enough. If I dressed Chris, I didn't dress him warm enough. If I made an A, she wanted an A plus. On the day I received my bachelor's degree, she wanted to know why I hadn't graduated magna cum laude. On the day I received my master's, she wanted to know why I had accepted a job in Ohio rather than New York City. Or Chicago.

Things were better those last thirteen years. She realized Sam would never come back to her—I never understood why she wanted him—and she stopped worrying about Joshua. She was happy, and I was happier to be around her. But I never told her how much she hurt me all those years.

And I never told her I love her. We always had other things to discuss—superficial things—but we never talked about feelings.

When I left, I was escaping from the demons of my childhood and my weaknesses as a man. When I saw the Grand Canyon, I took flight. I don't want to go back until I'm sure I won't become enslaved again.

I'm grinding my teeth for the first time since I left Chicago. I rub the back of my neck, trying to relax, until I find a beach. I walk in the waves, gazing at the horizon. I stand barefoot in the sand and surf until my teeth stop grinding, my muscles stop tightening, and tears stop clouding my vision.

Part Two

I pull into San Francisco after three days of making my way slowly up the coast. In Los Angeles, I found Abdullah. I don't know who or what I'll find here.

I've been driving around for forty minutes when I spot a religious center. The sign says it's Baha'i. I've never heard of them. Are they a remote branch of Christianity? This is my time to explore. They have a service tomorrow morning.

I find a nice beach area just north of the Golden Gate Bridge. I take out my sleeping bag, forgetting about city codes. All night, though, I toss and turn. I don't want to wake up and find my car gone.

In the morning, I find a restroom and wash up. I trim my beard the way Abdullah showed me. I get to the Baha'i center about fifteen minutes before the service starts.

A woman with a long, flowing skirt greets me. "Hello. Are you new here?"

"I'm just passing through."

"Welcome. My name is Lily." She absent-mindedly fingers her graying ponytail. "We're always happy to meet new friends. Please make yourself at home."

This isn't like any church I've ever gone to. I look around. No crosses. I find a seat and wait for the service to begin.

No minister stands in front, awe-inspiring in his robes. Different people rise and read words sounding more spiritual than Biblical. The music comes from a sitar instead of a pipe organ.

When the service ends, everyone starts talking. Lily comes over. "Will you stay for refreshments? I'm sorry, I don't think I caught your name."

"Brad." Dull and matter-of-fact. Not lilting like Lily.

"Please help yourself. And feel free to ask questions."

She excuses herself, returning a few minutes later with the sitar player. "Brad, this is Dave."

His hair is nearly as long as Lily's. He's younger though—couldn't be more than thirty. "I'm glad you could join us. Are you familiar with the Baha'i religion? Do you have any questions?"

"I've never heard of Baha'is before. I don't think you're a branch of Christianity."

"Not at all. We believe in unity. Humanity is one. The world is one. Rather than separating ourselves into different religions we should unite. Baha'is believe in universal peace."

I talk with Dave for the next two hours and I like what he's saying. The tension is completely gone from my shoulders and neck as I listen to him talk about unity and peace.

Finally, it's time for us both to leave. "I'm glad to have met you, Brad. I hope you find what you're looking for."

"Do you have anything I could read?"

"I'm glad you asked." He leaves for a moment and returns with a thin book and several pamphlets. "The inquiring mind is a healthy mind. You are on the right path."

We shake hands and I head for my car. I put the book and pamphlets into my back seat, next to my sleeping bag. The Qur'an must be somewhere back there. I never promised Abdullah I would read it.

San Francisco is nice, but I want to stay on the road. I get back on Highway 1 and drive up along the coast. Before stopping for the night, I buy a sandwich and a flashlight. I eat my sandwich on the beach and use the flashlight to help me read one of the pamphlets. I drift to sleep on the sound of waves and the words of peace.

In the morning, while eating pancakes, I remember what Uncle Rob said. He's right. I should take some time for myself. Beth will be okay. On my way out of the city, I drop another postcard in the mail. I tell her I love her and miss her, but I can't come home yet. She has to understand.

I contemplate the teachings of the Baha'is as I drive north. Unity. Respect. Freedom. Peace. I have always believed in these. I haven't always practiced them—not when I was competing with two other guys for the next position in the firm—but maybe it's time to approach life from a new angle.

I wonder if a new religion would make a difference. Being religious helps my brothers cope. It has never done anything for me, but I could give it a try.

This area is more mountainous. I pull into a small state park in the late afternoon. I don't want to negotiate these curves in the dark. I eat the dinner I bought along the way and take out my flashlight.

When I wake up, I'm convinced I have found something. This is too easy. I'll look for a Baha'i center in Seattle. I wonder if they have a conversion ceremony.

Once I convert, will I go home? My problems haven't gone away. I still feel restless. Is a new religion enough?

This is the most difficult driving so far. The road twists through the mountains, with drop-offs steep and frightening. Celeste handles the curves well, but I need to check her brake fluid.

I stop long before dark and park at a rest stop about sixty miles short of the Oregon border. I'll miss California. In Chicago, all we ever hear about are the problems here, but it's where I found my solution.

In the morning, I buy more brake fluid and check Celeste's steering and transmission levels. I eat pancakes at a local restaurant and give her a chance to rest.

After Seattle, I should head back to Chicago. I'll find a Baha'i center there and adjust to a new way of life. Beth and the boys will join me. Together we can find freedom and peace and have the life I've always hoped for.

Celeste and I have come a long way together over the past thirty years, but we've never gone through the mountains before. She doesn't have four-wheel drive, and she's never had to handle anything this steep. She's a good car, but I don't want to overdo it. I pull into another state park only twenty miles into Oregon.

I take out my flashlight and read. Peace. That's what I've been missing. I never had it. Even before my father started beating me, my life was never peaceful. They fought all the time. He cursed her and she cried. Sometimes he hit her and walked out. Sometimes I made him hit me instead. When he hurt her, she needed me to take care of her. And life was never peaceful.

Except when I went to my grandparents' house. Not Dad's parents. That grandmother always yelled at me to wash my hands, pick up my toys, stop making noise. That grandfather glowered and treated me like an intruder.

My best times were the hours I spent with Mom's parents. That grandmother held me and read to me and showed me how to love learning. That grandfather taught me jokes and riddles and showed me how to have fun. I was twelve when they both died, six months apart, and I thought the world had ended. Uncle Rob flew in for their funerals. After Grandpa died, I asked Uncle Rob to take me back with him. He smiled and said he would see what he could do. When he left without me, I hid in my bedroom and cried all night.

I didn't immerse myself in sex and drugs the way Joshua did. I worked hard in school so they would be proud of me. Mom said they were watching me from heaven, and for a couple of years I actually believed her.

I fall asleep and dream about my grandparents. I walk into their house. Grandma hugs me. Grandpa pats me on the back and tells me his best knock-knock joke. They listen when I tell them about my latest award. They make me feel like the most important person in the world.

I wake to the sound of the ocean and gaze at the blue sky and tall evergreens. It's beautiful, but I wish I was back at Grandma's kitchen table.

I've spent three days driving through Oregon. The ocean. The mountains. The massive redwoods I first saw in northern California. I never knew the world had this much beauty.

I drive up to Seattle on I-5, taking a detour to Mt. St. Helens. I was nine when it first erupted back in 1980. My teacher talked about it all week. We learned the science of volcanoes. Even then I wondered about the force behind the science.

On Wednesday afternoon, I pull into Seattle. I came here once for a conference. I went to the hotel and two days later I went back to the airport. All I've ever seen of the city was from the back of a taxi.

I haven't worked since Santa Fe and my funds are dwindling. I've heard about Pike Place Market. I head downtown, park near the market, and clean myself up in a restroom. I remove my wedding ring before asking around. After eight rejections, I land a job at a sandwich shop. I told him I just pulled into town. My ex-wife cleaned me out and I'm looking for a fresh start. He went through a messy divorce three years ago. I start tomorrow.

I buy a postcard of the Space Needle and tell Beth I'm looking for a new way of life. And I love her.

It's too early to settle down for the night, so I decide to drive around to get a feel for the city, heading north on I-5. After a few miles I pick an exit.

I'm looking for something interesting. A few miles off the highway, I discover a Buddhist meditation center. I know a little about Buddhism—mostly from my kung fu movie collection. Giving up meat, burning incense, and shaving my head don't sound appealing, but I can check it out.

A meditation will start soon. A couple of people nod at me as I walk in. I sit next to a friendly-looking woman. Everyone is quiet.

This is like nothing I have ever experienced. No music. No sermon. Just silence. I've had moments of silent meditation at the Grand Canyon and the ocean, but I never imagined group meditation.

The monk chants softly in another language before instructing us in English. It's very peaceful.

When the meditation is over, everyone stands and talks in hushed tones. The woman next to me says, "I don't think I've seen you here before."

"I'm new in town. Call me Brad."

"I'm glad to meet you, Brad. I'm Chelsea."

"Do you come here often?"

"Oh, yes. I could not make it through the week without my meditation."

Chelsea tells me she's a radiologist at a nearby hospital. She moved to Seattle after her divorce. Her ex-husband stayed in Missouri.

"I drove through Missouri several weeks ago and ate one of the best roast beef sandwiches ever in a place called Kingdom City."

"My aunt has a farm out near Kingdom City. I know the place you're talking about. I used to eat there all the time, but I'm more partial to their sloppy joes."

We talk for the next hour about Missouri and Seattle and life. Nothing about Buddhism. I didn't come here to pick up a woman. I have a wife.

Everyone else has left. The monk waits.

"They're kicking us out," I say.

She smiles. "Would you like to go for coffee?"

That sounds harmless enough.

"Sure."

"I know a great place. It's local. Forget the chains. Where's your car?"

When I point to my old friend, Celeste, Chelsea laughs. "You drove across the country in that?"

"She got me here, didn't she?"

"I have the beige car over there. Can you follow me?"

"No problem." It's dark, and beige is hard to see, but I'm looking forward to that coffee. I stay close all the way.

After we place our orders, she asks, "Why the road trip?"

"One day I felt like I had to get away. So I did." I don't tell her about the nightmares and plans of suicide. I also don't tell her about my wife and sons. She doesn't ask.

"That sounds romantic. Picking up and going wherever the wind blows. How long do you plan to stay in Seattle?"

"I don't know. I have a job over at the Market so I'll be here a few weeks at least."

"Let me show you around. Are you free tomorrow night?"

This is where I should tell her about my wife.

"Sure."

"Where can we meet?"

"Come by the sandwich shop. I get off at six."

We finish our coffee and bagels, and I walk her out.

"I'll see you tomorrow." She gives me a quick kiss and climbs into her car.

I go to my car, find a quiet place to park, and climb into my back-seat—feeling happy and slightly guilty.

On Thursday, Chelsea gives me the grand tour. We take her car and leave mine at the Market.

I like the atmosphere up here. Beautiful and free. Like Chelsea.

We end our tour at a seafood restaurant. My treat. She drives me back to my car.

"I really had a good time," she says.

"I did, too. You're a great tour guide."

She comes close and kisses me. For a few minutes, I lose myself.

What am I doing?

"I'd better go," I say, backing away. "We both need to work in the morning."

"What else do you want to see while you're here?"

"I have been curious about Mount Rainier. It seems to follow me wherever I go."

"Okay, I'll pick you up on Saturday and we can go hiking. Where are you staying?"

"Let's meet at your place."

"It's a date then," she says, handing me the directions. Another long kiss before I remember I'm married.

I watch as she drives away, and leap into my backseat.

A date? I should call and cancel. But I don't have her number. I should find something else to do on Saturday. She'll wait for me, and I won't show up. I have to get back to Beth. And Chelsea is only twenty-six. I'm old enough to be her father.

But I do want to see Mt. Rainier. There's no harm in going for a hike, is there?

On Saturday, I walk into her building and call her apartment. "I'm not ready yet," she says. "Do you want to come up and wait?"

"No, I'll stay in the lobby."

I can handle the situation. It's just a hike with a friend.

She appears about fifteen minutes later. "Sorry to keep you waiting," she says, kissing me lightly. We hold hands on our way to her car.

She heads south on I-5, and we talk. I go ahead and tell her about my family.

"I knew it," she says. "You look married. Do you plan to go back to her?"

"Sure. Someday."

Someday? Why did I say that?

She nods.

Mount Rainier looms on the horizon, appearing larger with every mile. When we reach the mountain, she drives up and parks at a secluded picnic area.

We walk a little. Then we eat lunch. She brought sandwiches. We hike again, and don't get back into Seattle until after dark. She invites me to her apartment.

"I'd better not," I say.

"I understand," she says. She gives me a little peck before I get out of her car and climb into my Toyota.

That sounds good, but it's not what happened. I have a bad habit of complicating my life.

We drove up the mountain and got out to hike before returning to the clearing for a picnic. That much is true.

I helped her unpack the food. Chicken, coleslaw, deviled eggs. Wine.

I told Lou I don't drink because of my brothers. That's not true either. I don't drink because of the blackouts.

I knew the smell of liquor before I could walk. As I got older, that smell told me I would be beaten before the night was over. I hid under the bed and waited for him to fall asleep. On a good night, he passed out on the couch.

Sometimes he claimed he didn't remember beating us. I knew he was lying. Until it happened to me.

I started drinking when I was in high school. The smell reminded me of my father, but it was the only way I could relax.

I didn't drink much, usually, but sometimes I binged. And every time I woke up the next morning in someone else's bed.

But I was younger then, I thought as she poured the wine. I can handle it now.

I drank a little and remembered the warmth. I emptied the glass and asked for more.

This morning, I woke up in Chelsea's apartment. I heard her humming in another room.

After a few minutes, she brought me breakfast on a tray and kissed me. "Good morning, sleepyhead."

I knew I was in a hell of a lot of trouble, but the last thing I remembered was drinking wine on the mountain.

She kept talking in this annoyingly cheerful voice. I finished the two bottles she brought for the picnic, she said, and insisted on stopping for more on our way into the city.

She went on and on about last night. I stopped listening and concentrated on the throbbing in my head. Until she got to the part about "moving in."

I looked at her. "What did you say?"

"You can stop pretending, sweetheart. I know you're sleeping in your car. You need to move in with me."

Sweetheart. Yeah.

"But I'm married."

"But you're not in Chicago, are you?" She came close and kissed me long and hard.

I almost stayed, but Beth's face flashed in my mind. "I'd better go," I said, looking for my shirt.

"Where do you think you're going?"

"Listen, it's been fun, but I can't do this."

My head already hurt before she started screaming. I managed to escape before she maimed me.

❧

I'm lying in the backseat and my head still hurts. I'm supposed to be at work. I'll tell him I was sick.

In twenty-five years, I have never cheated on Beth. When my head clears a little, I drop another postcard in the mail. I wrote her a poem.

> Hair of brown, caring eyes
> Words of love and loving sighs
> To Beth, my only love, my wife
> I want you always in my life
> And even though I'm far away
> I'll love you till my dying day.

I used to write her love poems all the time, during our early years. She teased me about my feeble literary attempts, but I know she loved them. She keeps them in a special box.

❧

It's taken me two days to feel normal again. My boss wasn't happy, but he gave me a second chance.

I just got off work, and I'm feeling restless. I should find a Baha'i center and make my conversion. I'll go back to Chicago and make a fresh start.

But it's getting dark and I don't feel like driving around. I want to go to sleep, but I can't sit still. I need a distraction.

I rummage around in my backseat and dig up the pamphlets I picked up at the meditation center. Maybe reading will relax me.

Buddhism has Four Noble Truths, one pamphlet says. First, all life is suffering. I can't argue with that. Most of my life has been suffering of one kind or another. Second, suffering is caused by desire. I desired Chelsea. Sometimes I desire one more drink. Most of my life, I've desired peace. Third, the way to end suffering is to end desire. That makes sense. I know it would work for me. Fourth, the way to end desire is through right understanding, right thought, right speech, right action, right livelihood, right effort, right mindfulness, and right concentration. I could do some of those—two or three maybe—but not all eight. Too much work.

Anyway, I can't go back to the meditation center. Chelsea won't be very relaxed if I show up.

~

For the next four days, I argue with myself. I need to find the Baha'is and go ahead with my conversion. I am suffering from my desires and I need to go back to Beth.

But I can't just jump into something. Up until the day I left Chicago, I had carefully planned out my life—family, work, everything. The unpredictability of my childhood left me craving for consistency. I still need that.

~

I find a Baha'i center and go there twice. Each time a guy named Dan comes over to talk to me. I enjoy listening to the sitar, and the words sound nice, but I'm just not sure. I have to head east out of Seattle anyway. I'll make my decision by the time I get to Chicago. Dan tells me the national Baha'i center is in Wilmette, not far from our home. I never noticed.

Every day, I make sandwiches. In the evenings, I drive around, enjoying the scenery and getting to know the city. One Saturday after work, I spot an Islamic center. There are cars in the parking lot. I wonder what's going on. I pop a couple breath mints and walk in, taking my shoes off in the vestibule.

There's a lecture. I sit down to listen. No one asks if I belong there.

After the lecture, they stand to pray. I decide to join them. I can keep the game going, pretending to be someone I'm not.

At the end of the prayer, the man next to me offers his hand. "As-salaamu alaikum. I haven't seen you here before. What's your name?"

There's only one Muslim name I can think of on the spot. "I am Umar."

He starts pulling me into a conversation, but someone interrupts. While he's distracted, I sneak out.

I have a good laugh back in the car. I'm Umar. Sure.

While getting comfortable in the backseat, I come across the Qur'an Abdullah gave me. I could read it. Maybe later. Right now I need to sleep.

I send postcards home once a week. And I explore. I drive to Mount Rainier again and hike up on my own. I head over to Puget Sound and catch a ride on a whale-sighting tour. It's beautiful up here. I wonder if Beth would consider moving.

I've been here for five weeks when I know it's time to move on. It's been nice, except for that little indiscretion with Chelsea. And the rain. One week, it rained every day. I like the people and the land-scape, and I even like my job, but it's time for Celeste and me to hit the road. I give my boss notice.

Seven days later, I say goodbye to Seattle and head east. It takes a few days to get through Washington, Idaho, and Montana. Great scenery. Mountains, farms, and open land.

When I get to Billings, I decide to head south. Denver is another city I've traveled to on business but have never been able to explore. I wonder what I can find there.

Part Three

For ten days I've enjoyed the fresh mountain air. The high point, literally, was in Colorado Springs, where Celeste and I made it slowly to the top of Pike's Peak. I stayed for hours, studying the land below. Breathtaking isn't a strong enough word. It is more.

I send Beth a postcard of Pike's Peak and tell her I made it to the top. I hope she's impressed.

I like it here. Denver is manageable, and the area outside of Denver is, well, beyond breathtaking. The right word hasn't been invented yet.

I don't need to work yet, but I want to stay in this area a while. I just landed a job at a small diner north of Denver. The Nugget is owned by an old man who's hired a young guy—not much older than Kyle—to manage the place. This diner also has its regulars. Jeff comes in for his coffee and bagel every morning. Ken always orders a bowl of chili for lunch. Christine has french fries and a diet soda while working the daily crossword puzzle. And there's Kate, who sits in a booth in the corner while eating her cheeseburger, everything on it, and types away at an old notebook computer.

Ken is usually good for a joke. Jeff is always in a hurry. Christine asks me for help with her crossword puzzle. And I enjoy teasing Kate because she is so quiet and intense.

After a week or so, Kate starts sitting at the counter with her cheeseburger and notebook. We talk while she writes. A week later, she comes without the notebook.

She talks while I fry the burgers. "So, I know you're from Illinois. I saw the license plates. How did you end up here?"

I smile. "What about you?"

She says she escaped to Colorado six months ago, leaving a husband and two children back in Columbus, Ohio. She's pursuing her literary career—writing newspaper and ezine articles during the day, and struggling at night with the Great American Novel.

She lived in Columbus most of her life. She was there, too, when I was a graduate student, but I don't remember seeing her. Her husband is a professor at the university.

"He teaches economics. Can you imagine anything more boring?" When I ask if she'll ever go back, she says, "How could I ever leave my mountains behind? They're the best inspiration I've found."

Every day we talk. She keeps asking about me, but I direct the conversation back to her. She tells me about her oldest, a girl who leads the cheerleading squad, and her thirteen-year old son who sulks in his room and always wears black. "I worry about him sometimes."

It sounds like she has reason to worry. Thank God I don't have those kinds of problems with my boys.

I keep sending postcards home. Mostly views of the mountains. I describe the fresh air and clear sky, and say I'll bring them here someday.

∼

I've been here for two months, and every day I like it more. Maybe I could convince Beth to move. I mention it in my weekly postcard.

Kate comes by one evening at closing time. I'm mopping the floor of the empty diner.

"I didn't expect to see you here so late. What about your novel?"

"I got stuck and I thought a little fresh air would help."

"Has it?"

"Not yet. So then I thought maybe you could help. Would you like to go for coffee? I know a great place a few blocks from here."

I know what happened the last time I had coffee with a woman. But Chelsea was a stranger. Kate is my friend. We are kindred spirits, both searching for something we couldn't find at home.

She still knows almost nothing about me. When we sit down with our coffee and bagels, she corners me. "So, what's your story?"

"I thought you wanted help with your novel."

"I do, but it can wait. Who are you, Bradley Adams?"

"Don't ask. I'd probably put you to sleep."

"You won't get out of it this time. You know almost everything about me. Now it's your turn."

"Okay, but remember, you asked for it." I tell her everything. My wife and sons. Why I left. I describe the Grand Canyon, the ocean, and the hallucinations. She listens intently. She actually seems to care about what I say.

"So you're sleeping in the backseat of your car? That can't be comfortable."

I laugh. "It's no big deal anymore."

She hesitates. Then she looks into my eyes and reaches for my hand. "Why don't you stay at my place?"

I look into Kate's eyes, and I like what I find. Friendship. Understanding. Acceptance.

I squeeze her hand. She smiles and looks down. "So what do you think?"

I recognize her offer for what it is. I have never cheated on Beth—except for that time with Chelsea, which I can't remember. This time I'm sober. And I accept. I have been lonely for a long time. And it will be nice to take a hot shower again.

She lives in a studio apartment about two miles from the diner. It's awkward, the first day or two, especially when she comes in for lunch. We try to act normal. Christine and Ken don't need to know where I live.

As the days pass, I begin to feel more comfortable. I talk with her about my search. She reads to me from her novel. We complete each other.

No more sleeping in my car. I have someone who is happy to see me at the end of my shift. And I am falling in love with her.

I'm not cheating on Beth. I am simply sharing my life with someone who understands.

I'm not cheating on Beth. She was too busy. She didn't know what I needed. She can't blame me for reaching out to someone else.

I'm not cheating on Beth. I tell myself that every morning when I wake up, before I take a hot shower and go to work. I almost believe it.

As I settle into a new life with Kate, my visions of Chicago grow dim. I sometimes remember my wife and sons. But I also know what I have here.

I don't know if I'll ever leave. I have my work at the diner, and the mountains, and Kate. Her novel is almost finished. My search is on hold. I'm happier than I've been in a long time. Twenty years maybe. I had forgotten how it feels to love a woman with all my being.

We've been together for more than three months when Thanksgiving rolls around. Mom was with Walt in Malaysia this time last year. She called the next day and laughed as she described eating squid for their Thanksgiving meal. My brothers and I took our families to Jean's house. She had the meal catered.

As the day gets closer, I guess I get quieter. On the Monday before the big day, Kate asks me what's wrong.

I tell her about my last Thanksgiving with Mom, all of us celebrating around her table. "Her turkey would have made the pilgrims jealous. She made all the fixings, from the dressing to the pumpkin pie. All from scratch. She always loved to cook, even when I was little."

If I close my eyes, I can still see her, in the kitchen of our old apartment, humming while she bastes the turkey.

"That's probably how she managed to put up with my father for so long. She went into the kitchen and lost herself in the recipes."

"So do you like marshmallows in your Jello salad?"

"It wouldn't be Jello salad without them."

She writes a shopping list. The next evening I find a turkey thawing in the fridge.

"You know how to cook a turkey?"

"Please," she says. "I've only been doing it for twenty years. Our house was always full of people. My family, his family, and two or three really obnoxious grad students or professors who didn't have families to go home to." She laughs. "I wonder what Geoffrey will do this year without me. He is completely lost in the kitchen."

The diner is closed on Thanksgiving Day, so I sleep late. I wake up to all the wonderful aromas of the day. Kate is standing in front of the oven, basting the turkey. I kiss the back of her neck. "It smells great."

She turns around and kisses me. "I want it to be special. Our first Thanksgiving."

It's a memorable day. Turkey and all the fixings, just for the two of us. We relax together after the meal. I try to concentrate on her, but once or twice my mind wanders back to Chicago. What are they doing right now? I block the thoughts and kiss Kate again. This is where I am.

As I go to sleep, I think about what she said. Our first Thanksgiving. How long is this supposed to last? Will I ever go back?

When I wake up, she's gone. I find her note on the bathroom mirror. "I went to get a jump on Christmas shopping. See you tonight."

I don't have to wait that long. She comes in at lunch time and sits at the counter. I kiss her. Christine and Ken don't care where I live.

"How was your shopping?"

"Fantastic. I can't wait till you see what I got."

"You can show me tonight."

"No, you have to wait until Christmas." She giggles.

She eats her burger and walks out humming "Jingle Bells." She bought me something. This is serious.

As I clean up for the night, I think about our relationship. It's been fun. Hell, it's been great. I love her. Her creative energy, her companionship, her caring. But how long am I supposed to stay with her?

When I walk into the apartment, she's acting like a kid. She won't let me hang my coat in the hall closet—that's where she hid the presents. I act excited, but I'm worried.

She goes to bed early. I pretend to watch TV while my mind wanders. Where is this relationship going? How long should I stay? I'm tired. I'll worry about it tomorrow.

I bolt awake. It wasn't a nightmare. It was a wonderful dream. In the morning, we went for a long walk. Later, we ate at an expensive restaurant, talking and laughing. At night, I held her close. And right now, I want her so much it hurts. Not Kate. Beth. Not the Beth who had to work late or the Beth who is always too damn practical. The Beth I fell in love with. The one who gave birth to my sons. The one I still love.

I lie in the dark and try to figure it out. In the morning, I kiss Kate and hold her close before going into the bathroom to get ready for work. I stare at myself in the mirror. And I know I am cheating on my wife.

After a dinner of Thanksgiving leftovers, I tell Kate a little about my dream. Not all. "Do you ever dream about your husband?"

"Sometimes. But Geoffrey never cared about me. He just wanted someone to wash and iron his clothes, raise his kids, and put dinner on the table by six."

I hold her hand and gently caress her fingers. "I still love my wife."

"So what does that mean?"

"I need to leave Denver. Tomorrow I'll give my notice at the diner. I want to stay, but I love my wife."

She doesn't ask me to leave her apartment. We spend the week as we've spent the others, but with sadness.

After my last day of work, I come back to say goodbye. "Have you thought about going back to him?"

"He'll never understand me. And I love…the mountains."

"I love you, too." I stay for three more days before I can force myself to kiss her goodbye and climb into my car.

I should drive straight to Chicago, without stopping. I need Beth. But I'm not ready to go home yet. I head west.

Celeste and I have done a lot of mountain driving by now, but the road west out of Denver is the most treacherous. I buy extra brake fluid, steering fluid, and oil to keep in my car, and check the levels often. One small failure of any major system, and I won't have to worry what to tell Beth about Denver. Once or twice, I wonder if that would be the best way to find peace. Ending my life. Ending my desires. But tumbling down the side of a mountain doesn't sound peaceful.

It takes me two days to get through the mountains, inching along. I breathe more easily as I leave the Rockies and cross into Utah. I park on the side of the road and spread out my sleeping bag under the stars, grateful I wasn't smashed to pieces against a mountain slope— an appropriate punishment for cheating on my wife.

While going through my things, all thrown together in the back seat, I found that copy of the Qur'an. I didn't promise him I would read it, but I will. I can always put it down. I crawl into my sleeping bag and begin, "In the name of Allah, the Most Gracious, the Most Merciful."

In the morning, I think about heading north to Salt Lake City to learn about Mormonism. I talked with two of their missionaries once. They gave me the Book of Mormon—it's on a shelf in one of the closets back home. I've heard of Mormons who still practice polygamy. I would really like to talk with them. Now I know it is possible to love two women.

But I head south instead, seeking answers again in the natural beauty. I take my time touring Zion National Park, Bryce Canyon, and the Grand Staircase. Always beautiful. Incredible. Awe-inspiring. As I read the Qur'an in the desert at night, I wonder who created all these magnificent places.

I buy a postcard of a desert scene. I haven't sent Beth anything since the night I moved in with Kate. I don't say much. Just that I love her.

Tomorrow I plan to drive further south, back into Arizona. I can see Rainbow Bridge, Monument Valley, and the Petrified Forest. I'm especially anxious to stand on the north rim of the Grand Canyon.

But when I wake up, I'm seized with an incredible urge to drive east. Not to Chicago. Back to Denver.

I find my way up to I-70 and head through the mountains. An early winter storm could hit, making the passage much more treacherous. I could drive up into Wyoming instead or go west into Nevada. I should go to Arizona. But I travel east, back to Kate.

It takes me two days, driving as quickly and carefully as I can. I arrive in the evening and knock at her apartment door.

She opens the door and stares at me. "You should be in Chicago by now."

"I went to Utah first. I saw deserts, canyons, and rock formations you wouldn't believe, but I couldn't stop thinking of you."

"So you think you can just come back to me?"

"I love you, Kate."

"How long will you love me, Bradley? Until you have another dream about your wife? I don't want to live that way."

"We've been married for twenty-six years. She's the mother of my sons. Of course I'll think about her sometimes."

"You need to choose. You can't have it both ways."

"I came back to you. Doesn't that mean anything?"

"And you'll stay until you're ready to leave again. I need more from you."

"But there's something special between us."

"There was, but you left. You made your choice."

Don't make me beg.

"Please, Kate, give me another chance."

"Go to Beth." She slams the door.

I slump back to Celeste and cry in my backseat, in the parking lot of her apartment building.

Part Four

As I drive into Wyoming in the morning, I keep beating myself up. Wasting my time on a woman I had no right to love. I should be in Arizona, at the edge of the Grand Canyon. Or in Chicago, back in my wife's arms.

When I settle in for the night, I pick up the Qur'an and come across verses about divorce. My parents' divorce was enough for me. I knew when I married Beth it would be for life. But if she knew about Denver, and Seattle, it would be over. I need to be careful.

I spend one night in Wyoming before heading into South Dakota. I drive through the Black Hills and head for the Badlands. They shot a cowboy movie there when I was a kid. Uncle Rob's only western.

I meander through the Badlands in the early afternoon, stunned by the beauty of the place. It doesn't have the spectacle of the Grand Canyon or the majesty of the mountains. It's a mystical beauty.

I pull off onto a small local road for the night, turn on the flashlight, and read passages about Allah. The Self-Subsisting. The Eternal. The Most High. I wonder about the power of Allah as I fall asleep, images of the Badlands running through my mind.

In the morning, I return to the Badlands. I don't know how I would describe this area to Kyle or Matt, if they asked. Like the Grand Canyon, it is rock formations. They say the formations were made by wind and water. I wonder again at the power behind the wind, behind the water.

Before leaving the area, I head south to Wounded Knee. As a child, I overheard stories of ancestors who tamed the west, killing Indians and buffalo on their way. Sam's family, of course. Two hundred people died here. Not as many as died in the plane crash, but their deaths were more senseless. I remember what I read in the Qur'an last night about the evil ones who lead men from light into darkness.

I buy a postcard of the Badlands and tell her about the mystical beauty—and ask if she would consider moving to South Dakota.

As the sun sets, I drive north to I-90. At Sioux Falls, I decide to keep going east rather than further north. The air is getting colder and I don't to be caught in a snowstorm.

I turned forty-eight today. Mom always made a fuss. But no card or balloons this year. I spent the day in my car and I wondered, does my birthday count now that the one who gave birth to me is gone?

I drive into Minneapolis on Christmas Eve and drop a Christmas card in the mail. It won't reach her in time, but it's the thought that counts.

We always stayed up late on Christmas Eve, wrapping presents and assembling bikes. Until last year. This year, I spend my evening reading the Qur'an.

When I wake up on Christmas morning, I want to celebrate, but I'm alone. I can't go to church in torn jeans and a sweatshirt. I go back to sleep.

Later, I read a little. I'm surprised to find verses in the Qur'an about borrowing money. I know Joshua and Umar are both strict about that, but I didn't know it was in their holy book. I'm more surprised to read about the birth of Jesus. I know Muslims don't celebrate Christmas, but the Qur'an refers to Jesus' birth as a special event.

At midday, I eat lunch at a Chinese restaurant with four other diners. An old man. A young couple. A woman my age. She smiles at me. I turn away and concentrate on my rice. Merry Christmas.

I drive to another rest stop and read some verses about fighting. Muslims fight. Everyone knows that. But I don't see the blood-thirsty love for violence I had expected. It's mostly about military strategy.

I set the book aside. I'm not in the mood.

It's Christmas and I'm alone.

I'm close to Chicago now. It would make sense to go home, but I'm not ready.

I've watched the sun set over the ocean, hiked in the mountains, and meditated in the Badlands. If I never do anything else for the rest of my life, I'll always have those moments. But now I'm more restless than ever. I could stay home for six months, maybe a year, before going back on the road.

I head north instead through Michigan's Upper Peninsula. Chuck, my talkative roommate, came from up here. He went on and on about the snowstorms and frigid winters. I may be driving into something. I should head south, but I can't. I send a postcard.

It's beautiful up here—snow-covered fields and frozen lakes. And no snowstorms.

I take my time traveling through the Upper Peninsula and back down through Michigan. On a Friday morning, I pull into Detroit and spot a mosque. I blend in with the crowd and do what everyone else does. Remove my shoes. Walk into the mosque. Sit and wait. Listen when the man stands up to give the sermon.

He talks about someone named Ibrahim and his search for truth. First, he says, Ibrahim saw the stars, and he began to worship them until he saw the moon, which was brighter. He worshiped the moon until he saw the sun which was, of course, much brighter still. He finally realized he shouldn't worship the stars or the moon or the sun, but the One who created them all.

The man tells of Ibrahim's journey to the west. He married once. Then he married again and had a son. Two wives. That might have solved my problem in Denver. But Beth wouldn't go for it, and Kate is already married.

Ibrahim named his first son Ismail. His first wife had a son, finally, when she was old, and they named him Ishaq. I recognize Ibrahim. He is Abraham. Mrs. Patrick, my old Sunday school teacher, taught us about him.

After the sermon, they stand up to pray and I pray with them. I did that once before, in Seattle, but this time when I go to bow down I feel something. A connection.

The prayer ends too soon. A man sitting next to me offers his hand. "Assalaamu alaikum, Brother. What's your name?"

"I am Ibrahim." Like before, in Seattle, I didn't think before saying it. This time it sounds right. I'm not Umar, but I can relate to Ibrahim.

"It's nice to meet you. My name is Musa. Have you lived here long?"

Another man comes over and starts talking to Musa about business. I quietly slip away.

This time it felt natural. To touch my head to the floor. To say my name is Ibrahim.

I head south toward Dayton. I know this area of the country. After eating, I drive east, pulling into a rest stop a little after sunset. I'm heading for Columbus.

Before going to sleep, I read a few verses of the Qur'an. It's interesting, but I don't feel inspired.

I don't know when the wind started blowing. I didn't wake up when the air became colder. I couldn't hear the sleet. I slept. And in the morning, I open my eyes to a roaring blizzard. My windows are iced up. My car is surrounded. I crawl deeper into my sleeping bag and wait it out.

I keep reading. A verse catches my attention. "He it is who created the heavens and the earth in truth. On the day when He says, 'Be!' it is."

When I was little and I went to Sunday school, before my father left, I learned about the Bible from Mrs. Patrick. She taught us songs and games, and told us stories from the Bible. Sometimes she took out the flannelgram and showed us pictures to go along with the stories. One day, she taught us about the creation. She said when God created the world He said, "Let there be light." Then she read from the Bible, "And there was light, and it was good."

I believed in God when I was little. I still do, one way or another. I don't want to hear how it was God's will that the plane crashed—I've never thought about God that way—but someone had to create the world. It wasn't just the river or the wind.

I fall asleep with questions, but find no answers.

~

When I wake up, I see the snow has stopped. I open my door a few inches. It is bitterly cold and I'm surrounded.

I rev my engine and try driving through the drifts, but they're too thick, so I put the car in neutral and get out to push. Cold wind blows in my face. Soon my cheeks are frozen. My ears ache. My chest hurts as I breathe in the frigid air. I climb back into the car to catch my breath. I won't be able to push her out of here. I'll have to dig. I step out of my car again and get to work.

I keep at it. A few minutes digging out and a few minutes thawing out. It never ends. My muscles ache and I'm exhausted, but I can't give up. After the snow plow comes through, I'll be blocked. My face stings. I can't feel my hands. I cough. My lungs burn. I keep digging.

When the plow comes, I wave at him. He does his best not to block me. I keep digging.

I've been at it for over two hours now and I'm finally clear. I get behind the wheel and slowly drive her out. She slides. I take my foot off her accelerator, steer her into the spin—stopping an inch or so from a parked semi—and ease her away.

I stop her in the middle of the parking lot, engine running, and get out to scrape her windows. I'm exhausted and half-frozen, but we're ready to go. I turn the heat to full blast and pull on a third sweatshirt.

It's nearly noon when I walk into a family restaurant, the kind that serves breakfast all day, and order a big plate of pancakes. I wrap my hands around a mug of hot coffee.

~

The highway is still slick, so I take my time driving into Columbus. The last time I drove this way, in the ice and snow, it was a few days after Christmas. Twenty-seven years ago. I had gone to Chicago to spend the holidays with Mom, but I kept thinking of Beth. I told Mom I couldn't stay. I drove straight through to Beth's parents' house and begged her to marry me.

As I pull into town, the memories keep coming. My old apartment, the one I shared with Chuck and Gary. My favorite pizza place. The corner where I stopped to talk to a pretty girl who was struggling to carry her laundry home in the rain, and offered to give her a ride. After we took her laundry back to her apartment, I asked her to eat lunch with me at the student center and I sat there, falling in love with her.

I find a booth and slide in with my burger and coffee, remembering the day my life changed.

She was a grad student, too, in her second year of studies in public health. By the time we graduated together the following May, she had agreed to marry me. We went to her hometown, where I married her in her parents' church on the first Saturday in June.

I miss those days, but I can't live on nostalgia. I finish my burger and leave.

On my way out, I see another memory. "You're back."

She shrugs. "Christmas was coming and I didn't want to spend the holidays alone. So I called him. He was upset with me for leaving, but he said he needed me. He admitted he's lost without me."

I don't know what to say. "I guess you're happy."

"He listens to what I've written, like you used to. We're going out to Colorado in a couple months. We might move there. So why aren't you home yet?"

Why does she care?

"I'm working on it."

"I'll never forget you, Bradley." She reaches out to touch me.

I turn and walk away—practically run away—from Kate's touch, and get the hell out of Columbus. As I head east out of town, I keep thinking about my memories and the two women I have loved.

~

They always go to bed early. I'd better not drop in on them after dark. I pull into a rest stop outside of Akron.

In the morning, I wash up a little before heading out. They'll be surprised enough to see me. I can't go there looking like a bum.

I'm heading to Youngstown—Beth's hometown—where we spent the first two years, the happiest years, of our marriage. I had a job with a small firm. She worked at a local hospital. Our jobs paid the bills, but they didn't consume us. We spent our evenings and weekends together, concentrating on our marriage and each other.

We were so happy. Then Mom started pestering me to move back to Chicago. Joshua was fifteen then and perpetually drunk or stoned. She was afraid he would end up dead or in prison and she needed me to take care of him. She found a job opening and nagged until I applied. I got the job, which paid much, much more than I was earning in Youngstown. We packed up and moved to Chicago. Life with Beth was still good, but never quite as good again.

I drive by our old apartment building and look up at the third floor. I wonder who lives there now. Could they possibly be as happy as we were?

Before I leave town, I have to see Don and Ann. I know how they'll react. I must enjoy suffering.

Don is shoveling snow. He needs to be careful. His father died of a heart attack twelve or thirteen years ago. He could hire someone to do that for him. And we bought him a snow blower a few years back—it must be sitting in his garage. But, knowing Don, I'm sure he enjoys the work. I just hope he takes it easy.

I park across the street and step out of my car. Don looks up. He goes back to his shoveling. Then he stops and looks again. "Brad? Is that you?"

"You shouldn't be shoveling that snow, Dad. What about the snow blower we got you?"

He carefully puts down his shovel. First he stares. Then he rushes over and hugs me. "You're alive. Beth is worried sick about you."

"You got quite a bit of snow out here. I had to sit through the storm just outside of Dayton, but I think Youngstown got more."

"Where have you been? What's going on?"

"Can I come in for a cup of coffee?"

"Come on." He grabs my elbow and walks in with me, calling as he opens the front door. "Ann, come quickly. Brad's here."

Ann trots up the basement stairs, carrying a basket of laundry. She puts down her load and hugs me tightly. "Brad. It is so good to see you. Where have you been?"

"Hi, Mom. What kind of pie do you have today?" She always bakes pies in the winter, nearly every day.

"Pecan. Your favorite. Sit down and I'll get you a slice."

Ann brings her pie and Don brings the coffee. He pours each of us a cup as we sit down together at the round oak table in their kitchen.

"It is so good to see you, Brad. We've all been very worried about you."

"I'm okay, Mom. You don't have to worry."

Don persists. "Why did you leave?"

I can't tell them I left home to kill myself. Don will have me committed. I have to make this sound good.

"I don't know what to say. You know I lost my mother and stepfather, and my father had died several months earlier. I couldn't make sense of it all. One morning I woke up and knew I had to get away. I've been on the road all this time, looking for answers." That wasn't much better than the suicide angle. It made me sound weak and confused.

"You didn't have to leave. You have family. Why didn't you ask for help?"

"I asked Beth for help. I couldn't get her to listen." Also not quite true. She did her best, but some things were beyond her control.

"She was worried about you. She said you refused to go for counseling."

Yeah. Like I'm going to pour my heart out to a stranger.

"Anyway, I've been searching. When I find what I need, I'll go home, but I'm not ready yet." That's true, though I don't remember when this became a search, and I don't know what I'm looking for.

Don looks me right in the eye. "Is there another woman? Are you cheating on my daughter?"

He has a gun collection he keeps locked away in the next room. Most of his guns are antiques, from as far back as the Civil War. I don't know if any actually works, and I don't like lying to him, but I won't take chances. It doesn't matter, because I left Kate. Or she left me. Whatever.

"No, it's just me. I realized how empty my life was. I have to find something to make living worthwhile again." That's a little too close to the truth. I need to be careful.

"You have your family. That should be enough. Do you realize how hard all of this is on Beth? She came home from work one day and you weren't there. She called here, frantic. Ann had to fly out there. They went searching for you and filed a missing person's report. Your name and picture were on the news. She was afraid you had gone somewhere to kill yourself. For over a month, she barely slept or ate. Until you sent that email. She still doesn't know where you are, or if you're ever coming home. For a while there, when the postcards stopped coming, she thought you were dead."

When the postcards stopped, I was living with Kate. "I can't go home yet. I'm not ready."

"But you must consider what this is doing to my daughter."

"Would you feel better if I called her?"

Why did I say that?

"It's not enough but, yes, it's better than nothing."

Ann brings me the phone. I don't want to call Beth. I'm not ready to talk to her, but I walked into that one.

"Are you two planning to sit here and listen?"

"We need to be here in case she needs us." Don is scowling. "And you had better not make my daughter cry."

I dial the number. It's still second nature. The phone rings twice. I hear her voice. "Hello. Mom?"

"Hi, Beth. It's me."

"Brad? Where have you been? What are you doing in Youngstown? Are you okay? Why did you leave us?" She pauses. "It's so good to hear your voice."

"I was in the neighborhood and I thought I'd stop by for coffee and pie. They're looking good, but you have to tell Dad to stop shoveling snow. It's bad for his heart."

"What are you talking about? Where have you been? When are you coming home?"

"I've been out to California and a few places in between. I'm heading for the east coast."

"Come home, honey. We need you."

"I love you, Beth, but I can't come home yet. I need more time."

"Why can't you come back? What do you need?"

"You don't know what I need. You wouldn't understand. But I can't come home."

"Please, Brad, we need you." She's crying now. I hope Don can't hear her. "You have to come back to us."

Something snaps. "That's all I ever hear," I shout. "What everybody needs from me. Why doesn't anyone ever think about what I need for a change? Why doesn't anyone take care of me?"

She's quiet for nearly a minute. I hear her softly sobbing. Then she says, "Do what you have to do. Come home when you're ready. I love you." The line goes dead.

I put the phone on the table. "She's gone."

Don glowers. "Did you make her cry?"

"I don't know. Probably. But she's okay."

"What happened just now?"

"I don't know." I grind my teeth and rub the back of my neck. "It all gets to be too much sometimes. I can't take it anymore."

Take it easy. If I'm not careful, Don will have me thrown into the loony bin.

"Brad, I think you need help. You're headed for a breakdown. Why don't you check yourself into the hospital for a few days?"

I knew it. I need to calm down. I pause a minute, close my eyes, and think about the ocean. They wait.

"No," I say softly, calmly. "I was headed for a breakdown, before I left. I had to get away."

That is too close for comfort.

"I don't understand. You have a beautiful wife who loves you, two healthy, intelligent sons. You had a good career and you were going places. How could you throw it all away?"

Good career? Yeah. I was headed for unemployment. Think, Brad, think. What does he want to hear?

"I don't know if I can make you understand. When my parents died, I started thinking about death."

That's good. I think he's buying it.

"I thought about all the things I never said to my mother. And I'm not getting any younger either. My career, my home, even my family. I felt trapped by them."

Don smiles a little. "Is that what this is about? When I was your age, I started to feel that way. I thought about death and all the dreams I would never fulfill. So I went out one day and bought a boat. I considered growing a beard, too, but the boat was enough. Every time I began to feel restless, I looked at that big boat parked in my driveway. Go back to your family, Brad. Go home and do something ridiculous, like buying a boat."

I did it. I'm on a roll.

"I can't go back, Dad. Not until I find what I'm looking for."

"How long will that be? And how will you know? Do you expect Beth to sit around and wait for you to have a magical moment of revelation? Life doesn't work that way. Life is about putting one foot ahead of the other."

"I don't know if it will be another month or another year. I love Beth and I will go back to her, but I need to do this first. I know about putting one foot ahead of the other. I've done that all my life. Since I was a child."

I'm losing it. I need to stick with the mid-life crisis angle. He understands that.

"Why did you come to see us then? You knew we wouldn't approve."

I smile. "I came because I was hungry for Mom's pie. Go read your journals, Dad. I'll shovel the walk."

"Eat lunch first," says Ann. "You must be hungry."

"I'm always hungry for your cooking."

She brings fried chicken and mashed potatoes to the table. It's great to eat home cooking again. In that way, she's a lot like Mom. But Ann is quieter, more submissive. She's the wife of a prominent physician and she's comfortable in that role. Mom was never quiet. And even when my father was beating her, I never thought of her as submissive.

After lunch, I go outside and pick up the shovel. A few minutes later, Don rides out of the garage on his snow blower. We work until dark. When we go back into the kitchen, Ann has the hot chocolate waiting.

"You're staying with us tonight, aren't you, Brad?"

"I was hoping you wouldn't turn me away, Mom. I could use a hot shower."

"Oh yes, I'm sure the showers in those motels aren't very good."

"I haven't stayed in motels. Most of the time, I've slept in my car."

Why did I say that? Another reason for Don to put me in a strait jacket.

He shakes his head. "You should stay here for a while and take a rest. It's no shame these days. Stronger men have broken under pressure. Stay in Youngstown for a few days, maybe a week or two. See someone and talk through your problems. Beth can fly out. She wants to help you."

He has to be kidding.

"No, I don't want to see Beth, not until I find what I'm looking for. And I don't need to have my head examined. I'm not broken. I was, before I left, but seeing the Grand Canyon, the ocean, and the mountains have made me whole. Having the freedom to explore and find answers on my own. That's all I need."

He takes off his glasses and rubs his eyes. "I don't know what to say. You have always been someone I could respect—ambitious and responsible. What happened to that man?"

"He was buried by his ambitions. He was strong on the outside, but fragile on the inside. I'm trying to build my inner strength."

No, that was way too honest. I don't need to go that deep.

"But what about Beth?"

"She has to be patient, because this is what I need to do right now."

Was that too defiant? I'm trying to sound confident.

Don grunts and walks off to get ready for dinner. I help Ann set the table.

"Brad, there's something I need to tell you. Beth said you were upset with her after your mother died because she tried to get on with life. Is that right?"

"I couldn't understand why she acted that way. I was tied up in knots and she was worried about running errands."

"There's something you don't know about my daughter. Death scares her. It scares her so much she tries to ignore it. She was twelve when my mother died. Has she told you about that?"

"I know Beth loved her grandmother. She talks about her sometimes."

"My mother died in a car accident. We were all devastated. Beth couldn't understand why her Grandma had to go away, and there was no one to comfort her. It took me a good month or two before I could accept my mother's death, so I know how you feel. The point is, I wasn't available for Beth during that time. Her brother and sister were still small, and Don was working long hours at the hospital. She had to go through it alone, so she learned to hide her grief.

"If you don't know her, you would think she was cold and uncaring, but she was deeply hurt by her grandmother's death. She didn't know how to grieve, so she just pretended everything was normal. Is that how she acted after Evie died?"

"She didn't seem to care. It was almost like she was glad my mother was gone."

"You've been married to her for how long? Over twenty-five years now."

"Yes, twenty-five years. No, it was twenty-six this last June, but I wasn't there."

I was with Chelsea.

"You should know your wife by now. Beth loved Evie. When she called and talked to me about the crash, she was crying."

"Beth never cried for my mother."

"She didn't cry in front of you because she knew how much you were hurting. She wanted to protect you."

"I wish I'd known that. It might have made a difference."

"Don told you I had to fly out there when you left. Beth was hysterical. Can you imagine? My oldest daughter is never hysterical. I flew to Chicago and helped her calm down. And we searched for you. We did everything we could, but we never thought to look in California. I love Beth. And I love you, too, Brad. You've been a part of this family for a long time. But it breaks my heart to see my daughter so sad and alone."

I don't know what to say. I hug her. "I'll go back soon, Mom. I promise."

"I believe you. And I hope, when you're finally ready, it's not too late."

~

She made chili for dinner. We eat quietly, with some small talk about the weather. After dinner, Ann changes the sheets in the guest room and Don reads his journals.

I've been sitting in the room with him, flipping through magazines, for nearly an hour when he comes to sit next to me on the couch.

"You're not feeling desperate, are you, Brad? You would let me know, wouldn't you, if you were desperate?"

Not anymore.

"If I had wanted to kill myself, I had plenty of opportunities. Plunging down a mountain, or walking into the ocean."

I never felt suicidal near the ocean, but that would have been a great way to die. Disappearing into the sunset.

"I just need answers. If I go home now, I'll be back out on the road in six months. I guarantee it. Think of it this way. This is cheaper than buying a boat."

He frowns and heads upstairs. I go to bed a few minutes later, but I don't sleep well. Don has given me enough guilt to make me toss and turn all night.

Ann makes french toast for breakfast. After we eat, I help her with the dishes. Then I tell them I have to leave.

Don is still frowning. "Stop and think about what you're doing to Beth."

"I've thought about Beth, and the boys, and my mother, and my brothers, all my life. I never had a real childhood. You know that. Now it's my turn."

Ann gives me a cooler full of food—enough to last for the next several days—including two of her pecan pies. Don and I shake hands and hug. "I'm sorry, Dad. I know you're disappointed but this is something I have to do."

"Drive carefully. And don't forget to go home."

"I won't."

I'm about to pull away when Ann says, "Oh, I almost forgot." She asks me to wait and sends Don into the house. He walks out with two large shopping bags.

I peek inside. Both bags are full. "What's all this?"

She smiles. "A Christmas present."

I watch as they grow smaller in my rearview mirror. They're still waving. There's no yelling or nagging. Just gentle advice and a frown. I wish my parents had been like that.

Before I leave town, I hesitate. West to Chicago? East to the unknown?

I miss Beth. I want to hold her in my arms again. If I go back, she won't ignore me.

I did make her cry. When I left, I was trying to protect her. Maybe I should call her. We could have a real conversation and I could explain why I'm doing this. But maybe she would cry.

This isn't about Beth. It's about Mom and Walt. And my father. And my childhood. And death. And truth. And...I don't know any answers yet.

I buy another postcard and tell her I love her, asking her, again, to understand. I head east.

∾

I'm still on autopilot, driving north to Niagara Falls, where we went for our honeymoon. It was nice, but we didn't see too much of the falls. This time, I'll try to find my answers in the mist.

I stop in a small town south of Buffalo, park for the night, and open the cooler. Pies, fried chicken, hard-boiled eggs, coleslaw. And that's only the top layer. I lean back in my front seat and have a picnic.

While eating, I read a few more verses of the Qur'an. There are stories in here about people like Joseph and Moses. I remember those stories. Mrs. Patrick told them.

When I finish eating, I look inside the bags. Sports shirts and casual pants. She remembers my size.

There's also an envelope, containing cash and a note: "Find a nice motel room. And you know where we are if you need us." Don wrote it. If my father had been like Don, my entire life story would be different. But my father took pleasure in making me suffer and I have to get rid of his ghost.

∾

My trip to Niagara Falls is nice, but not momentous. The falls are half-frozen. I stare at the icy formations. No answers here.

I go to a gift shop and buy a postcard. "Do you remember this place?" I write. "I love you more now than I did then." It's corny, but I think she'll like it.

I planned to make Albany my next major stop until I remembered Worcester. I drive into Massachusetts on a two-lane highway and find a quiet place where I can eat, read, and sleep. I wake up refreshed and pull into Worcester right around noon.

I don't know where Michael lives, but I know which college he attends. I ask for directions at three different gas stations before finding someone who will help. The others look at my out-of-state plates and mumble something about turning left at the doughnut shop. A lot of good that will do me. I've counted twelve doughnut shops since pulling into town.

I find the college and stop at a nearby grocery store to call his cell. I hope his number hasn't changed.

"Hello?" He sounds out of breath.

"How's my favorite nephew? Did I catch you at a bad time?"

"What? Uncle Brad? Is that you?"

"That's me. I'm in Worcester. Do you have time for your old uncle?"

"You are? Where in Worcester?"

"At a large grocery store near your college."

"I know which one you mean. I'll be right there."

A few minutes later, he pulls up in his silver compact, the car Mom gave him when he graduated. It still looks new. Michael always took good care of his things.

He hugs me tightly. "I can't believe you're here. It's great to see you."

"You're looking good. I like the beard."

"Yeah, it's coming along. I never thought I'd see you in a beard. Is there a story to go with that?"

"Just that I didn't feel like shaving. I like it. It's been especially nice when it's cold."

"I know what you mean. Let's go. You can follow me back to the apartment."

They have a nice place. He rushes to the kitchen and grabs a slice of pizza. "Sorry, but I have to get to class."

"How do you like it so far?"

"I'll tell you about it later. I have to run. Make yourself at home. I'll be back in a few hours." He rushes out the door with his backpack.

I check out the apartment. Their fridge is nearly empty. I remember those days. Chuck, Gary, and I lived on cheese pizza. We couldn't afford toppings.

I bring my stuff up from the car, including the food Ann gave me.

I eat a slice of pizza. I'm sure the boys will appreciate Ann's cooking.

I'm dozing on the couch when the door creaks open. I open my eyes. It's Marcus, Umar and Aisha's little brother, Michael's best friend. He stops and stares. "Brad? How did you get here? Where have you been? Everyone's looking for you."

I quickly sit up and pop a breath mint. "I, uh, pulled into town a few hours ago. Michael let me in. He had to leave."

"He has a full schedule on Wednesdays. So what's the story?"

"We'll talk about that later. How are you?"

"I'm good. Did Michael tell you I'm getting married?"

"We didn't talk much. Is she from around here?"

"She lives in Boston. Her name is Khadijah. Her parents remind me of Mom and Dad." He keeps staring at me. I think he saw the bottle before I rolled it under the couch.

"She sounds nice."

"She is. We're getting married at the end of May, after she graduates. The family is coming up for the wedding. Will you be back in Chicago by then, or do you plan to stay here?"

"I don't know."

"Are you hungry?"

"I ate pizza. I brought you boys some home-cooked food—I stopped in Ohio and my mother-in-law made sure I wouldn't starve. Help yourself. I noticed the empty fridge."

"We don't go shopping much. Pizza is easier. And I'll be married soon. Khadijah is a fantastic cook."

"Your mother is such a good cook. She didn't teach any of you?"

"She was so good at it, we didn't need to learn. My brother barbecues. And my sister can cook. She just doesn't like to."

Michael rushes in, half out of breath again. "Hey, Marcus, you're home. Assalaamu alaikum. How are you, Uncle Brad?"

"I'm great."

The boys settle in while I heat up dinner. Michael smiles. "Real food."

In the morning, I go out to stock up on groceries, stopping at a few cafes and diners to apply for a job. This time, I have an address and phone number. The fifth place I try has an opening. I start next Tuesday.

On Friday, Michael goes to an early class and comes back to take a shower. As he combs his hair, he asks, "Would you like to go with me to the mosque?"

I tell him about praying at the mosques in Seattle and Detroit, and mention I'm reading the Qur'an.

"That's fantastic. What do you think?"

"I always thought Islam was for people like your father. I love my brother, but he's different. I think you know what I mean. I never thought Islam could be for people like me, or like you for that matter. We're scientists, not visionaries."

"I used to think that, too. You're right about Dad. And Jeremy. But when Marcus converted, he and I started studying together. You might be surprised to learn how much science is in the Qur'an."

"Really. Science in a holy book. Aren't religion and science at opposite ends of the spectrum?"

"Keep reading. You'll find the science. So do you want to come with me?"

"Who should I go as, Brad or Ibrahim?"

"Who's Ibrahim?"

"That's the name I gave to a Muslim man after I had prayed next to him at the mosque."

"If you plan to be here for a while, you'd better go as Brad. And if you find enough science to suit you, you might decide to become Ibrahim."

"I doubt that. Okay, I'll go as your Uncle Brad. Just let me change." I shower and put on some of the clothes Ann gave me. If I'm going as Michael's uncle, I can't look like a bum.

At the mosque, Michael introduces me to his friends. One man gives me a chair. I observe from the sidelines.

The sermon is about marriage. He talks about choosing the right person and the proper way to treat a wife. Up until the day I left, I don't think I was a bad husband, but I wasn't as kind or attentive as I could have been. I was busy.

I wonder if Beth is thinking about that too. How the good old days weren't always that good. When I am ready to go home, will she still want me?

When they pray, I feel like bowing down with them. But I'm Michael's uncle. I can't be caught up in any lies.

On Saturday, the boys take me for a drive through New Hampshire.

"I didn't realize it was so mountainous up here," I say on our way back.

"Sure," says Michael. "There are some great places for skiing around here."

"Skiing? Do you boys ski?"

"Every chance we get," says Marcus. "Have you ever tried it?"

"No. That's another one of those things I never got around to doing."

"Let's do it tomorrow," says Michael. "We'll take you skiing."

"I'm too old." I laugh.

"You're not that old," says Michael. "I've seen people older than you on the slopes, some for their first time."

"Okay, but if I break my leg, you'll have to take care of me."

On Sunday morning, we drive to a place called Wachusett Mountain. It's not far from their apartment.

Michael and Marcus go to the advanced slopes. I start with lessons, learning how to start, stop, and turn. After two hours of instruction, I'm ready to try it on my own.

Abdullah told me I'm probably not afraid of anything, but as I look down the slope my heart beats faster. All this time, at the Grand Canyon and while driving through the mountains, I've avoided falling. Now I'm supposed to push myself down the slope, surrendering my body to gravity. I'm almost fifty years old. I don't like roller coasters. Here goes.

My first feeling is fear. I'm plummeting down, with very little control. Okay, I'm not plummeting. It's a small hill. But what if I run into someone?

After a few seconds, I feel free. I am skiing down the hill, submitting to gravity, with the cold air in my face. I reach the bottom too soon. Now I'll do it again.

This is great. The view is wonderful, but that's not what takes my breath away. It's the skiing itself. The slopes I'm on aren't very steep, but I can still feel the exhilaration.

After lunch, I feel confident enough to try an intermediate slope. I go for an easier one, but it's still steeper and has a few twists and turns. I can't believe I'm doing it.

Michael and Marcus are ready to leave, but I'm feeling at home on the slopes. Why didn't I ever do this before?

"We need to go home, Uncle Brad."

"One more time."

I enjoy another run. The wind in my face. The snow moving to make way for my skis. I surrender.

I want to go again, but Michael says, "We need to leave. I have a paper to turn in tomorrow."

I stare at him. "A paper? We've been playing all weekend while you should have been working? Why didn't you say something earlier?"

"I wanted you to enjoy your first weekend in New England."

"Michael, you've always been so responsible. Now I feel bad."

"Don't worry. I've written the second draft. Remember how you always told me to keep up with my work? I'm in good shape. I just need to type in the finishing touches."

We buy roast beef sandwiches on our way to the apartment. Michael goes to the computer and Marcus reads in the easy chair. I'm still flying down the slopes.

On Monday, I hitch a ride with Marcus into Boston. Another city I've always wanted to see as a tourist. He drops me off at the Boston Commons, the beginning of the Freedom Trail, and I see the sites I heard about in school. The Old North Church. The Boston Tea Party. The U.S.S. Constitution. My legs ache by the time I'm finished, but I enjoyed my day. I buy a postcard of the Boston skyline and tell Beth about skiing.

Marcus picks me up at Bunker Hill, at the end of the Freedom Trail. We talk on the way back, sitting in Monday afternoon traffic.

"If you don't mind me asking, Brad, why did you leave?"

I'll stick with the mid-life crisis angle.

"I'm getting older and I felt trapped by the daily grind. Later, I realized I was looking for something. When I find it, I'll go back."

"Have you talked with Kyle since you left?"

"No. I talked with Beth once, but not the boys."

"Have you ever thought how Kyle feels about you being gone?"

"I don't know why he would care. We spent most of our time fighting. Anyway, Kyle's a tough kid."

"I was fourteen when my father died. Kyle must have been about that age when you left."

"He was fifteen. Almost sixteen."

"I don't know if you remember, but I had a very hard time after my father's death. I was angry. My dad didn't choose to leave, but I blamed the world for taking him away from me. It took me several months to work through it. Losing a father, especially at that age, is very difficult. I still miss him greatly. I wish he could meet Khadijah. I want to call and ask for his advice. I will always feel his loss."

"I'll be back long before Kyle goes to college and gets married."

"But you're gone now, and this is an important time in his life. He needs you, even if he doesn't show it. And you chose to leave. I know Dad would have done everything he could to stay with us. It was Allah's will he died when he did, and I've tried to accept that. But you decided to leave Kyle. Believe me, that's how he sees it. Not that you left Chicago or left his mother or your job. You left him."

"I've never thought of it that way."

"Even though your father abandoned you?"

"That was different. I never beat Kyle."

"Your father beat you?"

I thought everyone in the family knew.

"For almost four years before he left."

"Didn't your mother stop him?"

"She never knew. He did it when she wasn't around. Anyway, he's been dead for nearly two years and I'm still working through my anger."

"Don't be surprised if Kyle is angry with you."

"What should I do? Call him? Send him a letter? Explain why I had to go?"

"Kyle doesn't care about your problems. He's hurt and angry. You can call him, if you want, but you really should go home. Don't get me wrong—I like having you here—but Kyle needs you."

"I can't go home yet."

"What are you looking for?"

"You talked about when your father died. I was forty-seven when my mother died and I still couldn't handle it. There were too many words left unsaid. And you talked about being angry. I'm still angry. My father left, my mother expected too much from me, and I never had a childhood. I need the freedom I didn't have when I was young."

A little too honest, but I can trust Marcus.

"What bothers you so much about the death of your mother? I think it's more than not saying goodbye."

"It wasn't right. It wasn't fair. You just said your father's death was the will of Allah. I don't buy it. Why would God be in the business of killing people?"

"I've thought about that a lot. Believe me. Can you imagine, Brad, if everyone who has been born was still alive? There wouldn't be enough room, enough resources. Allah has given each of us a life span. A friend of mine just lost his daughter when she was only three days old, but my grandmother is in her nineties and still going strong. Allah gave Dad fifty-six years. What's important is Dad did a lot with the time he had. About as much as any man could. Your mother was close to seventy, wasn't she? That was her life span."

She was sixty-seven. Nearly sixty-eight. She never made it to seventy.

Marcus honks his horn and curses at the driver who just cut him off. I've never seen him this tense.

"It's still hard for you to think about losing your dad, isn't it?"

He nods. "But he was a good man. I know he wouldn't have left me, not if he had a choice."

We ride the rest of the way in silence. I did leave Kyle. I never thought of it that way.

I go to work on Tuesday, but as I fry the burgers and eggs, I think about my son. Does he really think I left him?

Marcus told me I need to go home. That's what Don and Ann said, and Beth, but it sounded different coming from Marcus. He understands being a teenage boy without a father.

I work two weeks before giving them my notice. Seven days later, I say goodbye.

"I'd better think about heading home."

"I think that's a good idea," says Marcus.

"You're welcome here any time, Uncle Brad. And keep reading."

We hug, and I'm on my way again. I did some good while I was here. They have a full fridge and dinner cooking on the stove. I know I lived on pizza, but I want something better for my favorite nephew. And for Marcus, who is a very perceptive young man.

I don't go far, stopping just outside New York City. When I read, I look for the science.

In the morning, I take the train into the city. I can't help but notice the improvements to their system, but I'm not an engineer now, I'm a tourist. I see more on my one-day tour than I've seen on eight business trips into this city. I send Beth a postcard of the Statue of Liberty and put another postcard in the mail for Kyle. I tell him I miss him, and I'm working my way home.

I head south toward Washington D.C., taking it slow because I need time to think. I always stop early so I can read before I sleep.

I find the science. Astronomy, geology, and biology. Even embryology. Those verses amaze me: "Man We did create from a quintessence of clay; then We placed him as a drop of sperm in a place firmly fixed, then We made the sperm into a clot of congealed blood; then of that clot We made a lump; then We made out of that lump bones and clothed the bones with flesh; then We developed out of it another creation. So blessed be Allah, the best to create." Many people say Muhammad wrote the Qur'an, but he couldn't have known about the formation of the fetus in the womb.

I notice the next verse, too: "After that, at length, you will die." That's what Abdullah and Marcus both told me. Death is inevitable. They're right, but I don't like it.

I finish reading the Qur'an just outside of D.C. In a sense there is no ending. I could pick it up and start again, but I need to read another book now.

I walk into the National Cathedral and kneel down. I've never thought about becoming a Catholic, but it is a church. I try to find God in the stained-glass windows.

Before leaving town, I stop at a bookstore and buy a Bible. I have never read the Bible before. Most of what I know, I learned from Mrs. Patrick. I don't know, exactly, what it means to be a Christian. How can I consider being anything else?

~

I stop at Arlington and send Beth another postcard—a picture of the cherry blossoms. I send Kyle a picture of Lincoln Memorial. "I'll bring you here some day," I write.

On a Saturday afternoon, on a beach in North Carolina, I pick up a shell and remember Matt asking Mom and Walt to bring him shells from Malaysia. I pick up a few more and put them in my backseat. Then I buy a postcard, a picture of the ocean, and send it to Matt.

I stop at a church in Wilmington on Sunday morning. I'm glad Ann gave me those clothes. I look respectable enough. I know the songs. I sit through the sermon. It is all very familiar.

I spend Monday driving through South Carolina. I've never been here before, not even on business. I eat breakfast in Myrtle Beach and stop for lunch in Charleston. Beth once asked me to take her to Charleston, but I was busy.

We celebrated our twenty-fifth wedding anniversary six months before Mom died. Beth wanted me to take her some place special—a second honeymoon—but I had too much going on at work and I couldn't afford to take time off.

Instead we checked into a luxury suite in Chicago for the weekend. The first night was great. She forgave me for not taking her out of town and we rekindled our romance. In the morning, while she slept, I logged on to the computer and worked on my projects. By the time she woke up, I was so involved I barely noticed her. That night I watched the NBA playoffs on the TV in the front room and she cried while watching an old love story in the bedroom. The next morning we went home.

My diligence paid off. A month later I received another promotion, with a raise and a bigger office. I rewarded myself with a new Lexus. I didn't buy anything for Beth and the boys. I didn't think of it.

I walk through the streets of Charleston. This is what Beth wanted to see. The classic old buildings. The charm. I think about buying her a coffee mug, but she'd probably throw it at me. I'll bring her here someday.

I sit in an outdoor café, enjoying the atmosphere. After lunch, I stroll along the beach. I wish Beth were here.

I take my time driving along the coast down to Jacksonville—spending whole days wading in the ocean. On Thursday, I buy trunks and finally go for my swim. I plunge into the ocean and pull away from the land. The cold water. The waves. The seagulls flying overhead. I swim against the tide, feeling stronger than I have in years.

I pull into Jacksonville on a Saturday afternoon. In the morning, I decide to try a smaller church.

I recognize most of the songs, but there are others I've never heard. There is a sermon, as usual, but it's anything but boring. With all the "Amens" and "Hallelujahs," I start to get into the spirit of it.

The minister greets me on my way out. "Welcome. I'm glad you came to worship with us this morning. We're having a picnic here shortly. I hope you can stay."

"Sure. Thanks."

It's not like I have anywhere else to go.

There's wonderful food. Chicken and ham. I haven't eaten much pork on this trip—not since I started reading the Qur'an—but this is good ham. I load up on mashed potatoes, hush puppies, and pecan pie. I can never get enough pecan pie.

I don't talk to anyone. I watch. The children running and laughing. The men telling jokes. The women fussing over the children. They look like one large family.

As I head for my car, the minister stops me. "I'm glad you could join us, Brother. You're welcome here any time."

As I drive south, the feeling of family stays with me.

My Bible reading is coming along. First, I read through all the familiar stories—Creation, Flood, Abraham and Isaac. Then I got to Joseph and Moses. I read those in the Qur'an and the stories are almost the same. I skipped the book of Numbers, which is as boring as it sounds, but after that it became much more interesting.

I've enjoyed reading about Joshua and Ruth. I didn't know my youngest brother was named after someone in the Bible. Even in his wildest days he wasn't quite that fierce, but he would be the kind of person to bring down a wall. And the way he's turned his life around, sometimes it does seem like God is talking to him. My niece's name suits her well. She's kind, smart, and determined, like the woman in the Bible.

I'm a little north of Miami when I begin reading the Psalms. I know the 23rd Psalm. Mrs. Patrick made us memorize it. I didn't know about the others, though. Some of them are even more beautiful.

Most of the Psalms are happy, all about making a joyful noise to the Lord. But the one which touches me is the 22nd Psalm. I wish Mrs.

Patrick had taught me this one. "My God, my God, why have you forsaken me? Why are you so far from helping me, from the words of my groaning? O my God, I cry by day, but you do not answer; and by night, but find no rest." I used to pray, when I was little and my father was beating me. I wondered why God would let him do that to me. I wanted to ask Mrs. Patrick why God didn't love me enough to stop my father from hurting me, but I was ashamed.

❧

I decide to stay in Miami and work. I get another job at another diner and check out a different church every Sunday. Comparison shopping. Some are very staid while others have an excitement I feel in my bones. When I was an engineer, I wanted a quiet service on Sunday morning. Now, I welcome the excitement.

I think about checking out a mosque, but I would want to go as Ibrahim. I can't be Ibrahim at the mosque and Brad at the church. Not in the same city. I'm too old for that much confusion.

❧

My reading is getting more interesting. I really enjoy the Song of Solomon. If more ministers gave sermons on those verses, their churches would be packed with young men who want to hear about love and lust, and old men coming without their wives. I wonder how it got into the Bible.

I meet another woman. A waitress at the diner. Her name is Rose. She invites me for coffee one evening and I accept. After coffee, she asks me to her apartment and offers me a glass of wine. I can blame that love poetry in the Song of Solomon. And I've been watching the college students here on spring break. The next day, I send Beth another corny love poem. I give the owner my notice and work one more week.

I finish the Old Testament on my last night in Miami. Now for the Gospels. I know the story, but I'd like to read it all the way through.

I read about Jesus in the Qur'an, and in some ways the stories in the Bible are the same. The virgin birth. Teaching and performing miracles. But in the Qur'an he didn't change water into wine. Mrs. Patrick didn't tell us about that one either. She did tell us about the crucifixion and resurrection. I read those passages carefully. I'm fascinated when I come across the same words I found in the 22nd Psalm. "My God, my God, why have you forsaken me?" You don't have to be nailed to a cross to understand.

Paul's letters are interesting. Mrs. Patrick didn't tell us he'd been in jail. I think of Joshua's time in prison, when he was accused of terrorism. What Paul went through wasn't really that much different. I guess it all has to do with faith.

I like some of the things he says. Like in Corinthians when he talks about love. "Love is patient and kind; love is not jealous or boastful; it is not arrogant or rude. Love does not insist on its own way; it is not irritable or resentful; it does not rejoice at wrong, but rejoices in the right. Love bears all things, believes all things, hopes all things, endures all things."

I'm sure Beth knows that passage. And even though she worked too much and wasn't there every time I needed her, I know she tried. I hope she's ready to try again.

Another verse catches my eye. "When I was a child, I spoke like a child, I thought like a child, I reasoned like a child; when I became a man, I gave up childish ways." I am a man. I have a wife, two sons, and a mortgage, but there are still ghosts from my childhood. I can't see them or name them, but they're very real. I wish I knew how to get rid of them.

I'm passing through Tampa on a Friday, so I find a mosque and join the prayer. I am Ibrahim again, sitting on the floor. I stand and pray with the other men. I bow down and touch my forehead to the ground. I feel it. When the prayer is over I sit and try to hold on to the feeling.

In Tallahassee, I see one of those preachers who handles poisonous snakes and believes he won't get bitten because God will protect him. It's interesting, but I don't get anything from it. He doesn't get bitten. I don't know if God had anything to do with it or it was just dumb luck.

In Mississippi, I find a church where people speak in tongues. I watch as someone stands up and seems to be speaking in a different language. I listen closely. I can't understand what he's saying, of course, but it is a language, with the patterns and cadences of speech. Before the service is over, half of the church is speaking in tongues. Some roll around on the floor. I quickly head for the nearest exit.

I've traveled the east coast from north to south, reading the Bible and going to church. From liturgies and ritual to Amens and Hallelujahs. From snake handlers to holy rollers. I have been a Christian all my life, but I'm still not sure what Christianity is. What does it mean to me?

Part Five

I drive up north through Arkansas until I come to Missouri, eventually hitting I-70. I haven't been in every state, but I have traveled in a full circle around the states. I should head east now, back to Chicago, but I drive west instead.

I finish reading the Bible while driving through Kansas. It certainly ends with a bang. I'd heard about the book of Revelations. It would make a good action film.

I've saved the money Don and Ann gave me for a hotel. I head to Colorado Springs and find a small motel room with a kitchenette. Their money pays for a full month here. In a couple of weeks, I'll find a job for the money to take me home.

First, I need two weeks to be quiet. I have had many moments of solitude, but I have never been really quiet. I've traveled or worked, or stayed with someone. I take two weeks now to do nothing but read and think.

I sit in my room and think about everything I have experienced these last fourteen months. The religious experiences and the personal ones. I think about the beauty I have seen and the pain I have felt. When I return to Chicago, I'm determined to start a new life.

I spend two weeks thinking. You could call it meditating. You could call it praying. I stand, bow, sit, and kneel. I search for my soul.

I need to find a way to recapture the tranquility I felt while gazing at the Grand Canyon, the ocean, and the mountains. Even when I'm in the middle of downtown Chicago I want to be calm and serene. I browse through the literature to see what the religions can offer me. Each has a promise of peace.

In a pamphlet from the Buddhist meditation center, I find this quote. "Do everything with a mind that lets go. Don't accept praise or gain or anything else. If you let go a little, you will have a little peace; if you let go a lot, you will have a lot of peace; if you let go completely, you will have complete peace."

Let go. That's never been easy for me. Letting go means relinquishing control. When I was a child, my father had all the control and my lack of control allowed him to abuse me.

I look at a Baha'i booklet. The founder of the religion said, "Religion is the greatest of all means for the establishment of order in the world and for the peaceful contentment of all that dwell therein."

I have also heard religion is the greatest means for controlling others. The opiate of the people. I believe, possibly, religion can give me peaceful contentment.

In the Bible I find this verse. "Peace I leave with you; my peace I give to you; not as the world gives do I give to you. Let not your hearts be troubled, neither let them be afraid."

That's what I want. Peace. If Jesus gave it, how do I get it?

I find these verses in the Qur'an. "Those who believe and work righteousness—their Lord will guide them because of their faith; beneath them will flow rivers in gardens of bliss. This will be their prayer: 'Glory to You, O Allah!' And peace will be their greeting."

Those who believe and perform good deeds will have peace. Could I ever get to that point? No one has ever mistaken me for a righteous believer. I would have to work for peace.

I don't know which one I like. I'm tired. I'll think about it tomorrow.

Before sitting down to eat breakfast, I grab a piece of motel stationary. I need to make another list.

I know what my options are. I could become a Buddhist, Baha'i, or Muslim. Or I could simply learn how to be a sincere Christian. I could study other religions, but I don't want to spend the rest of my life searching. I need something now.

I can see merits in each way of believing. And I don't think it's my right to judge what's right or wrong for someone else. The question is, "What do I need from a religion? What is right for me?"

What do I need? What helps me get through the day? I jot down my thoughts as they come.

1. I need consistency and structure. I still don't like surprises.

2. I need rules. I've broken most of the Ten Commandments, and a few laws, but when I make my fresh start, it will help if I always know what is expected of me.

3. There have to be consequences. What happens if I don't pray, don't go to church, don't meditate? I need something to keep me in line. Heaven, hell, nirvana. Whatever.

4. I want a sense of brotherhood. I usually feel alone, even when I'm not. I need to belong somewhere.

5. I absolutely must have peace. When I go home, I don't want to be restless or haunted by nightmares again. I need something I can turn to when times get rough.

I read my list ten times. I don't know. Nothing is clear to me. I put the list aside and head out to find another job at another diner.

∽

I keep thinking with the spatula in my hand. I'm quieter these days than I've ever been. I don't know anyone's name here. I'm just the cook.

I need to make a decision, and I need to make sure it's right. Every night after work I think. And pray. And meditate. I study my list. What's right for me?

∽

I've worked at the diner for two weeks. I need to pack it up and head home. As I fry the burgers, I review my choices. When things are quiet, I take the list from my pocket and study it. An answer begins to form.

I decide to work for another week. It's not the money—I have more than enough to take me home. I need to be sure.

It happens one night. I have a dream. The clearest, most vibrant dream I have ever had. I'm praying next to my brother and I feel at peace—the same peace I felt at the Grand Canyon, the ocean, and the Badlands. My brother doesn't turn to me. He doesn't say a word. And even though I'm happy to see him, I don't want to talk. I am caught up fully in my worship.

I wake up and try to recapture the dream, but it's gone. I rub my eyes and look at my list. Peace, brotherhood, rules, consequences, consistency. I think I have it.

I drop my last postcard in the mail, telling her I'll be home on Thursday. I work three more days and spend one last night in Colorado.

Halfway across Kansas, I remember Kyle will be a senior next year. I'll help him pick a college and watch him go up for his diploma. I'll be a real father to him now. I check the road for the highway patrol and increase my speed.

I don't stop until I get to Missouri. I pass through Kansas City and pull into the rest stop near Boonville. After a short nap, I'm ready to drive straight through to Chicago.

When I pass Kingdom City, I think about Chelsea. I'd like another roast beef sandwich but, with my luck, Chelsea would be there visiting her aunt. I'm hungry, but I'll wait.

I pass through St. Louis. All this traveling, and I never went up in the Arch. One of these days, I need to come back this way. And I need to bring my family with me.

I'm in Illinois now for the first time in over a year. It has been one long and exhilarating year. My heart beats faster as I drive north on I-55, toward Chicago, and watch the dotted white line pulling me home again.

Turbulence

I pull into Chicago in the middle of the night, park in my brother's driveway, and sit in my car, waiting for the sunrise.

Brothers

I sought my soul, but my soul I could not see.
I sought my God, but my God eluded me.
I sought my brother and I found all three.

—Author Unknown

My oldest son, Jamal, and I have just come back from making the Fajr prayer at the masjid. Since the plane crash, I have been going to the masjid for all of the five daily prayers. I thought I knew death, but nothing prepared me for how it would feel to lose Mom.

Jamal always comes with me, whenever he's not in school. Together, we still feel the loss. It's been eighteen months, and the time for mourning has long passed, but the sadness remains. One day she sat in our kitchen, eating curry. Then she was gone. Both of us find the peace we need by standing shoulder to shoulder with our Muslim brothers.

Sunrise is still about twenty minutes away. Deep shadows cover the driveway. The morning rush hour has not yet started and the world seems calm. We are walking up the driveway when I see a figure in the shadows. It must be the neighbor's dog. I look closer and make out a human form. I pull Jamal close to me and get ready to hand over my wallet.

He whispers, "Joshua," and steps out of the shadows.

He has a beard. His hair is long, pulled back into a ponytail. Gray hairs streak through his hair and beard. I don't think I've ever seen him in torn jeans before. He looks so different, but I know him.

"Brad! Man, it is good to see you." I throw my arms around him.

We stand in the driveway for a long time, just holding on. I don't know what to say. Finally, I step away and look at him. "I was afraid I'd never see you again."

"I sent Beth a postcard saying I'd be back on Thursday."

"Yes, she told me. So you're still obsessive, even with that beard."

"Some things never change. How are you, Jamal? You're as tall as your dad now."

"I'm fine. We missed you."

"How are my boys?"

Jamal starts to answer, but I stop him. "They're okay. Kyle is over six feet now. Matt is doing well. Beth had to move. She's renting out the house."

"I wondered. I shouldn't have left like that but I had to, you know? I thought you, of all people, would understand."

"I'm trying to. Well, come on in. Let's go get some breakfast and you can tell us where you've been."

We walk into the kitchen. I send Jamal upstairs to get ready for school. "Can you tell your mom that Uncle Brad is here? And make sure Nuruddin wakes up and makes his prayers on time." Lately that boy has been as hard to wake up as I used to be. I hadn't expected that from Abdul-Qadir's son.

I turn to my brother. "Sit down, man. Have some coffee. Lots of cream, right?"

"No, I learned to drink it black."

"Beard, black coffee. Any tattoos?"

"I almost got one in Santa Fe, but I couldn't work up the nerve."

"I heard you went to find yourself. Any luck?"

"I found a lot. Some bad. Mostly good. It's been quite a trip."

"I hope you're home to stay."

"I hope Beth still wants me." He rearranges the salt and pepper shakers. "Walt told me he would come back and let me know what he found. I think they found it."

"I think so, too, but I keep telling myself it's just wishful thinking."

"No, this isn't wishing. It's something stronger. So I thought I should go looking for it myself. I used to love my life, but I had to get away."

"What did you find?"

"You'd better sit down first."

"I got to finish these pancakes first."

"I can wait."

I watch the surface of the pancakes bubble and wonder about my brother. He talks like Brad and acts like Brad, but there's something very different about him—beyond his new look.

Aisha walks in just as I'm putting the pancakes on the table. "Hi, Brad. Everyone has been worried about you."

"Hello, Aisha. How is Beth?"

"She knows you'll be back today. I think you'd better ask her yourself."

"I'll go see her in a little while. If she's willing to talk to me, that is."

"Yes, she'll talk to you."

"That's good. I was afraid she might want to slam the door in my face."

"I won't say what she wants, but she is willing to talk."

I put down the salt and pepper shakers, and look at Aisha. She turns to help Joshua. I wonder what she meant by that. What did Beth say to her?

All of the kids walk into the kitchen and take their places around the table. Little Maryam isn't a baby anymore. I wonder where Nuruddin is. Still sleeping, I guess. Jennifer isn't here either. She used to talk about going away to college.

"You were going to tell me what you found." Joshua brings over the syrup and pulls up a chair. "I'm sitting down. What is it?"

"Joshua, Aisha, I traveled all over the country. I slept in my car. Sometimes, I slept out under the stars. I met all kinds of people. I hallucinated in New Mexico, meditated with Buddhists in Seattle, worshiped with Baha'is in California, and knelt in the National Cathedral. I looked up to the sky, and out to the ocean, and touched my forehead to the ground. I read the Bible and I read the Qur'an. That's what I found."

Aisha raises her eyebrows. "What are you saying?"

"I haven't converted yet—I want to do that with you, Joshua—but I found what you two found when you went looking. I found Islam."

I can't believe I actually said it. Up until this second, I've fought it.

I stare at him. My brother.

"You want to be a Muslim?" asks Jamal. "Really?"

"Really. Say something, Joshua. I told you so, maybe?"

I don't know what to say. I just grab him and hold on. The tears come, too.

Maybe I'm dreaming. This is how I would dream it. He comes back, healthy and safe, and tells me that he's ready to accept Islam. It's too good to be true, but as I hug him, I know this is real. I feel his tears on my cheek and his beard against my neck. His strong arms hug me back.

"That's wonderful news," says Aisha.

I pull back. "You're serious, aren't you?"

"I've spent the last fourteen months searching, exploring, and experiencing life. I worked and traveled during the day. At night, I crawled into the backseat of my Toyota and read. In Los Angeles, I met someone named Abdullah who gave me a copy of the Qur'an. I read it, and it spoke to me. I asked questions, and it answered me. You know what I'm talking about, don't you?"

"Yes. I'll have some question or issue on my mind and when I pick up the Qur'an I find the answer right in front of me."

"That's it. That's it," he says, softly.

"So when do you want to convert?"

"As soon as I can. Right now."

"Go ahead and eat your pancakes first. And you'll probably want to wash up."

"A hot shower sounds nice. Do you have clothes I could borrow? I haven't done my laundry for a couple of weeks. And I'd better fix myself up before I see my wife."

"You might want to buy her flowers, too."

We finish eating. I get clothes for Brad and tell him how to make ghusl. While he's in the shower, I go haul Nuruddin out of bed and make sure he prays. Then I call Jennifer to come downstairs. She doesn't have classes until later today, but she needs to come see her Uncle Brad.

Hot water pricks my skin. It feels great. That shower in Colorado City never got past lukewarm.

I didn't know I had to take a special kind of shower. Joshua told me all the steps. Ghusl, he called it. I think I'm doing it right.

Do I really want to do this? I'll have to keep up with the prayers. No more drinking. And no more blackouts. No more women. Just Beth. I can't wait to see her.

I step out of the shower and dry off. It takes longer to get my hair dry. Maybe I should get a haircut before I go back to her. No, let her see me this way. She'll laugh. Then she'll take me into the kitchen and cut it herself. When she's done, she'll take me into her arms. I hope the boys aren't home. I'll take her on that second honeymoon soon and we'll get to know each other all over again.

I pull on the slacks and polo shirt Joshua gave me—we're nearly the same size. I'm glad he didn't give me any Pakistani clothes. They look comfortable, but they're not my style.

I pause before opening the bathroom door. This is it. I hope I'm ready.

We sit together in the family room. Aisha and the kids will be a little late for school today, but this is more important.

"Are you sure you know what you're doing, Brad? This is a life-long commitment you'll be making."

"You won't try to talk me out of it, will you?"

"I'd never do that. I just want to make sure you're ready. You'll have to keep up with the prayers. And Ramadan starts in a few days. Do you think you can handle fasting?"

"That's great. I've always wondered how it would feel to fast. It sounds like the perfect end to my journey."

"Just remember that no matter how hard your life gets, you have to keep up with it."

"Man, Joshua, you're the one who used to quit everything. If you can do it, I sure can."

"Okay then. Repeat after me. Ashadu ala ilaha ila Allah. Wa ashadu ana Muhammadu Rasul Allah."

He makes the shahadah. I never thought I'd hear those words

from Brad's mouth. "Are you sure you know what it means?"

"I testify there is no god but Allah, and Muhammad is the messenger of Allah."

"That's right. Assalaamu alaikum, Brother. Welcome to the ummah."

~

I did it. That wasn't so hard.

Joshua hugs me again. Then I hug each of the kids, except Maryam, who hides behind Aisha.

Jennifer smiles. "It's great to have you back, Uncle Brad."

"I wasn't sure you'd be here. I thought you wanted to go away to study."

"I decided to stay in Chicago." She glances at Nuruddin. Joshua doesn't seem to notice. He'd better start paying attention.

I stand up. "Now I need to see my wife."

"She might not recognize you," says Joshua. "Maybe you should get a haircut first."

"I'm sure she's changed, too. I hope we can learn to be a family again, changes and all."

~

We hug again before Brad leaves.

My brother is alive. He's back. He's a Muslim.

I watch as he drives away in the early morning light.

Coming Home

*Not everything that is faced can be changed,
but nothing can be changed until it is faced.*

—James Baldwin

Part One

I can't believe what I just did.

I've thought about it since Tampa. The sermon was about what it means to be a Muslim. He talked about the shahadah, the confession of faith. That's how I knew the meaning.

The dream convinced me. I was praying next to Joshua, and it was right. But now I wonder if I did the right thing. I should have waited. I should have gone home to Beth first. I shouldn't have jumped into this.

Joshua gave me the directions to her apartment. It's not far from the condo we lived in before Kyle was born. She always liked that neighborhood.

Aisha said Beth is waiting for me. I hope she still wants me.

On my way to her apartment, I drive past the firm. I don't miss it. Hendricks must be enjoying my office.

I pull into a grocery store. Joshua is right. I should buy flowers. What kind does she like? I bought flowers for her every week when we lived in Ohio, but I don't remember what kind. I stare at the display a few minutes, finally grabbing a bunch of roses. All women like roses.

I pull up to the high-rise. She knows I'm coming home today. I wonder if the boys are there. I can't wait to see them, but first I want to be alone with her.

I walk into the lobby and find her name on the directory. B. Monroe. Not Monroe-Adams anymore. Not Beth Adams. Not Brad and Beth. Not Mrs.

We used to joke about our last names. She reminded me Monroe was president, while John Quincy was his faithful cabinet member. I don't know if I'm related to John Quincy or not, but if so I must be descended from his brother Charles—he drank himself into an early grave.

It's an old building. I have to buzz her apartment. Once. Twice. Three times. Four times. She must have gone to work. Maybe she's met someone. I'll need to find a good divorce lawyer.

But I can't walk away. Not this time. Six times. Seven. "What is it?"

It's Beth. I've missed the sound of her voice.

"Hello? May I help you?"

"Hi, Beth. It's me."

"Brad." She pauses. "You are back."

"I miss you. Can I come up?"

"Yes." A second later she buzzes me in.

I get in the elevator, heading up to apartment 731. Our first apartment was 317. I wonder if she remembers.

Her apartment is in the middle of the hallway, between the elevator and the stairs. Like the rest of the building, the hall is nice, but old-looking. Worn green carpeting, faded yellow wallpaper, dim lighting. This was all she could afford without my salary.

I reach the apartment door and hesitate. What have I done? Beth stood by me all those years, and I walked away from her.

I knock lightly and wait. It takes several minutes. I hear her breathing on the other side.

Finally the door opens. She's more beautiful than I remembered. I smile. "Hi, Beth."

She stares at me.

"You look good," I say. "I like your hair that way."

"You look…different. Why in the world did you grow a beard?"

"Can I come in? I'll tell you all about it."

"First let me see your left hand."

"Why?"

"Hold up your hand. I need to see it."

I raise my left hand, and she smiles. "You're wearing your wedding ring."

"Of course. I wouldn't take it off."

Except for that time in Seattle, but that was to help me get a job. I didn't mean to pick up a woman.

"I searched the house for it. I thought there must be someone else."

Not when I left. And not now.

"Only you, Beth. Only you."

She takes my hand. "Come in."

The apartment is small. A tiny kitchen, a slightly larger living room, and a hallway leading to the bedrooms. She kept the green couch. We bought it six or seven years ago. We had some very nice evenings together on that couch, after the boys were asleep.

"I brought you flowers."

She takes the roses and frowns.

What's wrong?

"Are you ready for me to come home?"

"Sit down. We need to talk."

"I guess we do. Where are the boys?"

"Matt still has a few days of school before summer vacation. Kyle is asleep."

"Is his school out already? Does he have a job?"

"He dropped out of school last November."

"Dropped out? How could you let him do that?"

"He was bored and he wanted to quit. He's of legal age. There wasn't very much I could do about it."

I've been back two minutes and already we're fighting. I need to calm down. I think about the ocean. "All right. What is he doing now? Does he have a job?"

"He goes out with his friends every night and sleeps all day."

Is she talking about Kyle? How could he throw his life away?

"What about Matt? How is he?"

"He's quiet. He goes to school, fights with Kyle, plays video games. He is getting good grades, but he doesn't talk much."

I remember my little boy. He was always excited, always talking.

"What about you, Beth? How are you?"

"I go to work, make dinner, do laundry. At first I tried to keep up with my activities, but it got to be too much. Now I just get by."

"Maybe I shouldn't have left."

"Now what?"

"I want to come back."

"Tell me what you've found. I've been feeling pretty lost myself these last fourteen months."

"What can I do to make it up to you?"

"Tell me what you found."

I had no problem telling Joshua this morning, but how can I justify it to her?

"I don't know if you'll understand, but I've found peace."

I hope.

"That's it? You spend fourteen months away from us. You put me through hell wondering if you're still alive. You dump all your responsibilities and that's all you can give me?"

"It was a journey. When I left, I didn't know who I was anymore."

And I didn't care.

"But I found my self. And I found peace."

"Can you tell me how you found this peace? Because I sure could use some right now."

I have to tell her.

"I have spent the last fourteen months searching for my soul. When I came into town early this morning, I went to Joshua's house and asked him to give me shahadah. Before I came here, Beth, I said the words necessary for me to become a Muslim."

"A Muslim? Are you crazy? And Joshua found Islam right here in Chicago. Why did you have to leave? Why didn't you come home when I asked you?"

"I had to get away. That's all I can say."

I should say a lot more, but I can't.

"I was hoping for more from you, Brad. The man I married was strong, responsible, and committed to his family. Not some long-haired bum. You may have found yourself, but I don't know who you are."

I am strong and committed. I survived fourteen months on the road. And I came back, didn't I?

"I'm sorry. I'll make it up to you."

"Do you know what? I don't want to talk with you right now. I don't even want to see your face. If I leave in the next few minutes, I can still get most of my work done for today. You can go back to Joshua. I'm sure he'll take you in."

Doesn't want to see my face? I'd forgotten how arrogant she can get. I hold my tongue.

"What about us?"

"I don't know. I need time to think. You've had your fourteen months. Now it's my turn."

"What about the boys? I want to see them."

"I don't know if they'll want to see you, but you can try. Matt gets off the school bus at four. Kyle should be awake by then. I suggest you talk with them and see what they say. But I insist you call before five. I'll be home then, and I don't feel like talking to you again today."

She doesn't have to work late?

I almost say something, but the situation is bad enough. Instead I say, "I love you, Beth."

"I know, but I don't know if love is enough."

What's all this psycho-babble? Is she seeing a therapist? Maybe she's dating one.

"I guess I'll be at Joshua's house if you need me." I walk across the living room and open the door.

"I guess it was too much trouble to let me know where you were for the last fourteen months." She throws the flowers in my face. "And you forgot. I hate roses." She pushes me out and slams the door.

The hall looks dingier as I trudge back to the elevator.

Beth Speaks Out

So he came back. I guess that's him. It's hard to tell with all that hair. He's been traipsing around the country for over a year. Don't tell me he didn't have time to go to a barber.

He went to Joshua's house. Isn't that nice? I don't suppose he could have come to see his wife and sons first.

And on top of everything else, he's a Muslim. What is that? He never came to church unless I dragged him. Now he wants to be religious? Why can't he just learn to be a proper Christian?

He thinks I'm going to take him back. He must be crazy.

Part Two

Joshua's house is locked up tight and the cars are gone. I don't know where he's working now. When I left, he had that job at the restaurant, but I doubt he's still there.

I should go see Chris, but how can I explain to him what I've done. I barely understand it myself.

I park in Joshua's driveway and sleep in my car. I didn't sleep much last night, anticipating my reunion with Beth. I sure didn't expect to be sleeping in my car again.

I wake up to a rapping sound. Joshua's son, Muhammad, is knocking on the window.

"Assalaamu alaikum, Uncle Brad," he yells. "Why are you out here?"

I sit up, pop a couple breath mints, and open the door. "You don't have to talk so loud. Is your dad home yet?"

"No. He comes home at five."

"What time is it now?"

"It's four. We just got home from school. Where did you go today?"

Four!

I jump out of the car. "Is your mama home?"

"Yes. Why?"

This kid asks too many questions. "I need to use the phone."

"Okay. Let's go." He takes my hand and walks me into the house.

Aisha is in the kitchen, standing in front of the stove. I've never seen her without her scarf before.

"Um, hello, Aisha. Um, salam, um, I forgot how to say it."

"Oh, Brad." She shrieks, running into a corner of the kitchen. "Jamal," she screams. "Bring me my hijab. Right now!"

I wasn't supposed to see her without her scarf. I forgot.

"Muhammad said I can use the phone. I need to call my boys."

"Wait until I get a scarf on," she yells. "Jamal, where are you?"

"Just a minute, Mom."

"Come here, right now, with that hijab!"

"Okay, Mom. I'm coming."

We pass a few awkward minutes while Aisha waits to be properly covered. Jamal runs downstairs with a scarf, and then runs back up, taking two stairs at a time.

A minute later, Aisha comes to the front hallway, her eyes lowered. "Use the phone in the family room. I'll stay in here." She calls out again. "Jamal, come back here."

I pick up the phone and start to dial our old number, in Evanston, before I remember.

"Um, Aisha, what is Beth's number now?"

"I'll write it down for you. Jamal will bring it."

I hear her searching for pen and paper. By the time Jamal comes with the number, it's nearly 4:30. I quickly dial.

"Hello?" A deep, sleepy voice answers.

"Kyle, is that you? This is your dad."

"Dad? Where are you?"

"I'm in Chicago. At Uncle Joshua's house."

"You're back? Really."

"Yeah, I'm back. How are you, Kyle?"

"I'm cool."

"I want to see you."

"Why don't you come to the apartment? We moved, in case you didn't know."

"I came by the apartment this morning to talk with your mom. You were still asleep. She doesn't want to see me right now."

"I guess not. I don't blame her."

"Do you want to see me, Kyle?"

"Sure. I mean, if I don't have anything better to do."

"What about Matt? Is he there?"

"Yeah. Matt, it's Dad. He's back. He wants to talk to you."

It takes a few minutes. I hear them arguing.

"Go ahead," says Kyle.

"I don't want to," says Matt.

"Go on, moron. Talk to him."

There's silence, then a soft voice. "Hello. Dad?"

"Hi, Matt. How are you?"

"I'm okay."

"I missed you."

More silence.

"Say something, moron." Kyle badgers him.

"I don't want to."

"Hey, Dad, it's Kyle. Matt is being stupid."

"When can I see you?"

"Why don't you come over here?"

"Your mother doesn't want to see me."

"That's right, you told me. Okay, I'll try to come sometime tomorrow. I wrecked my car, but I can probably get a ride with someone. You'll be at Uncle Joshua's house, right?"

"Yes, I'll be here."

"Okay. Well, I gotta go. Talk to you later."

He's gone. Beth doesn't want to see me, Matt won't talk to me, and Kyle might come over if he can manage it. Three strikes, and I'm out. I should climb back into my Toyota and drive away. I don't seem to belong here anymore.

"Assalaamu alaikum." It's Joshua.

"Daddy's home!" Luqman screams.

"Isa, Brad is here." Aisha whispers a little too loudly. "He's in the family room."

"Okay. How's my little guy?" He wrestles with Luqman. I eavesdrop on their family moments, wishing I was somewhere else. Finally, Joshua walks into the family room.

"Assalaamu alaikum, Brad. Man, those are words I never thought I'd say. How are you, Brother?"

"My wife doesn't want to see me, my oldest son is a high school dropout, and my other son won't talk to me. And I think I broke a major rule when I walked in on your wife. I'm wondering why I bothered to come back."

"Don't worry. It'll work out. So, have you prayed Asr yet?"

"I know a little about the prayers, but I don't know which one is Asr. I haven't prayed since I left your house this morning."

"Okay, then that's the first thing you have to learn. Let's go to the bathroom. I'll show you how to wash up, and we'll get you started on your prayers."

"I don't know. Maybe this was all a mistake."

"Too late now, Brother. Let's go."

Joshua shows me, step by step, how to make ablutions and how to pray. He teaches me about the times for prayer. We pray together. Then we talk.

"Beth doesn't want me. She asked what I found, and all I could say was 'peace.' She's struggled alone all these months, just so I could find a little peace. I'm thinking about going back out on the road."

"Don't do that. You can stay here as long as you need. We just have to lay out a few ground rules."

"I guess the first rule is not to walk in on Aisha."

"That's right. All of our lives will be easier if you remember that."

"I don't understand. We've know each other for about fifteen years now, and it doesn't matter to me if I see her without her scarf. Besides, isn't a brother-in-law practically like a brother?"

"Not exactly. You can't stay alone in the house with Aisha either. It was okay today because Jamal was here and, in some ways, he's a man now."

"You mean my nephew has to protect his mother from me?"

"It's more complicated than that. Just go along with it, and you'll understand later."

"I don't have a choice, do I? Anything else?"

"Keep up with your prayers. And feel free to ask questions. I won't be able to explain everything, but some things will become clearer as you go along."

"When I came here this morning, I was excited about my fresh start. Now I'm confused."

"Now you understand how I felt."

"But you were used to being confused. This is new to me." Being confused is actually very familiar, but I won't tell Joshua that.

"You were gone for over a year, Brad. You can't expect everything to come together overnight."

"I guess not."

"Have you thought about getting a job? Maybe going back to the firm?"

"I don't want to go back to engineering."

And couldn't if I wanted.

"I'd like something less stressful. On the road, I stopped every few hundred miles to flip burgers. At the end of the day, the job was finished and I didn't have to worry about tomorrow. That's the kind of job I want."

Joshua laughs. "You have changed. You were always the most responsible person I knew."

"That's why Beth doesn't want me. She says I'm not responsible."

"You two always had a good marriage."

"Yeah, before I walked out on her."

An hour later, over dinner, we discuss the arrangements with Aisha. She repeats her ground rules and welcomes me into her home.

I tell them about my stay with Michael and Marcus. "Aisha, your brother is a very intelligent young man."

"Yes, I'm proud of him. I can't wait to meet his fiancée. She sounds wonderful. I'm sure they'll be very happy together."

Beth and I were happy once.

"Could you talk to Beth for me?"

"I'll try, but I don't think you understand what she's been through."

She doesn't understand what I've been through, either.

After dinner, Joshua and I drive to Chris's house. I thought about going alone, but, for the first time in my life, I'm not comfortable at the prospect of talking with Chris. I remember how he reacted when Joshua became a Muslim.

When Chris opens the door, Joshua puts his arm around my shoulders and grins. "Look who I found in my driveway this morning."

For two seconds, Chris just stares. Maybe it's the beard. Then a smile forms and he throws his arms around me. "Brad! You're back."

We hug. Joshua joins us. It's good to be with my brothers again.

"Come on in. Melinda," Chris calls out. "Look who's here."

Melinda greets me, but she's not smiling. "Hi, Brad. I heard you were back."

She talked with Beth.

"What did she tell you?"

She turns away. "Chris missed you."

"I sure did. Where have you been?"

Melinda stops on her way into the kitchen. "Go sit in the family room. I'll bring snacks."

"You don't have to bother," I say.

"It's no bother." She rolls her eyes and walks away.

Beth must have given her an earful.

"It is so good to see you," says Chris. "Where were you?"

"I was everywhere. I saw the Atlantic and the Pacific, and my faithful Celeste and I even made it through the Rockies."

"Why did you leave?"

"I couldn't stay. After the crash, I didn't know where to turn. And I couldn't find my answers here in Chicago."

I couldn't let my family know I was a failure.

"Why didn't you ask me for help?"

"I had to figure this out on my own."

"What's with the beard? I imagine it's hard to shave on the road."

"Sure is." I stop and rearrange the Christian magazines on their coffee table. "Chris, I pulled into town late last night and went to Joshua's house to tell him what I had found. He was ready to hear it, but I don't think you are."

"What is it?"

I rub the back of my neck.

Are there the right words to tell him?

"I went looking for my faith. And I found it."

"That's great."

I look right at him. "I found it in Islam."

Melinda is walking into the room, carrying a tray full of root beer and snacks. She gasps. Some root beer spills.

Chris stares at me. He looks at Joshua and again at me. Finally, he says softy, "You found your faith?"

"Yes."

"You're a Muslim?"

"Joshua gave me the shahadah this morning."

He sighs. "Welcome back, Brad." He takes the tray from Melinda. "Here. Drink your root beer before it gets warm."

"It's right for me, Chris."

"If you say so. Did you tell Beth?"

"Of course."

"That's why she was so upset," Melinda whispers.

"That's part of it."

"Do you know about Kyle?" says Chris.

"I know he dropped out. Is there something else?"

"He's usually intoxicated. He drives under the influence, and he was arrested once for possession of marijuana. We got him off that first time, but he's still drinking and using drugs. I've forbidden Isaiah from associating with him. He's a bad influence on my son."

It's been building since I learned Kyle wouldn't be graduating. "Would it have been too much for the two of you to look after my kid? For God's sake, Joshua, you know I looked after your kids. I took care of them when you left Heather, and again when you were in prison. And Chris. How about putting some of that piety into practice? Instead of watching my son destroy himself, why didn't you stop him?"

My brothers lower their heads. They're too ashamed to look me in the eye.

"They tried," says Melinda. "They spent time with Kyle and talked with him, but he didn't want to listen. He has a lot of anger."

"I talked with him this afternoon. He didn't sound angry."

"Have you seen him yet?"

"No, but he said he'll come see me tomorrow."

"He's very angry. You'll see."

"I don't know why. Joshua left his kids, and they practically fall all over themselves trying to please him."

"Brad, when I left my kids, they were little. When you left Kyle, he was becoming a man. He needed you more than ever. Nobody knew where you were, or if you were ever coming back. For a long time, we thought you must be dead. We tried, believe me. I'm still trying because I know something about anger and drugs."

Anger and drugs and dropping out of school. I always had high hopes for Kyle. All of his teachers called him gifted. When I left, he was fifteen and he had some issues. But nothing serious. Nothing he wouldn't outgrow.

"We let you down," says Chris. "But we did try."

"You're telling me my son has anger issues, and I deserve to be angry. But I'm too tired. I shouldn't have come back."

"You've been back less than a day, man. Give it time."

"A few days ago, I was in Colorado. I spent most of my time out west. It was hard to leave the mountains behind, but I missed my family. I drove practically non-stop. All the way home, I thought about reuniting with Beth, and helping Kyle get into a good college. I was ready to be a husband and father again, but I'm too late. I should have stayed in Colorado."

"Let's go home, man. You can sleep in a bed for a change. Things will look better in the morning."

"They can't look any worse."

"You're a Muslim. I wish you had told me first what you planned to do."

"So you could talk me out of it, Chris?"

"I don't know. Yes, so I could have talked you out of it. I have to tell you, I don't understand."

"I just spent more than a year on the road. You couldn't possibly understand."

"Maybe. Get some rest. We'll help you deal with everything later."

I hug Chris and climb into Joshua's car. I'm leaving Chris and going with Joshua. I'm homeless and Joshua is taking care of me. Everything is upside down.

While Joshua drives down the expressway, I gaze out the window, remembering Chicago. I watch other cars speeding by and wonder where they're going.

"I've ruined everything, haven't I?"

"What do you mean?"

"Two years ago, I had a solid marriage. Kyle was an achiever. I knew who I was."

"And you were close to Chris."

"Yes. That too."

Part Three

We get back to Joshua's and I haul my stuff out of the backseat. Mom's package is still in here. I'll open it later.

The roses lay where I threw them after leaving Beth's apartment. They look fresh. I carry them into the house.

Aisha greets us at the door. "How did it go?"

Joshua smiles. I've just noticed how often he smiles. "It will be okay. It just needs time."

I offer Aisha the roses. "Here. A small token of my appreciation for taking me in."

"You bought these for Beth, didn't you?"

"Um, yes."

"She hates roses. She thinks they're too cliché. You should have remembered."

"Yeah, well, I've had a lot to think about. What does she like?"

"You'll have to figure that out yourself."

What is it with these women? Have they formed a union?

We pray together in the family room. I follow the movements. It can't be too hard to learn. I really am a Muslim now, aren't I?

Joshua puts me in the large bedroom with Jamal and Nuruddin. Jamal sits at his desk, doing his algebra homework. I don't know where Nuruddin is.

"You need to wake up in the morning to pray," says Joshua. "Jamal will help you."

"I'll be up. On the road, I liked to wake up early to see the sun rise. I saw some sunrises you wouldn't believe."

"Did you take pictures?"

"Only in my mind."

"I'll take you to pray at the mosque tomorrow. You can meet the brothers."

"I went to Friday prayers a few times. Twice, I prayed with them."

"So you have been thinking about this. Have you thought of taking an Arabic name?"

"I have one. At the mosques in Detroit and Tampa, I told them my name was Ibrahim."

"That's a good name. What made you choose it?"

"The sermon in Detroit was about Ibrahim and his search for truth. I thought it fit."

"Do you mind if I call you that sometimes?"

"I don't know. I'm not used to it."

"I think it fits you, too."

He leaves to take care of his family. I think about my new identity. Abraham, or Ibrahim, had two sons, but neither of his kids was a drug-using dropout. I fall asleep worrying about my prodigal son.

When I wake up, it's dark and the house is quiet. I make my ablutions and go back to wake up the boys.

"Jamal." I shake his shoulder. "Jamal, it's time to get up."

He opens his eyes and smiles. "Assalaamu alaikum, Uncle Ibrahim."

He's a good kid. And it sounds nice. Uncle Ibrahim.

I go to Nuruddin and shake his shoulder. He groans and rolls over. "Nuruddin, you need to get up."

No response.

I wait downstairs for Joshua and Jamal.

For the first time, I can walk into a mosque as a Muslim. No more lies.

Joshua introduces me. The other men shake my hand and hug me. When Joshua became a Muslim, he talked about the sense of belonging. My wife and sons won't have anything to do with me, but at the mosque I feel accepted.

When we get back, Joshua sends Jamal to wake Nuruddin.

"I tried," I say. "But he wouldn't budge. What's going on with him?"

Joshua shakes his head. "He's Abdul-Qadir's son, but he's nothing like his father. Especially these last few months. He's changed." He sighs. "I'm trying."

Like you tried with my son, Joshua?

The bitterness remains, but I hold my tongue and help him get breakfast ready.

After breakfast, Aisha and the kids go to school. Jennifer heads to her classes. Nuruddin trudges back upstairs. Joshua and I clean up.

"I want you to go with me to the office," he says. "After lunch, we can go to the Friday prayer together."

"It sounds like you're afraid to leave me alone. I look different, but I'm actually quite harmless."

"I am almost afraid to let you out of my sight. I don't want you driving off again, chasing the sun. Come with me. You'll like it better than hanging around the house all day."

"What if Kyle calls?"

"You won't hear from him until sometime this afternoon. You know that."

Yes, I know.

We finish up the kitchen and go upstairs. Nuruddin is sleeping. I'm sitting on the bed, missing my family, when Joshua knocks. I pop a breath mint. "Come in."

"Here. You can wear this to the prayer." He gives me a long white robe.

"I don't know about that."

"Try it. It will look good on you."

After my shower, I put on the robe and look in the mirror. The outward transformation is complete—thoroughly hiding my internal confusion.

I don't ask Joshua where he works. I guess I can handle another surprise.

I used to plan everything. Beth teased me on Sunday nights when I decided which socks to wear for the coming week. She laughed as I ironed my ties. She called me obsessed. I think she liked that about me though.

I'm not surprised when Joshua pulls up to an old red brick building on the south side. It's not The Caring Center, but it looks the same.

"I've been working here for six months."

"Did Umar and you start this organization, too?"

"No. It's been around for nearly twenty years. When The Caring Center was shut down, they took in most of our clients. I convinced them to give me a job in program development. I'm still not allowed to work in funding."

I hadn't realized the bogus terrorism charges continued to haunt Umar and him. "You're still on probation? How many years has it been?"

"Three. We have two years left. We are allowed to travel now. Aisha and I may go for hajj soon. Umar and Safa went last year. Jeremy took Raheema soon after they were married."

"How are they? Any grandkids yet?"

"They're talking about it, but Raheema still has another year of college."

We walk down a narrow hallway to his office. It's a little place, about what I would expect for Joshua.

"How about that lawsuit against the prison? I guess you didn't get much. I thought you'd be driving a nicer car by now."

"It hasn't gone to court yet. Jared tells me they're stalling. He may go for an out-of-court settlement. I keep telling him I don't need the money, but he says it's about justice."

"Whatever happened to that consulting business Umar and you started?"

"We give presentations and workshops occasionally, but I'd rather do the work than just talk about it."

"Does Umar work here, too?"

"No, he's the director of a homeless shelter. He just finished his master's degree. In the fall, he'll start on his doctorate."

"Life goes on, doesn't it? I'm sleeping in my car and watching the sun rise, but everyone else is moving on. I had to leave. You do know that, don't you?"

"Why do you think you have to keep defending yourself?"

"Because I know I shouldn't have left, but I didn't know what else to do. If I had stayed, I would probably be in an institution by now."

Or washed up along the banks of the Chicago River.

"What was making you crazy?"

"It was seeing Sam before he died. And losing Walt. But mostly it was Mom. After Sam left, she depended on me, but I never realized how much I depended on her."

All of that is true, though the fight with Hendricks was the last straw.

"Why did you leave your things? The suits, the Lexus."

Because I was planning to kill myself.

"I decided to strip myself of everything except the barest of ne-cessities. A few old clothes. My Toyota. Some cash. And our family picture."

Joshua smiles again. "Aren't you the one who always took two suitcases on a three-day business trip?"

"I was many things I'm not now."

"I know how that feels. Well, I've got to get to work. I'm develop-ing a project to help boys in this area who don't have fathers in their lives."

"Does it include your nephews?"

He looks up from his computer. "I'm sorry, Brad. I tried."

"I'm going for a walk. I miss the outdoors."

"Be back by noon."

"I'll be back."

As I leave his office, I have no intention of going back. Why didn't he take care of my boys? He takes care of his own kids. He's develop-ing programs for kids all over Chicago. After all I did for him all those years. He thinks he's doing me a favor by letting me stay in Jamal's room. It's nice to sleep in a bed again, but I can do without. I almost miss the backseat of my car.

I remember this neighborhood. I was almost sixteen when Mom moved us to Lincoln Park. This is where I grew up.

My father hated this area. Too many black people, he said. Though that's not the way he said it. I can still hear him cursing "those people." He screamed at the neighbors. Then he screamed at Mom and me.

I pass a high school with a sign out front, congratulating this year's graduates. Kyle should be thinking about graduation. What happened to my son?

Joshua's children have graduated. Chris's children are graduating. That's right. Isaiah is in the same grade as Kyle is. As Kyle was. He'd better know I won't show up for his graduation.

Why couldn't they love my son the way they love their own? Would Joshua let Michael or Jeremy drop out? No way. Would Chris let Ruth or Isaiah leave school? Not a chance. Why didn't they love my son enough to stop him from ruining his life?

Michael is studying engineering but my own son, my pride, is a dropout. I worked hard to take care of my family while Joshua traveled halfway around the world and got himself mixed up in terrorist allegations, but his son is a success and my son is a failure.

I won't go back to Joshua's house except to retrieve my Celeste. Did he forget who taught him everything and who rescued him every time he got into trouble? Now he thinks he can rescue me.

I don't belong here anymore. I'll see Kyle, then I'll leave. Maybe he'll want to come with me. That's it. I'll take him with me and we'll get to know each other all over again. I'll make him into a son I can be proud of. Beth couldn't handle him, but his father is in charge now.

I'm far away from Joshua's office, but I'll always know these streets. This is where I learned to be a man.

No more handouts. Especially not from Joshua. He can barely take care of himself.

I'll let him take me to my car. Then I'm gone again. I'll go to the apartment, tell Kyle to pack a few things, and we'll hit the road together.

For the first time in thirty-six hours, I know who I am and what

I'm doing. Forget Beth. Forget Joshua. Forget Chris. I don't need them. All I need is my son and my freedom.

I walk quickly back to his office. I'm across the street from his building. All I needed was a little resolve. I'm different, but I will never be weak.

I step off the curb, thinking about our road trip. Kyle and me on the open highway. I'll get that boy straightened out. By the time I'm finished with him, he'll be ready to go to college. I hope he still wants to be an engineer, like he did when he was little.

I'm thinking about Kyle. I'm not thinking about the car speeding toward me. Not until it makes contact and I'm flat on my back.

The brakes screech too late. The black car which hit me speeds off. Another car stops and a young man comes over.

"Are you okay?"

"Sure." I try to stand, but there's too much pain. I fall back to the pavement.

"I'll call for help."

I lie helpless on the curb while he crouches next to me. He must be Kyle's age. Would Kyle stop to help a stranger?

When the ambulance arrives, Joshua comes out of his building to check out the commotion. While they're loading me into the back, he walks over and grabs my hand.

"Brad, man. I didn't know it was you."

"I'm fine. Don't worry about me."

"I'm right behind you. You're not alone."

"Call Kyle, will you?"

Part Four

I don't remember exactly what happened when they brought me in. Noise. Commotion. Bright lights. I must have been in shock.

I wake up in a hospital bed, my right leg encased in plaster all the way up my thigh. It doesn't hurt as much now. I notice the IV in my left arm. They're loading me with painkillers.

The doctor walks in maybe twenty minutes later. "Your right ankle and your leg are both fractured. I had to operate. You will stay here tonight for observation. Any questions?"

I have a million questions, but my mind is too foggy to put together a cohesive thought. I wave my hand and he turns to leave. I hope his surgical skills are better than his bedside manner.

He stops in the doorway and says, "You're fortunate. With that kind of impact, your injuries might have been much more severe. Be grateful there's no paralysis."

"Today must be my lucky day," I mutter.

I stare at my immobilized limb. The father-son road trip will have to wait.

I close my eyes. I'm tired. I give up.

When I wake up, Joshua is sitting next to the bed. "How are you, Brother?"

How am I? He asked for it.

"I'm angry."

"At the guy who hit you?"

"At you. Why did you have to give me shahadah? Everything was fine until then. Beth was waiting for me. My leg was whole. I was looking forward to my son's senior year."

"Kyle dropped out before you made shahadah."

"And whose fault was that? You couldn't watch my kid for fourteen lousy months? Your kids would have starved if it wasn't for me. Do you know that?"

"Yes, Brad, I know."

"It's your fault my kid dropped out of school. It's your fault I'm in this damn hospital bed."

"I guess the plane crash was my fault, too."

"Maybe it was. If you hadn't become a Muslim and gone to prison, then Mom and Walt wouldn't have had to work to get you out of there, and they wouldn't have gotten married, and they wouldn't have gone to chase some ridiculous dream. At least Walt would have gone alone and not taken Mom down with him."

I was screaming at him. Now I'm crying. I don't want to do this, but I can't stop. He puts his arms around me.

When I'm calm, he says, "I called Kyle and told him about the accident. He said he'll come in a few hours."

"Good. Great. Is Beth coming, too?"

"I don't know."

"I can't go anywhere for a few weeks. Is that bed in Jamal's room still available?"

"Yes, I think it is."

"Aisha won't feel strange about me staying there?"

"No. She's okay with it."

"I lost my health insurance."

"Don't worry. It's taken care of."

"Can you show me how to pray with this damn cast on?"

Kyle doesn't come. In the morning, I call the apartment. Beth answers.

"It's Brad. I'm hurt."

"I heard."

"Are you ready to talk to me now?"

"No."

"Can you put my son on the line then?"

"Which one?"

"You know which one. Kyle, the dropout."

"He hasn't come home yet."

"Where is he?"

"How am I supposed to know? He's probably passed out on someone's couch. Maybe he spent the night with his girlfriend. But he could be lying in a ditch somewhere. He could be unconscious and choking on his own vomit. He might have experimented with harder drugs and overdosed." Her voice sounds flat and tired.

"He's done this before?"

"Every weekend. If the police don't come to my door by noon, I'll know he's still alive."

"What is wrong with this boy?"

"Like father, like son."

She doesn't know what she's talking about. "Can you tell him I called?"

"Tell him yourself." She hangs up.

I punch my leg. Wrong leg. I grit my teeth and buzz the nurse to ask for more morphine.

~

Joshua checks me out on Saturday afternoon. I haven't heard from Kyle yet.

The good news is I shouldn't need more surgery. The bad news is I'm grounded for the next six weeks. A nurse comes in and asks me to sign some forms. "You need to keep your leg elevated. Don't put any weight on it. No stairs."

Joshua and Aisha decide to put me up on the couch in their family room. Just when I was getting used to sleeping in a bed again.

Jamal brings my stuff down from his room. Joshua collects my dirty clothes. Aisha fixes up the family room and brings extra pillows to make me more comfortable. At dinnertime, they carry everything into the family room and eat with me. Jamal fixes my plate.

"I can't believe they released you so soon," says Aisha. "You should have stayed another day at least."

"That's how it is these days. Too many patients, too few beds.

Sorry for all the trouble."

"It's no trouble. When do you go back in?"

"I have an appointment in two weeks."

"My mom will be in town soon. Do you want her to take a look at it?"

"Don't bother her. Just because Sharon is a nurse doesn't mean she has to take care of the world. By the way, how is your grandmother these days?"

"Still going strong. I think she'll make it to one hundred, insha Allah."

"Some days, I think she's stronger than I am," says Joshua. "So I have a bum arm and you have a bum leg. Jamal, will you push Uncle Ibrahim around the Ka'aba in a wheelchair when he goes for hajj?"

"Sure I will."

Hajj. Will I have to do that?

"I'll be as good as new in no time. Though I guess I never will beat you at soccer."

We have a normal family dinner. The boys talk about their summer vacation, which starts next week. Maryam shows off. Jennifer tells me about a feature she wrote for the college paper. They're a family. I can't remember the last time Beth and I had a dinner like this. We were always running to the next activity. And all that running didn't ease my pain when I lost Mom, didn't help me find answers, and can't save our son or our marriage.

Joshua tells me Ramadan starts tomorrow. "You can't fast—not with your injury—but we'll be fasting. Muhammad wants to fast whole days this year."

"I can't fast? I was looking forward to it."

"See what the doctor says in two weeks. Right now, you need to build up your strength. I'm sure you need your pain pills, too."

Need them? I practically crave them.

They wake up early and eat. I watch. Later Jamal brings me

scrambled eggs and coffee. "Mom said you need to eat."

"Tell her thanks." I wait until he leaves before picking up the fork.

At noon, he brings chicken soup and a sandwich. I'm the only one eating, besides Maryam. This is humiliating.

I call my boys again on Monday afternoon. Matt answers.

"Hi. It's Dad. How is everything?"

"Okay."

"Do you like school this year?"

"It's okay."

"Do you have friends?"

"A few."

"I miss you, Matt."

"Hold on, you can talk to Kyle."

They argue again. Finally Kyle says, "Hey, Dad. What's up?"

"I hoped to see you this weekend."

"I got busy. You know how it is. I heard about your accident."

"I'm okay, but my leg is busted up pretty badly."

"That must hurt."

"Yes. I won't be able to walk on it for a while."

"So you want me to come?"

"That would be nice. I miss you."

"Yeah, I missed you, too, for the first month or so. But life goes on."

"You're angry."

"Who? Me? Listen, I gotta go. You can stop calling. We're doing great without you." He hangs up.

This boy is making me crazy.

Umar brings his family over on Monday night. After dinner we talk.

"It's good to see you, Brad. So good."

"I've heard you'll be a doctor soon."

"I'm going for it. Tell me about your journey. You were about the last person I expected to accept Islam."

"You're telling me. I don't know where to start."

"Start from the beginning."

I tell him about Santa Fe and trying to find truth through peyote. "There were moments when I thought I had discovered all the secrets of the universe, but when I came down, I didn't know anything."

"Yes, the use of psychedelic drugs in an attempt to achieve a higher spiritual awareness. I read an article about that recently. Evidently the highs can create a sense of omnipotence."

"They do. But if the highs are heaven, the lows are hell. I didn't need that kind of trip."

"You have a strong sense of survival. You would never allow yourself to get that low."

Is that what kept me from sliding into the canyon?

"Try coming home to learn your son is a drunk and a dropout. That's lower than I ever thought I'd go."

"You do realize it's not your brothers' fault."

"I'm working on that. Joshua has treated me so well. It's hard to be angry."

But it's still not right.

We talk for over an hour. Before he leaves, he gives me a book. "This will help you learn about Islam. Use this time for reading, before your life becomes busy again. And let me know if you have any questions."

"Just one, for now. Or two. Why is a brother-in-law different than a brother?"

"Aisha told me about that. It's simple. She can, potentially, marry her brother-in-law. She can never marry her brother."

"And she has to cover her head in front of anyone she could, potentially, marry?"

"That's right."

"But why does Jamal have to be here when Joshua's not home? It sounds like he has to protect his mother from me."

"That's not it. Prophet Muhammad, peace be upon him, said if a man and a woman are alone together, the third is Satan. You've been around enough to know what I mean."

"And a brother-in-law is not the same as a brother."

"You've got it."

I have always enjoyed talking with Umar. Now we have more to talk about.

When Jeremy comes on Thursday, he tells me he's going to be a father. They just found out.

"I'm sorry I didn't come earlier. Between family, work, and classes, I've been very busy."

Kyle should be busy with work and classes instead of partying all night and sleeping all day. I nod, swallowing hard. He doesn't mean to hurt me. "That's fine. I understand."

Part Five

Chris walks in on Friday afternoon. I'm napping. He touches my shoulder. "Brad. How are you?"

I open my eyes and smirk. "I'm glad you could finally make it. Where the hell have you been?"

He looks down. "It's not easy for me," he says, leaving the rest unsaid. "So how's the leg?"

"It hurts."

"Weren't you the one who taught me to look both ways before I crossed the street?"

"Probably."

He removes his glasses and rubs his eyes. "Are you still a Muslim?"

"Sure am."

"I don't know what to say."

"Why don't you just accept it's right for me?"

"But it's wrong. Why don't you see that?"

"You really think your way is the only way?"

"What do you think I'm doing in the classroom everyday? Do you realize I am teaching my students how to convert people to Christianity while I can't hold on to my own family? I'm afraid someone will stand up and say, 'Excuse me, Mr. Adams. How can you teach us about converting Muslims when your own family is full of them?' I feel like a damned hypocrite."

"If it makes you feel better, my conversion had nothing to do with you. I made my choice based on the evidence."

"Didn't you say you read the Bible?"

"I read both the Bible and the Qur'an. The Bible was nice, but the Qur'an spoke to me. Have you read it?"

"Parts of it. I need to prepare my students."

"You should read the whole book before passing judgment."

"Muslims don't accept Jesus Christ as their personal savior. That's all I need to know."

"Do you know what? I have been on my own my entire life. I

would rather stand alone when I go to meet God. I don't need a mediator."

"You're being fooled. I thought you were smarter than that. I also thought you loved your family."

"I do love them."

"Then why did you leave them?"

"I had to. What does that have to do with my conversion?"

"Satan is deceiving you. Wake up, Brad, before it's too late."

"I thought you had changed. I didn't know you still believed that fundamentalist crap."

His face becomes red and he turns away. He's almost as good at controlling emotions as I am, but I know he feels like hitting me.

I grasp his arm. "Take it easy. Would you feel better if I told you I've prayed more in the last week than I have since I was seven?"

He's still tense. "You prayed when you were young?"

"Sure. Don't you remember? Mom took us to Sunday School every week."

"I don't really remember. What did you pray for, a new bike?"

"I prayed Dad would stop hitting me. And he did. He left."

"Jesus answered your prayers then."

"God answered my prayers. I hope He's still listening."

"I don't know about that. What do you pray for now?"

"I pray Beth and the boys will let me back into their lives," I say quietly.

He relaxes.

"That's better. All this time, you never accepted Joshua, did you?"

"I didn't accept his conversion, but he's my brother and I won't turn my back on him. I pray every day for his soul. Yours too."

"Don't worry about me. I've found what I need. I'm laying off the beer now. That should make you happy."

"That's good. Beth put your wine collection in storage, along with the rest of your things. I'll be happy to help you toss it out."

I'd forgotten about that.

"Yeah, after my leg heals."

"I don't understand. First Joshua. Then Joshua's kids. Now you.

Why can't you see the truth?"

"Truth is relative."

"Don't give me that philosophical crap. You are talking about your soul."

"It's my soul, Chris. Leave it between God and me."

"That's what Mom always said. I pray for her, too, even though it's too late." He sighs. "You're not the only one who has a hard time with her death. And I want to see her in heaven, but I just don't know."

I've never thought about Mom's death in those terms. Whether she went to heaven. Or not. I don't want to think about it.

I reach over and touch his hand. "So you're mad at me for becoming a Muslim?"

"Not mad. Concerned. And very confused. The truth is so clear to me. I don't know why you don't see it."

"You and I see different truths."

"Are you still mad at me for not keeping Kyle in school?"

"Not really, but I have to be mad at someone. I'm not sure who to blame."

"Why don't you blame Kyle?"

"I don't want to drive him away."

"He hasn't come to see you yet, has he?"

"No, but he will. You think I'm going to hell now, don't you?"

Muhammad walks in and makes the call to prayer.

"I have to go," Chris says quickly. "I'll see you soon."

I snicker. "You don't want to be here when we pray."

"You and I used to be so close. What happened, Brad?"

"I had to find answers. On my own. You have to accept that."

"I won't keep arguing with you, but I will never accept it."

I study his face. A quiet anger simmers in his eyes. I don't know what to say. Muhammad lays out the prayer rugs.

Chris stands. "Take care of that leg. I'll see you soon."

I don't know whether to laugh or cry. We're throwing away a life-long friendship over a difference in faith. I don't get it.

～

On Friday night, Joshua takes his family to the mosque. They plan to break their fast there. Later Jamal and Muhammad will compete in an adhan contest. Sounds like a wild time.

Joshua brings me dinner before they leave. "Call my cell if you need anything."

"Don't worry about me."

Aisha hustles the children out the door. Nuruddin goes with them. Jennifer is with her mother. I'm alone for the first time since the accident. A quiet house. Nice.

I brood about Chris all day Saturday.

When Isaiah walks in on Saturday afternoon, I have my guard up. His father probably sent him here to wear me down.

He hands me a basket full of candy bars. Finally something besides flowers. I have so many damn flowers in here I could open my own shop.

"How are you feeling, Uncle Brad?"

"It hurts, but I'll survive."

"You had a rough homecoming. I heard Kyle doesn't want to see you."

"And I heard you're forbidden to speak to Kyle."

"Oh, that's just Dad. No, Kyle and I are cool. I called him on my way over here."

"And he said he'll see me when he has time."

"Something like that. He's hurt. He'll come around."

"I guess your father sent you here to help me see the error of my ways."

He laughs. "No, I just want to see how you're doing. And I want to ask you something."

"If I'm ready to repent and accept Jesus Christ as my personal savior?"

"I'm not Dad. I am a Christian, but I don't think I have the right to tell anyone else how to believe. I want to know about your journey.

It sounds incredible."

He sounds sincere. "Okay. I left Chicago and drove until I got to New Mexico." I tell him my story up to the day I pulled into Los Angeles, leaving out the part about the peyote. Now that Kyle is into drugs, I really don't want him to know. And I'm still trying to figure Isaiah's angle.

After an hour he looks at his watch. ""I have to go. Dad's expecting me home."

"He doesn't want you spending much time with me, does he?"

"He doesn't know I'm here. He thinks I went to the library."

"You lie to your father? What happens when you get caught?"

"Not too much anymore. I'm taller than he is." He grins. "I know I shouldn't lie, but I wanted to see you. And I'm not here to convert you."

"That's good. Your trip won't be wasted."

"I'll be back in a few days to hear more about your trip. I'm especially curious about why you became a Muslim."

"Sure. But you shouldn't lie to your father."

"I know." He hugs me. "I'll see you later, Uncle Brad."

Am I dreaming, or did Chris's son just ask me about Islam?

Beth Speaks Out

I was finally getting my life back on track. Matt stopped having nightmares. Kyle was talking to me again.

Then Brad showed up. Now he keeps calling and bothering me. He left me alone for fourteen months. Why can't he do it now?

On some level, I do still love him. But I can't go through all that again.

Part Six

I'm going crazy, lying here on the couch and staring at the walls. I like the attention, but I would rather be active and whole. And I still haven't seen my family.

I call Beth after Isaiah leaves. "Aren't you coming? I'm hurt."

"I know. Kyle is out with his friends."

"I want to talk to you. I miss you." I whine, which is not what I meant to do.

"Are you going to keep bothering me?"

"Yes," I say in a stronger voice.

"This is harassment, Brad. I could call the police and report you. And you managed to get along without me for fourteen months. Why now?"

"I'm ready to come home now." The whine creeps back.

"I'm not ready." She hangs up.

"But Beth—" She's gone. I don't know how much more of this I can take. I throw the phone across the room.

Everyone else is asleep. The house is quiet. My mind is racing. Beth and the boys. Chris. Isaiah.

I'm wiggling around, trying to get comfortable, when I hear a noise in the hallway. I look over. And I see them.

Nuruddin and Jennifer are standing at the bottom of the stairs. He has his hands all over my niece. She doesn't seem to have any objections.

I understand enough about Islam to know they shouldn't be doing that. I should stop them. I could make some noise to let them know they're being watched. I could threaten Nuruddin with my crutches. I could tell Joshua, who would go after Nuruddin with more than crutches.

Or I could keep watching like some sick old voyeur.

I cough and pretend to sleep. They look over, and resume their activities. This is interesting. I suddenly see many possibilities. I fall asleep thinking about where I can go from here.

When Joshua wakes me for the morning prayer, I think about telling him. Nuruddin is still asleep. No wonder. I go through the motions of prayer, but I can't get that scene out of my mind.

Joshua reads the Qur'an. I think about telling him when he's finished, but I suddenly realize how much power I have.

All day, I turn it over in my mind.

On Sunday night, I see them again. I was waiting for a repeat performance. I lie here and watch them, like a dirty old man. And I know what I'm going to do. Nothing.

My brothers don't know how much they hurt me by not taking care of Kyle. Now I have the chance to hurt them. I'll let Nuruddin continue to grope Jennifer. I'll tell Isaiah everything I know about Islam. And when Jennifer gets pregnant and Isaiah leaves Christianity they'll understand how I feel.

Part Seven

Isaiah comes on Monday. "Tell me more about your trip."

"I was driving down the street in L.A. when I saw someone who reminded me of your Uncle Joshua, so I parked and went to talk to him."

"Who was he?"

I tell him about Abdullah's kindness and trust, embellishing a little. I need to make Islam sound so good he'll wonder what he ever saw in the church.

I won't tell him the whole story. He doesn't need to know about my suicidal intentions, or about the Baha'is or the Buddhists. I won't talk about the Bible with him. And he definitely does not need to know about Chelsea, Kate, or Rose.

I need to call Abdullah some day. Will be he surprised when I tell him I converted, or will he say it was fate?

Getting revenge on Joshua is easy. Jennifer and Nuruddin do all the work, meeting at the bottom of the stairs each night. I don't keep watching—it's not right—but I don't stop them.

If I wasn't on this couch, Jennifer would be pregnant in no time. Just like her mother. They must be waiting for the old man to hurry up and get well. They wouldn't dare do anything upstairs—Joshua is a light sleeper—but down here, after everyone else is asleep and the lights are out, they are free to do what they want. I see them. I listen. I say nothing.

On Tuesday, I call Kyle and try to get through to him. "How is everything?"

"Okay."

"When are you coming to see me?"

"I don't know."

"I miss you."

"Whatever."

Matt isn't any better.

"I think about you all the time."

"I need to go," he says, handing the phone back to Kyle.

On Saturday morning, I call Beth again. "Why won't you work this out with me?"

"It's no use."

"But I want you back."

"Show me you're willing to change. Then maybe we can talk." She hangs up.

Change? What does she expect from me? I'm injured. I don't know what is wrong with this woman.

I think my plan is working. When Isaiah comes on Saturday afternoon, he asks more questions about Islam. I can't answer many of them so I give him the book Umar left. I haven't read it yet.

Nuruddin and Jennnifer are still going at it, hot and heavy every night. If Joshua found out, he would kill them both. Then he'd come after me.

Umar comes on Sunday afternoon. "I hope you're reading the Qur'an these days. There's more blessing during Ramadan. And you can take advantage of being incapacitated."

I've been too distracted to read much of anything lately. "That sounds like a good idea," I say. It's what he wants to hear.

On Monday, I glance at the Qur'an Abdullah gave me. Joshua set it on a nearby table. I could read, but I'm tired, and Aisha and the kids are gone. I have other ways to spend my quiet time.

I look at it every day. It mocks me. I enjoyed reading it on the road, but I don't feel inspired these days.

Every evening, about an hour before sunset, Joshua reads Qur'an with Jamal and Muhammad here in the family room. I listen. They recite aloud in Arabic. Very nice.

Today when they finished, Muhammad asked, "Why don't you read the Qur'an, too, Uncle Brad?"

"Don't worry. I will."

This kid is too nosy.

I don't want to read, but Muhammad reads the Qur'an every day. In Arabic. I won't let an eleven-year old show me up.

On Friday morning, I pick up my copy and let it fall open, reading a verse in the middle of the page. "And be not like those who forgot Allah." No problem there. I pray every day.

I try again in the afternoon. "Truly man was created very impatient—fretful when evil touches him and niggardly when good touches him." I haven't had much good touch me for a long time now.

While Joshua and his boys read Qur'an in the late afternoon, I open mine again. "Woe to the worshippers who are neglectful of prayers, those who want to be seen of men but refuse to supply neighborly needs." I pray. And I don't live anywhere so I don't have to worry about neighbors.

These verses sounded different to me on the road. I'm not connecting. I close my eyes and doze until Jamal brings my supper. Joshua is taking his family to the mosque again. I love a quiet house.

They come back late. Joshua looks into the darkened room. "Do you need anything?"

"No, um, I'm good."

He goes to bed. A few minutes later, Jennifer and Nuruddin are at it again. I watch with vicarious pleasure, missing my wife.

Joshua reads the Qur'an again in the morning after the prayer. I don't want Muhammad bugging me, so I pick up my copy and start from the beginning. All about following the straight path. I read this before.

They're still reading, so I keep going. Something about true believers—sure doesn't sound like me—then verses about the rest of us.

"Of the people there are some who say, 'We believe in Allah and the Last Day,' but they do not really believe. They think they deceive Allah and those who believe, but they only deceive themselves and realize it not."

I'm tired. I set my copy aside and close my eyes.

~

I've just finished lunch when Isaiah walks in. "I read the book you loaned me. It's interesting."

"I'm glad you think so." I'm about to launch into my spiel when I realize two things. First, Isaiah probably knows more about Islam than I do now. And second, I'm in no position to convince anyone because I am more like the people I read about this morning. The ones who deceive themselves. I won't admit my shortcomings to Isaiah though. I smile. "Tell me what you learned."

He discusses the beliefs and practices of Islam and even the history. "I find it all fascinating. There are some strong parallels between Christianity and Islam, but on other points they completely diverge." I nod a lot because I don't know what the hell he's talking about. This kid is smart. And he sounds like Chris, ready to give a sermon.

After he leaves, I replay his presentation. He doesn't want to become a Muslim. He just wants to learn. Isaiah always was a curious kid. It usually got him into a lot of trouble.

I can't manipulate Isaiah, so I can forget about getting back at Chris. What should I do about Joshua?

I watch Jennifer and Nuruddin when everything is quiet. I really should do something. She is my niece, after all. But I'm tired. I'll take care of it tomorrow.

~

In the morning, Joshua gives me the Sunday paper and Jamal brings my breakfast. Nuruddin is still asleep, I'm sure. I need to say something, but there's never a good time.

At night, Joshua takes his family to the mosque. I'm awake when they walk in. He appears in the doorway, carrying a sleeping child. "Do you need anything?"

"Yeah, uh, we need to talk."

"I'll be right back."

Ten or fifteen minutes later, he looks in again. "What's up?"

"Sit down in that blue chair. Pull it closer. I need to tell you something."

He does what I say. I've always been able to boss him around. When he was little I'd say, Joshua get me this or Joshua do that. And he would.

"You said you have something to tell me?" He stifles a yawn.

I've taken care of Joshua since he was a baby. Sometimes, when Mom got really depressed, I had to do everything—feed him, bathe him, change his diaper. Now I'm waiting for him to get hurt. In fact, I wonder what Jennifer and Nuruddin are doing right now. They both went upstairs. Aisha is up there, but she doesn't know she has to supervise them. I'd better talk fast.

"I should have told you earlier."

"What's going on?"

"You won't like it."

"What is it?"

"There's something you need to know. Are you calm?"

"So far. What's going on, Brad?"

"At night, when everyone else is asleep, I've seen Jennifer and Nuruddin making out." I blurt it out and wait for the explosion.

He stares at me. "Making out? Do you mean?"

"I'm not that old. I know what they were doing."

"Are you sure?" His voice is getting louder. Here it comes.

"Yes."

"How long has this been going on?" he shouts.

"A week or so, that I know of."

"Why didn't you tell me sooner?" They heard that upstairs.

"You'd better take care of it."

He runs up the stairs, two steps at a time.

"What the hell is going on?" he booms. The next-door neighbors heard that.

No one on the block could sleep with all this noise. Joshua has been screaming for the last ten minutes. Jennifer is crying and screaming. Nuruddin has the good sense to stay quiet.

Aisha comes downstairs, carrying Maryam and dragging Luqman behind her. She holds them in the rocking chair. Luqman is screaming, too.

"Brad, do you know what this is all about?"

"Jennifer and Nuruddin. I've seen them, when everyone else was asleep."

"You've seen them?"

"Don't make me spell it out."

"Oh," she says. She stops a moment, and continues rocking.

It goes on for over an hour. Finally Joshua stomps downstairs, holding Nuruddin by the arm. "I'll be back!" He slams the front door.

Jennifer sobs loudly for another hour before storming into the family room and tearing into me. "Why did you tell him? It's none of your business."

"The hell it isn't."

"Why should you care?"

"It's wrong." And he's my brother. I have to take care of him.

She gives me the finger, runs up the stairs, and slams her bedroom door.

Aisha shakes her head, closes her eyes, and keeps on rocking. Five minutes later, she carries Maryam back upstairs. Luqman is asleep on the floor next to the chair.

Joshua walks in around 2 AM. I'm waiting for him.

"Hey, Joshua, come here." It's dark and I can't see his face but I think it's safe to talk. "Are you alone?"

"They were together in her room." He speaks slowly, emphasizing each word. "I saw them." He sits in the easy chair and puts his face in his hands.

"Where did you dump the body?"

"He's at Umar's house."

"Will you send him back to Pakistan?"

"I promised Abdul-Qadir. He can stay. They have to get married."

"Is she pregnant?"

"They both swear it hasn't gone that far, alhamdulillah, but it's only a matter of time."

Luqman wakes up, screaming and reaching. "Daddy, I'm scared."

Joshua soothes him in the rocking chair. As I drift to sleep, I hear my baby brother softly weeping.

~

It's light outside. Too late to eat.

I pat Joshua's knee. "We need to pray."

He has always been a light sleeper. When he was a baby, he woke up at the slightest noise. And he cried. And our father got angry. And he beat me because Mom couldn't let him hurt the baby.

He sighs. "Yes, I need to pray."

He doesn't pick up the Qur'an after the prayer. He just sits. "I don't believe it. Abdul-Qadir's son. I trusted him."

"Don't forget Jennifer. She looked very willing."

"I'll talk with her, but Jennifer isn't a Muslim. Nuruddin is. And he's Abdul-Qadir's son."

"You really think they should get married?"

"It's the only way. They say they love each other, and it's already gone too far. They'll have to live here for now. Neither of them has a job, and Nuruddin can't work in this country. That's something else we'll have to deal with."

"How many of his bones did you break?"

"None. I felt like it, believe me. If it had been anyone else. But he's Abdul-Qadir's son."

"You keep saying that. Why?"

"Abdul-Qadir has been like a father to me. He took me in when almost everyone else had written me off. I don't know what happened to Nuruddin to make him disrespect his father this way." He walks slowly toward the stairs.

I haven't slept much these last few nights. I'm dozing when Jennifer walks in. "Uncle Brad?"

I force my eyes open. "What's up?"

"I shouldn't have talked to you that way."

"Did your father make you apologize?"

"He doesn't know I screamed at you, but if I'm getting married I need to start acting like an adult."

"Do you want to marry Nuruddin?"

She smiles. "I have wanted to marry him since the day he got off the plane, but I didn't expect it to be like this."

"Remember, Jennifer, your dad really loves you."

"I know. You were watching us, weren't you?"

"A few times, yes."

"Why didn't you say anything?"

I don't want to talk about it. "Have you thought about what to tell your mother?"

"I already called and told her I'm getting married. She'll be here soon."

The doorbell rings incessantly, punctuated by pounding at the door. She's here.

Heather starts up the minute she walks in. "What do you mean you're getting married? Who is this boy? When did all this happen? Why am I always the last to know? Where is your father?"

"Calm down, Mom. Dad's sleeping. I'll get him. You can go into the family room and talk to Uncle Brad."

"Brad? What is he doing here?" She walks in, still screeching. "Do you know what's going on with my daughter?"

I haven't seen Heather since she came to the memorial service to say goodbye to Mom. "Joshua's putting up with me for now."

"What about Beth? Are you two divorced or something?"

"I'd rather not discuss it."

"Well is someone going to tell me about my daughter?"

"I will," says Joshua, walking slowly down the stairs. "I thought Jennifer and I would come to your place later, but I guess she couldn't wait."

"I had to tell her."

"I know. So do you want to give your mom the whole story?"

"Okay. Mom, you know Nuruddin. That cute guy from Pakistan who came here to study and live with Dad. Anyway, the minute I saw him, I knew I was going to marry him. But he's real shy. We've known each other for almost two years and for a long time he would hardly even talk to me. But I finally got him to open up and we started getting to know one another. A few months ago, he finally kissed me. He is so handsome. Anyway, I love him so much and I know he loves me, too. He wants to marry me. And Dad is worried that I'm going to get pregnant or something, so he says it's better if we go ahead and get married now instead of waiting. Don't you agree?"

I think she said all of that in one breath.

Heather stares at Joshua. "He kissed her so they have to get married? That's what this is about? Are you crazy?"

"Did you hear what Jennifer said? They love each other. How long will it be before they take it further and she ends up pregnant? You and I both know that's no way to start a marriage."

"But he kissed her. That's all. She's going to get married and jeopardize her future because of a little kiss?"

Heather didn't see them. It was more than a little kiss. But I'd better keep my mouth shut.

"I'm thinking about her future," says Joshua.

"You could have fooled me. I think you want to enslave her to some hormone-driven Muslim boy. She's kissed other boys, too. Why this one? Because he's your best friend's son? Are you planning to sell our daughter for a herd of camels or something?"

"I know you're not that stupid."

"Mom, Dad, I have something to say. Please."

"Go ahead, Jenny." Heather sighs.

"Okay, first of all, Mom, I haven't kissed anyone since you guys made me break up with Brandon. You told me to wait, and I've waited. And Dad, I'm not going to marry Nuruddin because I'm worried about getting pregnant. I think we're both smarter than that. I want to marry him because I love him."

"What do you mean, you love him? What do you even know about him?" Heather's voice is piercing. Some things never change.

"I know a lot about him. He wants to be an architect. He's shown me some of his plans. He's very smart. And he loves me."

"Your father said he loved me, too. Before he cheated on me and left me with three little kids to take care of and not a dime of child support."

"That was almost twenty years ago," Joshua yells. "Are you ever going to let it go?"

"I'm telling my daughter about what scum men can be. She has to be careful. Weren't you preaching that a few years ago? Or is it different because this boy is a Muslim?"

"Why does it matter to you that he's a Muslim?"

"I didn't raise my daughter to become someone's slave. He'll probably lock her up in the house and keep her barefoot and pregnant."

"Is that the way I've treated Aisha?"

"That's the way you treated me."

"Mom, Dad. Stop it. Please." Jennifer is crying. "Just stop."

"Um, Joshua, Heather, I'm sorry to break up this tender family moment, but I wonder if I could say something."

"Are you some kind of expert? Apparently you're not living with your wife."

"Mom, let Uncle Brad talk."

"Look, Jennifer is a young woman now and she knows what she's doing. This isn't about the two of you. This is about your daughter. You two have been divorced much longer than you were ever married. Give it a rest."

"But I want Jennifer to have the kinds of opportunities I never had."

"I will, Mom. I'm going to school, and I'll keep going. In another year, Nuruddin will graduate and get a good job. And I'm not like you. I'm marrying someone I love."

"I thought I loved your father," Heather says in an acid tone, "and he walked all over me."

"That's enough, Heather. I have put up with your biting remarks for too many years. I'll warn you right now that I am not in a very good mood. I slept about ten minutes last night. Don't push me."

Heather ignores Joshua. She walks over to Jennifer and holds her daughter's face in her hands. "Are you sure, Jenny? Is this really what you want?"

"Yes, Mom. I'm sure."

"You won't let him treat you like a prisoner?"

"Never."

"You'll finish your education?"

"Of course."

"Are you going to become a Muslim?"

"No. Not yet anyway."

"Not yet." She throws up her hands. "You win, Joshua. All of our children will end up being Muslims."

"It's not a war, Mom. You and Dad have to stop fighting over us. Whether or not I become a Muslim, it won't be about what Dad wants. It will be about what's best for me."

"I don't know, Jenny. I've had so many dreams for you."

"I won't disappoint you. I love you, Mom," Jennifer says with a hug.

The hug softens Heather. She gazes at her daughter. "So when I do I get to talk to this boy?"

"He's at Umar's house. You'll have to go over there."

Heather looks at Joshua and giggles. "You wanted to kill him, didn't you? Okay, I have to get to know this Nuruddin. You can come with me, Jenny."

"I think Jennifer should stay here."

"It's okay, Dad. Umar and Safa will be there. I just want to see him. Please."

He shrugs. "Go ahead."

Before she leaves, Heather looks at me. "What's the story, Brad? Did Beth finally come to her senses and kick you out?"

"I just decided to spend a couple months on my brother's couch."

"Okay, don't tell me." She laughs again. "You Adams boys are all a little strange."

Joshua sighs, as he always does around his ex-wife. "Whatever you say, Heather."

After she leaves, Joshua picks up the phone. "That's done. Now for Abdul-Qadir."

He paces through the family room and kitchen, speaking Urdu in emotional tones. I wish I could listen in. All I know is what he says when he hangs up. "He agrees. They'll get married right after Ramadan."

"That soon?"

"Sooner is better. I just hope I can stay in the same room with Nuruddin by then. I'm stuck with him now." He shakes his head and walks away.

That's over. I didn't get back at Joshua, but I think I protected him again.

⁓

In the afternoon, I pick up the book Umar gave me. I want to be able to have an intelligent conversation with Isaiah. My reading answers some questions but creates others.

When Umar comes in the evening, I tell him. "Something is bothering me. I'm a little embarrassed to ask, but I need to know."

"Go ahead. I'll keep it confidential."

"Out on the road, I wasn't exactly a saint. There were some women. I lived with one of them for three months. Now I see how wrong it was."

"Three months. In Colorado, right? That's why you stopped sending postcards."

"It was easier for me to forget about Beth and concentrate on Kate."

How does he know it was Colorado?

"Beth was frantic. She called everyone, asking if we'd heard from you. She was afraid you had killed yourself. She read newspapers online, looking for your name. Your last postcard had been from Denver, so she flew out there, talked with the police, and searched homeless shelters. She even had to check out a body at the city morgue. She was planning to go there again when she received a postcard from Utah. That's when she decided to rent out the house."

"No wonder she's angry. But when I called her from Ohio, she asked me to come home."

"You refused. Two weeks later, she moved out of the house and let them repossess your Lexus. I think she had decided you were never coming home."

"If she ever finds out I was with another woman during those months…"

"I imagine, on some level, she knows."

"That's part of the problem. Also, this book says the punishment for adultery is death."

"The adulterer should be lashed. Some say stoned to death. But you weren't a Muslim yet, were you?"

"I started reading the Qur'an a few days after leaving Denver."

"Why did you leave?"

"I kept thinking about Beth."

"I'm glad it's over. And I have good news. Everything you did before you became a Muslim, all those indiscretions, doesn't count anymore. When you made the shahadah you started out fresh, with a clean slate."

"That's great." I laugh with relief. "I wish someone had told me that sooner. Hell, if everyone knew that, I bet more people would convert."

"But everything you do after making shahadah, you are accountable for that."

I need to be more careful.

Part Eight

On Monday, Joshua takes me to the doctor. My bones aren't healing as well as they should. The doctor reminds me to keep my leg elevated. I ask about fasting.

"I don't recommend it. You need proper nutrition to become stronger. I'm concerned about your health."

I laugh. "I'll be okay. I'm just getting old." I don't care what that doctor says. I need to fast.

I wake up early on Tuesday morning. I'm not hungry, but I manage to gulp down eggs and juice. I sleep a couple of hours and wake up thirsty. Very thirsty. I think about hobbling into the kitchen for a drink. Then I look at Muhammad. If he can do it, so can I.

I'm doing well until the pain hits, right around noon. I need my pills. I ask Luqman to bring me a glass of water.

The afternoon drags and I watch the clock, counting down the hours. Then the minutes. Joshua comes in and recites the Qur'an. I pick up my copy and try to concentrate.

With two minutes left, Muhammad brings me water and dates. I've never eaten dates before, but I guess that's the way it's done. I stare at the water and back at the clock. I watch the seconds tick off.

Finally Joshua stops reading and asks Luqman to make the call to prayer. His voice sounds clear and innocent.

I pick up the glass and take a sip. That tastes good. I drink more, gulping it down.

"Take it easy," says Joshua. "You'll get sick. Eat one of your dates."

I don't like trying new foods, but these dates aren't bad. I eat a little and drink more water before we pray.

After the prayer, I'm exhausted. I lean into a pillow.

"Assalaamu alaikum." Umar's deep voice rings out as he walks in with his family. The number of kids is doubled and the noise level increases dramatically.

"Brad fasted today," says Aisha.

"Congratulations. Your first fast."

I nod. I can smell the food. I wish they would go ahead and serve it.

Finally Jamal carries a plate in. I attack the chicken and rice.

After dinner, Umar tries to get a conversation going. While he's talking about some article he read recently, I drift away.

Joshua wakes me up a few hours later. "You need to eat. And you missed your prayer."

I'm not hungry but, piece by piece, I manage to swallow a pancake and wash it down with coffee.

After the morning prayer, I sleep. This fasting is exhausting.

My leg hurts. By noon I can't stand it. I pop a pain pill.

I count the hours, minutes, and seconds again, waiting until it's time to eat.

Ramadan is almost over. I fast every day, but I need my pills.

One day, Joshua sees me hobble into the kitchen for a glass of water. "What's up? Are you having trouble fasting?"

"No, I'm okay. I need water to help this pill go down."

"So you're not fasting today?"

"I'm fasting, but I need something for the pain."

"Sit down." He sighs. "We need to talk." He explains to me what fasting means. "No food. No drink. Nothing swallowed. Including medicine."

"But I need it. My leg hurts."

"Take the medication then, but that's not fasting. How many days have you fasted without the pills?"

"None."

"It's my fault. I should have talked you out of fasting. Don't try to fast again this year. Wait until you're on your feet again and I'll help you figure out how to make it up."

"Will I have to make up all thirty days?"

"All thirty. Once you became a Muslim, fasting in Ramadan became obligatory." He turns back to the food on the stove as I hobble to the couch.

Being a Muslim is more complicated than I expected. Do I really want to keep doing this?

～

Ramadan ends and Joshua borrows a wheelchair from somewhere so I can go to the Eid prayer. I never imagined this many Muslims in one place. Men in their robes, suits, or turbans. Women and little girls in brand new dresses. Little boys running and playing. It reminds me of that church in Jacksonville. This time I'm a part of it.

First we pray. Then the sermon—something about how Ramadan should have changed us. I don't know about that. We'll see.

After the prayer, we go to a restaurant and then back to the house where the kids play with their presents and the adults relax. It's like Christmas, but different.

Joshua hands me a package. "Happy Eid."

I carefully open the wrapping. He's given me two white robes, a round white cap like the one he sometimes wears, three books about Islam, two CDs with Islamic songs, and my own prayer rug. And a big bag of jelly beans. Nice.

～

Nuruddin is marrying Jennifer in a few days. Joshua invites him for dinner. Afterward, they come into the family room.

"Sit down," says Joshua. He still addresses his future son-in-law with an edge to his voice. "I don't like the circumstances of this marriage. You should have been honest with me. Why didn't you tell me you wanted to marry Jennifer?"

Nuruddin looks down. "I'm still in school. I wasn't ready for a wife."

"You shouldn't have let that stop you. If you had come to me, I would have said yes."

"Even though I can't support her?"

"You will support her. In a few months, you'll have your work permit. In the meantime, I'll help you. All you needed to do was ask."

"My brother had to work two years to give his wife a proper dowry and a good home."

"Most families in Pakistan are very strict about those things. Of course I want my daughter to be comfortable, but, more importantly, I want her to marry when she's ready. I don't believe in postponing marriage for lack of money. I helped Jeremy when he married Raheema. Why wouldn't I help Jennifer and you?"

"I was ashamed to ask."

"But you weren't ashamed to kiss my daughter."

Nuruddin sinks lower into his chair.

Joshua walks over and pats his shoulder. "I know you care for Jennifer, and I'm sure you'll be good to her." Nuruddin relaxes. He got off easy.

I climb into the wheelchair and go to the mosque for the big day. It's a simple service, with few guests and no catered dinner. Only cake and punch.

Michael flew in for his sister's wedding. He'll stay in town a few days, then fly back to Boston to see Marcus marry. We haven't had much chance to talk yet, but when he walked in he hugged me and grinned. "Assalaamu alaikum, Uncle Ibrahim. You found the science, didn't you?"

Chris refused to come. I talked to him a few days ago and he said he "will never set foot in a mosque." Isaiah is here. He lied to his father again.

I thought Kyle would be here, too. Kyle, Isaiah, and Jennifer used to be the Three Musketeers. Good friends, and sometimes partners in crime. Like the time they decided to spray paint Kyle's bedroom walls. Mostly in black. My son's new lifestyle doesn't leave room for family, I guess.

Beth sent a present to the house a few days ago, along with her regrets. Her note said she had a prior engagement. The truth is she doesn't want to see my face.

Nuruddin wears a white suit. The same one Joshua wore for his wedding. Jennifer wears a simple white dress with a thin white scarf covering her blond hair.

Heather and her husband, Peter, come up to me after the service. She has a transparent yellow scarf draped over her head. "I called Beth and I know why you're on Joshua's couch."

"You had to find out, didn't you?"

"You're a Muslim, too? What is wrong with this family?"

"I don't know, Heather. Maybe it's something in the water."

"Nuruddin seems like a nice boy, but I still don't like this marriage. She's too young. I haven't met his family. He'll probably take her to live in Pakistan. It's all Joshua's fault."

"For inviting Nuruddin to stay with him?"

"For becoming a Muslim. For going to Pakistan. Everything."

"For leaving you?"

"No." She puts her arm around Peter's waist. "That turned out to be the best thing he's ever done."

"Then why do you still give him a hard time over it?"

"I enjoy giving him a hard time. He knows that."

The newlyweds leave for a short honeymoon in the Wisconsin Dells. They'll come back to live in Joshua's house.

Sharon, Aisha, Umar, and Safa are ready to fly up to Boston. Even Sharon's mother is going. Joshua decided to stay here with me.

"You should go." I tell him. "I know Marcus wants you there."

"It's not a good time. Jeremy and Raheema are watching Umar's kids, but they can't watch our four, too. And you're in no shape to keep up with them."

"I could manage."

"It's too late. I don't have a ticket."

In the afternoon, he drives Aisha to the airport and returns with movies and pizza. He hands me a slice and puts in a martial arts film. We all sit together, Joshua, the kids, and me, and watch incredible stunts usually culminating in broken furniture.

It's good to be with family, but I wonder if I'll ever be with Beth and the boys again.

Part Nine

I've spent the last two months recuperating. My bones should have healed by now. I am off the couch and on crutches, and they gave me a new shorter cast—only up to my knee. The doctor said I will never be as strong as I was. I asked him if I'll be any good at soccer. He said if I wasn't good before, I won't be now. I like a doctor with a sense of humor.

I still haven't seen my boys. I call them nearly every day, and Kyle promises to come, but I hear the hostility in his voice.

Beth won't see me either. I don't know if she has someone else or she's just fed up with me.

Umar comes over a couple times a week. We laugh together when I tell him about being Umar in Seattle.

Isaiah comes, too. I finished reading that book about Islam and we have some good discussions about salvation, revelation, and predestination. He also talks to me about problems with his father. Despite Chris's pressure, Isaiah refuses to attend the Bible college. He's applied to Loyola University instead. He says his father barely talks to him now.

I've seen Chris just a few times in the last two months. He's different now. Quieter. He still thinks I'm going to hell. The last time he came, I asked him to help me reconcile with Beth.

"Don't get me wrong," he said, "but I'm not sure that's a good idea."

"What do you mean?"

"You wouldn't understand."

"What's the problem, Chris?"

"You're a Muslim now."

"And?"

"Beth is a Christian." He looked at me and said, a little too forcefully, "I don't want you to take her away from the church."

"I don't believe you."

"You're my brother and I care about you, but you're a Muslim."

"And you would rather see a broken family than risk her conversion? I do not believe you."

"I don't know how you can be so casual about faith."

I had to laugh. "During that last month or so on the road, my faith was all I thought about. I am very serious, but I'm not dogmatic. I think there's enough room for everyone."

"So you're not sure if Islam is the right way then?"

"Nice try. It's right for me, but I'm not so arrogant as to presume I know what's right for everyone."

"Arrogant?"

"Yes, and you'd better get your arrogant ass in line here. My marriage is ending. I am your brother. Will you help me?"

He took off his glasses and rubbed his eyes. "I believe in the sanctity of marriage, of course."

"Then help me save mine."

"You won't try to convert Beth?"

He had to be kidding. "You have known Beth for over twenty-five years. Has she ever let anyone tell her what to do?"

"You're right. Melinda and I will go talk to her."

"When did you get to be so uptight?"

"When my best friend abandoned me."

"I haven't abandoned you. We have different beliefs, that's all. And I wouldn't worry too much about Beth converting. I have a much greater chance of losing her."

"I never thought I'd never see Beth and you like this."

"I never thought we'd lose Mom. I never thought I'd be a Muslim. And I never thought you and I would have trouble talking to each other."

"I'm still praying for you."

"A little prayer never hurt anyone."

He frowned, but he was with me. I hope we can be close again.

I watch Jennifer and Nuruddin. The way they smile at one another. Holding hands. The physical closeness, as if they're joined by an invisible cord. I remember when Beth and I were like that.

Chris comes by in the evening. They went to see Beth. "She says she can't take you back."

"She won't even think about it?"

"No. She was adamant."

That's Beth. It's time to take matters into my own hands.

I ask Joshua to drive me to her apartment on Saturday morning. My ankle is still weak and I won't be able to drive for a few more weeks.

I ring the buzzer. She answers quickly this time. She doesn't know it's me.

"This is Brad. I won't leave until you talk to me."

"What if I call the police?"

"You won't."

"Kyle isn't home yet."

"I'm here to see you."

"Come on up."

She could sound happier about it.

She's waiting in the hallway, the apartment door open. "Make it quick. I'm expecting someone."

"A man?"

"I don't see why you would care."

A man.

"All right. I'll get to the point. I love you, Beth. I want to come back. I'm wearing my wedding band." I thrust my left hand into her face. "But I can take a hint. If you don't want to be married to me, say so. I'll find a lawyer and we'll make it official."

"I don't want to be married to you."

I used to love her decisiveness.

"You don't need time to think it over?"

"All I've done is think. I don't see how we can rebuild our marriage. I want a divorce."

"Fine. I'll get started on it Monday. My lawyer can talk to your lawyer, or whatever."

I turn to hobble away on my crutches. Then I hear him. "Dad. Wait."

"Matt, get back in here."

"No. I want to see Dad."

He's getting tall. My little Matt. He's in my arms and I'm holding him tight. The crutches hit the wall on their way to the floor.

"Dad, don't go away again." He's crying.

"It's okay, Matt. I'll be back to see you. Your mother and I will work something out."

"I want you to come back, Dad."

"I can't. It's too complicated. I just can't." I kiss his cheek. I didn't realize how much I missed him.

She gives us a few minutes before she calls him. "Matt, I need you to get back in this apartment. I mean now."

"I have to go."

"I know. Listen to your mother. I'll see you soon."

He bends down to retrieve my crutches and comes back for one more hug. Then he's gone. She slams the door.

I haven't lost both my sons.

～

All day Sunday, I'm depressed. My marriage is finished. I always thought we had a chance.

In the afternoon, Joshua and Aisha take the kids to the lake. They ask me to come. I tell them I have a headache. While they're gone, I sit on the couch and try to figure out where to go from here.

～

On Tuesday, the doctor finally takes off the cast. It's good to be free, but when I try to walk I nearly fall. Joshua supports me to the car. When I get back to the house, I practice walking.

On Wednesday, I decide to get a job. I need a lawyer, and I'm practically broke. I ride in with Joshua and hobble around the south side looking for work. I'm very careful crossing the street.

It takes me a week to land something. Another diner. He notices my limp and says I won't be able to keep up. I tell him about my diner experience. I'm a drifter, living with my brother and trying to settle down. My beard needs trimming, but it gives credibility to my story.

I haven't found a lawyer yet. I'm not looking. I don't want this divorce.

I work hard to show the owner I can manage. When I come home from work on Friday, my second day on the job, all I want to do is stretch out. I'm about to limp upstairs. Joshua stops me.

"Hey, Brad, let's go sit in the kitchen a minute."

"I really want to go to bed. I'm beat."

"This won't take long. Aisha and I need to talk with you."

He looks serious. What's wrong? I sit at the table and turn to Aisha. "Did I break another rule?"

"It's Beth and you," she says. "You're going to walk away from your marriage, and your brothers are going to let you do it, but it's not right."

"Don't blame me. I've tried. She doesn't want me."

"Then the family needs to get involved. We need to sit together—you and her, someone from your side and someone from her side—and talk it out."

"I don't think it will make a difference."

She wags her finger and says in that teacher voice of hers, "It doesn't matter what you think. It's in the Qur'an."

"I guess we'll do it then."

Part Ten

I'm nervous. I hope this works. I don't want a divorce, and I don't really believe she does either. We just need to get past this rough spot.

I can't sleep. I can't sit still. And I can't find a chance to be alone. All weekend Joshua watches me, just like Beth used to. He follows me when I go upstairs. He stares at me when he thinks I don't notice. And Umar comes over every day, talking with Joshua in hushed tones. I'm being paranoid.

If this doesn't work, I don't know what I'll do. Go back to the Grand Canyon and try again?

The great reconciliation effort is scheduled for Monday evening. Beth wants to have it at Chris's house. Fine with me. I want my brothers there, and she wants her sisters-in-law. I want Umar to mediate and, surprisingly, she agrees. I was afraid she would drag that busybody minister of hers into this.

When the parties have all arrived, the women amass on one side of the room and the men gather on the other. Umar sits in the yellow plaid easy chair in the middle, like a great judge of old. In spite of the seriousness of the gathering, I can barely stop myself from laughing at the scene.

Umar starts. "In the name of Allah, the Most Gracious, the Most Merciful."

I glance at Beth. She won't demand equal time?

"We're coming together," Umar continues, "to reconcile Brad and Beth. I want each of you to state the problem, as you see it. Brad, you go first."

I've been practicing what to say. I don't want to stray from my story. "When that plane went down, my world turned upside down. And you were never there for me, Beth. You were more worried about your job.

"Yes, I went away. You don't know how I felt. I had to find peace. I

196

found it, and I came back to you. But now you don't want me.

"We had a great marriage. Over twenty-five years together. I could have been a better husband, but it wasn't so bad. I love you, Beth. I need you to love me again."

I feel like crying. I have to do a better job of controlling myself.

"Beth, it's your turn."

Everyone waits while Beth sits there silently. She looks down and shakes her head. Finally, she looks right at me.

"I didn't want to do this. Umar had to talk me into it, but he's right. This has gone on too long."

What? The way she keeps rejecting me?

"Everyone thinks we had the perfect marriage. They don't know the hell you've put me through all these years. The late night 'meetings.' The weekend binges. It has to stop."

"What the hell are you talking about?"

"Do you want me to say it? You're an alcoholic, Brad, and I'm sick of it. As long as you're still drinking, I can't take you back. I won't put up with it again."

I stand up and shout. "You're crazy. You don't know what you're talking about."

Umar grabs my arm. "Settle down, Brad. We're here to help you. This isn't just a mediation. It's an intervention." He looks into my eyes and says very slowly, "You must stop drinking. It's the only way you can save your marriage."

I look at their faces. They're all staring at me. "What the hell is going on?"

"It's time for you to address your problem," Umar says quietly.

"What problem? I don't have a problem. You're the ones with problems if you believe what she's saying about me." I look at Joshua and Chris. "What's wrong with you? You don't believe her, do you?"

"Brad," says Joshua, "I found your stash in Jamal's closet." He starts shouting. "You have been drinking in my son's room. And you said you were a Muslim."

"Calm down," says Umar. "Brad, we came here tonight so we can get you into treatment."

"You're all in on this? Joshua, Chris, Aisha, Melinda? All that talk about reconciliation was a lie? You lied to me."

"You've been lying for a long time," says Joshua. "It's time to face the truth."

"I'm willing to reconcile," says Beth, "but I can't even think about it until you stop drinking."

"I haven't had a drink in months. I'm a Muslim, remember?"

"That day when you walked in on me," says Aisha. "You were drunk, weren't you?"

Not drunk, exactly. After Beth threw me out, I bought a bottle of wine and finished it off in my car. Just one little bottle. Not enough to make me drunk.

"And the day you got hit by that car," says Joshua. "You were drinking then, too."

"I was upset about Kyle and I needed something to take the edge off. Just one drink."

"Just one drink?"

"Maybe it was a six-pack. So what? My son is a dropout."

"And you are a Muslim. Are you going to drop out of that?"

Umar shakes his head. "We're not here to blame you, Brad. You have an addiction. You need help."

"Addiction? How did we get from a couple of drinks to an addiction?"

"A couple of drinks?" says Beth. "Toward the end, you were drunk almost every night. And every time you called me from Joshua's house, I could tell you'd been drinking. When you came over a couple of weeks ago, you could barely walk straight."

"I was on crutches."

"Don't even try, Brad. You've fooled the rest of them, but you can't fool me. I'm tired of protecting you and helping you keep your little secret. I won't do it anymore."

Chris is still quiet. I look at him and smirk. "Why aren't you hitting me over the head with the Bible?"

"I know you have a problem, Brad—I've known it for a long time now—but I've had a hard time accepting it. Beth told me about it the day you disappeared. You were running away, weren't you? It's time to stop running and face your problem."

"What is wrong with you people? I have told you a million times why I left. Are you deaf?" I walk over to Chris and shout into his face. "And I do not have a problem."

"Brad. Brad." Umar puts his arms around me. "We're here to help you."

I shake myself loose. "I had to drink. Business contacts. How in the hell do you think I made all that money? I never heard Beth complain about the money I brought home. And I can control it. I haven't had a drink for a long time."

"You're drunk now, aren't you?" says Joshua.

"Of course not." He glares at me. "I was a little nervous, all right? I needed something to take the edge off."

Joshua gets up and paces around the room.

"I don't have a problem. I can stop anytime I want."

"Then why didn't you stop when you became a Muslim?" Umar asks.

"I meant to. But the way Beth treated me. And Kyle dropping out. It's their fault. They're the ones who make me drink. Why aren't you blaming them?"

"Don't even go there," says Beth. "That's a lie and you know it. It's you, Brad. You're an alcoholic, just like your father."

"I am nothing like my father!" I scream. "Nothing! Don't you dare!" She's lucky I haven't beaten her before. Now she's really asking for it. I throw myself at her, my fist raised.

Umar tackles me. I fall on my face. "That's enough." He yanks me to my feet. "Let's go."

My brothers jump up and join Umar. The three of them grab my arms, restraining me. They force me outside and shove me into the backseat of Umar's car. Umar gets behind the wheel, Joshua goes in front, and Chris climbs into the backseat with me. Umar takes off.

"What the hell are you doing? You can't do this to me."

"We're taking you to get the help you need."

"Let me out of here." I try to open the door. It's locked. "Where are you taking me? This is kidnapping. I can have you arrested."

They're silent. I throw my weight against the passenger door. It won't budge.

"Settle down," says Umar. "This is for your own good."

"You bastards don't know anything about what I need. Let me out of this car!" I thrash, kicking the back of the seat. Umar ignores me.

Chris grasps my arm. "Settle down, Brad," he says in a soft voice. "Take it easy. It's going to be okay."

Now I cry. "You can't do this," I say over and over again between my sobs. "Leave me alone."

Chris takes off his seat belt and puts his arms around me.

I want to hit someone. I should hit Joshua for ratting on me, but he's too far away. I can't hit Umar. He's driving. I can't hit Chris either. He's the only real friend I've ever had. I bury my face in his shoulder and cry like a baby.

～

We've been on the highway for a while now. I can't fight them. They have me trapped like an animal, and I know Umar could take me down any day of the week. I'm tired. Beth is right. It has to end, but I don't have anything to kill myself with. If only I could open this damn door.

Chris is still holding me. I concentrate on his lifeline as I fall asleep.

～

I wake up as Umar crosses the bridge into St. Louis. My head hurts. How did I get here?

I feel sick. I need to rest.

～

I hear the call to prayer—it must be a dream. I feel Umar's hand on my shoulder. "Let's pray."

Umar, Joshua, and I pray at the rest stop. I go through the motions but I can't think. My head hurts and my mind is swimming. I'm happy to climb back into the car and close my eyes.

"Are you hungry?" says Umar. "We'll stop soon."

Roast beef. I want a roast beef sandwich, with mashed potatoes and green beans on the side. My mouth waters. I fall asleep again thinking about roast beef.

"Wake up, Brad." It's Chris. What's he doing here? He should be in Chicago.

I open my eyes and remember the ugliness of last night.

Umar, Joshua, and Chris escort me into the truck stop. I order roast beef. And coffee. I need a cup of coffee. Hell, I need the whole pot.

After eating, we get back on the road. We're in the middle of nowhere. Even if I could get away, I wouldn't know where to go. "Where are you taking me?"

"A rehab center in Colorado," says Umar. "They're expecting you."

"You can't make me stay."

"By the time we get there, I think you'll realize how much you need it."

They take turns driving. Umar and Chris take turns sitting with me in back. Joshua ignores me.

We pull into Colorado Springs in the early afternoon. The mountains. I missed them. It's good to be back, I guess.

Umar drives up to the compound. Sprawling brick and wood structures blend into the mountain scenery. He turns to me.

"Are you ready to admit you have a problem, Brad?"

I don't know. My wife betrayed me. My son is a drunk, like his old man. My brothers hate me. I'm a liar and a hypocrite. And right now my hands are shaking so badly and I can't make them stop. Do I have a problem? I think my whole life is just one big problem.

"I've lost it all, haven't I?"

"Not yet, but you're close. Are you ready to do something about it?"

I don't think they'll let me blow my brains out.

"Do I have a choice?"

"If you don't sign yourself in, you will lose the support of everyone you love. Your brothers have always stood with you, but, if you don't walk into that building, they are ready to put you out on the streets. Am I right?"

"Yes," says Chris.

Joshua nods. "Yes," he says softly.

"So are you going to admit you have a problem and do something about it, or do you want to spend the rest of your life sleeping under the stars?"

"I don't want to go in. I'm not ready. Give me a couple more days," I plead.

At least let me have a drink first to help me get through it.

Umar glares at me.

This is it. Do or die.

I don't know what to say. No more one-liners. No more lies. I stare at my shaking hands. "You win."

"Let's go." Umar and Chris get out of the car. Chris brings my gym bag from the trunk, and he and Umar escort me into the main building. Joshua stays in the car.

Umar walks me through the process. I steady my hand long enough to sign myself in. They hug me, and then they're gone. Leaving me alone with my problem.

Beth Speaks Out

Melinda and Aisha help me stop shaking.

"You did the right thing," Melinda says softly.

"I agree," says Aisha. "Now he'll finally get the help he needs."

I keep picturing his face. His expression when I called him an alcoholic. He always depended on me to keep his secret, but I couldn't do it anymore.

Maybe I should have done this sooner. I knew he was drinking at Joshua's house, and I often thought of warning Aisha, but I was afraid she wouldn't believe me. Brad puts on such a good act. I should know.

Oh, but I hated to do that to him. I'm the last person he could depend on. Aisha and Melinda embrace me while I weep.

Aisha left a few minutes ago. Melinda asks me to stay with her tonight. I'm tempted. She says she'll bring Matt here. Kyle is with his friends again and won't be home until morning. I should stay. I don't want to be alone.

But I need to keep my life on track. I can't give in to my emotions. I'll sleep in my own bed, and in the morning I'll go to work, as usual. If I follow my routine, everything will be better.

He almost hit me. That's only the third time he's ever tried. Two weeks after we met, he drank too much at a party, and when I took the car keys he got a little rough. I should have given up on him then and there, but there was something about him. To this day, I don't know what it is.

He hit me on the night before he left. He walked in the door, drunk again, and I screamed at him. I shouted my ultimatum—he had to either go into rehab or pack his bags. He slapped me. I ran into the bedroom and cried myself to sleep. In the morning, I ignored him. When I came home from work, he was gone.

Melinda and I finish our herbal tea, and I drive home to Matt. They told me I did the right thing. Why do I feel so awful about it?

Joshua Interrupts

I should have gone in with him. I couldn't. He brought that poison into my home. Into my son's room. While they're inside, I stare at the pine trees and cry for the brother I've lost.

Most of my childhood memories are of Brad. When I was three, I dreamed I was being chased by a big dog with huge teeth and woke up screaming. Brad held me until I went back to sleep. Every day after school, Brad fixed my afternoon snack and helped me with my homework. On the street, Brad stopped the other kids from pushing me around and showed me how to defend myself.

He has always been there for me. When I was seven, I got busted for swiping a video game. Brad settled things with the owner. When I was sixteen, I got hauled in on a DUI. Brad bailed me out and promised not to tell Mom. While I was trying to get custody of my kids, Brad kept me up-to-date on their progress. When I was in federal prison, Brad kept my family fed and clothed. All my life, it has always been Brad.

When I was little, I thought he could do anything. That impression didn't change much as I got older. The day he told me about the abuse was the first time I saw any weakness in him. After Mom died, he kept sinking lower, but I never imagined he would be this low.

On the way here, Umar asked him how long he's been drinking. Off and on, he said, for more than thirty years. Most of my life.

I uncovered his stash on Friday morning. Jamal couldn't find his jacket, so I went up and dug through his closet. Brad was downstairs when I found it. I swear I wanted to kill him. I called Umar instead. He talked to Beth and arranged the intervention.

We planned it all out. I would pack Brad's clothes. Beth would confront him. If things got too rough, Umar would give the signal. As it turned out, we didn't need anyone to tell us he had gone too far.

I had to pretend I didn't know. I watched closely, trying to stop him from drinking again, but he must have another stash somewhere, because he came to the intervention drunk. I found one bottle in his gym bag. When I get home, I'm going to tear the house upside down.

I want to hit him. I want to hug him. I don't know what to do. I sit in the car and stare at the trees.

~

As we drive back to Chicago, I search my memory for signs of his alcoholism. He was a teenager when he started. I was just a kid. Do I know who Brad really is? How much of his personality comes from his addiction? The dry sense of humor? The obsession? The need to always be in control?

Beth told Chris about it when Brad disappeared. I didn't find out until the postcards stopped. Those were rough days. I think we all imagined him lying dead in an alley somewhere.

But he came back and said he wanted to be a Muslim. I thought his conversion was real.

Why wasn't he strong enough to overcome it? I used to drink, and Islam got me past it.

No, I should say Abdul-Qadir got me past it. Without him, I never would have given Islam a chance.

I wasn't strong enough to help my brother. While Umar and Chris sleep, I drive into Chicago, shedding tears over Brad's failure—and mine.

Seeking Normal

*The longest journey of any person
is the journey inward.*

—Dag Hammerskjold

Part One

The first thing they did was look through my bag. The guy held up my bottle of pain pills.

"What's this?"

"I broke my ankle a while back and I need the pills."

He smirked. "I bet you need them."

They put me into detox, giving me medicine to ease the tremors and hallucinations. I don't want to go through that again.

I've been here a week. They tell me I'm through the worst of it. I hope so.

Umar left me with a prayer rug and a copy of the Qur'an. For the last week, I've been too sick. As the sun sets on my eighth day here, I take out my prayer rug and fall on my knees, asking Allah to take me back.

I've spent a lot of time with a counselor these past two weeks. His name is Hank. At first, I told him I didn't want to talk about it. He respected that. We sat in his office until my time was up. I turned my face away and kept my arms crossed. He pretended to do paperwork at his desk, glancing at me every few minutes.

The next day, he asked again. I gave him my name and hometown. That's it. He didn't push me. As I left, he said, "See you tomorrow, Brad." I grunted.

On the third day, he told me he was an alcoholic.

I laughed. "They let drunks work here?"

"I stopped drinking over twelve years ago, but I will always be an alcoholic. So will you."

After his confession, I opened up a little. I think he can help.

We don't just talk about the drinking. We talk about my feelings about drinking. The cravings. The situations that make me want to drink myself into oblivion. The deceit. The many lies I told to hide my secret. The pretense. The things Beth did to cover for me. Both of us pretending we were the perfect family.

Then we get into why I drink. No matter how I tell it, all roads lead to Sam. Hank wants to know how I feel about my father. I tell him even the thought of Sam makes me nauseated.

~

He says I need to apologize to all the people I hurt. The list is too long. I write down a few names—Beth, Chris, Joshua, Kyle, Matt. I could add many more.

Yesterday, I wrote them each a letter. It took me all day, writing and rewriting. Thirty-one wads of paper went into the trash. I mailed the letters today. I hope they read them.

~

I have to attend group sessions every day. One woman in my group likes to tell her whole life story. Over and over again. Don't ask Gerry how she is unless you have an hour to kill. A kid named Terry is always angry. He reminds me of Kyle. One of the men, Carl, is an engineer. Brittany, an aging debutante, wants to talk about her affairs. A grandmother named Jill had everyone fooled. I don't tell them too much about myself. They're strangers. But it helps to know I'm not alone.

Some of them have visitors. I'm glad no one comes for me. I don't want them to see me like this.

~

Hank wants me to tell my story. When did I start drinking? Why? I won't share my life with strangers. He respects that. He gives me a week to write out the sordid tale. His only condition is I must be honest.

210

I had my first drink when I was six. My father gave me a can of beer and ordered me to drink it. He laughed when I fell over and started throwing up. He would have given me more if Mom hadn't stopped him and threatened to expose his drinking. He beat her for interfering with his fun, but he never did it again.

I didn't have another drink for almost eight years. I didn't want one. I got into the weed first, back in seventh grade.

I was in ninth grade when I went to a party where everyone was drinking. It gave me a nice high, especially when I combined it with the weed. I forgot all the pressures of home and school.

The thing is, it didn't affect me. Not in a bad way. I continued to make good grades and impress my teachers. All week, I was the model student. On the weekend, I went out and binged. Mom never caught on. Some mouthwash, or a few breath mints, and I could walk straight into the house and tell her about my marathon study sessions. Because I always got good grades, she always believed me.

My drinking was heavier in college. There were so many opportunities. I rarely got roaring drunk. It helped me relax so I could focus.

I cut back a little when I went to grad school—the work was harder—but I still managed a binge at least once a month. A guy can't always be serious.

On the day I met Beth, I had a hangover from a night of heavy partying. All morning my head pounded, but when I saw Beth I forgot about my headache.

We'd been together for two weeks when I asked her to party with me. We walked into the place and I grabbed a beer. At first she refused a drink, but I kept bugging her until she took a wine cooler. I think she sipped that same cooler all evening. I got wasted.

When it was time to leave, she grabbed my car keys. I wrestled her for them. It was all in good fun. She won.

I guess I got a little aggressive though. The next day, she gave me an ultimatum. If I wanted to keep seeing her, I had to stop drinking. Completely. She promised to help me beat my addiction.

It was amazing. For eight years, I'd hidden my problem from everyone, but the first time she saw me drinking, Beth knew. That's one of the main things I love about her. She's the only one who can cut through all the crap and see me for who I am, and love me anyway.

It took some effort, but by the time I proposed to her, I was completely dry. It was New Year's Eve and everyone was drinking. I held tight to Beth and resisted. That night, I knew we were invincible.

I stayed away from it for a long time. We got married, settled down in Youngstown, started living the American dream. Life was great.

Then we moved back to Chicago. Three weeks after unloading the moving van, I dove back into the bottle. I had to. Mom nagged me every day about Joshua, who was always in some kind of trouble, and I was under pressure at work. I needed something to give me an edge.

I settled into a routine. Working my tail off at the office. Relaxing in the bar before going home. Wine with dinner. Another drink or two to help me sleep. Beer on the weekend. If I had a really hard week, I binged on Friday night.

I took a class on wine-tasting and started my own modest collection. I wasn't a drunk. I was a connoisseur.

Beth hated my drinking, but she loved me. She complained, but she wouldn't leave me. After a while, I guess, she got used to it.

I continued to keep up the façade. Chris was a full-blown fundamentalist by then, so I never drank in front of him. Once he saw a six-pack of beer in our fridge and lectured me for a full hour. I bought another fridge and hid it in the basement.

Mom saw me drink, but she didn't know I had a problem. Only Beth knew. She kept my secret for twenty-six years.

After Kyle was born, I cut back to one drink after work and a glass of wine with dinner. I might have a few beers on the weekend, but I almost never got drunk. I smoked instead. I started smoking when I was thirteen. When Kyle was little, I puffed away at a pack or more a day.

That lasted until Matt came along. We rushed him to the hospital when he was three months old because he could barely breathe. They told us he had asthma. Beth nagged until I gave up tobacco. I tried gum, but it didn't do anything for me. The economy was bad that year and the firm had a round of lay-offs. I worked long hours to keep my job and maintain our lifestyle. I had to drink just to sleep at night.

By the time Mom died, I was drinking as much as I had in college. Seeing Sam again. That's what did it for me. I had to drink to blur the memories.

On that Saturday, when I knew Mom was gone, I walked away from the computer, picked up a bottle, and went to bed with it. I didn't crawl out for three weeks.

But I kept pretending. No one knew, except Beth. I even fooled Umar, who has probably seen his share of drunks down at the homeless shelter. Maybe I should have become an actor.

When I went back to work, I had a hard time keeping up appearances. I was drunk in Des Moines. I was drinking the night I fell down the stairs. Before, I could separate drinking and work. (Except for that one office party where I got totally bombed and, according to Beth, acted like a complete idiot.) After Mom died, the lines blurred until there were no more boundaries. Hendricks saw it. So did Ted.

So after that fight, I knew I was finished. I went out and got totally plastered. I don't know how I made it home. That conversation with Kyle and his girlfriend happened a different time. I think she was there that night, but I could barely put two words together.

If Beth knew I had lost my job, she would force me into rehab. But if I was going to stop drinking, I needed to do it on my own terms. No nurses sticking me with needles. No doctors examining my head. No screaming roommates shaking with the DTs.

Anyway, when Beth saw me like that she laid down the law. If I didn't go into rehab by Saturday, she was kicking me out. I knew she meant business. Rehab or the street. So in the morning, I told her I didn't feel well. She repeated her ultimatum and left.

I had to get out of there fast. I searched the house, looking for cash. Beth had a couple hundred in one of her dresser drawers. I found Matt's birthday money in his piggy bank. Kyle had a little cash from his weekend job. I took it all. Then I grabbed the keys to the Toyota.

Forget what I said about leaving so I could kill myself. I wanted to die, and when I was standing next to the Grand Canyon it seemed like a real good idea for a second or two. Until I slipped and nearly fell in.

I got into my car and drove, and I didn't drink for an entire week. Well, except for a few beers here and there. I didn't drink heavily until I went out on the town with Lou.

Lou was one of the best drinking buddies I ever had. We had a lot of good times in that apartment up over the diner. I wasn't going to let Molly dictate my life. For a few weeks, I threw peyote into the mix. You could call Santa Fe the high point of my trip.

After Santa Fe, I drank off and on, depending on my mood. I didn't drink as much in California—not when I was with Abdullah, anyway. I'd had a little to drink before going to see Uncle Rob that first time. When I sobered up, I went back and apologized.

I got roaring drunk on the night I spent with Chelsea. I really don't remember what happened. I just know where I woke up.

In Denver, the mountains calmed me the same way the ocean had. I cut way back, down to a drink or two a day. Then I moved in with Kate. She had a bit of a problem herself. We made a wonderful pair. She said the vodka helped her write, and proceeded to name all the famous authors who had turned their alcoholism into literary masterpieces.

Kate's drinking is what attracted me to her. Beth hates to drink, and she only did it when I nagged her to join me. In Kate I found someone who validated my desire.

It took me so long to make it through the mountains because I was sure I would go over the edge. I inched along, not able to stop drinking but not ready to die.

After I started reading the Qur'an, I cut back again. There were a few days, here and there, when I didn't drink at all. At least once a week, I decided to stop. I just needed one more drink.

On Christmas Day, after eating lunch in a Chinese restaurant with four total strangers, I sat in my backseat and drank myself into a stupor. After that, very few hours passed when I didn't have alcohol in my system. I wasn't drunk when I walked into the mosque in Detroit. I stopped to get something on my way out of the city.

I made sure I was sober enough when I got to Youngstown. They're Baptists. The wine cooler Beth sipped at that party was her first drink. They never knew about my drinking, and I didn't want to ruin it, but I did sneak a little that night in their house, just before I went to sleep. I needed something to help me relax.

I tried not to drink in Worcester—I didn't want my nephew to see me that way—but Marcus caught me on the day I arrived. He never came right out and said it, but I think he couldn't wait for me to leave.

As I made my way down the Atlantic coast, all bets were off. I'd drink one day, drive the next. Sometimes I drove drunk. I don't know how I avoided getting myself killed. From New York to Mississippi, I rarely stopped.

Somehow, I managed to stay sober in that motel room in Colorado Springs. I didn't have a drop for nearly five weeks. And a very mild withdrawal. I would have to call that a miracle.

I drank a little on my way home, but it was a farewell celebration. I thought when I became a Muslim I would be done with it.

I never meant to take another drink, but Beth threw me out, and I couldn't face my life. After that, I was back to full speed. I was living in Joshua's house, and I had to find places to hide my stash. Joshua discovered one of them. I wonder if he's located the others yet.

It was hard to keep up after I broke my ankle, but I couldn't stop. Some days, I had to rely on my pain pills for a buzz. I devised ways to visit my hiding places without them noticing. When they went out, I called in my order to a nearby liquor store. They delivered.

Once, I had to get really creative. My stash was almost gone, and I was low on cash and getting shaky. Then I remembered my wine collection in storage. I had to get to it.

Joshua and his family left for the mosque and I limped to my car. I drove with my left foot and hobbled into the storage place where I told them an elaborate story, complete with military duty overseas—that's how I broke my ankle—and a wife on her deathbed. She wanted her dead brother's shirt—he died fighting for our country, of course—to give her comfort. By the time I was finished, everyone in the place was crying. They let me in and I smuggled out my wine, wrapped up in some of my old shirts. I laughed all the way back. I found some new hiding places and had a good old time.

No one knew. I hid it from Chris and Joshua. I was never pulled over by highway patrol. I even got away with it at work.

Well, almost. Ted knew something was going on for at least a year before I left. I almost never drank at the office, but when I went out of town I wasted my evenings in the hotel bars. A few times, I came late for my morning meetings. Once or twice, I fell asleep at my desk after lunch. I couldn't have kept it going, especially after that last promotion. More hours, more responsibility. More alcohol. They tolerated my indiscretions because when I was sober I was one hell of an engineer, but after Des Moines I was finished.

So why did I drink? Was it Sam's fault or mine? He got me started, but I kept it up. I can't blame Sam for everything, but my muscles tense every time I think of him.

I went to the clinic last week for blood tests and a full physical exam. I haven't had an exam that thorough since Matt was born. I go back today for the results.

The news is worse than I expected. I just thought I was old and tired. I didn't know I was sick.

I have alcoholic hepatitis, which means my liver is still functioning, but not the way it should. I also have diabetes. No more pecan pie. On top of that, there's the high blood pressure and the osteoporosis. Which would explain why my bones took longer to heal. And I need glasses. I knew my vision was getting worse, but I didn't know the drinking contributed to it.

The doctor sits down with me and discusses the full range of health problems associated with long-term alcoholism. He warns cancer could be on the horizon. Both of my parents had cancer, so the deck is already stacked against me. And I will need to go on a strict diet to prevent more damage to my heart and pancreas.

"You will probably also notice some memory impairment. Have

you had difficulty with your short-term memory?"

I crack a smile. "I don't remember."

He laughs. "A sense of humor will help. I know this is a lot to digest. Do you have any questions?"

Millions of them. But I need time to sort it all out.

I shrug. "Thanks for telling me."

"Believe it or not," he says, "it could be worse. And you must not return to drinking. If you do, I predict you will be dead within two years."

Two years. Matt is eleven now, almost twelve. I would be dead by the time he started high school. I wouldn't live to see Kyle reach twenty. No college graduations. No grandkids.

I want to live.

Today in the group we talked about our low points. Hitting bottom, they call it. When you know you can't do it anymore and you're willing to put an end to it. Gerry's low point came when her husband left, taking the kids with him. Carl got drunk at an office party and went after the boss's wife. Like me, he doesn't have a job to go back to. Terry's parents threatened to cut him off without a dime. Brittany woke up one morning and realized how lonely she was. She slit her wrists. Her landlord found her in time. Jill had an accident with two of her grandkids in the car. One of the kids barely pulled through.

I've had a lot of low points. My brothers probably think their rejection finally forced me into rehab. That was just the icing on the cake. My lowest was when I went after Beth. I love her, yet at that moment I could have killed her. I fought going into rehab, even after that, but I knew I was finished. If Umar and my brothers hadn't forced me into the car, I know I would have killed myself.

I tell the group my story. It's no more sensational than what anyone else has experienced. They nod. Carl pats me on the back. "That's beautiful," says Gerry through her tears. She's always crying about something. Hank smiles. "Thank you for sharing, Brad." What he means is thank you for finally opening up. You're getting there.

~

Umar chose this place for me. He knows how much I love the mountains. There must be dozens of rehab facilities in Illinois, but I'm glad they brought me here. Whenever I feel tense, I gaze at the scenery and remember those five weeks in meditation. If I did it then, I can do it again.

~

They talk a lot about spirituality here. In private sessions and in groups. I've told Hank about my journey to Islam. Yesterday, I mentioned parts of it to the group. I pray in my room. I read the Qur'an before I go to bed each night. I keep asking Allah to give me another chance.

I've been here for five weeks when another Muslim walks in. I guess just because we're not supposed to drink doesn't mean we all don't. It's like they keep telling us here. You've got to put in the effort.

~

Six weeks ago, I signed myself in. Six weeks without a drink. It's been over twenty years since I could say that. I'm going home tomorrow. Not home exactly. I don't have a home.

I wake up, say my prayers, pack my clothes back into my gym bag, and sit on my bed, waiting for them. I read the Qur'an while I wait. I'm pacing by the time Chris and Joshua arrive.

Chris smiles. "Are you ready to get out of this place?" He hugs me.

Joshua doesn't say anything. When I look at him, he turns away.

Hank comes to say goodbye. "Good luck. I don't expect to see you here again, unless you decide to come back as a counselor."

"We'll see."

He hugs me. "Take care, Brad. You'll be fine."

Chris puts his arm around my shoulders and walks with me out to his car. Joshua carries my gym bag. I sit in the front seat while

Chris drives. Joshua is quiet in back.

We stop for lunch in a small town just inside the Kansas border. I order an open-faced roast beef sandwich. It tastes better now.

No one knows what to say. They don't want to talk about my alcoholism, but I know they're thinking about it. I don't want to talk about it either. It sits there on the table like the proverbial elephant.

We finish eating with just a little small talk among us. Ruth has another year at the Bible college. Raheema had an ultrasound. It's a girl. They don't say anything about Kyle. Another elephant.

I finish my roast beef, and Chris asks, "Aren't you going to order the pecan pie?"

"I can't." I tell them about my health problems.

"That's tough." Chris pats my arms. Then he calls the waitress over and asks her to bring low-fat, sugar-free ice cream. It's not too bad, but I miss the real thing.

Before we go back on the road, Joshua gets the prayer rugs from the car. We find a secluded spot in the field next to the restaurant. Chris waits in the car.

We've driven for an hour or so when Chris says, "Don't worry. You're going to make it."

"No sermons about the demon rum?"

He reaches over and pats my shoulder. "I don't think you know how much you mean to me."

We stop at a highway motel near Topeka. Chris orders pizza. When Joshua and I take out our prayer rugs, Chris goes to find the ice machine.

After the prayer, I turn to Joshua. "Did you get my letter?"

He nods.

"I'm sorry."

"I know, but it hurts."

Chris walks in with the ice. Joshua turns away.

I try again after the morning prayer. "I mean it, Joshua. I'm sorry."

He looks down. "I want to forgive you. I think I could forgive the fact that you went back on your faith. I know you have an addiction, and it's hard to beat. But you brought that wine into my son's room. That's what gets me."

"I'll make it up to you. I'm a real Muslim now. You'll see."

He reaches for me and cries. I hold him, just like I did when he was a little, after he woke up from a nightmare.

I try again after the morning prayer.

It takes us nearly a full day of driving to get to Chicago. It's dark by the time Chris pulls up in front of Joshua's house.

Joshua turns to me. "Are you coming in?"

"Am I still welcome?"

"Get your gym bag."

Chris steps out of the car for another long hug. Joshua and I pray downstairs before I crawl into my bed in Jamal's room.

I need to go to an Alcoholics Anonymous meeting every day for the next three months. Ninety meetings in ninety days, they say. If I don't show up, they won't come and drag me in, but they can't guarantee my recovery without it. Umar found a local group. Joshua offers to go to my first meeting with me.

"That's okay," I say. "It's a very exclusive club. Alcoholics only."

"I am an alcoholic."

"What are you talking about? You haven't had a drink in almost twenty years."

"But you know how much I used to drink. I couldn't stop. That's why my friend Mahmoud sent me to Pakistan. He and Abdul-Qadir got me through it. And even though I haven't had a drink in seventeen years and three months, I will always be a recovering alcoholic."

"Sam was an alcoholic. Did you know that?"

"I could have guessed."

"I didn't have to guess. I lived it. The smell made me sick to my stomach. But the first chance I had, I followed him into the bottle."

"Why didn't you tell me? I could have helped."

"I couldn't admit I had a problem. I'm still trying to grasp it."

"I found your stash in the basement."

"I know. I checked."

"And your stash in the garage. Along with a couple bottles in the bathroom and a bottle behind the family room couch."

"What about the stuff I stored in my car?"

"That's the first place I looked. Umar and Chris helped me clean it all out."

We go to the meeting together. I don't say much. Joshua tells his story. And he says even though it's been nearly twenty years, he can still remember. A guy who is new to the meetings, like me, asks how he's managed to stay sober. He says, "My faith gets me through it. One day at a time."

So that's why Umar and Chris had to help him take care of my stash.

On the way back, he says, "In Islam, the punishment for drinking is forty lashes."

I let out a short, bitter laugh. "I think I could handle that. I've been beaten before."

"He really did a number on you, didn't he?"

"More than you'll ever know." More than even I can understand.

Part Two

Joshua keeps me on a short leash. He asks me to go in to work with him, and gives me simple tasks to keep me close by. He makes sure I'm in bed before he goes to sleep. I know he has my car keys. I guess it will take a while.

I've been out of rehab for a week when Umar comes over with a message.

"Beth called me today and asked about you. When I told her you were back, she said she wants another meeting."

"Really."

"She's worried about you, Brad."

"Sure she is."

I feel sorry for everything I put her through, but she betrayed me. Even after six weeks in rehab, I can't quite let it go.

"I told her we would meet tomorrow. What time is your meeting?"

My meeting? Say it, Umar. I go to AA.

"At six."

"I'll tell her to come at eight then."

"This isn't another setup, is it?"

"No, but you have to admit you needed it. Would you have agreed to an intervention?"

"I would have climbed into my car and never come back."

"This time it's for real. You have my word." He pats my shoulder. "Don't worry, Brad. You're on your way."

"Why do I feel like I'm going nowhere fast?"

"It takes time. Be patient with yourself."

"I know. One day at a time."

Sometimes I think if I hear that phrase one more time I'll vomit.

"What are you doing to get back to normal?" he asks. "Have you looked for a job?"

"Joshua doesn't seem to think I'm ready."

"I'll talk to him. You're headed in the right direction."

~

I head out with Joshua again in the morning to start my job search. Before I take off, he hands me a phone.

"My work number, home number, and Umar's cell are all on speed dial. Call if you need anything."

Like a drink?

"Sure, I'll call."

There aren't many diners around here anymore. I think about going back to the old place, but he was hard to work with, even before I went into rehab. I don't need his abuse.

I pass a lot of liquor stores, nearly one on every block. I know at least one is owned by a Muslim. I went in there on the day I broke my ankle. When I made my purchase, he looked me up and down, standing there in the white robe Joshua had given me.

"Are you a Muslim? Why do you drink?"

I snickered. "Why do you sell it?"

He shrugged and said, "It's a living."

What a pitiful way to make a few bucks.

Today, I'm able to walk past every one of them. I grip the phone and look straight ahead.

The problem is I have to be honest. Hank drilled that into me every day for six weeks. No more lies. No more hiding. Honesty, honesty, honesty.

A mile from Joshua's office, I find a place with a "Help Wanted" sign in the window. They look busy. I walk in and order a cup of coffee. When things have calmed down, I ask about the job.

The guy asks about my experience. I tell him I've worked in different diners across the country.

"How do I know you'll stay on?"

"Chicago is my hometown. My family is here. I don't plan on hitting the road again."

"Where have you worked in Chicago?"

Tough question. He doesn't need to know about my engineering background. He just wants to know if I can handle the work. "I had a job at another place several blocks away. The Silver Dollar."

"Why did you leave?"

Tougher question. Hank told me to be honest about my addiction. He said dishonesty fueled the alcoholism. "I, um, I have a little problem. I just spent six weeks in rehab."

"Drugs?"

"Alcohol."

"How long have you been sober?"

"Seven weeks and one day."

He looks me up and down. "How do I know you won't hit the bottle again?"

"I guess you don't."

He nods slowly. "Seven weeks and one day, huh? It's one day at a time, isn't it? I've been sober for five years, eight months, and six days. One day at a time." He pats me on the back. "I'd better get you into an apron and show you where everything is."

Halfway through my orientation, he says, "You don't have to tell everything about yourself."

"But they keep talking about honesty."

"There's a balance. I'll help you find it."

Bill Green bought this place nineteen months ago. He calls it "High and Dry." I hadn't noticed the symbolism. I think I'll like it here.

We go to Chris's house on Tuesday for a real stab at reconciliation. If it doesn't work this time, that's it. One thing I learned on the road is it's not that hard to find a woman. And my life is complicated enough already.

When I walk in, Chris hugs me. He hugs me all the time now. I'm glad we're close again, but I don't understand why being a recovering alcoholic is better than being a Muslim.

Beth finally saunters in, a man by her side. She brought her boyfriend? I take a good look at his face. She brought her pastor.

"Brad, you should remember Pastor Mueller. Not that you went to church much. I'm sorry, Umar, but I need someone who understands my perspective."

If Umar's annoyed, he doesn't show it. He shakes hands with the good reverend and says, "Let's get started."

First he invites Pastor Mueller to offer a short prayer, which he does with great enthusiasm. Then Umar says, "In the name of Allah, the Most Gracious, the Most Merciful. The last time we met, Beth indicated she would be willing to consider reconciliation, if Brad received treatment for his alcoholism. Brad has just returned from rehab and he is making positive steps toward rebuilding his life."

Mueller nods. "I'm glad to hear it." I hope he keeps his mouth shut. I know people in that church.

"Beth," says Umar, "what else is there besides the drinking? What do you need from Brad?"

"Do you really want to hear it? Okay, Brad, remember you asked for it. The drinking was a big part of it. Huge. The last few years, I couldn't recognize my husband anymore. And when I look at him, I still don't see the man I married. All I see is that beard and that, that ridiculous ponytail.

"I tried. God knows I tried to save our marriage. I begged him to go for counseling or into rehab, but he fought me every step of the way. Then, suddenly, he was gone, choosing the bottle over me. And even though I know he's stopped drinking, I can't get over all those years of lying and neglect. You didn't talk to me, Brad. You didn't tell me you were afraid of going into rehab. You just left. No note. No phone call, except for that once when my father forced you to talk to me. All I got from you was a lousy postcard once a week. Sometimes not even that. There were weeks when I knew you must be dead, and it tore me up inside.

"While you were off finding peace, I had to keep this family going. Your brothers helped, but not nearly enough to make up for your absence. And when you did come back, you yelled at me for letting Kyle drop out of school. Do you think I wanted that? It's your fault, Brad. Not mine. Not your brothers'. You turned your back on your son, and that's why he's an alcoholic and a dropout."

I know she's right, but I won't give in that easily.

"First of all, I wasn't afraid."

Okay, maybe a little.

"I thought I could do it myself. And didn't you see how much I was hurting? I thought I was headed for a complete breakdown. If you had paid attention to me, rather than worrying about your work, I wouldn't have needed to tell you. You would have known."

"I tried to get you to go to someone for help. You refused."

"I didn't need someone. I needed you, but you were too busy with your damn career."

"You have always resented my career. All you ever wanted was a little housewife to give you children and fulfill your needs."

Mueller interrupts. "This would be more productive if you would reflect on what you hear the other person say. Try not to make it personal."

Yeah, right.

I attack her latest remark. "That's a bunch of crock and you know it. We have always been partners. And I was happy to have a wife who is smart and independent, but I wanted a wife, not a roommate."

"So I wasn't by your side every minute of the day. Someone had to keep things going. And you left without a word. At least I deserved a good fight before you walked out that door."

"You don't understand. You'll never understand what I need."

"It's still all about you, isn't it? What about me, Brad? What about my needs?"

"All right. What do you need?"

I can reflect. Mueller should be happy.

"When you left, I needed a husband who would fulfill his responsibilities. Now I just need you to leave me alone."

"Then I guess it's over."

"That's what I have been trying to tell you."

I turn to Umar. "Are you satisfied? We tried. It won't work."

Aisha answers. "I'm not satisfied. You're only thinking about yourself. Have you ever considered Beth's feelings?"

Joshua jumps in. "He's apologized for leaving. He wants to make it up to her, but she refuses to give him a chance."

"Why should she? How does she know he won't take off again, or go back to drinking?" Melinda sounds angry.

"She can't simply throw away their twenty-five years as husband and wife. Marriage is too important to be taken so lightly." I've never heard Chris raise his voice to his wife.

There are too many people in this room.

Umar clears his throat. "That's enough, all of you. We need to stay focused on Brad and Beth. You two are not hearing one another. You have both been hurt, and you are both concentrating on your own pain. Can you look at the issue from the other person's perspective?"

"Beth keeps saying what a lousy husband I was. Is that you want me to say? That's all in the past. What about now?"

"You keep pushing me, Brad. You must have your reasons, but I don't see how anyone could be so self-centered."

"That's not quite what I meant," says Umar. "For twenty-five years you had a partnership. What held you together all that time? Can you draw on that?"

"I love you, Beth. How many times do I have to say it?"

"You don't love me. You only needed me to support your addiction. Our marriage was over years ago."

"Why do you always have to be so damn stubborn?"

"Why do you always think you're right?" She looks down. "I can't do this, Umar." She grabs Mueller's hand. "Let's go."

The reverend starts to protest, but Beth pulls him away. Stubborn.

I want to leave, too. I could go for a drive. Find a place where people understand me.

Umar grabs my arm. "I know what you're thinking. Don't do it."

When we go back to the house, Joshua pretends to help Jamal with his science homework while waiting for me to sleep. I am tired. I give up.

～

In the morning, Joshua drops me off at High and Dry. "Don't forget to call if you need me."

Yeah, sure.

Twice I drop the orders, french fries and burgers flying. I clean up while customers wait. After the lunch rush, Bill puts his hand on my shoulder. I jump.

"Having a bad day?"

"A bad life."

"Tell me about it."

We sit with our coffee and I talk about Beth. "She is so damn stubborn."

"That's what you said to her? No wonder she walked away."

"What should I have said?"

"Not that. I messed up my marriage, too. She left while I was still drinking, and she refused to come back after I quit. I don't know much, but I can tell you what not to do."

Over the next hour, Bill helps me sort things out. Before I leave for the night, he puts his number on my speed dial. "Call me anytime, day or night."

After dinner, I go to the computer and send her an email. "I'm sorry. Can you give me another chance?" I wait for an hour. She doesn't reply. I think about taking a walk, but Joshua is in the kitchen. I stomp upstairs and fall into bed. Maybe I can sneak out after he goes to sleep.

But he walks into the bedroom and sits with Jamal, discussing the James Baldwin novel my nephew is reading for class. I fall asleep, their voices droning in the background.

He drops me off in the morning with his usual reminder. I grunt.

The place is busy all day, which is good. It keeps me from thinking.

Umar comes by after dinner. "Beth called. She says she's willing to give it one last try."

I should have known she would come through. I can always depend on Beth.

Umar's glare wipes the smugness off my face. "Be careful, Brad. If you spout off like you did last time, you will lose her."

He's right. I need to be very careful.

Part Three

We meet again on Friday night. Same people, same scene. When Beth walks in with Mueller, she glances in my direction and quickly turns away.

Umar begins. "Last time, we descended into insults. Let's see if we can keep it civil this time. Beth, would like you start? Why did you request another meeting?"

"I don't know. Maybe I'm crazy. But when Brad apologized, I thought we should try again. God knows I'm used to giving him chances. This is it, though. I'm barely able to function with all this stress."

Be careful.

"This has been hard on both of us," I say. "I just want to work things out with you."

That was civil.

"I know, but I can't get past all the hurt. And I don't know who you are now. I can barely stand to look at you. I don't want to hear about how you found Islam. Frankly, I don't see how we can make this work."

"But you haven't tried. You've barely talked to me since I came back."

"What am I supposed to say? I'm not usually one of those women who keeps a running list of hurts in her head, but there are so many. Drinking, abandoning us, becoming a Muslim, looking like a bum. And it's still all about you. Do you ever think about us?"

All the time.

"Not as much as I should, but I miss you."

"You say that every time, but I'm tired of words. Can you tell me how anything will be different?"

"I'm not drinking. That's something."

"And how long do you think that will last?"

"I'm doing the best I can, okay?"

Be careful.

"I think we should just go our separate ways. You can see Matt whenever you want. Our lawyers will divide up the property. I want to get on with my life."

"I want to be part of your life, Beth. Please let me in."

"We can barely talk to each other. Tell me how we could possibly live together."

"Can't we try?"

"And how is that supposed to work? I let you back into my life as if nothing happened? You can forget about that."

Umar interrupts. "This is much better. You are actually talking."

"But talk can't change the way things are," says Beth.

Umar looks at Mueller. "Could I speak with you privately for a few minutes? I want to see if we're on the same page."

Beth protests. "What do you have to say that you can't say in front of me?"

Mueller pats her hand. "Don't worry. I'll make sure your concerns are addressed."

They huddle for ten minutes in a corner of the room, gesturing, nodding, and shaking their heads. We wait. She won't look at me.

When they come back, Mueller says, "Go ahead."

"Thank you." Umar looks at me, then at Beth. "I hear two people who are hurt and angry. I also hear two people who still care about one another. Our judgment is that you two must work through your feelings toward one another before you can decide on divorce. You cannot do this adequately with your current living situation. So, Brad, you need to move into Beth's apartment."

"What? Just like that? You expect me to take him back?" Beth turns to Mueller. "I thought you were on my side."

"Think about it," he replies. "You need to be sure of your decision. If things don't work out, you can still go through with the divorce."

"You're not taking him back," Umar explains. "Brad will move into your apartment, but you will be roommates, nothing more. If you decide to resume your marital relationship, there will be no more talk of divorce. Or, if, after four months, you both agree you cannot stay together, you may begin divorce proceedings."

"Four months? I don't think so. This has already dragged on too long. I'm ready to move on."

With another man.

A lump forms in my throat.

"But you have an investment in this marriage," says Umar. "Two sons and twenty-five years together. Think about what a divorce will mean to your boys."

"I don't see how it would change anything. He's been out of our lives for almost two years now."

"Four months is a long time," says Mueller, "but the decision to divorce should not be taken lightly."

"Give your marriage another chance," says Umar. "If it doesn't work, you'll know you did everything you could, and you can move on without regrets."

Beth plays nervously with her hair. "My apartment only has two bedrooms. I won't ask the boys to give up their space, and he is definitely not coming into my room."

"I assume you have a couch," says Mueller.

"Yes."

Umar smiles. "Brad, you've slept in your car and outside on the hard ground. I think Beth's couch will be sufficient."

It's not Beth's couch. It's our couch.

"Sure."

"Any other objections, Beth?"

"I don't know. I don't like it."

"What do you have to lose?" says Melinda.

"It will be inconvenient, but you'll feel better knowing you made the effort," Aisha adds.

"Four months? Are you sure?"

"Yes." Both Umar and Mueller answer. I wonder how Umar managed to convince the good reverend.

"Not a day longer. Okay, let's get this over with. When do we start?"

"It's late tonight. Why don't you let Brad move in on Sunday?"

"I hope you two know what you're talking about." She frowns. "What if we feel like killing each other before the four months is up?"

"I'm not worried about that," says Umar.

"I'll see you on Sunday then." She walks out quickly. Mueller shakes hands with Umar and follows her.

Four months. Is that enough time to convince her how much I love her?

Beth Speaks Out

I need to have my head examined. Why did I tell Umar I wanted to reconcile? I should have moved a thousand miles away and forgotten Brad ever existed. But there's something about him.

I thought reconciliation would be more like counseling. I didn't expect this whole business of having to live together. But Pastor Mueller agreed with it. He's helped me get through these last couple of years. I have to trust someone.

I know what Brad expects. He thinks he'll walk through that door and I'll throw myself at him. What a fantasy. I'll let him live here. That's all.

I can't let myself get close to him. I can't let him hurt me again.

Part Four

Hank advised me not to make any major life changes for the next twelve months. One rule broken.

I'm nervous. I want Beth to fall into my arms the minute I walk in, but I know that won't happen. I wonder how she'll treat me.

At least I'll get to be with the boys. I haven't seen Kyle since the day I left—about eighteen months now. He must look different. I hope we don't start fighting again.

Don't make any changes, Hank said. He was right. Every morning I feel shaky. Every night I can't sleep. I need just one drink to calm my nerves. I call Bill instead. Three or four times a day. Every time I call, he says just the right thing to keep me going.

I don't work this Sunday, but I drop by High and Dry on my way to Beth's place. Bill and I have coffee together.

"I didn't expect to see you today," he says.

"I'm on my way over there. I want everything to be the way it was before I left, but I'm afraid to get my hopes up."

"The way it was? When she was working long hours and you were drinking yourself into an early grave? I thought you were more ambitious than that."

"You know what I mean. How it was in the early days, before my drinking got in the way."

"That was a long time ago. You have to be realistic. It will probably be awkward at first. At least your wife is willing to try."

"That's right. You know how it is."

"I see my kids three days a week. That's all I need."

We finish up and I climb into my Toyota, ready to meet the challenge. I hope.

I grab my gym bag and my sleeping bag, and buzz her apartment. She takes a long time to answer. She knows it's me.

"Hello, Brad."

Finally.

She buzzes me in.

As I ride up in the elevator, I think about how much I dread living in this building for the next four months. If we reconcile, the first thing I'll do is move us somewhere else.

She meets me at the door. "Before you set one foot in this apartment, I have a few ground rules. First, one drink and you're out of here. Second, you will not enter my bedroom. In addition, you will not start a conversation with me. If you are suffering, please do it quietly. We will be roommates, nothing more. You will clean up after yourself and cook for yourself. You will provide your own food and toiletries. I expect you to keep your area of the living room clean. And exactly sixteen weeks from now, I expect you to be gone. Here's your key. Any questions?"

It's no use.

"Thanks for the key."

"There's the couch. Make yourself comfortable, because you'll spend the next sixteen weeks there." She turns to walk down the hall.

"There is one thing. I'll have to say my prayers. Do you know which way is northeast?"

"Don't say your prayers when I'm around. I don't know which way is northeast. You used to be an engineer. Figure it out."

"Are the boys here?"

"Matt is. Kyle's out again."

"Can you tell Matt I'm here?"

"I suppose." She calls down the hallway. "Matt, your father is here."

He comes out of his room and runs into my arms. Beth walks away.

I don't see Kyle until Monday afternoon. He's walking around in a t-shirt and boxers. He looks like he just woke up.

"Hi, Kyle. How are you?" He's taller. He's put on some weight, too. He was always bulky, but it used to be muscle. Now, I think most of it is fat.

"Oh. Hi, Dad. I guess we're stuck with you for the next sixteen weeks." He yawns in my face. I smell his breath. Could he be drinking this early in the day? And why would Beth let Kyle bring alcohol into the apartment? Is this a set-up? I try to forget the smell. I need to go pray.

Kyle is still standing there, staring at me. I wonder why I was so anxious to see him. Who is this man and what has he done with my son? "How have you been?"

He yawns again. "I'm good." He reaches back and scratches his butt. "Never been better." He turns to go back to his room. "See you later."

I make my ablutions and bow down to Allah in my corner of the living room.

Beth and Kyle do a good job of ignoring me, but Matt talks to me every afternoon. I ask him about school and his friends, and he asks me about my journey. I tell him about my adventures, and how much I missed him. He says he missed me, too. He's a good boy.

I've lived in the apartment for a month. Beth has kept her promise to treat me like a roommate, and I've kept my end of the deal, but I keep trying to win her over. I clean up around the apartment before she comes home, fix a shelf in the kitchen, and take care of the leak in the bathroom. I also pay some of the bills. One evening when she walks in with a couple bags of groceries, I take them from her and begin putting things away.

"You don't have to do that."

"I know."

"It won't work."

"What will?"

"Nothing. This four month deal is only a formality. We can't save our marriage. There is no marriage left to save."

"There was. We had a good marriage, Beth. Don't you remember?"

"The first few years were good, but I'm too busy to live in the past."

"Every night when I go to sleep on that green couch, I remember those evenings after the boys went to bed and everything was quiet."

"That was so long ago. We had different lives then. We had our house. You had a real job. Some of it was nice, but it's gone."

"I miss those times."

"We can't live in the past," she repeats.

I turn to look at her. "Why did you stop loving me?"

She turns away. "I try not to show it, but I still care. It's not enough, though. It was enough when I was twenty-two. Not now."

"I have been sober for twelve weeks and two days."

Which isn't easy when Kyle is drinking in his room down the hall.

"What else do you need from me?"

"You can't give me what I need. I married an engineer, not a short-order cook. I need a man who can shoulder the burden and take responsibility for his family, not someone who speaks wistfully about sleeping in the desert. I've listened to some of your talks with Matt about life on the open road. It sounds romantic, but I'm a realist. Once, you and I wanted the same things. I still want the stability you scorn, but you want the adventure I'll never be able to share with you."

"What if I change?"

"You could take your suits out of storage and get another job in your field, but you could never go back to being who you were. Your experiences have changed you."

"Do you want to forget about the three months we have left? I'll tell Umar we tried and it won't work."

"No. I didn't want to say this, but I like having you here. Matt is happier than he's been in years, and Kyle is coming around. You can stay. As long as you stay on the couch."

"Is there someone else, Beth?"

I need to know for sure.

She looks at me. "I started seeing him two months before you came back. By then I was sure you would never return. He's an accountant—he still wears suits. What about you? Did you have any encounters on the road?"

I didn't want to tell her, but I have nothing more to lose. "Some. There was a woman in Denver. She wanted to be a writer."

She presses her lips together. "That's what you were doing in Colorado."

"Yes." I look down.

"We have both moved on."

"Can I ask for one small favor? Could you stop seeing your accountant until the divorce becomes final? We are still married."

"What about the woman in Denver?"

"It was over long ago."

"I promise I won't see him while you're living here. Is that good enough?"

"I don't deserve to ask for more."

"Thank you for putting away the groceries. If you want, I can cook for you sometime."

"That would be nice."

I love you.

She talks to me a little now. Nothing important. Just "Hello" and "Goodbye" and "How was your day?" It's something.

Kyle smiled when I came home today. Now I know why he's hated me. You can't love someone who makes your mother unhappy.

I come home from work on a Thursday afternoon and collapse into the couch. I get around well now, but my ankle hurts after eight hours on my feet. I prop up my leg.

Kyle walks out of his room and sits next to me. "How's the leg doing?"

"It's okay, but I'm not up to full strength."

"I heard you telling Matt about your trip. How was it up there in the mountains?"

We sit together on the couch and I tell him about the cool fresh mountain air and the exhilaration of watching eagles fly overhead. Even in my alcoholic haze I couldn't help but notice the beauty. We're still talking when Beth comes home.

Every afternoon for the next week, I tell him about my trip. I describe the desert, the ocean, and the Badlands. And I apologize for never taking him there.

One day he asks, "Tell me honestly, Dad. Why did you leave?"

"My drinking got the best of me. I knew Mom would put me in rehab and I wasn't ready to let go." I look him in the eye. "I'm worried about your drinking, too. I started when I was a little younger than you, and it took me way too long to quit."

I'm still tempted.

His eyes harden. "Are you telling me what to do?"

"Just be careful. I don't want you to learn the hard way."

"So you're saying you left so you could keep on drinking?"

"Pretty stupid, wasn't it?"

"Real stupid. And couldn't you at least have said goodbye?"

"I did everything wrong. But I felt trapped. I had to get away."

"That's how I see it. I was trapped at school. I had to get out of there."

"But Kyle, you're talking about your future. How could you throw everything away?"

"How could you?"

"I'm sorry." I put my hand on his shoulder. He pushes my arm away and trudges back to his room. The door slams.

Thanksgiving comes around and we all go to Joshua's house for the meal. I try not to think about last Thanksgiving with Kate. I wonder if she's cooking a big meal for Geoffrey this year. I wonder if she's still drinking.

Kyle won't talk to me, but Beth is showing signs of thawing. Yesterday she sat with Matt and me on the couch and listened to my story of skiing in Massachusetts.

We're halfway through our period of enforced togetherness. She made a large pot of chili this afternoon. In the evening, she brings me a bowl.

"I said I'd cook for you sometime. Don't worry, there's no pork in it."

"Thanks. That was nice of you."

She fixes a bowl for herself and sits next to me. "So you remember this couch."

"Some of the best moments of my life were the times I spent with you right here."

"We forgot about our schedules and concentrated on each other."

"We talked about our hopes, our fears, our plans for the future."

She smiles. "You're the one who picked this couch. I thought it would be too dark, but when we got it home, I knew it was perfect."

"One of the last times I held you here was the night Mom and Walt came for dinner, right before they left. You made seafood, which was a bit ironic. Later we cleaned up and relaxed together, enjoying the quiet. After the plane crash, you never had time for me."

"Every day you withdrew further into the bottle. I had to take care of things."

"I wouldn't have withdrawn if you had been there for me."

That's not really true. I was so addicted by then it wouldn't have mattered what Beth did. She knows that.

"I would have been there for you, but I had to take over your responsibilities."

"We were at cross purposes, weren't we?"

"I suppose we were."

"But is it enough to lose a marriage over?"

"It's not just that. It's the months after that, when you were off finding yourself and I was a struggling single mother. That's what did it for me."

"It must have been hard."

"You have no idea. Juggling work and the household, taking care of the boys and managing the finances. Lots of women do it, but I was thrown into it without warning. And on the day I married you, the last thing I expected was you would abandon me."

I reach for her hand. It's a reflex action, from over twenty-five years of being together.

She looks into my eyes.

I pull her close to me. She doesn't resist. I kiss her. We sit together on our green couch and start to relive one of my fondest memories. We're close again.

But she stops me.

"No, Brad."

"Yes, Beth. Please."

"In two months you'll be gone, and I'll be on my own again. That's the way it has to be."

"Why don't you want me, Beth?"

"I do want you, but it won't work."

"It will work. We just need to try."

"No, Brad. I love you, but it's no use." She pulls away and rushes down the hall to her bedroom.

I kick the couch. I pace. I call Bill. I pray. Allah, please give me strength.

Part Five

Living with her has been harder since that night. Sometimes I think I should take my gym bag and go back to Joshua's house until I find a place of my own. I'm tired of this farce. But I want to be close to my boys. And I want to be close to her.

A week after the chili incident, Umar invites us over for an impromptu barbecue, taking advantage of an unseasonably warm day before the start of another long winter. I don't want to go, but Chris and Joshua will be there. The four of us climb into my old yellow friend, Celeste, and pretend to be a family.

Matt says, "What's this?"

It's the package for Mom.

"Nothing important." I put it in the trunk and hit the road.

"I can't believe this old thing still runs," says Beth.

"This is a cool car," says Matt. "You did a great job."

Kyle hasn't said anything to me for a long time.

The barbecue is okay. When I was on the road, I occasionally remembered moments like this—talking and playing soccer with my brothers—but I remembered them as being happier.

Thankfully, no one asks about our marriage. They can probably tell.

Everyone is quiet on the way back. When we get out of the car, Matt holds up a handful of seashells. "I found these back here."

"Yeah, I picked those up for you on the beach. I know you like shells."

"You were thinking about me?"

"I thought about you a lot. And Kyle, too."

"And Mom?"

"Especially Mom."

As we walk back into the apartment, before Beth goes to sit in her room, I ask her, "Do you remember the day we met?"

242

"That was so many years ago. I have more important things to think about."

"It was raining. You were carrying your clothes home from the laundromat. I offered you a ride in my brand new, yellow Toyota Celica. Remember? You're the one who named her."

"My mother always told me not to accept rides from strangers. I should have listened to her." She walks away.

Beth and Kyle avoid me. Only Matt makes me feel connected. There are so many things I never knew about him. I guess I neglected Beth and Kyle, too, all those years when I thought I was being a good husband and father.

I am feeling better about myself. The meetings help. Bill helps more. Islam helps the most. Now I pray with my heart. It makes a difference.

My forty-ninth birthday comes and goes. Beth doesn't say anything, but when I walk in from work, Matt says, "Happy birthday, Dad!" and hands me a homemade card.

"Thanks." I pull him close. He's only an inch or so shorter than me, but he's still my little boy.

Four weeks left. I've done my best. She was right. It's no use.

Joshua calls on Wednesday morning to tell me he's a grandfather. "Raheema had the baby this morning. It is a girl."

"Congratulations, old man. Grandpa Joshua. You'd better get used to it."

"I'd better." He laughs. "Yesterday Jennifer told me she's pregnant. I can't wait to be called grandpa. And that makes you a great uncle."

"I feel my age every morning. Tell Jeremy and Raheema congratulations. I'll come visit my little grandniece in a few days. Maybe I can persuade Beth to come with me."

"How are things?"

"Keep that bed in Jamal's room ready."

"You're welcome here any time. You know that, Brother."

"I know." Someone still wants me.

Beth walks in and heads straight for her room.

"Wait. I have good news."

"What?" she says sharply.

"Raheema had her baby."

She smiles. The first smile I've seen since the night of the chili. "That's nice. Jeremy and Raheema are a sweet couple. I'm happy for them."

"Would you like to go with me to visit them?"

"I don't know. I do want to see the baby. While you were gone, Jeremy and Raheema often came to visit, and they never came empty-handed. It would make sense to go together, I suppose. Let's go on Saturday. I'll stop by the store tomorrow and buy something sweet and frilly. It will be fun picking out clothes for a little girl."

"You never did get your daughter, did you?"

"No, I never did."

I reach for my wallet and offer her some bills. "This is my share."

"I'll take care of it. I'm used to taking care of things." She turns and heads for the kitchen. Halfway there she stops and looks at me. "Would you like chicken for dinner tonight?"

"Yes, chicken would be nice."

She won't let me contribute to the present, so I'll buy something on my own. I stop at a store on my way home from work, but I don't know what to buy for a little girl. I don't know what to buy for a boy either. Beth always took care of those things.

I wander around the store, trying to get my bearings. I don't know what babies need. Beth knows. I finally settle on a little pink teddy bear. I hope she likes it.

I'm walking out with the teddy bear when I notice the florist's shop next door. I glance at the display in the window. I remember.

They make a nice arrangement for me and put it in a fancy vase. I walk into the apartment and place the vase on the kitchen table.

She walks in thirty minutes later, puts down her briefcase, and heads for her bedroom. I wait while she changes and relaxes in her room. She'll be out soon. I sit on the couch and pretend to read the paper.

She must have had a rough day because she stays in there longer than usual. Finally she walks into the kitchen. I listen. She laughs.

I hear the sounds of pots and pans, and the refrigerator door opening and closing. A familiar aroma wafts through the living room. An hour passes. She hasn't said anything. Maybe I was wrong.

I'm still pretending to read the paper when she walks out of the kitchen and calls Matt for dinner. I wait for her to say something. She ignores me.

I did it again. She hates them. I lie down on the couch and close my eyes.

"Brad."

I open my eyes. She's standing over me.

"Would you like to come eat with us?"

"Sure."

The orchids are in their vase, in the middle of the table. Beth hums as she pulls up her chair.

"Matt, could you pass the meatloaf to your father?"

That's what I smelled. Her meatloaf. She made it all the time when we were first married. Later, she confessed it was all she knew how to cook back then. She knows I have always loved the way she makes it.

She's a beautiful baby. They've named her Nadia. Jeremy is grinning. I remember feeling that way when Kyle was small. It's too bad they stop being cute.

We give Raheema the presents. Beth bought several little outfits and some practical baby things. Raheema examines a pink dress and smiles. "Thank you so much, Aunt Beth. It's beautiful."

When I give her the pink teddy bear, she sets it aside. "Thank you. It's cute."

I hope Nadia likes it.

Raheema lets me hold the baby. I'd forgotten how tiny they are. I keep remembering Kyle.

We stay for an hour maybe before heading back in silence.

"She's a beautiful baby," I say finally.

"She is. Those dark eyes and her thick black hair. And that little round face."

"She must get her hair and eyes from Raheema, but do you remember Jeremy when he was small? He had the roundest little face I've ever seen on a child."

"It seems like it was only last year. Now he's a father."

"Do you remember when Kyle was born? He was the most beautiful baby I have ever seen. Smart, too. He smiled at me on the day he was born. Did I ever tell you that?"

"All the time. Everyone else said it was gas, but I always thought it was a smile. He talked before he could walk. He was a good baby." She sighs. "I wish I had stayed home with him longer instead of going back to work. He'll never need me like he did then."

"I wish I had spent more time with him when he was young. I always thought I was a good father. Now I remember how much I neglected you and the boys."

"You tried. You cheered at their games and helped them with their schoolwork. You were a good dad, when you were sober. It wasn't all bad."

"But it was bad enough. Don't you ever wish we could start over?"

"Haven't you noticed the gray hairs? I'm not the young grad student you fell in love with. I have a grown son, and a retirement plan, and I'm tired. I'm too old to start over."

I reach for her hand. "Does your accountant know you have a weakness for strawberries? Has he seen that scar on your right knee, and does he know you got it from falling off your skateboard when you were eight? Does he know you practically lived off peanut butter and jelly during your two years of grad school? Has he seen you come in from a snowball fight, your entire face red from the cold? Has he seen the look in your eyes as you nurse your newborn son? Could he ever know you the way I do?"

She pulls away. "We can make new memories of our own," she says softly.

"Wouldn't you rather adjust to a new life with this old guy than try to start fresh with someone new?"

She's quiet. When we get back to the apartment she goes to her room. I pray before stretching out on the couch. It takes me a long time to fall asleep. I wish I could reach her.

My Son

It is a wise father that knows his own child.

—William Shakespeare

Part One

I'm jolted awake by the phone. It's dark. I dash to answer, glancing at the clock on my way. 2 AM. It can't be good news.

"Hello?"

"I need to speak with the parents of Kyle Adams."

He doesn't need to say another word. My son. My chest constricts.

"This is his father," I say quietly.

"Your son has been in an accident." I barely hear the rest. When I hang up, I know Kyle is still alive, he's in the hospital, and I need to go to him.

We need to go. I quickly get dressed and knock on her bedroom door.

"Beth, wake up."

She has always been a sound sleeper. When Kyle was a baby, I brought him to her for his midnight feedings. When he finished, I burped him, changed his diaper, and put him back in his crib. I miss those times. I didn't know how happy we were.

I knock again. No answer. I walk softly into her room. She looks so peaceful. I wish I could let her sleep. I could go to the hospital alone. In the morning, I'd tell her how I panicked, only to learn he needed a few stitches. We would laugh. Beth would thank me for letting her sleep through it.

But he said we need to come immediately. I think it's more than a few stitches this time.

I touch her shoulder. "Beth, Kyle is in the hospital."

She shoots up. "What happened? How is he?"

"They just called. He's been in an accident. We need to go."

"Give me two minutes."

We drive silently through city streets, hoping for the best, and fearing the worst.

We walk into the emergency room. "We're the parents of Kyle Adams."

"Have a seat, please. Someone will be with you soon," the woman at the check-in desk says.

She turns back to her work. We sit on the hard plastic seats.

She said soon. It's only a minute or so, but it feels like eternity.

"Mr. and Mrs. Adams?" It's someone in a white coat.

"How is our son?"

"He's critically injured and needs immediate surgery."

"What's wrong?"

"He has several broken bones and internal bleeding."

"Can we see him?"

"Not yet. I'm sorry. One of you needs to sign the forms so we can get him into surgery."

"I'll do it." I'm walking to the nurses' station when I hear a loud moan. That's what you can expect in an emergency room. Some people can't control themselves.

I'm nearly finished filling out and signing forms when a nurse says, "You should go take care of your wife."

"Are you talking to me?"

She points in the direction of the plastic chairs. Beth is doubled over, sobbing. Is that Beth?

I need to go to her. I sign my name without reading and pass the stack to the nurse. "Make sure my son gets into surgery." I rush to Beth.

Beth never gets emotional. She is never frantic. That's what Ann said. Is this how she acted when I left? Is this what I did to her?

I hold her tighter.

Gradually she calms down. I stroke her head.

"He'll be okay." I don't know if I believe that.

She's still crying. She whispers, "My baby," over and over again.

The hours pass. We sit on the plastic chairs, waiting for someone to tell us he's okay. No one comes.

I glance outside. It's getting light. I need to pray, but I hate to leave Beth. I could skip it this time, or at least wait until we hear from the doctor.

But I don't want to become weak again. And I need to pray for Kyle. I kiss Beth on the head. "I have to pray, honey. I'll be right back."

She holds on. It's hard to tear myself away. "Come soon," she whispers.

I find a corner, face Makkah, and say my prayer, asking Allah to let him live.

As I'm finishing, two nurses walk by.

"Have all the parents been notified?"

"I don't know. It's so sad. Only one of those kids is still alive, and they don't know if he'll make it."

My eyes blur. I quickly wipe them and go back to Beth.

We've been here for nearly four hours. Still no word.

"Will he be okay?" Beth whispers.

If I were talking to the calm, rational Beth, I would discuss my hopes and fears with her. I would probably even tell her what I overheard. But she's not the rational Beth, she's the frantic mother. I stroke her head.

"He'll be okay."

"What about Matt? He'll wake up and wonder where we are."

"I'll call him."

"Come right back."

I'm not sure how to break it to Matt. I use general terms—accident, hospital—and tell him, "Don't worry. He'll be okay."

I planned to stop lying, but this isn't the right time.

"I need to be there, too, Dad."

"I can't come for you. I'll let you know."

I hang up and call Joshua. I know he's awake.

"Kyle was in an accident. We're at the hospital. Matt is at home. Could you bring him?"

"I'm on my way."

I go to Beth and wait.

We're still waiting when Matt walks in with Joshua, Nuruddin, and Jamal. Beth holds Matt close to her. I shake hands with Joshua and the boys.

"We don't know yet. He's still in surgery. Pray for him."

"I am."

"Could you call Chris and let him know?"

"No problem. What about Beth's family?"

"She'll call them when we know something."

Joshua goes to make the call. We wait.

Chris walks in and hugs me. Theological differences don't matter now.

"He'll come through it. He'll be okay."

I don't think Chris believes that any more than I do.

We're still sitting, numb, when a doctor approaches. We've been here for over five hours.

"Mr. and Mrs. Adams?"

"How is he?"

"He came through the surgery. We were able to stop the bleeding. We're doing everything we can for him."

"Where is he? Can we see him?"

"He's been admitted to intensive care, in critical condition. You two may see him now. Everyone else will have to wait here."

We follow the doctor, our hands clasped.

"He's in a medically-induced coma," says the doctor. "Don't expect any response."

He takes us to Kyle. I wasn't prepared for this.

He is completely immobilized. A black metal device—I think it's called a halo—surrounds his head and extends to his chest. He has an oxygen mask, and tubes running down his throat. His chest is bare, encased in bandaging. He lies there, still and pale.

He looks broken. Can he be fixed?

"Can I touch him?" Beth says softly. The doctor nods.

She holds Kyle's hand and whispers words of love. She caresses his fingers.

"We're here, Kyle. Come back to us."

At first, all I see are the machines and equipment keeping him alive. Then I stare at his face, partially obscured by the oxygen mask and the feeding tube. He has whiskers on his chin, but he looks like my little boy again. I used to go in to kiss him goodnight and stare at him, wondering at the miracle Beth and I had created. Now I ask Allah to heal my son, whom He created.

Beth keeps talking to him. Softly. Gently. I have so many things I want to say, but the last time we talked, we argued. I don't want to upset him. I stay quiet.

My son. I never took the time to really know you. I hope it's not too late.

～

She stays by his bedside, leaving only to call her family. Don and Ann will fly out. Her brother and sister can't come, but they say they'll pray for us.

We keep a silent vigil. Wake up, Kyle. Be well again. Be whole. I love you.

I leave to talk with my brothers. Chris will meet Beth's parents at the airport. Joshua will take care of Matt. Matt wants to see Kyle, but they say he's too young. I don't want him to see his brother this way. Bruised, broken, and much too still.

Don and Ann arrive early Monday morning. We all hug. Then we turn back to Kyle.

We've had so many hopes and dreams for him. Now our only hope is he won't die.

～

Bill calls after the breakfast rush. I was supposed to be at work.

"Are you okay, Brad?"

I tell him about Kyle. "I don't think I can come in yet. I need to be here."

"Of course you do. Don't worry about it. But are you okay?"

"The last thing I need right now is a drink."

"I'll pray for him. Let me know, will you?"

～

Wednesday is Christmas Day. My first Christmas as a Muslim. No one celebrates. We all watch Kyle, waiting for signs he'll come back to us. I know he's heavily sedated, but I keep willing him to open his eyes.

On Thursday morning, Pastor Mueller walks in and takes Beth aside for a moment of prayer. I follow. "Whatever you say to my wife, you can say to me."

He looks at our clasped hands. "That's good." He says a long prayer. I wait. After he leaves, I go to the corner to pray.

On Saturday afternoon, Kyle's doctor takes us aside. "His condition is still critical, but there's a very good chance he'll come out of it."

"Thank God!" says Beth. We hug.

"Alhamdulillah," I whisper.

"But," Dr. Brooks continues.

I don't want to hear "but."

"He does have a spinal cord injury."

"What does that mean?"

I hope I'm wrong.

"There is paralysis."

He's alive. I should be thankful.

"Will he walk again?"

"There are several new treatments available, but with the level of damage Kyle has sustained, I would have to say it is very unlikely."

"How certain are you?"

"I wouldn't get my hopes up," he says quietly. He might as well be shouting.

Beth puts on a smile. "He's alive. That's what counts."

While Beth and Dr. Brooks discuss the details of Kyle's condition, I remember the day I was hit by the car. I wish I was the one with the spinal cord injury.

What will this mean for his future? No more football, that's certain. He can still become an engineer. Being disabled didn't stop Hendricks from worming his way into my job. But this is my son we're talking about. This kind of thing happens to jerks like Hendricks. Not Kyle.

He'll live. I need to remember that.

But he will probably never walk again.

I plan to return to work on Sunday. I'll need to work twice as hard to pay these medical bills. I go back to the apartment on Saturday night for the first time since we received the phone call. Beth stays with Kyle. I ask Chris to come with me and clean out the beer from Kyle's room. I don't trust myself.

I pick up the accumulated mail and newspapers. It's on the front page. The accident. I stare at the picture. There's almost nothing left of the car. I put the paper down and try to wish it away. A moment later I look again. There were six kids in the car that night. Chicago watched as five families buried their children. One clings to life.

I try to settle into the couch, but I'm restless. I call Bill, who offers to stay the night. He arrives as Chris is leaving.

"Thanks for helping my brother," says Chris.

Bill smiles and pats my back. "We've got to stick together."

We alcoholics. We addicts. It's an exclusive club. The price of membership is steep.

I stop at the hospital on my way to work. "Call me if anything happens."

"I will," says Beth. "Don't you think he's looking a little better?"

I nod, but all I see are the ventilator, the feeding tube, and the halo. My son is in there somewhere.

We have a large lunch crowd and it's noisy. I rush the burgers and fries, and worry about Kyle. What if I can't hear my cell phone? Whenever I can, I check for messages.

It never rings. He's still alive.

Tonight is New Year's Eve. The first time in over twenty years I've spent the holiday sober.

Don and Ann are eating in the cafeteria. Beth sits next to Kyle. I stand at the window, thinking about New Year's past. The room is quiet except for the hum of the machines keeping our son alive.

Beth speaks over the silence. "It's been almost sixteen weeks."

I glance at her. "I'd better pack up my gym bag."

She walks over and touches my shoulder. "I want you to stay."

"Are you sure?"

"You're Kyle's father. He needs two parents waiting for him when he wakes up."

"Am I still your husband?"

She smiles. "Do you remember the night you proposed? It's been twenty-eight years. Can you believe it?"

I gaze at the black sky. "The world was ours that night. I thought we could accomplish anything as long as we were together."

She touches my cheek. "And we can."

We're still kissing when Don and Ann walk in. They stop in the doorway. We pull away from each other, embarrassed.

"Beth, would you like to go home tonight?" says Ann. "We can stay here with Kyle."

"No, I need to be here. Dad and you need to rest. Brad will give you a ride back to the hotel."

"Are you sure?"

"Yes, Mom. I need to stay here with Kyle until he wakes up."

We all know better than to argue with Beth. Thirty minutes later, as we're walking out, she grabs my hand and squeezes it. "I'll see you tomorrow."

"Yeah. I'll see you."

After dropping Don and Ann off, I call Bill. "I just left the hospital. Would you like some company tonight?"

"I'm having a little party with my kids. You're welcome to join us."

On my way there I pick up two large pizzas—no pepperoni—and a couple bottles of Coke.

∾

On Wednesday evening, while Beth and her parents eat dinner, I sit alone with Kyle and study him. He has Beth's soft brown hair, high cheekbones, and small round mouth. He has my eyes. I want to see his eyes again.

He's the man who ignored me. He's the boy who used to depend on me. He is my son. I touch his face. "Kyle, it's Dad. I love you." That's all I can say.

∼

Eighteen days after the accident, Dr. Brooks says he'll cut back on the sedatives and start bringing Kyle out of the coma. "It's up to him now."

While I rush to fill the orders, I wait for the call. "He's awake," she'll say. Every day, I wait.

∼

On Sunday afternoon, she calls. "They're removing the ventilator. He's ready to breathe on his own."

"Is he awake?"

"No, but he's breathing. That's a start."

When Kyle was a newborn, I came home from work and Beth would say, "He smiled" or "He looked right at me." We were excited all evening about every small milestone. Now we feel a little better because he can breathe.

His breathing is strong, but by Thursday he still hasn't come out of the coma. It's been nearly a month. Will he ever wake up?

∼

On Sunday morning, he moans. That's all. But it's something. We call friends and relatives to share the news.

On Tuesday evening, he moves his right hand. Beth gasps. "Did you see that?"

On Friday, he moves his left hand. Beth calls me at work. "He's coming back to us."

We go through another week of increments. A twitch. A moan. Occasional agitation. When he moves his head slightly on Thursday, Beth jumps. "He's waking up."

"No," says Don. "It was involuntary."

On Saturday, I'm removing a basket of french fries from boiling oil when my phone rings. I drop the fries and grab the phone. "What happened?"

"He opened his eyes."

"I'll come as soon as I can."

My arms and legs sting in places where the hot oil splashed. I quickly rinse my burns. After cleaning up the mess and feeding the lunch crowd, I tell Bill I need to go.

"Stay with your family tomorrow," he says. "I'll be okay."

I nod and rush out the door.

"Kyle, you're awake." I burst into his room.

"He's sleeping now," says Don.

"But Beth said he opened his eyes."

"He did. The doctor says he will go through periods of sleeping and wakefulness before he's completely alert."

"How long will he sleep?"

"There's no way to tell."

I touch his hand. "Wake up, Kyle," I whisper.

I call Joshua and ask him to keep Matt. I'm not leaving.

On Sunday afternoon, Kyle's eyelids flutter and he mutters. His vital signs are good. I call Bill and my brothers with the update. We wait.

On Monday morning, he opens his eyes and stares for a full two minutes and twenty seconds before closing them again. Beth kisses his cheek. "That's it, Kyle. Good job."

On Tuesday, he raises his hand and seems to be reaching. Beth rushes to him. "I'm here." He seems to smile.

On Wednesday, he acts agitated. Random violent movements. He mutters unintelligibly. His heart rate increases. Beth soothes him. A nurse administers a mild sedative.

Not much happens on Thursday. He opens his eyes twice, briefly. That's all.

On Friday, he opens his mouth and tries to speak. I can't understand what he's saying. He breathes rapidly. The nurse keeps a watchful eye.

"He's calling for Amy," says Beth.

How can she tell?

"Who's Amy?"

She pulls me aside and whispers. "His girlfriend. She died in the crash."

On Saturday, he reaches for Beth and says, "Mom." She grasps his arm and cries.

He's still awake when Dr. Brooks walks in to examine him. Fifteen minutes later, the doctor leads us outside.

"Kyle is showing remarkable progress."

"What about his spinal cord?" I ask.

"I can't be certain until he's fully awake and I can order more tests, but based on his movements and a preliminary exam, I would say the paralysis is in the lower area. Probably a T-9 or T-10." He indicates the area on his own back. "Basically, he is paralyzed from the waist down. He will need months of therapy to increase his upper body strength and learn how to live with his disability, but he has made tremendous progress."

Therapy. Disability. Those aren't words I want to hear in connection with my son.

Before we walk back into the room, Beth turns to me. "Do you remember the day we went to see Jeremy's baby? I said I regretted going back to work when Kyle was small. I want to make it up to him now. I've decided to quit my job and take care of him. What do you think?"

"What about the health insurance?"

"It won't cover most of these bills, especially since Kyle knowingly rode in a car with a drunk driver, and he himself was drunk. They rarely pay out in those cases. I've already spoken with social services. They'll help us find assistance."

"If that's what you want, then you should go ahead. Do you think it's time to put the house up for sale?"

"I'll miss it, but I don't think we have a choice."

Bill calls in the evening, at his usual time. "Are you okay?"

I ask about rearranging my hours to accommodate a second job. "Assuming, of course, you still want me to work for you."

"Go ahead and look for that job. I'll make the arrangements."

Bill isn't just my sponsor. I feel he's been sent by Allah to watch out for me.

On Monday, Kyle stays awake. They remove the feeding tube and put him on a soft diet. Beth feeds him pureed bananas, just as she did seventeen years ago. He's groggy, but responsive. He's alive.

I spend every hour I can with him. On Thursday, he says, "Dad." I hide my tears.

He's progressing rapidly. On Friday, he asks to see Matt. On Saturday, he asks about his friends.

"Where's Amy? What about Steve?"

"Don't worry about them right now," says Beth. "You need to concentrate on getting well."

He persists. "Where are they? I want to see them."

"They can't come right now."

"I have to see Amy."

"Settle down, honey," Beth says. "We'll talk about them later."

"Where is she? I need to see her." He's becoming agitated.

"It's okay, honey. You have to stay calm."

"No, I need Amy." He's sobbing.

Beth tries to soothe him, but he pushes her away. I buzz for a nurse.

"Where's Amy?" he cries out. "Why won't you let me see her?"

Beth continues to calm him until the nurse comes with a sedative. He eases back into his pillow.

Our son is alive. Now we have to tell him his friends are dead.

He sleeps soundly. But on Saturday morning, when I'm alone with him in the room, he asks again.

"Where's Amy, Dad? I have to know."

I can't tell him. I look away. "Wait until your mother gets back. She'll tell you."

"I want to see her. I need to know she's okay."

I pat his arm. "The important thing, Kyle, is you're back. We thought we had lost you."

"Are you back?"

"Yes, your mother and I worked things out. I'm back."

"That's great," he says, but he's frowning.

"Hold on." I rush out and wait for Beth in the hallway. When she heads for the room, I stop her. "You have to tell him."

"I don't think he's ready yet. It might delay his recovery."

"But he won't give up. We can't keep sedating him."

"And you want me to tell him?"

"You're closer to him. I didn't even know Amy."

"Yes, you did. They've been together since they were fourteen. She came to our house all the time."

When he was fourteen, we lived in Evanston and I was still an engineer, but I don't remember.

"I don't know what we should do."

"We should talk to Dr. Brooks first," says Beth.

"I agree, but you'll have to find a way to stall him."

We walk in together. He's waiting. "Mom, I need to see Amy."

"You must be hungry."

"No. I need Amy. Why won't you let me see her?"

"Wait until you're stronger, honey."

"Seeing Amy will make me stronger."

"Let me talk with Dr. Brooks first, okay? Now open your mouth and eat some of this delicious oatmeal."

He obeys. I never realized what a fantastic mother she is.

The minute Dr. Brooks walks in on Monday morning, Kyle asks. "Will you let me see Amy?"

"I'm sorry. No visitors outside of immediate family until you are out of ICU."

"How long will that be?"

"A few more weeks."

Kyle closes his eyes.

I grab Dr. Brooks outside. "I don't like it. He thinks he's going to see her."

"See who?"

"Amy."

"Is that his girlfriend?"

"She died in the accident. He needs to be told."

The doctor sighs. "Put it off a little longer if you can. He will be upset no matter when you tell him, but he's still very vulnerable. I'm afraid this news could impede his recovery."

"But when he finds out he'll think we lied to him."

"Yes, but he'll be better able to handle it."

I need to find another job. A garage near the hospital needs a mechanic. It's not engineering, but I can work with my hands. Working with machines. That's why I became an engineer in the first place.

I go there Tuesday before work. When the owner asks about my experience, I show him my old friend Celeste. "I have rebuilt this car from bumper to bumper. Check out her fuel system. Two hundred and fifty miles to the gallon. She runs on solar energy and vegetable oil. I just took her on a 12,000 mile trip around the country. Mountains, deserts, she handled them all."

He takes ten minutes to examine my work—looking under the hood, studying the fuel and exhaust systems, checking out my revamped interior. I start tomorrow.

Bill schedules me for evenings and weekends. I wanted to stop working so hard.

Kyle has been awake for three weeks. They just moved him out of ICU. Tomorrow he starts therapy.

When he's all set up in his new room, he asks, "Can I see Amy now?"

Beth answers. "No, honey, you can't."

"But she can visit me now, can't she?"

"No, she can't come."

"I thought you liked her."

"I do, Kyle."

"Then why won't you let me see her?"

Beth comes closer and puts her face next to his. She whispers, "I'm sorry, honey. You can't see her."

"But I have to. What's wrong?"

Beth shakes her head, tears running down her cheeks. Kyle looks at me. I look down.

"No! She's okay!" he shouts. "I was right next to her. I wouldn't let her get hurt. Where is she? Why won't you let me see her? You're lying! Nothing happened to her. Tell her I need her. I know she'll come." He sobs. "Tell her. I need her." Beth holds him close, like she did when he was little, but this nightmare won't go away.

A nurse gives him a sedative. He falls asleep in Beth's arms.

I stop by in the morning on my way to the garage. "How are you feeling, Kyle?"

He turns away.

I come again after closing up the diner. Beth meets me in the hall. Her eyes are red.

"They took him to therapy, but he refused to try. He won't even talk to me."

"I guess he needs time to mourn. He was very close to Amy, wasn't he?"

She nods. "I think they planned to get married someday."

Every day it's the same thing. Kyle won't try, won't talk, and barely eats. Beth brings Mueller in but Kyle turns away. I ask Umar to come. He stays with Kyle for thirty minutes. On his way out he shakes his head. "Give him another week."

We're spending our lives waiting. Will he live? Will he wake up? Will he get over losing Amy?

Don and Ann are flying back to Ohio. I drive them to the airport on Thursday night.

They haven't said anything about the time I showed up on their doorstep. Don waits until we're halfway to the airport. "I suppose you worked out whatever was bothering you."

"I guess you know I'm a Muslim."

"I don't understand that, but you're back with my daughter and grandsons. You have a regular job—two jobs, even. It's not what I would have chosen, but Beth seems happy."

"I'm trying to make it up to her."

"Next time you feel an itch, Brad, go out and buy a boat."

"Whatever happened to your boat?"

"I sold it last year to another middle-aged man. He told me later his wife went through the roof when he brought that thing home, but it made him happy, and she got used to it. Now they go fishing together every weekend."

I hug them at the airport.

"We'll be back in about a month," says Ann. "I need to spend more time with my grandsons."

"I'll see you two in a month then."

"You will still be here, won't you?"

"Yes, Dad, I'll be here."

Kyle is still mourning and I can't stop worrying. Two days after Don and Ann leave, I duck into a convenience store for a carton of cigarettes. I haven't smoked in twelve years, but I need something to get me through this. When I walk into the hospital room, Beth smells my clothes and frowns.

I shrug. "It's better than going back to the bottle."

"Don't do it around us."

My brothers come nearly every day, usually bringing their sons with them. Chris disapproves of my new lifestyle, but he always shows up when I need him.

For eight days Kyle has barely eaten, barely spoken. Beth cries often. I don't know what to do.

Every day, Matt has tried to get through to him. Talking about video games and telling jokes. Tonight when Joshua brings him, Matt goes over and hugs his brother. I don't think I've ever seen them hug.

"Don't worry," says Matt. "You'll be okay."

Kyle lifts his arms. Matt goes closer. Kyle breaks down.

My eyes blur. Joshua hugs me. It's great to have a brother.

I'm wiped out. Besides work and the hospital, I still go to AA two or three times a week. Bill comes with me.

A new guy showed up tonight. At the end of the meeting we're standing around, drinking coffee and smoking, when a woman walks in and takes his arm. "How was your meeting, Nick? Are you ready to go?"

"Celia?"

"Brad? What are you doing here?" She laughs nervously. "Never mind."

"They say it's genetic."

"They're probably right. This is my husband. Nick, this is Brad, my half-brother."

I put down my cigarette and shake his hand. "Welcome to the club." I turn to my sister. "What about you?"

"I never drank. My job was to take care of our father. Anyway," she says, her arm around Nick's waist, "we're making a clean break with the past."

"Good luck with that. I still can't escape his ghost."

"He was a hard man to live with, but in some ways I miss him."

"I guess you do." I sure can't imagine wanting him back.

"It's nice to see you, Brad. Take care." She hugs me. "We'll have to get together sometime."

"Sure."

As Bill and I head for my car, I silently curse Sam and the legacy he left his children.

"You never said you had a sister," says Bill.

"The first time I met her was when our father died. He left us for her mother when I was seven. It's not Celia's fault he left. But I can barely stand to think of Sam."

"It's not your fault either."

"Yeah."

～

Kyle is talking now and cooperating with the therapist. Beth told him about his other friends, and he took it well. I guess he's worked through his grief.

The police came to question him last week. Thank God he wasn't driving, or he'd be facing manslaughter charges. His friend, Steve, was the driver. He's buried now.

Three boys come to visit on a Saturday, more than two months after the accident. Greasy hair, torn jeans. They're loud, too. I watch, looking for a reason to kick them out.

One boy says, "You really laid one on, didn't you?"

"Yeah," says Kyle, "that was one hell of a hangover."

"What was the car doing when you went over that hill?" another boy asks.

"Hundred, maybe a hundred and ten. We were flying." Kyle sounds proud.

"I wish I'd been there."

"You'd be dead." Kyle laughs.

"Yeah," says the first boy, "he'd be good and dead."

I hold my tongue. After they leave I lash out at Kyle.

"Do you think it's funny? 'One hell of a hangover.' Five kids died in that crash."

"I know, Dad." He turns away.

Maybe I came on too strong. I put my hand on his shoulder. He pulls away from me.

On the last Saturday in February, Beth sets up a miniature Christmas tree in the hospital room. Chris and his family walk in loaded down with presents. It's important to Beth to have this belated festivity. I don't celebrate Christmas anymore. I watch.

I receive presents, too. New shirts, pants, and pajamas from Beth. New shirts and a Bible from Chris. Don and Ann sent new shirts and a model sailboat. Are they trying to tell me something?

At night, we go back to the apartment and Beth finally gives me a haircut. Handfuls of black hair drop to the floor. When it's done, she smiles. "That's my present."

"You won't ask me to get rid of the beard, will you?"

She strokes my cheek. "No. I think I would miss it."

Our marriage is back on track. After New Year's Eve, we both knew. No fireworks. Just comfort.

～

I want to connect with Kyle, but I'm afraid of saying the wrong thing. I end up saying nothing at all.

He leaves the hospital tomorrow. They'll take him by ambulance to a rehab center in St. Louis. It's the closest we could find specializing in paraplegic injuries.

I want to fix our relationship before he goes. When Chris comes I ask him, "How do you connect with your son?"

"You love him."

"Of course I love him. What else?"

"It's not always as easy as it sounds. Be firm. Be his friend. Make sure he always knows you love him."

"That sounds too easy."

"Try it."

Later, I ask Joshua. He tells me, "Treat him the way you wish our father had treated you."

That is easy. "I wish Dad had loved me."

Joshua smiles. "You just answered your own question."

I think I have this figured out, but I ask Jeremy when he comes.

"I haven't been a father very long," he says, "but I have been a son. My dad was always there for me. I hope I can be as good a father as he is."

I find it amusing that Joshua is a better father than I am, but the proof is in the pudding. He has five sons, all happy and secure. I have two sons. I'm awkward with Kyle, and I'm still getting to know Matt. I don't know why I can't connect.

～

Before Kyle and Beth leave for St. Louis, I take another stab at it.

The ambulance is waiting and Kyle is ready for the trip. "I'll miss you," I say.

He's silent.

"I hope you do well so you can live a normal life."

"Normal? How can I ever be normal again?"

I don't know how to respond. They take him away. "I love you, Kyle," I whisper.

Beth Speaks Out

I put the phone down. Brad sounds like he's doing well. I hope he doesn't do anything stupid.

I lean against the headboard and stare at the TV. There's nothing to watch. I walk to the window and look out at the hotel parking lot, missing my family.

Kyle's therapy is progressing nicely. I go to the center every day to see how I can help. Most of the time, I do nothing but watch.

Today, he got into the pool. He started out slowly, but before the end of the session he was swimming. It was great to see him active again. For a few minutes, I think he forgot about his disability.

I need to go to sleep. I want to be at the center early in the morning. He has a basketball game. I can't wait.

Before I sleep, I fold my hands. "Please, God, take care of them. Make Kyle strong. Help him get used to his new life. Protect Matt. Let him know how much I love him. And please, God, please help Brad stay sober."

Part Two

Matt and I manage, day by day. We eat a lot of hamburgers. He spends a lot of time alone.

Beth calls every night with an update. At first, Kyle refused to try. Slowly, she says, he's coming out of his shell. When she called tonight, she was frustrated because a staff member told her not to come to the center tomorrow. They want Kyle to be more independent.

"He needs me."

"I know he does, honey, but they know what they're doing."

"I'm his mother. I need to be there."

I don't tell her I'm glad they're making her stay away. She wouldn't understand.

They've been gone for a month. Matt and I drive down on a Friday afternoon. Kyle is watching TV with other patients. A roomful of wheelchairs.

Matt runs and hugs him. "Hey, Kyle."

I offer my hand. "Hi, Kyle. How are you?"

"Hi, Dad. Glad you could come."

He takes us to the room he shares with another boy. "Look at this." He hauls himself out of the wheelchair into his bed, and back again.

"Cool," says Matt. "Could you teach me how to do that?"

"Sorry. It's a special skill. Only a crip can do it."

Crip. The term makes me uncomfortable, but I stay quiet. I soon learn from listening to Kyle and his roommate that many of the boys refer to themselves this way.

I'm a drunk. Who am I to judge?

"That's great, Kyle," I say. "You're really getting the hang of it."

"You should see him." His roommate, Joey, pipes up. "He wins the races almost every night."

"Races?"

"Wheelchair races. We have them in the hallway when no one's looking."

Boys will be boys.

I talk with Kyle and Joey for another hour before heading to the hotel. Joey is from Kansas City. He's only thirteen. He was shot by a boy who had a grudge against his cousin.

On Saturday, we check Kyle out for the day. He swings almost effortlessly from his wheelchair into the front seat of Beth's rental car. As I stow his chair in the trunk, he says, "Next I'm going to learn how to get my chair in and out of the car."

I finally take my family to the Arch. We walk through the museum exhibit on the ground floor before getting in line for the ride up. The capsule is small and claustrophobic.

When we reach the top, I stand behind them, observing their expressions of awe as they survey the city from 600 feet up. This is great. I need to take them to the Grand Canyon someday.

Matt and I leave on Sunday afternoon. Kyle says goodbye in the parking lot.

"Thanks for coming, Dad. It's good to see you."

"Keep up the good work," I reply. Not I love you. I miss you. We hug one more time before I hit the highway.

I am impressed with Kyle's progress. He's adapting well, but I can't help wishing he was headed for college.

His chair is top-of-the-line. An ultralight racing model. I could never have afforded it without Chris's help. He came to me one day soon after Kyle was released from ICU.

"He's looking great, so why do you keep rubbing your neck?"

"He has special needs now. I never thought I'd see my son in a wheelchair, and I don't know how we'll pay for it. Not to mention the months of rehab he'll need."

"Look, Brad," he said, "you were the executor of Mom's estate. When you left, the job went to me. You probably didn't notice, but she left a sizable inheritance. She also made a provision for each grand-child to receive something special when he or she turns eighteen."

"Is that right?"

Could she have known?

"She bought Michael a car and gave Jeremy and Raheema a fur-nished apartment. Ruth and Jennifer have received something from the fund. Now it's Kyle's turn."

"So Michael gets a car and Kyle gets a wheelchair." I couldn't keep the bitterness out of my voice.

"Between the fund and the inheritance, there should be enough for a specially-equipped vehicle for Kyle to drive."

"As long as he doesn't drive drunk."

"That will be your job. It's my job, as executor, to make sure Kyle has what he needs."

"What would Mom say if she were here?"

"She would do everything she could for him. You know that."

So Kyle is staying at a top-notch rehab center and driving a hot-rod wheelchair. But it's only a consolation prize.

Beth and Kyle have been gone for nearly two months. I pick Matt up from school at midday so we can leave early for our monthly visit.

Halfway there, he wants to stop for food. He eats all the time these days. He's growing out of his clothes, too. Maybe Beth can take him shopping tomorrow.

We walk into a fast food place and I give him money. "Get what-ever you want. I'll wait over here."

"Aren't you eating?"

"No. Today is the first day of Ramadan. I'm fasting."

And my doctor just warned me to lay off the burgers and fries.

"Aren't you hungry?"

"A little. I'll be okay."

"If you're not eating, I won't eat either."

I laugh. "You're a growing boy. And look how skinny you're getting. Pretty soon there won't be anything left. Go on, get your food."

When we're back on the highway, he says, "Jamal and Muhammad fast. I think Luqman even fasts sometimes. Why can't I?"

"Your cousins are Muslims."

"If I become a Muslim, will you let me fast?"

I turn to look at him.

"Dad, watch out!" He shouts.

I turn back to the road, narrowly missing the slow car in front of me, and catch my breath. "Yes, Matt, if you become a Muslim, I'll let you fast."

On Saturday, Beth wants to go somewhere special for lunch. "I found the nicest little Italian restaurant. You'll love it."

"I can't, Beth. It's Ramadan. I'm fasting. You and the boys go ahead. I'll stay at the motel."

"Oh," she says. "I guess we'll eat burgers then."

Before I left, Joshua told me I wouldn't need to fast while traveling, but I have to do this. I screwed up so badly before. It took me all year to make up those days I missed, with a lot of encouragement from Joshua. This year I want to get it right.

I'm working almost as many hours as I did as an engineer. But now when I get home, I don't write a report. I collapse.

I'm dozing on the couch when someone buzzes. Matt gets it.

"Who was that, Matt?"

"Michael. He's coming up."

I force myself awake. Michael graduated last week. Joshua went to Worcester for the ceremony. I wish I could have been there.

I open the door and spot him walking down the hall. When he sees me, he picks up his pace. We hug tightly.

"Congratulations, Michael. I am so proud of you."

"Not as proud as I am of you. You're still my role model."

I put on the coffee. "Sorry, I don't have much in the way of refreshments."

"Don't worry about it. Let's just talk."

"Have you found a job yet? It shouldn't be hard, not with your qualifications."

"Didn't I tell you? I was drafted. They let me complete my degree, but I report to Brownsville in August."

"No, I didn't know that." What a waste of talent.

The month has gone quickly. I'm starting to enjoy the fast. Last night, as we ate a late dinner together, Matt said he wants to fast, too. He woke up early this morning and ate suhur with me. He's serious.

At noon, we head out on our monthly trip to St. Louis. "Do you want to stop somewhere for lunch?" I ask him.

"No, I want to keep fasting."

He sleeps most of the way. We pull into St. Louis two hours before sunset. I wake him when we get to the rehab center.

"Is it time yet?" He rubs his eyes.

"No, not quite. How are you feeling?"

"I feel great." He yawns.

We're visiting in Kyle's room when I notice the time. I take the dates and water I brought and hand some to Matt. Beth watches quietly as he imitates me.

He fasts with me on Saturday, too. Beth frets. "Aren't you hungry? You're growing. You need to eat."

"But Luqman fasted eleven days this year. If he can do it, so can I."

She frowns, but stays quiet.

On Sunday morning, I take a shower and wear my best clothes.

"Why are you all dressed up?" Beth asks.

"Today's Eid. I'm going to the prayer."

"Okay. Matt, get ready for church."

"I'm going with Dad."

"But you're not a Muslim." She pauses and looks at me. "Is he?"

"Not yet," says Matt.

She presses her lips together and tugs on her hair, but she lets him come with me.

After the prayer, we meet Beth and Kyle at the rehab center and go for lunch at that Italian restaurant. While we eat, Beth discusses Kyle's progress and many other things, but she avoids talking about Islam. We haven't fought since Kyle got hurt. We'd both rather keep it that way.

Four months after they loaded Kyle into the ambulance, we make the final trip to bring him home. Aisha has loaned me her van.

I walk into Kyle's room. "Are you ready to go?"

"Yeah, sure." The enthusiasm is gone.

"Are you all packed? Matt, help me carry your brother's things out to the car."

Kyle says goodbye to his friends. Matt gets Kyle's suitcase. I try to help him with his wheelchair.

"I can do it myself. Don't you know that by now?"

"I wanted to help."

"I don't need your help."

He has trouble pulling his wheelchair into the van. I move forward to lend a hand. "Butt out," he says. "I've got it."

All the way home, he's quiet. Matt chatters. He insisted on moving his things to the living room to give Kyle more space in the bedroom.

"You don't have to make such a big deal out of it," says Kyle.

Beth and I exchange glances. I thought he had adjusted to his disability.

Part Three

We're finally bringing Kyle home, seven months after the accident. He's been in a bad mood all day. By the time we arrive, I'm not feeling very festive myself, but I try.

"Welcome home," I say as he navigates his chair through the doorway.

"I never liked this apartment," he says.

I had planned to move us out of here if Beth took me back, but Kyle was hurt and Beth quit her job. We'll have to make the best of it.

Kyle settles into his room. I order pizza for dinner. He pulls his chair up to the table, and we sit down to eat together as a real family again. For the first time ever.

"So, Kyle, what are your plans now?"

"I don't know, Dad. I just got home. Give me a break."

Beth shoots me a look. I'll try to be more diplomatic.

"How does it feel to be home?" Beth asks.

"It's okay. I missed my room. Thanks, Matt, for giving up your space."

"No problem. Hey, Grandma bought me a new game. You want to try it out?"

"Sure. But you're not going to beat me. I still got it."

We're cleaning up when Chris and Joshua arrive with their boys and more food. The boys sit around the game, playing and snacking. My brothers and I sit around the table, talking and eating.

"I know you're happy to have him home," says Chris.

"Of course I am."

"You're rubbing your neck."

"The problem is where do we go from here?"

"I didn't think you worried about that anymore," says Joshua.

"I never stopped worrying. And haven't you noticed? The long hair and jeans are gone."

"Everything will come together as long as you love him," says Chris.

"Of course I love him. But..."

"No buts. He needs your love, but he's so much like you he's too stubborn to admit it."

"You're saying I'm stubborn?"

My brothers laugh. I give up.

"Forget about your past dreams and expectations. Work with Kyle on his own terms."

The bitterness. It won't go away. "That's easy for you to say, Joshua. Michael is an engineer. Jeremy is in college. Isaiah is headed for college, too. And you don't have to worry about getting a phone call at 2 AM."

Joshua's smile disappears. "My kids are doing well, alhamdulillah, but you know how messed up I was. And while you were making big bucks, I was throwing my life away. Neither of you knew how bad off I was. There were times when I desperately wanted to get away from it all. Forever. And what I needed was a father who believed in me. When I found that—in Abdul-Qadir and The Doc—I found the strength I needed to pull myself out of it. Don't resent me, Brad. I know what hell feels like, because I've been there. That's why I can give so much to my sons."

He's talking about suicide. I never knew he'd gone that low. "But Kyle has everything he needs to succeed. He just has to try."

"He doesn't have everything. He doesn't have you. You would support him if he were in college and if he hadn't been in that accident. You would support him if he weren't a paraplegic."

"I've never said that, Chris, not to him or anyone."

"It shows. Give him the support he needs. Love him unconditionally and you'll see him succeed, in his own time and his own way."

"Is that how you treat your sons?"

"All of my children. Every kid has problems now and then. Melinda and I decided long ago that no matter what happens we would always love them. And they know it."

Joshua grins. "Even if they became Muslims?"

Chris shakes his head. His jaw tightens. "Let's not go there."

He doesn't know Isaiah is curious about Islam.

Part Four

Joshua and Chris leave. I'm ready to go to bed. Kyle and Matt are still playing the video game.

I put my hand on Kyle's shoulder. "Don't stay up too late."

"Yeah."

"I'm glad you're home."

"Yeah, me too." His eyes never leave the screen.

I walk down the hall and cuddle with Beth.

"Your brothers gave you a hard time?"

"I'm not that bad, am I?"

"You are a little uptight. You like to talk about your months on the road. What if you had met a young man like Kyle during your travels? How would you have treated him?"

"That's different. Kyle is my son."

"I know. You have an investment in his future. But it is his life. You didn't like Evie telling you what to do, but that's exactly how you treat Kyle. Don't worry about his future right now. Just be grateful he's alive."

"I have been worrying about his future since the day you told me you were pregnant."

"All those sunrises and you're still obsessive."

"I am glad he's home."

"Then show him." She kisses me. "I'm glad you're home, too."

Our family is together again. That was the hard part. Now I have to figure out where to go from here.

We have a quiet Sunday. I don't have to work. Beth cooks large meals. The boys play their games.

In the evening, Matt reads a book. Kyle goes into his room and turns on the music. I knock.

"Can I come in?"

"Sure."

The music is loud, and unpleasant to my aging ears, but I can take it. I sit on the edge of the bed and reach over to pat his leg. Then I remember. I pat his arm.

"What's the name of this group?"

"Silver Sky."

"I was into heavy metal. Iron Maiden, that kind of thing. Gramma hated it."

No response.

"She loved the Beatles. I know you've heard of them."

"Everyone has."

Let him know how much I love him, my brothers said. But I won't get sentimental. I don't know how a father should talk to his grown son. It's not like I had a role model.

"Well, I'd better get ready for work tomorrow."

"What do you have to do? Put grease stains on your coveralls? You can leave if you want. Don't make lame excuses."

"I know. Look, Kyle, maybe we should talk."

"I heard you talking to Uncle Chris and Uncle Joshua about me."

"It wasn't about you really. It was about me." I hesitate.

Maybe I should open up.

"I was never close to my father. You know that."

"Everyone knows about Sam."

"He left when I was seven. It was hard, being without a father, but I was happy he was gone."

Kyle listens to the music. I keep talking.

"I was glad he left because the beatings stopped."

"You didn't beat me, Dad. You ignored me."

"I know I was gone too long. I'm sorry."

"You think I'm talking about when you left? It started way before then, when I was seven or so. You were almost never around, and when you did come home, you went straight to your computer. Except when you were drunk. You were never there for me."

"That's not true. I made it to all your games."

"Yeah, so you could brag. But when our team lost, you came home and hit the bottle. Anyway, you can't go to my games now.

Wheelchairs don't perform well on the football field."

"There are other things you can do."

"Hah! I knew you couldn't make it ten minutes without talking about my future. That's all you ever talked to me about."

"Isn't that what a father is supposed to want for his son?"

"Maybe, but you never seem to care about who I am."

He's right. I don't know what to say.

I stand up. "I guess I'd better get ready for work tomorrow."

We go along, day after day. Everything else is good, but Kyle and I can't connect.

I've worked at the garage for six months when I see an old acquaintance—or should I say nemesis. He stares at me.

I should ignore him, but I won't be rude. "How are you, Curt? Enjoying that new office?"

"You look familiar, but I can't quite place you."

I should tell him I'm mistaken and leave it at that, but I guess I still enjoy suffering. "I'm Brad. Brad Adams."

"Adams. So you didn't get swallowed up by the wilderness. I heard about your little odyssey." He stares at my coveralls. "What are you doing in a place like this? Don't tell me you work here."

"I sure do. Getting back to basics." I hold up my grease-stained hands.

He laughs. "Are you serious? You're even crazier than I thought. Still hitting the sauce, I see."

I feel like hitting him. "It's none of your business, but I've been sober for several months now. In case anyone asks."

He's still laughing. "Wait until I tell them where I found you."

"Sure, Curt. Nice to see you, too."

He pays his bill and drives off in the Lexus I just fixed. For the next couple of weeks, he'll have a good laugh at my expense. A year ago, it would have been enough to make me drink. I won't go back, but I should have left a nail in his tire.

Three days later, a few minutes before closing time, a shiny black Jaguar pulls in. I know that car. I practically drooled over it the day Ted first drove it to the office. At one time, my greatest goal in life was to have a car like that.

He steps out. "Hi, Brad. You're looking good. Curt told me where I could find you."

Why is he looking for me? More humiliation?

"How are you, Ted?"

"I'm fine, but I've been worried about you. You disappeared without a trace. Are you okay now?"

"Better than ever. I'm sober and doing the work I love."

"The work you love? You're an engineer, not a mechanic. The place hasn't been the same since you left."

Sure.

"You have Hendricks. I know he loved stepping into my place."

"Curt's a good engineer and a great salesman, but he doesn't have your instincts for structure. Why did you leave?"

I have to laugh. "I was about to be canned. Wasn't that reason enough?"

"I didn't want to fire you. I planned to put you on leave and insist you check into rehab. Is that why you took off?"

"Basically. You weren't going to fire me?"

"You have talent. You shouldn't be wasting your time in a place like this."

"Is that an offer?"

"It could be. Come to my office tomorrow morning and let's see what we can work out."

He climbs back into his car, waving as he pulls away. I tell my boss I'll be a little late tomorrow. He raises his eyebrows, looks in the direction of Ted's car, and nods.

I don't tell Beth, but I think about it all night. He wasn't going to fire me. Would I have done anything differently if I had known?

I leave in the morning, wearing my coveralls, and stop at the storage facility to change into one of my old suits. It's been more than two years and I can still knot a tie. I throw my coveralls into the backseat and hit the expressway.

I walk in and head straight for the elevator. Eyes seem to follow me. Are they really looking, or is it paranoia?

I see Tamara on my way to Ted's office. "Oh, Mr. Adams. It's so good to see you. Are you back?"

I wave at her and keep walking. I don't want to talk about it.

His door is open. I knock.

"Come in, Brad. It's good to see you here again. You look better in a suit and tie."

I sit down. "What do you have in mind?"

"You're not as patient as you used to be."

"I'm sober now. No liquor to dull my edge."

"Let's get down to business then. You can't go back to your old position of course."

"Of course."

"But I can bring you back on as a senior engineer. No business trips. You'll stay in Chicago and supervise our projects here. I don't know if you've heard, but the transit system you helped develop has been very well received. Now they're looking to expand. You'll work with a team to see the project through to completion. Your salary will be less than you made when you left, but considerably more than you can earn as a mechanic." He writes down a figure and slides it over.

That's quite an offer. Coming back in as a senior engineer. No dealing with city councils in hick towns. It will be just the machine and me again. It's too good to refuse.

But I have to think this over. Is it really what I want? I'd have to wear suits and bring work home. Could I handle the stress?

More money. One job, not two. More time with my family.

Ted is waiting, watching me. "What do you think?"

I rub my neck and clear my throat. "That sounds good. Can you give me a day to think about it?"

He frowns. "You need to think? I thought you'd jump at the offer."

"I should."

Should I tell him what's bothering me?

I lean forward. "The thing is, Ted, I know what kind of pressure

I'd be under, and I don't want to slip. Do you know what I mean?"

Alcohol and engineering. I did both for so long. I'm not sure I could separate the two.

Ted rubs his hands together. "Yes, I know what you're trying to say, but you're recovered now, aren't you? Of course, I wouldn't tolerate a relapse. Do you think that's a possibility?"

I drank when I was an engineer. I also drank on the road. Whether I'm a cook in a diner or a senior engineer, it doesn't really matter. My job didn't make me drink. That was just another excuse.

"It's always possible. No alcoholic is completely free of it. Are you willing to take that chance?"

"If you think you can do it, the offer still stands."

I could talk with Beth first, but I know what she'll say. Money is tight. I can't turn this down.

I rearrange two silver paperweights at the edge of Ted's desk. He waits.

"I need to give notice at my other jobs. Could I start in two weeks?"

"That sounds reasonable. I'll expect to see you bright and early on the twenty-fourth."

We shake hands. He walks me out. "We'll see you in two weeks."

I drive to the garage in my suit. I vowed I wouldn't go back to engineering. I didn't want a job with that much responsibility. But we need the money. And I am an engineer.

I slip into the restroom to change. I have a brake job waiting.

I tell my boss at closing time. "I've enjoyed working here."

He looks up from the computer. "But you had a better offer."

"Yes. I start in two weeks."

On his way out, he puts a "Help Wanted" sign in the window.

Beth is in the kitchen. I kiss the back of her neck.

She turns around. "You're late. Where have you been?" She looks at me closely. "Did you stop anywhere on the way home?" she says in an accusing tone.

I produce the flowers from behind my back. "Only to buy these."

She laughs. "They're beautiful, but we can't afford orchids."

"Now we can." I tell her about my return to engineering.

She puts her arms around my neck. "That's wonderful, Brad, but are you sure it's what you want?"

I kiss her. "What I want is to buy you orchids every week."

Don and Ann come into town the next day. Beth tells them the news.

"You're back where you belong," says Don. "That's great, Brad."

Everyone is happy about it. I'm still not sure, but I can't turn it down.

I don't see them much during their five days here—I still have two jobs to hold down. They spend most of their time with Kyle, taking him places and buying him things. He has more games, more music. He's more spoiled.

I go back tomorrow. Yesterday, I said goodbye to the garage.

This morning, I worked my last few hours at High and Dry. When I told Bill about the offer, he didn't say much. This morning, he reminded me to call if I need him. I promised I would, but I think I'll be okay now.

Everything is good, except for Kyle. He's been home for nearly three weeks and all he does is sit in his room, listening to that music, coming out only to eat. He could be studying for his GED. He could be checking out colleges. He could get a job. I hold my tongue.

I've been nervous all week. My suits just came back from the cleaners. I ironed my ties this morning. Beth laughs as I sort out my socks. She goes to the closet and brings out my briefcase.

I fold one of my prayer rugs and put it in the briefcase. I didn't tell

Ted I'm a Muslim, but it shouldn't be an issue. We have a few other Muslims working at the firm. Maybe I can pray with them.

Everything is ready. I sit on the couch with Beth and hold her.

Kyle comes out of his room and wheels into the kitchen. A minute later, someone buzzes from downstairs. "I'll get it," says Kyle.

He whispers into the intercom. Something's up. He talks for a few seconds. Then he wheels restlessly around the apartment. After a couple minutes, he says, "I think I'll go get some fresh air."

"Where are you going, Kyle?"

"Just out to the hallway."

"Who was that on the intercom?"

"Wrong number."

"Get back here, Kyle."

"I'll see you later." He leaves the apartment, slamming the door on his way out.

What's up?

I turn to Beth. "You don't think he's stupid enough to…"

"Get him."

He's already in the elevator. The door closes. I take the stairs, running, and pray my ankle won't give out. By the time I get to the first floor, he's headed out the front door to a waiting car.

"Kyle, come back here."

He ignores me.

A bunch of kids are standing around a car in the parking lot. They laugh when they see my son in his wheelchair. "Hey, Kyle, nice set of wheels you got there."

"Just wait. I'll get this chair roaring. A couple of months, I can challenge you to a race."

"You're not going anywhere, Kyle." I catch up to him and grab his chair.

He pulls away from me. "Leave me alone."

"Hello, Mr. Adams," says a boy in a blue football jersey. "We were just asking Kyle if he wanted to go to the library with us."

"My mother used that one on her parents. No more parties for you, Kyle. Let's go."

"I'm a man. You can't tell me what to do."

"You're a man? Do you have a job? Do you pay the bills? Do you do anything all day besides listen to that damn music and play those damn games?"

Another boy in a red shirt speaks up. "Really, Mr. Adams, it's no problem. We'll have him back in an hour, max." I smell the beer on his breath. I also notice the car keys in his hand.

"Let's go, Kyle."

"No."

"You're coming with me if I have to carry you upstairs. You kids can go now. But you—" I point to the one in the red shirt. "You are in no condition to drive. Didn't you kids hear about the five teens who were killed on the night my son lost the use of his legs? I suggest you either wrestle the car keys from your friend here or take the L home. Or if you want, I can call your parents."

"Don't bother. See you later, Kyle." Blue shirt turns to red shirt. "Dude, give me those keys."

They fall into the car. Kyle resists as I wheel him back. It takes several minutes just to get him into the elevator.

He's quiet. But when we get to the apartment, he turns around and screams. "You had no right to do that. Those were my friends. You stood there and totally embarrassed me. I'm not your little boy. You can't tell me what to do."

I scream right back. "The hell I can't. Look at yourself. Have you already forgotten how you ended up in that chair? Five of your friends are dead. Your legs are useless. Doesn't that mean anything to you?"

"You don't get it. You'll never get it."

"You're not stupid, Kyle. Why do you insist on destroying yourself?"

He stares at me. For the first time, I notice the pain in his eyes. "What do I have to live for?" He spins around and goes to his room, slamming the door.

Beth is crying. "Doesn't he remember the accident? What is he trying to do?"

"He wants to destroy himself." I hold her for a minute before pulling away. "I'm calling Joshua."

He comes twenty minutes later. It's been a long twenty minutes. I kept putting my ear to Kyle's locked door, hoping he wouldn't do something stupid. I couldn't hear anything over the music.

I quickly tell Joshua what happened. "I don't know what he's thinking, but I'm worried."

"I'll talk to him." He knocks. "Hey, Kyle, man. How you doing?"

"Leave me alone."

"Hey, man, open the door."

"Go away and leave me alone."

"Is that how you treat your favorite uncle? After I came all this way to see you? Come on, dude. Let me in."

The lock clicks. Joshua walks in and closes the door.

Beth and I huddle on the couch while Matt sits quietly nearby. Kyle won't do anything while Joshua is with him, but Joshua can't stay here all night. How will we take care of our son?

We sit. It reminds me of those long hours in the waiting room when we didn't know if he would live or die. How could he forget?

Two hours and thirty-six minutes later, Joshua and Kyle emerge. They've both been crying. Joshua turns to Kyle. "Go on, man."

Kyle hugs Beth. "I'm sorry, Mom." He looks down and mumbles, "Sorry, Dad."

"What's going on?" Beth cries.

"Those other kids in the car, they were my best friends. I knew Steve since we were in kindergarten. Terry and I played football together. And Amy. I loved Amy. I was going to marry her. No one ever talks to me about them. Everyone just tells me how lucky I am to be alive. I don't feel lucky. I should have died too."

"So you were willing to get into another accident?"

"Why not? It's better than living like this. You said it, Dad. My best friends are dead and my legs are useless. What's the point?"

"Kyle, no. You can't think like that." Beth puts her arms around him.

"What should we do, Joshua?"

"Kyle says he never had counseling about the deaths of his friends. You can't heal the body without healing the soul."

"I was just so happy he was alive. I never thought. I don't know. What do you suggest?"

"He wants to come home with me. We'll set him up in the family room and treat him like one of our boys. I'll do what I should have done while you were gone."

"Is that what you want, Kyle?" says Beth.

"Yeah. Dad and I are just making each other crazy. Uncle Joshua gets it."

"I love you, Kyle. I hope you know that."

Why couldn't I say that to him earlier?

"If you love me, let me go with Uncle Joshua. No offense, but I have to get out of here." He turns to Beth. "Mom, you've been great, but I have to go."

We help him pack his things and carry them down to the parking lot. Joshua brought the van.

I stand at his open car door, wanting to hold on, and swallow hard. "When can I see you again? When will you be back?"

"That's funny," he says. "That's what I would have asked you before you left. I'll be in touch." He closes the door, and they're gone.

Part Five

Beth, Matt, and I head back to the apartment. I try to hold her hand on the way up, but she pulls away.

She moves around in the kitchen for a few minutes before storming into the living room. "What is wrong with you? Why did you drive him away?"

"What are you talking about? I saved him just now. He was going to do it again."

"Why was he going to do it? Why did he think his life was so worthless?"

"I don't know. I haven't understood anything about Kyle since I came home."

"You haven't tried to understand him. You've driven him away. The way you pressure him, it's no wonder he's trying to escape."

"Escape from what? I don't see him doing a hell of a lot of work around here. If you ask me, I think we raised one spoiled kid."

"He's not spoiled. He's hurt. And he needs our love and support."

"He'll get my support when I see him getting off his ass and doing something with his life."

"He just came home. He needs time. Stop trying to control him."

"Somebody had better tell him what to do because he doesn't seem capable of doing anything on his own."

"Stop pushing him. Let him feel comfortable enough to make his own choices."

"He sure is making good choices these days, isn't he?"

"You know a lot about good choices, don't you? Drinking, leaving us, leaving the church. Oh, and now you're taking Matt away from the church, too. You're a real expert."

"Matt? What does he have to do with this?"

"As soon as I left town, you started filling his head with your strange ideas. Praying on the floor and fasting all day. I won't let you do that to my son."

"He's my son, too, and he has the right to make his own choices."

"So Matt can make choices, but Kyle can't?"

"Kyle can't seem to do anything these days but sit in that damn chair and play video games. He's ruined his life."

"What do you expect? Look at his role model. I knew you were a drunk the minute I met you. I should have walked away and never looked back."

I'm trying. Doesn't she see that?

"Let's not go there," I shout. "Yes, I'm an alcoholic. I'm sober now. Aren't you satisfied? Or maybe you liked me better as a drunk."

"Is that a threat?"

"You could call it that. You have no right to blame me for what's going on with Kyle."

"I have every right to blame you. It is all your fault."

"I'm trying. I don't know why he won't work with me."

"Because you're trying to make him into something he's not."

"I'll tell you what he is. An invalid. A cripple. A bum. Anything else?"

She slaps me. My cheek stings. "Don't you dare talk about my son that way." She runs into the bedroom. Her room again.

Matt pretends to be reading. I'm glad he's not looking. I don't want him to see me cry. I wash up for my prayers, but I can't concentrate. She's right. I'm nothing but a drunk.

I pace nervously. I stop and stare at my car keys hanging by the door. I just need a little fresh air. I won't go far. I grab the keys and walk out, slamming the door behind me.

Most places are closed at this time of night. But not the bars. I drive past five of them, gripping the steering wheel until my knuckles turn white.

I'm losing my family. Allah knows how hard I've tried. It won't work.

I need a little something to take the edge off. Something to numb the pain. I signal, but I don't stop.

I drive over to High and Dry. Locked up tight for the night. I park in front, frozen. Up the block, another neon light calls me. I should call Bill but I left my cell at the apartment.

I close my eyes. Why don't I know how to be a father? Sam left all of us, not just me. This isn't Sam's fault. Something is lacking in me. I can't connect.

I haven't connected with very many people in my life. Walt maybe, but he connected with everyone. Others, I control. Or I pretend to be close when I know it's superficial. Kate and I lived in a fantasy world in the Rocky Mountains, but I was as disconnected from her as I am from everyone else.

Everyone except Beth. She and I are connected at our souls. Yet I keep driving her away.

Before Sam died, he told Joshua he needed to control the people he cared about. Will I die lonely and bitter, as he did?

I put the car into gear. There's only one way I can connect. I head for the neon lights.

Someone's shouting. I look in my rearview mirror. Bill. I stop.

He jogs up to my car. "I forgot my phone at the diner. What are you doing over here?" He notices my shaking hands. "Come inside. You can tell me about it over a pot of coffee."

We sit down and he listens. Me and Kyle. Me and Beth. Me and the emptiness I always feel. We talk until dawn. I pray before heading to my car. As I put it into gear, Bill says, "Why did you come here? There's a bar just up the street."

"That's where I was headed."

He pats my shoulder. "I'm glad you found me."

Beth is in the kitchen when I walk in. She stares, studying me.

I shake my head. "Not a drop. I was with Bill all night."

She throws her arms around me.

"I'm sorry," I whisper.

"I'm sorry, too." She strokes my cheek. "Why did you leave?"

"I didn't think you wanted me."

"I didn't. Not last night." The way she says it, I know I'm forgiven.

"You're right. It is my fault. I've pushed him away, and he may never come back."

"Don't you know how much he loves you?"

"He sure doesn't act like it."

"He's hurt. Give him time."

"I don't think it will ever work between us."

"Brad, on the day you left, Kyle was in tears. He insisted we drive around looking for you and begged me to call the police. He barely slept for the first five weeks. Until you sent that email. Then, when I didn't hear anything for three months, we both thought you were dead. He shut himself off. That's when he quit school and started drinking.

"I tried to provide him with some sense of security, but just as he was beginning to feel comfortable again, I had to return the Lexus. Then we moved. You know how much Kyle loved that house. He's the reason we bought it in the first place.

"Think about it. How long has it taken you to get over being left by your father?"

"I never got over it."

"Then I think you're asking far too much from your son."

"Joshua and Aisha will take care of him, won't they?"

"They'll take good care of him."

As we clean up from breakfast, I mull over what she just told me. Kyle quit school because he thought I was dead. He thought I was dead because I stopped sending postcards. I stopped sending postcards because I was living with Kate. Falling down the side of a mountain would have been a less painful punishment for my infidelity.

As I help her load the dishwasher, I ask, "Beth, many people in my life have left me, one way or another. Why do you want me?"

"Aside from your rugged good looks? Because I know how much you love me. And it is wonderful to be loved by you."

Part Six

I wish I could stay home with her today, but I'm an engineer again. I head for the shower. It takes me exactly one hour to get ready. Did I used to spend twenty minutes shaving?

I kiss Beth goodbye, and Celeste and I hit the expressway. As I follow the dotted white line back to the office, I drink my second cup of coffee—I'll have to make it on caffeine and adrenaline today.

Traffic slows to a crawl. I inch along for ten minutes before coming to a complete stop. There must be an accident. I grind my teeth.

I walk into Ted's office ten minutes late and mumble something about traffic. He nods and walks with me to my new office.

It's decent, though not nearly as nice as my old one, where Hendricks is. Half as big. Standard issue desk. A window overlooking the parking lot. But it will do.

Ted hands me a file. "This is where we are on the mass transit project. They're keeping the L, with major upgrades—including several of your recommendations. Curt and Hussein are overseeing the project. Curt travels extensively, so I plan to minimize his participation. You will need to work closely with Hussein to meet the deadlines. The city expects the entire upgrade to be completed by June 30, 2021. That gives you ten months. Do you think you can do it?"

When I made those recommendations, I was stumbling through nightmares and alcohol. If I did that well before, I should burn rubber now. "I know I can."

"Read this first. You'll need to meet with Curt and Hussein so they can bring you up to date. Can you handle that?"

I know what he's trying to say. "Sure. Don't worry about it."

He leaves. I get another cup of coffee and start reading.

I've spent three hours and twenty-eight minutes going through the materials. They worked hard on this. Hendricks is a good engineer, but that doesn't mean I have to like him.

I'm not used to sitting behind a desk. I stretch and rub my eyes. Lunch time. I call a sandwich shop with my order. I don't plan on going out for lunch anytime soon. I need to avoid my old haunts.

I'm finishing up my roast beef sandwich when Hendricks calls me into his office. My old office. Hussein is here.

"Look what the grizzly bear dragged in," says Hendricks. Hussein laughs.

I need to stay professional. "Okay," I say, opening the file. "Let's get started."

We spend the next two hours hashing out details of the system and debating our options. Hendricks is telling a story about his recent run-in with city hall when I glance at the clock. I wait until he finishes the story.

"That's interesting, Curt. I need to excuse myself a minute. I'll be right back."

"Sneaking a drink?"

"No, I need to pray. I'm a Muslim now. Would you like to join me, Hussein?"

Hendricks laughs. "I didn't know you went all the way to Arabia."

Hussein laughs, too. "You go ahead. Take your time."

I escape into my office, take out my prayer rug, face Makkah, and raise my hands in submission. I ask Allah to make me patient.

When I go back, Hendricks shoves my file at me and says, "Draw up a timeline. And make sure we don't go over budget."

I'm still familiarizing myself with the specifications. I'm not ready for that kind of an assignment, and Hendricks knows it. "I'll have it for you tomorrow morning." I grab the file and retreat.

At 5:03, I'm still far from done. Ted walks in.

"How was your first day back?"

I continue typing. "It was good."

"You didn't say anything about becoming a Muslim."

"I converted over a year ago. I planned to mention it later."

"Make sure your prayers don't interfere with your work. Remember we're on a tight schedule here."

"It won't be a problem."

"Fine. Well, it's good to have you back. I'll see you in the morning."

I work for another two hours and fifty-two minutes before I can pack up and go home. I've read through the material a second time and drawn up a detailed timeline. I'll review the budget before going to sleep tonight.

The elevator isn't working again. As I head down the stairs, I begin to feel dizzy. I grip the railing and walk carefully, step by step. My chest feels tight. I sweat. I focus. One step at a time. Finally I make it out of the building and breathe in the night air. I play the CD of ocean sounds as I cruise down the expressway.

Beth is in the kitchen. She kisses me. Then she looks into my eyes. "You're late. Is everything okay?"

"I had to work. I didn't stop anywhere."

"Thank God." She hugs me.

How long will it take before she trusts me?

She and Matt already ate. She heats my dinner and sits with me while I eat.

"I talked with Kyle today. He sounds lonely."

I miss Kyle.

"I'm sure he'll be fine."

"How was your first day back?"

"They kept most of my original recommendations. Can you believe it? I wrote those before I was sober. Imagine what I can do now."

She smiles. "I know you'll be wonderful."

It's good to be home.

When I finish, she takes my plate. "Why don't you go rest?"

I stretch out on the couch. I'm glad I don't have an AA meeting tonight. I'm nearly asleep when someone buzzes. Beth gets it.

"Umar's here." She goes back into the kitchen.

I wait for him at the door. We hug. "I'm sorry for dropping by so late," he says.

"I'm glad to see you. Come on in."

"How was your return to engineering?"

"It went well, but I'm beat."

"I heard about your problems with Kyle last night. Are you okay?"

I tell him about my midnight ride. "Bill was there for me."

"That's great." He strokes his beard. "I wanted to talk with both Beth and you. Do you have a few minutes?"

I call Beth. She brings coffee and cake.

"Thank you," says Umar. "Sit down, Beth. I know about the trouble you had with Kyle last night, and Brad just told me what happened after Joshua left. You know that alcoholism takes a toll on the entire family. Have you heard of Al-Anon? Many people don't realize they're separate from Alcoholics Anonymous. They run support groups for the friends and families of alcoholics."

Beth nods. "I went to a meeting once, about eight years ago."

I didn't know that.

"You haven't gone recently?" Umar asks.

"How can I, with everything else going on? And Brad isn't drinking anymore."

"But you lived with his addiction for over twenty years. You must have lingering emotions about that part of your life. And Brad can you tell how important it is to know you're not alone."

That's why I keep going to my AA meetings. I hope Al-Anon can help Beth trust me again.

"I'll consider it," she says.

"Good. After hearing about last night, I thought I should talk with you about family support, but it's late and I don't want to be a bother. Brad, would you like to pray with me before I leave?"

I haven't prayed with another person since making the Eid prayer in St. Louis. It's good to be shoulder to shoulder again.

Before he goes, Umar says "Call me anytime. And remember you can always call on Allah."

"I tried to pray last night, but I couldn't concentrate."

"I want you to remember this phrase. 'Subhan Allah.' Glory be to Allah. You can say this when you're distressed. Say it a thousand times if you need to. That's the easiest way to call on Allah. And I promise, He'll answer."

～

It takes me fifty-six minutes to get ready in the morning. I'm improving.

I grab a cup of coffee and go to meet with Hendricks and Hussein. They're co-conspirators. Hendricks belittles me and Hussein encourages him. I ignore them and present my work.

Ted walks into my office as I'm finishing my prayer. Hussein refused to join me.

"I saw your timeline, Brad. That's what I'm talking about. You're an engineer. Did I say I'm glad to have you back?"

"I think so."

"You're a Muslim. I have to say I'm surprised, but there shouldn't be a problem as long as it doesn't interfere with your work."

He said that before, too. Maybe he is ready to retire. But now Hendricks is next in line.

Beth calls at ten minutes after two. "I went to Joshua's house, but no one was home. Do you know where Kyle is? I don't have a job to go to. I'd like to see my son."

I call Joshua at his office.

"Kyle is with me," he says. "I'm putting him to work. Answering phones, stuffing envelopes. Later, I want him to interact with the kids."

"He has a job?"

"It's volunteer, but he's not sitting around moping all day."

"Is he happy?"

"Happier than he has been. Give him time, Brad. Did you realize how much he misses his friends? He was deeply in love with that girl. Amy. Did you know that?"

"Not until the other night."

"Kyle has a lot of issues to work through. I'll keep him active during the day. Umar will counsel him three or four evenings a week. Be patient. And trust me. I'm your kid brother, but I'm not a loser. And neither is Kyle."

"Beth wants to see him."

"Tell her to come down to the center. We can always use another volunteer."

"Sure. I'll talk to you later."

"Assalaamu alaikum, Brother."

"Yes. Walaikum assalaam."

I call Beth and tell her where she can find our son. As I review my budget projections, I think again about my relationships. Everyone else knows me better than I know myself. I still have some issues to work through, too.

Discovery

All men should strive
to learn before they die
what they are running from, and to, and why.

—James Thurber

Part One

Beth worked at the center for two hours today. "I wasn't able to talk with Kyle much, but I watched him. He was smiling. Do you know how rarely he has smiled these last few years?"

No, I guess I don't.

Umar comes over as we're cleaning up from dinner.

"Assalaamu alaikum. Can I fix you a plate?"

"Walaikum assalaam. No, I ate. Can we talk?"

We sit on the couch. Beth starts the coffee.

"I just met with Kyle. I won't tell you everything he said, but there are some things he wants you to know."

"Such as?"

"He wants to be close to you, but he says you keep putting up barriers."

"I've tried. He won't talk to me. If there are barriers, he's the one who's put them there."

"Tell me about the barriers."

"He listens to that damn music. When he's not listening to music, he's playing those games. Between the music and the games, he has completely tuned me out."

"What have you done to break down the barriers?"

"I tried to talk to him, but I don't know if he heard me."

"Brad, your son has several issues to work through, but I think you have some very solid issues of your own. And I'm guessing they have very little to do with Kyle. Am I right?"

He's perceptive.

"I've done everything I can to change the direction of my life—the road trip, the counseling in rehab, going to AA, practicing Islam, returning to engineering—but it keeps coming back. My father, my mother, and Walt."

"I know you were devastated by the deaths of your mother and Walt. What is it about your father that still bothers you? The fact that he left you? The fact that he's dead?"

"No, it's the fact that he beat me regularly for nearly four years before he left. He apologized before he died, and I thought I had closure, but I can't make it go away. My problems with Kyle don't help. I don't understand it, Umar. My father beat me, yet I was able to make some sort of peace with him before he died. I never laid a hand on Kyle. What right does he have to be angry with me?"

"Have you ever spoken with a counselor about the abuse?"

"Most of my life, I've been too busy. And I don't really want to think about it. I have talked with Beth."

"Didn't you discuss this with your counselor in rehab?"

"No. I had other problems to deal with."

"I think it will help if you work through your feelings about the abuse."

"For over twenty years, no one knew, except Beth. It was another twenty years before I told Joshua. Most of the family knows now. I already feel too vulnerable."

"When I had my breakdown, I learned that sometimes we have to let ourselves become vulnerable. It may be the only way to become free."

"You know what you're talking about, don't you?"

"You may not like me so much once we get started. I need to ask you some tough questions. You don't have to answer if you're uncomfortable. Are you ready for your first challenge?"

"Do I have a choice?"

"Not if you're serious about rebuilding your relationship with Kyle."

"Go ahead."

"You said you never laid a hand on Kyle. Can you say honestly you have never beaten him, at any time?"

"Never," I answer quickly. Umar looks at me, expecting more. "But I have felt like hitting him. Sometimes, when he was little, I went so far as to get my belt. And now, too, I want to hit him. I have to do something to get his attention. When I have those feelings, I walk away. I never want to hurt him the way my father hurt me."

"So your feelings about the abuse are affecting your relationship with Kyle. I think it would be a good idea if I counseled you as well as your son. I won't be able to discuss anything he's told me, unless I have his permission, and I won't divulge—to anyone— anything you say. After you've both made some progress, I want to have joint sessions with Kyle and you. What do you think?"

"I don't know. Joshua wears his heart on his sleeve. That's not me."

"It is risky to talk about feelings you've tried to bury, but I believe counseling will help you understand yourself and, in the process, help you become closer to Kyle."

"When I came back, I thought I knew myself. It's only after dealing with Kyle that I'm not so sure. If you really believe this will help, I guess I could try it. But I just started a new job and our budget is tight. We don't have the money for that kind of luxury."

Umar smiles. "You're family, Brad. Don't worry about that."

"I don't take handouts. Even when I was on the road, I always worked for my food."

"Family members help one another. That's all this is."

"At least let me take care of your cars. Oil change, tune-up, you name it."

"I'll do that. Let's try Mondays and Thursdays for now. I'll come by about this time and we'll talk. Is there any place in the apartment where we can go for complete privacy?"

"There's Kyle's room."

"That will work. There is one other thing, Brad. I haven't seen you at the Friday prayers. Which mosque do you attend?"

"I don't go. You know how hectic my life has been. I don't have time. And I work. I can't get away."

"You need to make time. It's a requirement for all Muslim men. And by law, your boss is required to allow you time off for the prayer, as long as you're able to complete your work."

"I didn't know that."

"Talk to your boss tomorrow. Come to the prayers. It will help."

"I'll try."

Hendricks will love that. But Ted is still my boss. It shouldn't be a problem.

Umar has cake and coffee, and we pray together before he leaves. Standing shoulder to shoulder always helps.

In the morning, I tell Ted about the Friday prayer. He shakes his head. "I know the law. What is it with you, Brad? Alcoholic to fanatic?"

I'm not a fanatic. Just a believer.

"It won't affect my work."

On Friday at noon, I drop by Hussein's office and ask if he wants to come. He glares at me. "I have too much work. You'd better get serious, too, if you know what's good for you."

Beth volunteers at the center two or three hours a day. I take a long lunch break every Friday. Umar comes twice a week to help me work through my problems. We spend a lot of time talking about the abuse and my resentment over my lost childhood.

The project is on schedule, but Hendricks and Hussein continue to mock me. I don't need this. There are days when I'm tempted to turn in my resignation, but I want to see this project through to completion.

I haven't seen my son since the night Joshua took him away, over a month ago. I miss him, but I'm afraid of saying the wrong thing and driving him further away. I tell Umar this when he comes on a Thursday evening.

"You two do need to meet, but I appreciate your caution. Do you want me to talk with Kyle and see if he's ready?"

"Of course."

My talks with Umar do help. I hadn't realized how much I still hurt. I'm a grown man with gray hairs and crow's feet, but I still feel the pain and humiliation of the little boy, standing there with his pants down.

When Umar comes on Monday, I ask again about seeing Kyle.

"He misses you, and he wants to see you, but I don't think either of you is ready."

"He wants to see me? That's real progress."

"Kyle never stopped loving you. He felt bad about leaving, but he had reached the breaking point. You know how that feels, don't you?"

"You could say that."

"And you still have emotions you have not dealt with. Why do you always feel you have to be in control?"

That's a strange question.

"Someone has to be in charge."

"That's not what I mean. You are very constrained in the way you interact with others. And you seem to have the need to control the people you love. Especially Kyle, but I have noticed it in your other relationships, too. Why is that?"

"I don't know. That's the way I am."

"You were only seven when you father left, but I want you to think back. Did your father control your mother?"

"That's an easy one. He was very controlling."

"Give me some examples."

"I'll put it this way. There were only two decisions my mother made which my father didn't approve. One was to go to church every Sunday. The other was to have Joshua. I was young, but I knew what it meant to get rid of something. I remember him screaming at her to 'get rid of it.' Once when Joshua cried for hours. he shouted, 'I told you to get rid of that damn thing.' I think he wanted to hurt the baby. My mother carried Joshua almost all the time when my father was home. When she couldn't, she asked me to watch the baby for her. I was young, but I knew what she meant."

"So your father controlled everything else your mother did? Where she went, what she wore, what she cooked for dinner?"

"Everything."

"Tell me about your paternal grandfather."

"I didn't see him very often. My father hated him. When Dad was drunk, he ranted about 'the old man.' After my father left, we never saw my grandfather again."

"How did he interact with your father?"

"When 'the old man' was around, my father was quiet. Timid even. But after my grandfather left, Dad beat me for no reason. After my father died, I learned his father had beaten him. I was proud I had broken the cycle, but my relationship with Kyle isn't much better."

"Brad, where was your mother when your father abused you?"

"I don't know. Out, I guess."

"Did she go out often?"

"No. My father wouldn't let her go anywhere. She didn't have a job then, I know that. She didn't have any friends either. Sometimes she went to visit her parents, but she always took us with her."

"So where was she?"

"I don't know. Maybe she was shopping. What does that have to do with anything?" Sweat trickles down my face and my palms are moist.

Did Beth turn up the heat?

"Did your mother know about the abuse?"

"Of course not. She wouldn't have let him do that to me."

"But he made all the decisions. He controlled her. How could she have stopped him?"

"She tried to stop him. I know she tried."

"What happened when she tried?"

"I don't know."

He grasps my arm. "You're safe now, Brad. What happened when she tried to stop him?"

I can see it. "He hit her. And he beat me harder when she tried."

"So she knew."

I can't answer. My eyes blur and I can't swallow. The earth opens up beneath me. I'm falling.

Umar reaches out and grabs me. He holds me by the shoulders and stops my descent.

"She tried to stop him. She did. He hurt her."

"Yes, Brad. She tried. She loved you. She tried to protect you. You're safe now."

He holds me tight. I cling to his lifeline until I'm on solid ground again. Then I let go and wipe my eyes. I can see now.

"She knew," I say quietly.

"Yes, she knew."

"I thought if she really loved me she would have stopped him. But she couldn't."

"No, she couldn't."

"She did try."

"I'm sure she tried. She loved you, Brad."

"Yes, she loved me. And I loved her. I miss her." My eyes blur again, but I wipe them clear.

"She was your mother."

"We never talked about it."

"I'm sure it was painful for both of you."

"I didn't tell her I love her. I didn't say goodbye."

"She knew."

I stand up, still fighting for control. "You won't tell Joshua, will you? What my father wanted to do to him?"

"The only way he'll find out is if you tell him."

"What about Beth? Should I tell her?"

"That's up to you. If you think you should."

"I feel different."

"I'd like to come back tomorrow. Is that okay with you?"

I nod. "That sounds like a good idea."

He pats me on the shoulder. "Remember, Brad, you're safe now."

I tell Beth about it before we sleep. "I didn't realize, all these years. My mother knew, but she couldn't stop him."

"The two of you never discussed it?"

"You know she wouldn't have wanted to talk about it. And I had buried it so deep inside. I didn't want to remember."

"How do you feel, now that you know?"

"Horrified, at first. How could she have stood by and let me be hurt? Then I remembered that she tried, but he hit her, too. He beat me while she cried for him to stop."

"I wonder why, with all that abuse, she spent so many years wanting him to come back to her."

"It doesn't make sense. But Sam was very controlling. I guess he had her under his spell."

"You should be proud of yourself. You've broken the cycle."

"With your help. But there have been times, both long ago and more recently, when I've felt like beating Kyle. I could never hit him, though. I walked away instead."

"I thought you were being distant." She looks into my eyes. "That's why you lashed out at me."

"Forgive me. I don't know where I would be without you."

I'm glad I told her. She holds and comforts me. By the time I fall into my pillow, I can accept everything I've learned about myself today.

I won't tell her—or anyone else—about Joshua. He feels good about Sam now. I won't take that away from him.

As I drift off to sleep, I think about my new insights. That last year or so before he left us, Mom and I both lived in fear of him, but we forged an alliance against him, bonded together in a common cause. She depended on me to help her, but she couldn't really help me. She had to protect the baby.

That's who Joshua is to me. The baby. And I still have a hard time thinking of him any other way. He'll never know how hard Mom and I worked to make sure Dad didn't get rid of him.

Chris was there, but he wasn't there. He played with his toys, oblivious to the danger, and Dad left him alone. I think Dad loved him more. I don't know why.

My eyes close and my breathing slows. Random pictures flash through my mind. They come into focus. Him hitting me. Her stopping him. Him hitting her. Him pushing her down the stairs.

I scream and reach out, trying to keep her from falling, but I'm too damn slow.

She tumbles down, crying out, her arms flailing. She hits the floor. The sound echoes.

I run down the stairs and crouch beside her. She doesn't move.

I'm still screaming.

She puts her arms around me. "What's wrong, Brad?"

I open my eyes. Beth is holding me.

"What's wrong?"

I can't speak. I bury my head in her chest and sob.
She soothes me back to sleep.

~

In the morning, she asks me about the nightmare.
"Don't ask."
I stay in my office all day, reviewing the specifications. When Hendricks calls, I say I'll get back to him. As I pore over the figures, the images run through my mind. I force myself to concentrate. I pace. I think about going out for lunch. I call Bill.

When I get home, I'm still restless. I pace while waiting for Umar. "Subhan Allah. Subhan Allah. Subhan Allah. Oh Allah. I need you."

"What's wrong, Brad honey? Don't you want dinner?"

"I can't eat." I pace, my stomach in knots.

When Umar comes, I grab him and drag him to Kyle's room. I quickly shut the door. "It's my fault," I say breathlessly.

"What's your fault?"

"They were all ready to go to church, but I was reading and I wasn't ready. He kept yelling at me to put down the damn book. Finally I got dressed, we all walked out into the hall, and he slammed the door. Then he screamed at me again, right there in the hallway, because I was 'too damn slow.' He raised his hand to hit me. Mom grabbed his arm. So he started in on her. He slapped her a few times. Then he pushed her. She stumbled and fell down the stairs. She wouldn't wake up. There was blood. The ambulance came and took her away. She almost died. Joshua almost died, too."

"Joshua?"

"Joshua was born too early because my father pushed her down the stairs. She was trying to protect me and they almost died. It was my fault."

The pain grips me. I double over, shaking and sobbing.

Umar holds on, keeping me from falling into the pit.

I'm shaking, moaning. Remembering. Mom lying on the floor. Blood. I call for her. She doesn't move. Some lady grabs me and holds me while they take her away. Grandpa comes for Chris and me. Grandma comforts me while I cry myself to sleep. I want my mommy.

I lie on Kyle's bed, still shaking. I want my mother, I moan.

I open my eyes and look around. I'm on Kyle's bed, covered with a blanket. Umar is sleeping on the floor next to the bed. Matt sleeps in the far corner, near the door.

"Umar," I whisper. "Wake up."

He opens his eyes and rubs his face. "How are you?" he says softly.

"I don't know."

"It wasn't your fault. You know that now, don't you?"

"I don't know."

"You don't have to pay for the sins of your father."

I can't answer.

"Let's pray."

After the prayer, he pats me on the back. "Will you be okay now?"

"Why did you stay?"

"I needed to be here when you woke up."

"Won't Safa be upset?"

"I called and told her not to wait up. Don't worry about me. What about you? Are you okay?"

"I guess I am."

"I'll come back tomorrow night. You're almost there, Brad."

Am I? I feel like I'm a million miles from anywhere.

"Call me if you need to talk. I'll see you tomorrow, insha Allah."

He gives me a warm hug before going out into the night. I glance at the clock on my way to Beth. 2 AM. I crawl into bed, close to her. She puts her arms around me.

I wake up, remembering. They rushed her to the hospital. I didn't see her again for twenty-six days. Grandma told me she would be okay. Grandpa said I had a new baby brother. They kept reassuring me and telling me not to worry.

But I thought she was dead, lying there at the bottom of the stairs. It was my fault. I thought I had killed her.

~

After the morning prayer, I get ready for work, but I can't do it. I lie on the bed, in my suit and tie, and pull the covers over my head.

Beth calls Ted, gets Matt off to school, and comes back to hold me.

I sleep. When I wake up, I pray. I tell Beth about the day my mother almost died. She comforts me.

I struggle through the day, sleeping a lot and eating a little, until Umar comes. We go to Kyle's room. He asks again, "Are you okay?"

"I think so."

"It wasn't your fault. It was an accident."

"I should have stopped reading so he wouldn't be angry. I should have caught her and kept her from falling."

"You were just a child. There's nothing you could have done."

"I should have protected her from him."

"You were only seven years old."

Seven. Five years younger than Matt is now. Luqman is seven, isn't he?

"You're almost there," says Umar. "I need to ask you a few more difficult questions. Let me know if you can't handle it. Will you do that?"

"Yes."

"Did you love your mother?"

"Yes, of course."

"Do you think she knew how much you loved her?"

"I think so."

"Good. Who else do you love?"

"I love Beth, of course. And I love my sons."

"Then why can't you show it?"

"Beth knows I love her."

"What about Kyle?"

I don't want to face it, but there's no way around it. Finally, I have to confess. "I don't know how to love him."

Umar nods. "Go on."

"The truth is I didn't want to be a father. I spent most of my childhood taking care of my brothers and I didn't want to be responsible for anyone else. But I loved Beth and when I married her, I knew she wanted children. I thought if I kept putting it off she would forget about it, but she wouldn't give up. One night we had a long talk and I told her about the beatings. We talked for weeks until I thought it didn't bother me anymore. I loved her, and I wanted her to be happy, so I finally agreed we should have a baby.

"I was with her the first time we heard the baby's heartbeat. We had created a new life. That's the day I fell in love with our child.

"When Kyle was born, I was ecstatic. He was perfect. And he didn't make a move without us watching. We were in awe of our son.

"Things were good for the first several years. But then he started school, and Matt came along, and we got busy. I spent a lot of time at the office, trying to make a name for myself, and I drank to escape the pressure. Suddenly, I realized Kyle wasn't so cute anymore. I was still proud of him, but I was more interested in his accomplishments. I could go to the office and brag about my son—the best athlete and the smartest in his class. I put our family picture on my desk and people commented about my good-looking boys. I felt good because I'd found another area of life in which I could succeed.

"I do love him. If I didn't love him, I wouldn't have spent sleepless hours at the hospital. I would have let him get into that car, the second time. I wouldn't have called Joshua. I wouldn't have come back.

"But every time we talk, we end up fighting. And when I look at him, I'm no longer in awe. I feel disgusted at the way he has thrown his life away.

"While my father was beating me, I decided to be successful in life so I could show him how wrong he was. And I have been a success at almost everything I have ever attempted. But my son is a failure and he doesn't even care. I do love him, on some level, but I don't know how to love a failure."

My monologue exhausts me. I close my eyes and put my face in my hands. Umar puts his hand on my shoulder.

"First of all, Brad, you didn't create Kyle. Allah did. I'm sure you know that."

I look up. "Yes, of course. But when Kyle was born, I didn't have that concept."

"It seems to be a small point, but it's important. If you see yourself as Kyle's creator, it would make sense that your success hinges on the success of your creation. But if you see Allah as the One Who created Kyle, you will realize you are not in control of Kyle's destiny. You helped give him life, and you have given him a home and a proper education. At some point you have to step aside and let him meet the world on his own terms."

"But he's wrong."

"How do you know that? By whose standard do you judge him?"

"Everyone knows you don't just drop out of high school. Every-one knows you have to go to college and get a job. Everyone knows you don't get into a car with a drunk driver behind the wheel."

"Does everyone know it's wrong to hate your father? Does every-one know a man shouldn't walk away from his family? Doesn't every-one make mistakes?"

"But we're talking about his future."

"It's his future. You've taken care of his needs. If you've done your job properly, you should be ready to let go."

"So he can die next time?"

"No. Stopping him from getting into that car was an act of love. Kyle may not appreciate that yet, but it would be easier for him to recognize your love if you didn't criticize him all the time."

"But a father has to correct his son and keep him from making a damn fool of himself."

"Any father, or your father?"

Sam's angry face flashes. "I can't do this anymore. Not now. It's too much."

"I understand. I want to leave you with one thought. Your father didn't just beat you. He didn't just punish you. Your father abused you. He violated your rights to a safe environment and a childhood free from fear. You have every right to be angry about what he did to you, but be sure not to take your anger out on Kyle."

"I don't. How can you say that?"

"Think about it, Brad. Put it in the back of your mind and chew on it while you're studying your diagrams. You're making real progress. I think you're almost ready."

"How much longer?"

"That depends on you, and on Kyle." He smiles. "You two are very much alike."

"I want to see my son."

"He wants to see you, too. Soon, I think. Very soon."

We pray together before he leaves. After the prayer he hugs me. "You're safe now, Brad. Remember that."

When he's gone, I find comfort again with Beth. I've been ignoring Matt. I know that. I just don't have anything to give him right now. I hope he understands.

Part Two

On Thursday, Umar says, "I want you to tell me everything you have learned about yourself."

"That's a tough one. Okay, I'll give it a shot. I am controlling, like my father. I have a hard time loving people, like my father. I never wanted to be a father in the first place. After Kyle stopped being cute, I didn't know how to connect with him. And I can't accept him because of his failures. Is that it?"

"You've forgotten something."

"I'm afraid to ask what it is."

"You were abused. Your rights were violated, and it was not your fault."

"It was my fault. He didn't beat Chris. There was something wrong with me. I should have been able to make him love me."

It's a short session.

"Okay, Brad. Calm yourself and we'll pray."

After the prayer, he hugs me and whispers, "It is not your fault."

We're standing at the door when he gives me an assignment. "Before we meet next Monday, I need you to write a letter to your father. Write it by hand. Tell him everything you've ever felt about him. You can show me the letter if you want, or you can burn it. It's up to you. The important thing is to get your feelings down on paper."

"I don't know if I can do that."

"You can. Remember, he can never hurt you again."

I tell Beth about the letter before we go to sleep.

"That sounds like a good idea."

"I don't think I can do it."

"Why not?"

"I could never talk back to him. He beat me harder. Then he beat Mom for giving him a 'worthless son.'"

I still hear his voice.

"He's dead, Brad. He can't hurt you."

"He can't love me either."

"No, he can't. But I always will."

On Saturday afternoon, I sit in Kyle's room and try to write. I start thirteen times and throw each one in the trash. The effort is exhausting.

I lie on Kyle's bed and close my eyes. After a few minutes I see him. Holding the belt over his head. Bringing it down so hard I hear the rush of air. Hitting me while I scream, blood trickling down my legs. Laughing softly as my mother falls down the stairs.

I pick up the paper, grab the pen, and write through my tears. I am seven years old again. I feel the hatred and pain of that boy. I write, with no thought to form. I write without pause until finally my words are exhausted. When I finish my letter to my father it is twenty-one pages long.

I don't have to read it. The words have been written on my soul all these years. I take the letter into the kitchen and set it on fire. I place the burning pages in the sink and disable the smoke detector so I can enjoy the inferno. I sit on the counter and watch them burn. I imagine my father screaming for mercy from the fires of hell.

When all the words have been reduced to ash, I feel a rush of exhaustion. I run a little water to make sure the fire is out, reconnect the smoke detector, and go back into Kyle's room. I fall into his bed and sleep deeply.

When I wake up, two hours later, the apartment is still quiet. Beth and Matt went out so I could have the solitude I needed to conquer my father's ghost. It's done now. He is dead. And I feel whole.

I pray. After the prayer I know what I have to do.

I lock the apartment door and climb into my old yellow Toyota.

I drive down the expressway, following the dotted white line.

Part Three

Their cars are parked in the driveway. He should be here. I have to see him.

Aisha looks surprised to see me. At least she has her scarf on.

"I need my son."

"I don't know. I guess…"

Joshua appears in the doorway. "Come on in. He's in the family room."

This is his bedroom now. I barely notice the posters on the wall or the dresser in the corner. I focus on my son, sitting in the middle of the room in his wheelchair.

There's nothing to say. I hug him tightly. And he hugs me back.

When I pull away, I study him. I can see my little boy in his eyes. I don't know why I didn't see it before. I'm sure it was always there.

"Do you know how much I love you, Kyle?"

"Yeah. I love you, too."

We hug again. How could I have forgotten how to love him?

"Are you ready to come home?"

"Are you sure you want me?"

"I'll help you pack."

"I don't think all of my things will fit in the Toyota," he says.

"We'll take some now and come back later for the rest."

He says goodbye to Joshua, Aisha, and the kids. I thank Aisha and hold Joshua close to me. He's not the baby. He's the man who rescued my son. And me.

"We're going to miss Kyle," says Joshua. "He's a great kid."

I clasp my son's arm. "I know."

"Why don't you all come back for dinner tomorrow?" says Aisha. "You can get the rest of his things and I can say a proper goodbye to my seventh son."

"We'll do that."

Joshua and Jamal help me carry some of Kyle's things out to the Toyota. Kyle climbs into the car, folds his wheelchair, and stows it in the backseat.

Beth and Matt are putting away groceries. Beth's mouth opens wide when Kyle rolls through the doorway.

"You're back!" says Matt.

"You better not have gotten into my stuff."

"Welcome home, Kyle." Beth hugs and kisses him, and cries a little. Kyle and Matt go off to do what brothers do. My wife turns to me.

"I saw the ashes in the sink."

"I finally killed the beast."

She pulls me close. "I knew you could do it."

I go down to the car to get Kyle's things. On my last trip I spot the package for Mom, still in my trunk. I tuck it under my arm.

We spend a quiet evening at home with our boys. Nothing momentous, but it's the best evening I can remember. Ever.

Before we go to sleep, I sit on the bed and open Mom's package. Beth watches.

I find a dark blue scarf, two books about Islam, and pictures of Mom, Walt, and some other people. There's a note.

"Assalaamu alaikum, Evie. You forgot your scarf in the hotel room. I have enjoyed knowing you. Please accept these books as my gift, and let me know if you have questions. I am very happy to have you as my sister in Islam. Wassalaam, Huda.

"P.S. Harun sends his salaams to your husband."

Beth gasps. "Evie became a Muslim? And Walt? They never said anything."

"I guess they wanted to surprise us."

Shock is more like it.

I fall asleep picturing Mom. She's happy.

We buy a plant on our way to Joshua's house. A very small way to show our appreciation.

Umar hugs me in the doorway. "I knew you could do it."

"That's why you kept putting off a meeting."

"I knew when you were ready you wouldn't need my help. But I would like to come tomorrow and sit with the two of you, if it's okay."

"Sure. And I hope you keep coming—as a friend."

During dinner, Joshua says he wants Kyle to continue working at the center. "It might turn into a paid position."

"What do you think, Kyle?"

"Yeah, Dad, I want to keep going."

"I'll drop you off on my way to work, but you have to wake up early."

He laughs. "I haven't slept late since Uncle Joshua brought me here. Anytime I wouldn't get up in the morning, they sent Luqman in to get me."

Luqman laughs too. "And I got him good."

When Aisha brings dessert, I tell them about the package. "Apparently Mom and Walt became Muslims."

"That would explain the last email I received from Walt," says Joshua. "It came on the day of the plane crash. They were standing in front of a masjid and Mom was smiling. She looked happier than I've ever seen her."

I can think of only one thing to say. "Subhan Allah."

Before we leave, I ask Aisha why she called Kyle her seventh son.

"I have three sons of my own, and Michael and Jeremy. And Nuruddin. Until now, Kyle was just another nephew, but in the past weeks he has become part of our family. My seventh son."

We enjoy a quiet Sunday evening. Kyle and I don't talk about our problems. I'm afraid to disturb the peace.

On Monday, I drop him off at the center. He's still working when I pick him up at six. He does look happy.

After dinner, we go our separate ways and wait.

~

Umar and I walk down the hall. He knocks on Kyle's door. "Can we come in?"

"It's open."

Kyle is lying on his bed with headphones on. When we walk in he sits up, takes off the headphones, and turns off the music. I don't know if it was Joshua or Aisha who taught him some manners, but this isn't the first time I've seen it in the last two days.

"Go ahead and sit down," Kyle says.

We all get comfortable. Umar clears his throat.

"I'm very happy the two of you have reconciled. That's a tremendous step, but there may still be underlying issues. I want to meet with you so we can set some ground rules and make sure the lines of communication stay open.

"I promised from the outset that I would not divulge anything either of you has told me in confidence. It will be up to you to decide how much you want to reveal. But I would like each of you to share one thing you have learned. Who would like to go first?"

"I will," says Kyle. "There's something you need to know about the accident, Dad. We were drinking—it was something we did—but they were all good. I lost my two closest friends that night. You knew them, too. Steve was at our house all the time. And you knew Amy. Maybe you don't remember. She had long brown hair and the sweetest smile I've ever seen.

"Amy is the only one who wasn't drinking that night. Because she was going to have my baby. I was going to get a job and we were going to get married. And I was trying to figure out how to tell Mom and you. It was hard because you two weren't getting along and I didn't want you to fight about me."

"What?" I sputter. "She was—?"

"Wait," says Kyle. "You'll get your turn. I have to say this. Steve, Amy, and I were sitting in the front seat. Steve had just bought this car from a guy at his job and we wanted to see how fast it could go. We were speeding over a hill. Amy screamed. That's the last thing I remember until I woke up. Then Mom told me they were all dead. Amy was dead. And Steve and Terry and their girlfriends. What you didn't know was that my baby died, too, that night."

He's crying. I don't know how to respond. He was in love with someone I don't remember meeting. He wanted to marry her. They were going to have a child. I should have known.

I reach for him, but he stops me. "There's something else, too, you need to know. Almost every night, I dream I'm out there on the field. Usually it's football, and sometimes it's soccer. My legs are strong and I feel whole. Then I wake up. And the first thing I see is my wheelchair. I need you to promise me something. Don't you ever tell me what I lost. Because I know. Believe me, I know." He looks at me, a tear rolling down his cheek. "That's all I wanted to say."

"Go on, Brad," Umar says quietly. "It's your turn."

My problems have been far from trivial. For over forty years, I was burdened with anger over my father's abuse, guilt over what happened to my mother, and confusion over my mother's inability to save me. But all these don't seem relevant now, not in the face of what Kyle has been going through.

They're waiting. I shake my head. For a moment I can't speak. I wipe my eyes and clear my throat. "I planned to tell you about problems stemming from my childhood. Things I have continued to struggle with. I wanted to explain why I push you so hard. But what I wanted to say doesn't seem so important now. I didn't realize what you were going through."

"And what if you had known? Would you have yelled at me for getting myself into that situation? Would you have reminded me I should have been headed for college? Would you have stopped me from marrying her?"

"Probably. But I've learned some things these past few weeks and I promise I will never turn away from you again. Whatever it is, we can work it out."

"That's what Amy said. She told me not to worry. As long as we were together, we could do it."

"She sounds like your mom."

"She was like Mom. They got along real well. You liked her, too. You just don't remember."

"Did Mom know about the baby?"

"I was going to tell you both the next day, even though I knew you would scream at me and probably scream at each other. Don't tell her, okay? It will just make her sad."

"I won't." He's opened up to me. I feel more comfortable being candid about myself. "I don't know if this will help, but I had a similar experience. I was sixteen when my girlfriend got pregnant. We went to the abortion clinic together. Her own parents didn't know. We broke up three months later."

"That's bizarre. You got rid of your baby. I wanted my baby, but it's gone." He looks down. "Do you remember when you brought me back from St. Louis?"

"You weren't very happy about coming home."

"It had nothing to do with home. Amy said our baby would be born around that time. Man, I can't believe you got rid of your kid." He glares at me. "Did you want to get rid of me, too?"

I've never given much thought to the incident. It happened. I took care of it. It has taken my son to make me feel ashamed of myself. I look him in the eye. "No, Kyle, I have always wanted you."

Ever since I heard your heart beat.

We hug again. I think we've broken the barrier. When I sit up, I notice tears on Umar's cheeks. I pat his shoulder.

"It's a good thing this is our last session," he says. "I've lost my objectivity."

After Umar leaves, Kyle and I sit with Beth. He talks to her about his feelings for Amy and, in spite of what he said, he tells her about the baby. We cry together.

Beth wipes her eyes. "We need to visit Amy's family."

"They didn't know she was pregnant. She was going to tell them the same time I told you."

"Then we don't need to tell them. But you love their daughter, and you were with her in the moments before she died. I can almost imagine their pain, because for a while I thought we would lose you. I think it will help them, in some small way, to talk with someone who loves Amy almost as much as they do."

Before we go to sleep, I hold my wife close. "I didn't know what Kyle was going through."

"Amy was such a sweet girl." She's quiet for a minute or two. "Brad, do you think he will have a normal life someday? Get married and have children? Or did he lose everything when the car crashed into that tree?"

"I wish I knew."

"I hurt for him. It's so hard to see my baby hurting."

Our family has been through so much. We're together now, and we're surviving. Alhamdulillah.

Closure

To each is a goal to which Allah turns him;
Then strive together (as in a race) towards all that is good.
Wherever you are, Allah will bring you together,
For Allah has power over all things.

—Surah 2 (Al Baqarah):148

Part One

Beth calls Amy's mother on Tuesday and arranges to visit them Sunday afternoon. She mentions it as we're finishing dinner.

"At first I didn't know what to say. I've spoken with her only a few times before. But I think she wants to see us. I suppose if you lose a child, you would reach out to anyone who knew your child."

"Did she say anything about me? Was she angry?"

"She asked how you were. Why would she be angry, Kyle?"

"Because I asked Amy to go out driving with us that night. She should have stayed home."

"It wasn't your fault. She knows that."

"Then whose fault is it?"

"Kyle," I say, "at least ten things might have happened differently that night. Amy could have stayed home. You could have taken her to the movies instead. You all could have stayed sober, which would have helped more than anything. But all the ifs and could haves don't change what happened. I spent many months thinking about the ifs and could haves which would have saved Gramma and Walt. But things happen, and often it's no one's fault."

"When did you become a fatalist?" asks Beth.

"I wouldn't call myself a fatalist. After Mom died, I started thinking about life and death, and I finally realized there are many things which are simply beyond our control."

"Sort of the 'eat, drink, and be merry, for tomorrow we die' philosophy, isn't it, Dad?"

"Not quite. More like pray, be careful, and be kind because we don't know how long we have. Can I tell you what Islam says about life and death, Kyle?"

"Sure."

I glance at Beth, waiting for her protest. "Go on," she says.

"Each of us has a life span which was written before we were born. Some people, like my father, live to be in their sixties or beyond. Others, like Steve and Amy, die when they're only eighteen. It would seem fairer if my father, who was cruel and self-centered, had died when he was young, and if Steve and Amy, who were kind and caring, had lived to be old. But it doesn't always work that way. You survived. I saw a picture of the accident scene in the newspaper, and I found it hard to believe anyone could have lived through that. God gave you a longer life span, and He expects you to do something with it. That's what makes me think you have much better days ahead of you."

"I hope so." He smiles a little. "Dude, first we eat dinner together. Then you start talking about God. Are you really my father? Where is the real Brad Adams and what have you done with him?"

"Yeah," says Matt. "I bet our dad was kidnapped by aliens when he was in the desert. How do we know you're not an alien?"

"Oh, that reminds me," I say in my best alien voice. "I need to phone home." Beth laughs. The boys don't get it. That was way before their time.

Umar and I drive to the prayer together on Friday. Something has been bothering me. I mention it on our way to the masjid.

"Kyle told his mother about the baby. It's very sad, but I'm torn. The child was illegitimate, and Kyle was drunk on the night of the accident. Now that I'm a Muslim, I have a hard time accepting that behavior."

"Did that kind of behavior bother you before?"

I snicker. "Of course not. My attitude then was boys will be boys."

"And you've admitted to committing adultery, not to mention your alcoholism."

"You know how it is. You were there once."

"And I have an illegitimate son. It took me years to reconcile my past with my life as a Muslim. We both know how it is. So why are you surprised?"

"I'm not surprised, just disappointed. I want my son to be better than me."

"He is better. You took your girlfriend to an abortion clinic. He planned to marry the girl."

He's right.

"What can I do?"

"Be there for him. Don't confront him. Teach him about Islam."

"I don't know if he would listen."

"Brad, I have known you for over fifteen years and I never hoped you would become a Muslim."

"Do you know how angry I was when Joshua converted? I thought he was throwing his life away."

"Isn't that what you were saying about Kyle a few weeks ago? Have you tried talking to him about Islam?"

"A little. He finds it hard to believe I'm talking about God. All those years, even when I did go to church, I never discussed it."

"How did he react?"

"He listened."

Umar nods. "That's a start. You're a practicing Muslim now. I know they've seen you pray."

"Yes. Beth is careful about the food she buys. She won't eat pork anymore. And they respect my prayer times."

"That's more support than many converts receive, especially when you're talking about a long-term marriage and teenaged children. And if Kyle hasn't done anything worse than what you or I did, he still has a chance. Also, don't forget about Matt. He is still innocent. Do your best to keep him that way."

I still have a lot to learn about being a father.

Amy's parents live in Evanston, near our old house. We finally closed the sale a couple of weeks ago. The old days were far from perfect, but I miss that house.

We get out of the car and go silently up to the door. Beth rings the bell. The woman who answers is thin and middle-aged. She has sad eyes. "Hello. Please come in."

She leads us into their living room. A gray-haired man stands to greet us.

"I'm Randy Hawkins. This is my wife Pat."

"I'm Brad Adams. I think you know Beth, and of course you know Kyle."

"How are you these days, Kyle? Are you adjusting?"

"I'm okay, Mrs. Hawkins."

"You used to call me Pat. We've known you for such a long time. You were almost part of our family."

"Yeah."

"Mr. and Mrs. Hawkins, I'm so sorry we have to meet this way. I've been out of touch with my son and I didn't realize until recently how much Amy meant to him. I want to express my deepest condolences. I can only imagine how it feels to lose a child."

Randy's voice is strained. "She was such a sweet girl, everything I could have wanted from a daughter. Pat and I are doing the best we can to accept her death and move on, but not an hour, sometimes not a minute, goes by that I don't think of her."

"It's harder, too," says Pat, "because our family and friends avoid talking about her. They think if they mention Amy it will make us sadder. They don't understand. We never forget. It's good to see you again, Kyle. I know you loved Amy. I wish things could have been different."

"I wanted to marry her."

"I know," says Pat. "She told us."

Randy clears his throat. "Kyle," he says, "I'm going to ask you a difficult question. I'd appreciate an honest answer. Was my daughter pregnant?"

Kyle's face turns red. "She told you?"

Pat is wringing her hands. "I found the box for a pregnancy test underneath her bed when I went in to clean up. I wasn't able to go in there at all until a few months ago, and then it was difficult. When I found the box, I wasn't sure what to do. I didn't want to bother you."

"She wanted to tell you," says Kyle. "We were talking about it that night. I would get a job, and we'd get married, and I'd take care of her. I never thought I would lose her."

Randy walks over and comforts Kyle as he cries.

"I should have taken care of her," Kyle sobs. "She shouldn't have died. It should have been me instead."

"No, Kyle, don't say that. Don't ever say that." He holds Kyle and they cry together.

I watch. Randy lost his daughter, but he is comforting my son in a way I never have.

After several minutes, Randy walks back to his chair. "Do you mind if I talk about that night? There's something you need to know."

Kyle is still crying. He nods.

"My wife and I were in bed. The policeman rang the bell. When I woke up and heard him at the door, somehow I knew what it meant. I was tempted to stay in bed and pretend he wasn't there, but he kept ringing. I got out of bed and confirmed it. My daughter was dead. I woke Pat and told her. Then we had to tell our other children. The officer sat with us for a while. We all cried together.

"After an hour or so I felt restless. I needed to see the place where she had died. I left Pat and the kids, and drove to the accident site. It was mostly cleaned up by the time I arrived, but the car was still there. That car looked like it had gone through a trash compactor. There was almost nothing left. I learned Amy had her seat belt on. She was trapped. The place where the car hit the tree, that's where she was sitting. She died instantly. Kyle, you flew through the windshield. I saw where you landed. I saw it all."

He closes his eyes and buries his face in his hands. We wait.

After several minutes, he's able to go on. "I knew all of the kids in that car had to be dead. It was four days later, during Amy's funeral, when someone told me you were still alive. I could scarcely believe it. I called the hospital every few days to check on your condition. I had to know. I wanted you to live." He stops again.

"I wanted you to live," he says softly. "I knew if you survived, it would be a miracle. Your survival gave me hope. There's a reason you're still alive. Why God spared you. We weren't very religious before the accident, but now we go to church whenever we can. We need to find answers. I know the answer for you, Kyle. God has something very special planned for you. You need to get out there and find out what it is."

We stay for another hour. They talk about Amy. Her sweetness. Her spirit. Her dreams. We page through the picture album. I remember her now. She was a beautiful girl.

I'm impressed by their strength. They've buried their daughter, but they still care for my son. No bitterness. No recriminations. Only sorrow.

As we leave, Pat and Randy hug Kyle. "Take care of yourself," says Randy. "Come to visit us sometimes. You're still like a son to us. And remember, you're meant to do greater things. That's why you're still alive."

"I'll remember," he says quietly.

When we return home, I pray and read Qur'an. And I think about Randy and Pat. Their strength. Their compassion. Their example.

The visit with them has changed Kyle. He helps Beth do the dishes and assists Matt with his math homework. During dinner, he tells us he's planning to study for his GED.

"That's great."

"And Dad, after I pass my GED, do you think I could have a car? Uncle Chris said I could get one specially equipped and Gramma's estate will cover it."

"Why do you need a car?"

"I need a job. And I want to take some college classes."

The words I've waited to hear.

"There will be restrictions. No drinking, of course, and no friends who drink. I'll hold you to a curfew, too."

"I'm finished with drinking. You know I haven't had a drop since that night. I can't. Even watching beer commercials makes me sick to my stomach. Drinking is what killed Amy and our baby, and put me in this chair. I won't forget that."

Part Two

The toughest part of my life these days is at the office. I do my work and meet my deadlines, but I have to put up with a lot of crap from Hendricks and Hussein. On Tuesday, I take Hussein aside.

"Why are you always on my case? You're a Muslim, aren't you?"

"Yes, but I am not an extremist, like you."

"Extremist? I don't have any bombs in my briefcase."

"You wear a beard. You interrupt your work to make prayers. You leave your job on Fridays to attend the mosque. Those are the ways of our grandfathers. We live in the West now and we must adapt ourselves to this culture."

"I'm from this culture. Why do you think I converted?"

He shakes his head in pity. "If you had asked me, I would have told you not to do it."

I don't know how to answer that. I walk away.

I miss working with Bill. We stay in touch, but it's not the same. I miss the garage, too. No office politics. Just the machine and me.

I'll stay until this project is completed. Then I'm out of here. If I'm careful, I can save enough to open my own garage.

On Wednesday morning, Ted tells me he's decided to retire in a few months. "My position will go to Curt, of course, but you'll take over Curt's place. You'll be back in your old office."

I might as well say it.

"Actually, Ted, I won't be here very long. After my work on the L is completed, I plan to resign."

"Are you leaving on another trip?"

"No, but I miss having grease under my fingernails."

He shakes his head. "What happened to you, Brad?"

"I found peace."

"I don't understand." He walks away.

Beth is restless, too. "Kyle doesn't need me now, and that's good. When he was in the hospital, I was afraid he would be helpless for the rest of his life, even though I knew what a paraplegic can accomplish. But he's actually getting his life on track."

"He's more on track now than he was before the accident."

"Having you here is a major part of that. He needed you more than he'll ever admit. I have a problem though. I'm bored silly. I volunteer at the center, and that's rewarding, but I need something more demanding."

"I always knew you weren't housewife material."

"I need to go back to work, Brad. It would help our finances. And I miss the challenge. Getting stains off the kitchen floor just doesn't do it for me."

"Do you want to go back to the hospital?"

"Not really. I did that job for so many years, and I was good at it, but I want something new and exciting."

"Any ideas?"

"Not yet. I don't know what else I can do."

"When I was on the road and needed cash, I stopped to find a job in a diner. While I flipped those burgers, I had time to think about what I really wanted to do. Fix cars."

"Not engineering?"

"We can talk about that later. You're very talented, and I know the world is crying out for you to use your skills again, though I will miss those home-cooked meals." I pat my middle-age paunch.

"You must have learned a few tricks at those diners. Why don't you cook at home for a change?"

"I just might do that."

"Are you sure you won't miss having a little wife at home, anxiously awaiting your return?"

"I'd rather have a happy wife."

She comes closer. "I am happy."

Beth sent her resume to several places last week, including the center. They have an opening for director of health programs.

We're getting there.

I'm not the only one getting my life together. On Saturday afternoon, Beth and I were browsing through a bookstore when I spotted a newly released novel. She finished it. I picked it up and flipped through the pages. Oh my God. She changed the hero's name to Bradley. That is my name, but she's the only one who's ever called me that. It sounds more romantic, I guess.

Beth looked over my shoulder. "What's that?"

No more lies. "I knew the author. In Denver."

Beth studied the photo on the back. "Nice looking."

"But nowhere near as beautiful as you." I pulled her close.

"Brad, we're in public. Let's go look at the bargain books."

"You don't want to read it?"

"Not unless you want to let an accountant I know do our taxes."

"Let's move on."

Part Three

We moved last weekend—just in time to have Thanksgiving at our place. Our new house has four bedrooms and no stairs. I'm using the extra bedroom as a library and prayer room.

Bill helped with the move. He tells me he just hired a new guy. Fresh out of rehab.

My brothers carried boxes, too, along with Jeremy, Jamal, Nuruddin, and Isaiah.

Jennifer came, but she was busy with her baby. Kyle took a look at her son. "Nice looking kid. Good thing he didn't take after you."

Jennifer whispered to the baby. "Don't listen to him. He was dropped on his head as an infant."

"But I still have my looks." Kyle grinned.

Isaiah shouted, "Hey, Kyle," and tossed him a vase.

Jennifer shrieked and shielded her baby. Kyle caught the vase and pumped the air. "Yes!"

Beth scolded, "Are you three at it again?"

Everything is back to normal.

Beth started her new job at the center last week. We take turns cooking dinner.

I walk into the house after another long day of dealing with Hussein and Hendricks. Kyle picks up the mail. A minute later he shouts. "Yes!"

"What is it?"

"I passed my GED. I am on my way."

I hug him. "I'm proud of you." I'm learning to open up, a little.

I walk into the kitchen to start dinner, and Kyle picks up the phone. When I come out, he's still talking to Randy.

Randy told Kyle there is a reason he's still alive. I told him that, too, but it sounded more convincing coming from Randy. Even to me. Kyle has a destiny to fulfill. It's fate.

~

I haven't spoken with Abdullah since we said goodbye in the parking lot, nearly three years ago. I still have his number in my wallet. After dinner I pick up the phone.

"Hello?"

"Assalaamu alaikum, Abdullah."

"Walaikum assalaam. Who is this?"

"It's Brad. The guy with the yellow Toyota and the pepperoni pizza."

It takes him a moment, then he laughs out loud. "Brad. How are you? I'm glad to hear from you. Did you ever find what you were looking for?"

"Didn't I just give you salaam? You can call me Ibrahim."

"You're a Muslim? By Allah, that's what I hoped for. How?"

"By reading the Qur'an you gave me."

"What do you think now about fate?"

"I was talking with my son about that the other day. There might be something to it."

"Your son? So you're home now. How is everything?"

"We've had some rough times, but I think we'll be okay."

We talk for the next two hours. I tell him what I've been through. He tells me he'll graduate next May. He hopes to get married soon after.

"I'd better let you go," I say. "Let me know if you're ever in Chicago."

"I'm coming that way in August, insha Allah, to meet with other Muslim film makers."

"That's great. I'll show you around, and you can get to know my sons."

He says he'll email me. I can't wait to see him again.

When I hang up, I think about fate. Leading me to Abdullah. Bringing me to Islam. Protecting my son. Sometimes Allah does allow people to die in plane crashes. But Allah also saves people—in ways we can never imagine.

Epilogue: Beth Speaks Out

We're living the life I've always dreamed of. I'd come to believe it would never happen.

When I was talking with Melinda yesterday, I mentioned the package from Malaysia. It's been a few months now. She wasn't surprised. She told me a letter had come to their house from someone named Harun, offering condolences on the deaths of Evie and Walt.

"I'll never forget one of the lines," Melinda said. "'Now they are with Allah.'"

"How long ago was that?"

"Shortly after Brad disappeared."

"You never said anything."

"I didn't know what to say."

"How did Chris take it?"

"He doesn't want to talk about it, but it has disturbed him deeply. Can you imagine?"

No, I can't imagine. Evie is the last person I would expect to convert to any religion. Besides Brad, that is.

I am trying to understand. I've started reading one of the books Huda sent. Brad doesn't know. I'm very satisfied with my church, but there must be something about Islam. It won't hurt to investigate.

Brad turned fifty today. We had a quiet celebration, just the four of us. I know he doesn't like a fuss. After the cake and ice cream, I handed him an envelope.

"What's this?"

"Tell Ted you need some vacation days."

He opened the envelope, studied the contents, and hugged me. "It's perfect."

"It was Kyle's idea."

The envelope contained four airline tickets. In three weeks, we're going exploring. The itinerary includes Los Angeles, Colorado

Springs, and the Grand Canyon.

    I think I'm ready for a little adventure.

About the Author

When she was twelve years old, Jamilah Kolocotronis took her first long-distance family trip—a three week vacation to California, including a day at Disneyland. Two years ago she finally visited her fiftieth state—Vermont. She has always enjoyed traveling down the open road, looking for the next adventure. Jamilah lives in Wisconsin with her husband and sons.

Her published books include *Islamic Jihad, Innocent People,* and the first two books of the Echoes Series—*Echoes* and *Rebounding.* Visit Jamilah's website at http://jamilahkolocotronis.writerswebpages.com.